Chasing a Dream

Chasing a Dream

Beth Cornelison

Five Star • Waterville, Maine

First Edition
First Printing: September 2006

Published in 2006 in conjunction with Tekno Books.

Set in 11 pt. Plantin by Christina S. Huff.

Printed in the United States on permanent paper.

Library of Congress Cataloging-in-Publication Data

Cornelison, Beth.
    Chasing a dream / Beth Cornelison.—1st ed.
        p. cm.
        ISBN 1-59414-514-8 (hc : alk. paper)
        I. Title.
    PS3903.O765C47 2006
        813'.6—dc22   2006012789

To my son, Jeffery—believe in yourself.
Dreams do come true!

Prologue

LOCAL BUSINESSMAN RILEY FANNIN FOUND DEAD,
APPARENT SUICIDE

A ripple of uneasiness shimmied through Tess Sinclair as she reread the newspaper headline. *Fannin.* She knew that name. But from where?

"Randall?" She peered over the top of the paper to the man seated across their opulent living room on a black leather couch.

He glanced up from his business magazine with an impatient glare. Accustomed to Randall's short temper and not sure her curiosity warranted upsetting him, Tess hesitated.

"What?" he asked irritably.

Tess drew a deep breath and plunged forward. "Don't you have a business associate named Riley Fannin?"

Randall's glare darkened. "My business dealings are none of your business. It would behoove you to remember that."

She nodded, trying to appease him. "Yes, I know. I only ask because the paper says he died. Apparent suicide."

Randall dropped his gaze to his magazine again. "Good riddance."

"Randall, that's an awful thing to say!" Tess gaped at him, disconcerted by his callousness, though she shouldn't have been. After twelve unhappy years of living with Randall, she

7

should have learned to expect such coldness from him. Deep in her soul, the naive and idealistic girl she'd been when they met still harbored a tiny hope that somehow, someday, Randall would change. But after twelve years, Randall still hadn't deigned to marry her, although he called her his wife and took all the privileges. To Randall, Tess was just another possession, bought with his money and subject to his iron will.

Now, as he glowered at her, a muscle in Randall's jaw twitched, a sure sign he was getting angry. Tess's defenses went on alert.

"The man was weak. A nothing. And I don't tolerate weakness, Tess. You should know that better than anyone." He paused, and his menacing dark eyes found hers. "Get me a scotch."

Obediently, she rose from her chair and crossed to the wet bar to pour his drink. Her hand shook as she poured, knowing how alcohol encouraged Randall's fits of rage. She was adding ice to his glass when she remembered where she'd heard Fannin's name. "The call."

"What?" Randall groused.

Tess spun to face him when she realized she'd said the words aloud. "I . . . I said 'the call.' You had a call last night from someone about Fannin. I overheard because the answering machine picked up at the same time you did."

Randall narrowed a speculative glare on her and slapped his magazine aside. "You were eavesdropping on my phone call?"

She swallowed. Why had she brought it up? Better that he'd never known. "Not on purpose. I swear. The machine came on while I was starting dinner. I had raw chicken on my ha—"

"Shut up!" Randall surged to his feet. His dark brown eyes

glittered with wrath as he stalked toward her. When she'd met him, Randall's swarthy good looks had been appealing. Now his height and dark features seemed more intimidating, especially when he used his size advantage against her.

Her grip tightened on the crystal highball glass while fear squeezed her lungs. *No. Not again.*

Hand trembling, she held the scotch out to him. He knocked it to the floor with a swift lash of his arm. "What did you hear?"

Panic swelled in her chest as she met the blaze of fury in his eyes. He clenched his jaw, flexed and fisted his hands at his sides, waiting for an excuse to use them.

A pit of despair, the gnawing sense of being trapped and at his mercy, filled her gut. She marshaled what courage she could and fumbled with the two-carat diamond on her left hand. On nights like tonight, her jewelry felt like a noose.

"Nothing really. I—"

With a jarring smack, the back of his hand connected with her cheek. Pain streaked through her and weakened her knees. She tasted the familiar metallic flavor of blood and had to suppress the urge to vomit.

"Don't lie to me, Tess. Don't ever lie to me." His tone was frighteningly calm, like the lull before a Texas tornado. "What did you hear?"

Frantically, Tess tried to remember exactly what the man on the phone had said to Randall. The call had puzzled her, she recalled, and the male voice had been unfamiliar.

We took care of Riley Fannin. He won't be a problem anymore.

Tess caught her breath when the man's strange words came back to her, and she jerked her stunned gaze up to Randall's.

You idiot! I told you never to call me on this line! Randall had answered.

Sorry, boss, I thought—

But whatever the man had thought had been lost when Randall slammed down the phone, disconnecting the call.

Now, Tess blinked in disbelief as the significance of what she'd heard sank in. Icy fingers of horror clawed at her. "You killed him," she rasped.

"Give me some credit. I'm not stupid enough to dirty my hands with such things."

No, of course not. Randall wielded his power and position like a despot. He'd have had one of his many minions carry out the seedy details.

"But you knew about it. You . . . ordered his murder. Didn't you?" Just the idea made Tess nauseated, light-headed with shock.

A sarcastic grin tugged one side of Randall's thin lips. "You always were the smart one, weren't you? Which is why I've always kept you out of my business affairs. I didn't need your bleeding-heart, sanctimonious morality interfering with the way I do business."

"Murder is not business! It's criminal! It's evil!" She should have kept her mouth shut. She knew what it meant to challenge Randall. But everything inside her and everything she believed, balked at the obscenity of what she was learning.

Randall stepped closer, grabbing her arm with a viselike grip. She gasped as his fingers bit into her arm.

"Are you threatening me?" he growled, his nose shoved close to her face.

"No!"

"Good. Your sister wasn't smart enough to keep her whoring mouth shut. I'd hate to have to deal with disloyalty from you the way I did with her."

Tess's stomach somersaulted, and she shook her head in confusion. "Angie? What does this have to do with Angie?"

"Only that when she got a notion to hold my business

10

dealings against me, she, like Fannin, learned how I deal with traitors."

Bile rose in Tess's throat as she processed this new insight to her sister's thirteen-year-old murder. She'd been living, sleeping, having sex with the man responsible for her sister's death! A man for whom murder was a business tool. She'd known he had a bad temper, known he became violent when she angered him, but had never imagined the scope of his malice or his immorality. And now that she knew the true extent of Randall's treachery, what could she do?

"Her pimp owed me money," she heard Randall say, though her mind already reeled with the implications of his previous revelations. "He handled Angela when she stepped out of line, and I forgave his debt. A simple business transaction."

Tears of rage filled her eyes, her own safety forgotten in the shadow of the horrid truths she was learning.

"You bastard," she muttered with every bit of venom that seethed inside her.

Randall jerked as if hit. Fire erupted in his eyes, and he shoved her backward with a force that knocked the breath from her. Crystal tumblers and wine glasses shattered around her as she crashed into the wet bar and slumped to the floor.

"How dare you speak to me like that!" Randall delivered a sharp kick to her ribs. "I took you in when the only other way you could have survived was as a whore. I laid the world at your feet, bought you everything money could buy! And this is the thanks I get?" Another bone-jarring kick. "You ungrateful bitch! I ain't gonna take it!"

On some level, through the haze of pain, fear and loathing, she heard Randall's language slip into the street slang he'd grown up using. The lazy speech pattern he worked meticulously to avoid as an adult and a respected San Antonio businessman. His regression spoke for the extent of his fury . . . and her danger.

"I swear, woman, if you ever rat me out, I *will* kill you."

Tess shuddered and closed her eyes, squeezing back her tears.

"Think about that if you have any half-assed ideas about taking what you know to the cops. The cops can't touch me. I've made sure of it."

She was sure of it, too. How else had he gotten away with his crimes for so long?

He'd hidden his vile business practices from her well, kept her ignorant to the extent of his evil nature. But she should have known. Had she turned a blind eye to the signs of his wickedness in self-preservation? Had she been too stupid to see what was right before her? More importantly, now that she knew who and what Randall Sinclair was, how did she survive? How did she look at herself in the mirror, knowing how he paid for the clothes on her back, the jewels on her hand?

She heard the rasp of his pants zipper and cringed. The beatings were bad enough without humiliation heaped on top.

Tess searched for answers, prayed for guidance. She knew she had to leave, had to get away from Randall somehow. She'd find the conviction and courage to do what she should have years ago.

Her mind set, she began planning her getaway.

Chapter One

Tess clutched the steering wheel with a death grip and checked the rearview mirror once more. Her escape seemed flawless, yet she knew better than to relax. Randall would come after her.

Fear clawed at her, accelerating her pulse. Nudging the gas pedal, she urged her new Jimmy to eat up the miles of Texas highway just a little faster. The farther she got before Randall discovered her flight, the safer she would be.

She worried her lower lip and sighed. "Safe" was a relative term, and she doubted she would ever consider herself truly free of danger. Randall never forgot a betrayal.

Dark clouds loomed overhead, eclipsing the late morning sun. Driving rain obscured her view and made the interstate treacherous. But she pushed on.

Her survival, her sanity depended upon fleeing the parameters of Randall's power and influence. She needed to fade into the sweet obscurity of the American populace. Without any specific destination in mind, she headed across the plains of South Texas, leaving behind a nightmare beyond anything she'd ever imagined.

She'd had to act quickly. Too quickly. Spontaneity had never been her strong suit, but under the circumstances, she couldn't afford the time extensive planning would involve.

Her affronted ethics had compelled her to act. Panic had guided her escape. Desperation now led her quest for seclusion and anonymity. Certain only that she had to make a new life for herself, Tess plotted her next move while she drove.

She'd avoid large cities where Randall could have contacts. A newcomer in a small town would draw too much attention as well. Someplace about the size of—

Thunk!

Tess gasped. The loud bump and pull on the steering wheel jerked her out of her deliberations. A gunshot? Her gaze flew back to the rearview mirror. A fresh surge of adrenaline swept through her. Her heart thudded against her ribs, and her hands shook.

The steering wheel slipped in her sweaty palms, and the Jimmy listed to the right. In her distraction and in the blinding rain, she must have hit something on the road and damaged a tire.

"Oh, no." Her chest tightened with dread as she eased to the shoulder. Not only would changing a flat tire waste precious time, but stranded along the side of the interstate, she became a sitting duck. She'd be an easy mark for one of Randall's lackeys who had no compunction about using her for target practice.

Sucking in a deep breath, she fought the swell of panic rising with the taste of bile in her throat. The swishing windshield wipers kept time with the steady cadence of the June rain on the car roof while Tess quieted her jangling nerves. Pressing the heels of her hands against her closed eyes, she curled her fingers into her hair and counted to ten.

You can do this. Just stay calm and think clearly.

After cutting off the engine, she glanced around the floor and realized that, in her haste to change vehicles, she'd left her umbrella in the BMW she'd traded for the dark blue Jimmy.

Digging her cellular phone from her purse, she turned the device on to call a tow truck. Then hesitated.

With a groan, she discarded the idea. She had to learn to take care of herself, survive alone, and she might as well start now. Besides, the less attention she attracted, the better.

From the glove box, she withdrew the owner's manual for the Jimmy she'd owned for less than two hours. Hands trembling, she studied the instructions for changing a tire then tossed the manual on the passenger seat.

With a heavy sigh, she opened the door and stepped out into the torrent. The warm summer rain dripped from her hair and nose. After retrieving the jack and lug wrench from the storage space in the back of the truck, she set to work.

Having positioned the jack under the car frame as the instructions in the manual described, Tess threw all of her body weight into loosening the lug nuts on the tire before levering the truck. Within minutes her muscles ached from fighting the stubborn nuts, which refused to budge. When the wrench slipped in her wet hands and clattered to the pavement, she growled her frustration. She dropped onto the ground and, despite the puddles she sat in, leaned back against the truck.

Surrendering to the tears that stung her eyes would be easy. Though distraught, discouraged and drenched, she mustered enough strength in her quivering muscles for another try.

Giving up was not an option. Quitting now meant certain discovery, defeat, even death. She didn't delude herself for a minute by hoping that Randall would forgive her flight, ignore the damning things she'd learned about him, and allow her to live.

Memories of his rage the night she'd confronted him with the truth knotted her stomach and persuaded her to struggle to her feet for a second attempt with the stubborn lug nuts. Grasping the wrench with a grip as firm as her resolve to rid herself of Randall's menace, she jammed the tool in place and tugged with all her might.

"Looks like you're having a little trouble."

Tess's heart slammed against her ribs at the sound of the male voice. Her hands stilled. A pair of muddy hiking boots appeared in her peripheral vision. She eased her gaze over to study the man's shoes while her mind raced.

Was he one of Randall's men? Should she run? Could she defend herself with nothing more than the lug wrench?

As she raised her head, her gaze traveled up a pair of long legs, clad in blue jeans, and past slim hips to a broad and imposing chest. Though not what she'd call muscle-bound, the stranger's torso, clearly delineated beneath a clinging, wet T-shirt, looked strong and capable of inflicting harm if he so chose. Her 110 pounds held no chance against his brawn.

Gulping a breath, she dragged her gaze to his face, shadowed under a black cowboy hat, and she searched for her voice. "I—I can handle it."

The man squatted beside her, his long legs splaying wide. "Are you sure? I don't mind giving you a hand if you want to get out of this rain a little quicker."

On eye level with him now, she surveyed the stubbled cheeks and square jaw of the man she estimated in his late twenties. "I'm already soaked, so . . . I . . . thank you anyway."

Bright blue eyes stared at her from under the dark rim of his Stetson, and his mouth curved in a lazy grin. He reached for her, and Tess shrank back with a gasp. The fingers that curled around her grip on the wrench felt surprisingly warm as he gently pried the tool out of her hand.

"I'm afraid my rearing won't allow me to take 'no' for an answer. My mama would tan my hide if she found out I'd let a woman change a tire in the rain when I could've done it for her."

She lifted her chin a notch, grabbing for the wrench again. She needed it for a weapon if nothing else. "Well, I won't tell your mother, if you don't."

His grin blossomed, lighting his face with a handsome smile that caused a flutter in her pulse. He put a hand under her elbow and stood, drawing her to her feet as well.

"Come on. Stand back. I'll take care of this."

The idea of locking herself safely in the car appealed to Tess enough to let him slide the lug wrench from her hand. "All right."

Stepping away from him, she wrapped her arms around her chest to ward off the chill of the rain and the nip of apprehension that shimmied down her spine. She watched him remove his hat long enough to push wavy hair, as black as his Stetson, off his forehead.

He moved into position beside the flat tire and fit the wrench in place. She heard him grunt as he tugged until the lug nut gave. While he continued working, his attention riveted on the task, she rounded the front bumper to take refuge in the driver's seat.

Locking her door, she then searched for something to dry her hands and face but didn't find anything. Nothing short of a hair dryer and a complete change of clothes from her hastily packed suitcase would do her much good anyway. She surrendered to the idea of being wet and closed her eyes, leaning against the headrest.

She focused on relaxing her tense muscles and gathering her wits. The car jostled while the dark-haired cowboy finished changing the damaged tire. The full-sized spare that came with the car proved a fortunate option she'd taken for granted when she picked a Jimmy from the dealer's lot. Basic transportation, something Randall wouldn't recognize, had been her only concern when she'd switched cars that morning.

A rap on her window pulled her from her musings, and she opened the window a crack to speak to the man who stood by her door.

"All done. Where do you want me to put these?" He held out the jack and lug wrench.

"I'll take them." She lowered her window enough for him to pass the tools in to her. Relief that she could now get back on the road mingled with gratitude for the tall, handsome cowboy who'd come to her aid. She fished some money from her purse, and a smile found her lips as she met the man's blue gaze. "Thank you so much. You don't know what this means to me."

You may have just saved my life.

Waving off the money, he flashed her a warm smile. "No problem." He stepped back then paused, narrowing his eyes. "Can I give you a little advice?"

She eyed him suspiciously. "Excuse me?"

"Gettin' in the truck while I was working . . . you could've made the truck fall off the jack."

"Oh." She stared at him blankly for a minute, until he stepped back from her window.

"Just remember that next time." He gave her a wink as he turned away.

The tension in her chest eased, and she cranked the engine, eager to make up for lost time. When she checked her mirrors for a break in the traffic, she spotted the man on the shoulder of the road behind her car, hoisting a backpack and stooping to pick up a guitar case. While she watched, he turned and struck out along the side of the road, passing the passenger side of her Jimmy and moving on.

She'd been so preoccupied with worry and her suspicions of him that she hadn't realized he had no car until that moment. Staring at his retreating back, Tess told herself all the reasons why she'd be crazy to offer him a ride. The risk she'd be taking by picking up a stranger didn't outweigh the guilt of leaving him to walk in the rain. Common sense forbade her from anything as foolish as letting a strange man in her car.

But . . .

Compassion for the friendly cowboy with the lazy grin swamped her, battling with the voice of reason. Tess shook off the jab of tender emotion and shifted the Jimmy into drive. While she waited for a truck to pass and allow her room to pull out, she glanced again at the lonely figure of the man hiking along the side of the road.

He may have saved your life, but you have to look out for your well-being. You're on your own now.

On her own.

The thought stuck in her mind. She hated the idea of being alone, of being vulnerable.

Randall's men would be looking for a woman traveling by herself.

A woman traveling by herself.

Her breath caught. Her good Samaritan's presence would provide a decoy, protecting her from the men looking for her. Her hands squeezed the steering wheel, and her head swam as she considered her options.

How dangerous could a man carrying a guitar be? Would a man with any intent to hurt her have bothered changing her tire? When he'd had a chance to harm her, he hadn't. He'd proven himself a help, not a hazard. Having the cowboy riding beside her would help throw Randall's men off her trail and aid her escape.

Her mind set, Tess blasted the horn and eased the Jimmy up beside the man.

He cast her a sidelong glance and slowed his pace. When she stopped and rolled down the passenger window, he stepped up to the Jimmy and ducked his head to peer inside. "Yes, ma'am?"

"Would you like a ride?" She wondered if he heard the tremor in her voice. Clearing her throat, she squared her shoulders and added, "It's the least I can do to repay you."

Running a hand over his face to wipe away the rivulets of rain dripping from his hair, the cowboy tugged his mouth in a lopsided grin. "You don't owe me nothin'. Glad to help."

She knitted her brow and regarded him warily. "You don't want a ride? But . . . but it's raining and—"

"I never said I didn't want a lift, just that you don't owe me one." Bracing a hand on the passenger door, he leaned down to meet her gaze more directly. "You sure you don't mind? I'm awfully wet."

Her cheeks twitched nervously when she tried to smile. "That makes two of us." She licked her lips and nodded. "I'm sure. You can put your pack in the back."

For several seconds he studied her. His piercing gaze sent shivers skittering through her, and she shifted uneasily. "Is something wrong?"

Her question snapped him from his daze, and he shook his head, his easy-going grin returning. "Naw."

Moving to the back door, he slid the guitar case across the seat and unloaded the backpack from his shoulders with a fatigued sigh. She watched with interest as he pulled back the protective rain-flap at the top of his backpack and extracted a dry shirt. Next, he removed the plastic grocery bag he'd torn and draped over the top of the guitar case. Using the shirt, he wiped the guitar case dry then opened it to check the instrument. Apparently satisfied everything was all right, he snapped the case shut and closed the back door. Before climbing into the front seat, he removed his cowboy hat, shook the excess rain from it and tossed it on the backseat.

When he climbed in the passenger's seat, he turned a kind smile to her and fastened his seatbelt. "Where you headed?"

"Where are you headed?"

"I asked you first." His eyes brightened in good humor, and he flashed her a roguish grin.

Tess responded with a tight-lipped frown and a cool glance. Anxiety squelched her sense of humor and spawned uncharacteristic impatience in her. She glanced in her side mirror as she pulled back onto the road in front of a large camper that lumbered slowly toward them. "See that camper behind us?"

He checked the mirror on the passenger-side door. "Yeah."

"That's my parents," Tess lied, causing an uneasy quiver in her stomach. The fib chafed her conscience. "They just saw you get in my car, and they'll be behind us every inch of the way."

The cowboy faced her with a keen gaze, and Tess's heartbeat stumbled. Could he tell she was lying?

"So they'd know, right off, if I tried to rape or murder you." His expression remained impassive. "Is that what you're saying?"

His blunt reply startled her, but she straightened her spine. "Yes." It bothered her that he'd read her motives so easily. But she was, admittedly, a horrible liar. Coupled with her distaste for dishonesty, she had little experience with this type of deceit, flimsy as it was.

21

Turning his gaze toward the windshield, he wearily rested his head on the seat. "I'll keep that in mind."

"So where are you going?" Tess repeated tightly. His insouciance and evasive answers chafed. His casual manner seemed to mock the urgency of her situation.

He regarded her silently for a moment before answering, his expression inscrutable. "Nashville."

He returned his gaze to the rain and the road.

"Nashville? That's got to be a two-day drive from here. Were you really planning to walk the whole way?"

Arching one dark eyebrow, he gave her a brief, sideways glance. "If I couldn't get a ride from a considerate stranger."

She heard a note of challenge in his voice, as if he dared her to belittle his intentions.

"Well, I don't necessarily plan to go that direction." Flexing her fingers then wrapping them back around the steering wheel, she peered across the front seat and met a level gaze.

The corner of his mouth lifted, and an unexpected warmth lit his eyes. "I didn't think you were. I appreciate the ride as far as you're willing to take me, just the same."

His unwavering politeness and calm in response to her coolness plucked at her conscience. Despite her nervousness, she had no reason to act rude.

Dividing her attention between her passenger and the road, she assessed him more carefully. A couple days' growth of black beard shadowed his cheeks, giving his boyishly handsome face a manly edge. The mellow scent of damp leather from his hiking boots and the clean aroma of June rain clung to him, blending with the new-car smell of her Jimmy.

Noticing her appraising gaze, he stretched his right arm across his chest to offer his hand. "Justin Boyd."

She glanced down at his hand before giving it a quick

shake. "Tess Carpenter." She used her real name without giving it any thought. Randall had insisted she take his name, for business appearances, even though they'd never legally wed.

"Nice to meet you, Tess. So, where are you folks headed?"

Tess pondered his use of the plural "you folks" before she remembered her story about the occupants of the camper behind her. "Uh, camping."

She winced at the lame response that sprang to her lips.

"Anywhere in particular or just wherever the mood strikes you?" Humor laced his tone.

"Colorado." She blurted the first state that came to mind. "In the mountains."

"Never been there. I bet it's beautiful."

Tess, who'd only seen the Colorado Rockies in pictures, bluffed again. "It's our favorite camping spot."

"Where are you from?"

Clearly he felt it necessary to make small talk, but she grew increasingly uncomfortable with the lies that tumbled unbidden from her lips each time she answered one of his questions.

"San Antonio . . . uh, formerly," she amended, realizing she shouldn't give away too much information about herself.

Confusion darkened his expression. "Formerly? Where do you live now?"

"I . . . uh, nowhere . . . yet." When his puzzled frown deepened, she added, "I'm looking for a new job and . . . I'll move wherever the new job takes me."

"Ah." He nodded his understanding. "Same here. When I get to Nashville, I plan to take any job that will pay the bills while I work toward my ultimate goal."

"Which is?"

"A recording contract," he said matter-of-factly, as if he'd just told her the sky was blue.

"What?" A tiny laugh of disbelief bubbled from her.

The warmth in his expression faded, and his stony reserve made her swallow her laugh with a twinge of regret. Determination blazed in his eyes then, and he set his jaw with a stubborn rigidity.

"You're not the first person to laugh, but you won't be the last. I will, when my name's at the top of the Billboard Hot 100."

The certainty in his voice and the fire in his eyes convinced her that he just might be right. She wished she had the same optimistic confidence in her future.

"I'm sorry. I didn't mean to laugh at your aspirations. I just didn't . . . well, it just took me by surprise. It's not every day you meet a rising star."

He narrowed his gaze on her as if trying to decide whether to find any sarcasm in her last statement. "I know it won't be easy. I'll be one of thousands beating on producers' doors. But unlike most of my competition, I have three things on my side."

He held up his fingers as he counted them off to her. "Talent and time."

"Time?" Tess shot him a questioning glance.

"I intend to stay in Nashville, beating on doors and playing my demo tape for anyone who'll listen until I get what I want. I flat out refuse to give up."

His dogged determination was the attitude she needed for her own mission. His optimism sparked an ember of hope in her, and the tension squeezing her chest loosened its grasp a bit. She smiled at him for the gift of reassurance he'd unwittingly given her. "That's two things. You said three."

"I did?" His eyes grew dark, and he turned his gaze toward

the front to stare out the windshield. "The third one is kind of private. I don't usually talk about it."

"All right." She understood painful secrets, private motivations for desperate acts. Turning her attention back to the highway, she acknowledged the escalating jitters inside her. The more she learned about Justin, the more the restless flutter grew. But why? Shouldn't she feel calmer with more evidence of his harmlessness? In fact, her predicament posed him far more of a threat than he apparently posed to her.

A flash of understanding followed on the heels of that thought. Guilt yanked her gut in a knot. Her desperation to have a decoy, her selfish motivation for offering him a ride, didn't justify putting this man in danger. She'd fled Randall because her morals and her deeply rooted ethics wouldn't allow her to stay with a man so void of decency or conscience. She couldn't live with the guilty secret he'd sprung on her. Literally. Randall would kill her to keep her silent.

The thud of her pulse echoed in her ears. Her conscience castigated her for putting Justin in harm's way. A dull ache of remorse settled in her chest.

A moment of thick silence passed before he spoke again softly. "The third reason is an angel . . . named Rebecca. She's with me. I know she is."

He flicked an uneasy glance toward her. The fleeting smile she gave him seemed to reassure him.

"This was as much her dream for me as it was my own. She bought me the guitar when I was ten." Affection, tinged by sorrow, filled his voice. The low, even timbre resounded inside her and increased the guilty ache in the center of her chest.

He'd trusted her enough to confide in her. His unwarranted faith in her made her selfish endangerment of him even more unconscionable. Though she knew that the anonymity of strangers sometimes made such openness easier, his honesty and trust in her created an unwelcome bond with him.

She saw pain in his eyes when he looked at her, and her heart wrenched. Then slowly, like the sun spreading its rays across the horizon in the morning, his lazy grin returned, and a gentle warmth shone from his eyes. "With Becca on my side, I can't lose."

His optimism calmed her. He'd managed, if only for a minute, to distract her from the daunting fear that had set her on the road, fleeing for her life. His easy-going charm made her smile, and his confidence and tenacity encouraged her. "You know, Justin Boyd, I believe you just might be a rising star at that."

For a moment he appeared stunned by her compliment. Then he curled his mouth in a sheepish grin. "Sorry. I get a little carried away sometimes." He lapsed into another brief reflective silence. "Nobody that I left behind shared my faith in my dream. Rebecca's the only one who ever did. I tend to get defensive out of habit."

Tess's gaze drifted to him again before returning her full attention to the road. "No offense taken."

In fact, she admired the conviction and aspirations of this blue-eyed, stubborn cowboy. That's when the irony hit her.

He wanted fame, and she needed obscurity. He was aiming for the spotlight, and she had to find the shadows. While Justin chased a dream, she was running from a nightmare.

Chapter Two

Justin watched in the side mirror as the camper that had followed them for the last couple hours pulled off at an exit Tess didn't take. She drove on, oblivious to the loss of her tail, and he grinned. He'd suspected she invented her tale of camping with her parents, but he now knew without a doubt that she'd lied. Not that he blamed her for devising a ruse to dissuade a would-be attacker.

The camper's departure brought Justin back to his initial reaction when she'd offered him a ride. *Why?*

The milk of human kindness didn't usually override the potential danger a hitchhiker posed to a woman traveling by herself. Most women would have passed him by without a second thought.

Something had her spooked. A simple flat tire couldn't account for the tension that wound her tighter than a guitar string. Gripping the steering wheel so hard her knuckles blanched, sitting ramrod straight and checking her mirrors more often than a fashion model, Tess vibrated with enough anxiety to set him on edge as well.

As if to prove his point, her cellular phone rang at that moment, and Tess jerked at the muffled trill. Her hazel eyes widened with apprehension, and she stared at the phone as if she'd discovered a rattlesnake in the truck. Catching her lower lip in her teeth, she glanced back at the road, ignoring the ringing phone. She'd already eaten off all her lipstick, chewing her lip until it looked ready to bleed.

"Want me to get that?" He aimed a finger at the persistent phone.

"No!" The alarm in her expression melted to chagrin when she met his puzzled gaze, and she took a deep breath, blowing it out slowly through pursed lips. "I . . . I don't want to talk to anybody right now. It's—"

Before she could finish, Justin picked up the phone and punched the power button to stop the incessant ringing. "There. They can leave a message."

As Tess turned her attention back to the road, she lifted a trembling hand to rub her temple.

"Are you all right?" He studied the harsh lines of worry that creased her otherwise attractive face. She nodded unconvincingly.

While she stared out at the road, her expression haggard, he allowed his gaze to linger on the comely woman. Other than the dark circles beneath her eyes and tiny worry lines at the corners of her mouth, her flawless skin radiated health and looked satiny soft.

His fingers itched for the privilege to comb through her mane of ashen brown hair or playfully tweak her pert nose. His lips twitched, longing for a taste of the twin chocolate brown freckles on the side of her slim throat. He wanted to sample her fragile, pink lips, as well, and soothe the irritation her nervous habit of biting them caused.

Having molded to her form as they dried from the rain, her silky blouse and khaki shorts hugged her slender body, revealing her graceful, womanly curves. Coupled with her obvious agitation, her petite size added a certain vulnerability to her appearance that disturbed him. Justin dismissed his uneasiness, loath to examine its source, and contributed his own disquiet to her jitters.

When he spotted the elaborately jeweled band on her hand, he sighed. She might be a common man's lustful fantasy, but she was also some damn lucky man's wife.

"So, why didn't your husband come with you on this trip?"

To his amazement and consternation, Tess's face drained of color, and her eyes darkened with what he could only call fear.

"Husband? Who says I'm married?"

"That rock you're wearing was my first clue." He tipped his head toward her left hand, which still squeezed the steering wheel for all it was worth. She raised her hand and stared at the ring for a second or two in silence.

Her tongue darted out to wet her lips before she tugged the band off her finger and shoved it in her pocket. Returning her gaze to the road, she stared ahead silently with wide, doe-like eyes.

He sat frozen, watching her while an eerie intuition prickled the back of his neck. Her obvious fear, her attempt to hide the evidence of her marital status, and her deafening silence prodded a dormant guilt and woke his protective instinct.

"Rebecca, you can't ignore the problem and think it will just go away!"

"Leave me alone, Justin. I can handle him."

Shifting in his seat, he searched for a safe, lighthearted topic of conversation that would dispel both her anxiety and the flash of painful memories that unexpectedly haunted him. Distracting her from her troubles didn't seem like much help, but he felt compelled to do something that would ease her palpable distress.

"So what line of work will you be looking for when you settle . . . wherever?"

29

A quick glance. Hesitation. A nibbled lip. "Marketing."

"The research side or are you—"

"So, tell me, cowboy, where are you from?"

He heard the false animation she put behind the question, a cheer that didn't reach her eyes. Clearly her life was not open for discussion.

"Cowboy?" Following her lead, he arched an eyebrow and gave her an amused grin.

"Yeah. You've got the hat, the guitar, the whole Nashville thing."

"And that makes me a cowboy?"

Tess sighed. "Forget it."

He sensed her withdrawal as he watched a shadow cross her face. Her reaction to his teasing stabbed him with guilt without fully understanding why. "I'm from a little town in west Texas that I'm sure you've never heard of."

She lifted her chin. "Try me."

"Wellerton."

Her sculptured eyebrows drew together in a frown. "Never heard of it." She peered over at him with a reluctant grin.

His own smug smile said, *I told you so.*

Her face brightened marginally as she shook her head. "And do you have a wife and cowbabies waiting for you back in Wallerton?"

"It's Wellerton. And no. No wife, no cowbabies. Just an ex-girlfriend."

When she turned to him, her gaze slid down his body then slowly back to his face. "Her loss."

Even though she hadn't touched him, his skin tingled in the wake of her visual caress. Heat erupted in his groin, and he gritted his teeth, fighting the flare of desire. Despite her compliment, he knew a tryst with a stranger couldn't be further from her mind, and casual sex had never been his style. His conscience wouldn't allow it.

Redirecting his thoughts down a safer path, he gave her a lopsided grin. "Do you have any other family?"

Her expression grew somber. "My parents died when I was fourteen, and my sister was killed when I was sixteen."

"I'm sorry," he mumbled while biting back the chuckle that fought to surface when she gave her ploy of the camper away. Despite his efforts, a grin split his face.

"What about y—" She stopped abruptly and furrowed her brow. "What's so funny?"

"I'm sorry. Truly. I'm not laughing at your loss."

"Then what?"

"You lied."

"What?" Her eyes widened with dismay.

"About the people driving the camper behind us." Justin chuckled harder as her slip dawned on her, and she flushed a bright pink.

"I was—"

"They pulled off at an exit about ten miles back. I figured out the rest."

Hazel eyes full of worry and vulnerability turned to him, fueling the intuition that lurked in the recesses of his mind. Shoving his suspicions aside, he covered her hand on the steering wheel and brushed her knuckles with his thumb. "But don't panic, Tess. I'm not a criminal."

She yanked her hand away and locked her gaze on the road. "I bet you say that to all your victims."

He laughed. "Yep. Every single one."

Her scowl expressed her concern, and he regretted his teasing. Once again, her uncertainty pricked his curiosity.

"So why did you pick me up if you're worried that I might be a bad seed?"

She hesitated, then the corner of her mouth curled up. "Your guitar."

"Huh?"

"I figured a serial killer wouldn't be carrying a guitar." She cast him a sheepish grin.

"Then you haven't heard of the great Nevada guitar murders?"

Her grin faltered, and her eyebrows snapped together. "What?"

When Justin grinned again, she scowled at him. "You're not funny." But the corner of her mouth twitched before she looked away.

The slight improvement in her disposition encouraged him. A success, no matter how small, still qualified as a success. Seeing the shift in her mood fed his need to fix her broken spirit.

"So if you're headed to Nashville, may I presume that you're a *country* musician?" She said the word as if it were something offensive.

"I take it you don't like country music."

"You'd be right."

"What did country music ever do to you to earn such a bad rap?" He crossed his arms over his chest and settled back in his seat.

Tess gave him an unladylike snort. "Nothing, I guess."

With that admission from her, Justin leaned forward to snap on the radio. He scanned the radio stations, under a disapproving glare from Tess, until he found a country station. When he swiveled to retrieve his guitar from the backseat, Tess clicked off the radio. "No, thanks. I'm not interested in a free concert."

Studying her profile, he ignored her admonition and took out his guitar. He arranged the instrument, his prize possession ever since Rebecca had given it to him at age ten, and turned the radio on again. This time when Tess reached for the knob, he batted her hand away. She raised a startled gaze to meet his.

With a growl, she put her hand back on the steering wheel, her teeth clenched. A bouncy Garth Brooks tune came on the radio, and Justin sang and played along, grinning broadly as he watched Tess grimace.

He belted out the refrain about a long-necked bottle, and Tess groaned.

"Oh, God. Spare me!"

Justin chuckled and leaned closer to sing in her face, knowing his actions, no matter how they irritated her, kept her from dwelling on the unknown threat that rattled her earlier.

She glanced at him and grinned. "Oh, my woman left me, and my poor dog died," Tess crooned to her own tune in a mocking, off-key howl.

He continued singing and playing, not only unperturbed, but amused by her teasing. When he sang louder, she matched his volume.

"My truck broke down. My beer is flat. I can't find my cowboy hat!"

His laughter interrupted his duet with Garth, and a giggling Tess pressed a hand to her flushed cheek.

Warmth spread through him and puddled in his gut. A spark lit her eyes, rewarding his efforts to humor her. When the song ended and a ballad began, he reached for the radio knob.

Now Tess swatted his hand away. "Wait. That one sounds pretty."

Sitting back, he studied her face, and a self-satisfied grin crept to his lips. He picked up the melody on his guitar. The song was a duet, and whenever Tim McGraw sang with his wife, Justin added his voice. Tess glanced at him with the soft glow of intrigue reflected in her eyes. When the song ended, he turned off the annoying car dealership advertisement that followed. "So you approve of country ballads, huh?"

She shrugged. "Maybe." She flicked another glance at him. "You have a nice voice."

The compliment caught Justin off guard, but he smiled his appreciation. "Thank you." His voice sounded husky, and he cleared his throat before adding, "Your singing needs work."

Now Tess laughed, a lilting, beautiful sound, sweeter to his ears than Faith Hill's ballad. His stomach chose that moment to growl loud enough to wake the dead.

A grin still graced her lips when she faced him. "Hungry?"

Chuckling, he ducked his head. "Yeah, how'd you guess?" Except for the peanut butter crackers he'd devoured last night for supper, he'd not eaten since breakfast the previous day.

"Do you want to stop? There are several restaurants at this next exit."

"This is your show, so you pick. I'm just along for the ride."

His deferral to her preference seemed to startle her. "Well, uh, how about . . . hamburgers?" She made her suggestion tentatively, as if afraid to give the wrong answer.

"Fine by me."

Puckering her brow, she added, "Can we make this quick? I don't want to lose more time than we have to."

He shrugged. "Sure."

Why the rush? he wanted to ask but swallowed the question.

As Tess took the exit and pulled in at a hamburger chain restaurant, Justin checked his cash reserves. He'd budgeted only so much money per week, needing his limited funds to last him until he reached Nashville and found employment somewhere. He'd have to maximize his lunch purchase with a minimum of outlay.

Any crowd the restaurant might have had at lunchtime had dispersed hours ago, and the drizzling rain apparently kept any late afternoon snackers away. Tess pulled into the deserted parking lot and cut the engine.

A frown darkened her face, and she bit her lip again. Only after she'd cast a wary glance around the empty lot did the tension in her expression relax. "I'm only going to use the restroom. I'll meet you back here once you get your food, okay?"

He reached back for his hat and gave her a nod. "Yes, ma'am."

She wrinkled her nose as she peeked up at the dripping clouds then opened her door with a sigh.

Hustling out the passenger's side, he splashed through the puddles, jogging toward the restaurant door beside her. They parted ways inside, and he stepped up to the counter to place his order.

A minute later, while he waited for his hamburgers, he saw her leave the restroom and stop at the outside door to watch the rain a moment before venturing back to the truck.

He glanced away only long enough to check the progress of the teenager filling his order, only long enough to see the girl stuff a bag of French fries in his sack and start wrapping his sandwiches. Then he looked back outside for Tess.

And his heart lurched in horror.

Chapter Three

Tess hadn't seen the man coming.

One second she crossed the parking lot, keys in hand, eager to get out of the rain. The next second a strong hand clamped over her mouth, stifling her scream. Another hand snaked around her waist, and a brutish arm hauled her up against a stout body.

Panic surged through her. Fear squeezed her chest. Her keys clattered to the pavement.

"Get in the car," a deep, menacing voice ordered. Something hard jabbed her side. She heard a loud click, like the cocking of a gun. The man thrust her toward a blue sedan.

Acting on survival instinct alone, she twisted and fought as her captor shoved her toward the waiting car. Adrenaline strengthened her, but her certainty that she would die if she got in the sedan fueled her struggle.

The man's grip around her middle tightened. His gun dug deeper into her ribs. The hand over her mouth suffocated her, and her lungs burned with the need for air. Clawing at his hand, she prayed for deliverance, for oxygen. When he lifted her from her feet, she thrashed wildly. She kicked the knees of her captor in a desperate battle for her freedom.

Suddenly, his grasp weakened. Asphalt bit her hands and knees as she crashed to the ground with a jarring thud. Ignoring the pain that streaked through her limbs, she groped frantically for her keys. Tears blurred her vision. The rush of blood in her ears muffled all but the drumming of her heartbeat.

She didn't waste time wondering how she'd won her release. Focused only on fleeing, she searched futilely for her keys. Finally, her fingers touched metal. At the same time, a muscled arm wrapped around her waist again. The powerful man dragged her to her feet.

"No!" She wrenched around and flailed at the assailant who'd imprisoned her in his grip.

"Tess! It's me!" Justin caught her wrists and held off her blows.

Confusion stilled her momentarily. A groan called her attention to the man sprawled on the pavement at her feet. Clutching the back of his head, the wounded stranger turned dark, feral eyes up to meet her stare. With a growl, he swiped a hand toward her feet. Justin jerked her by the wrists away from the sweep of the man's arm.

She stumbled as her cowboy-savior tugged her toward the parked Jimmy. Her gaze locked in terror on the dark scowl of her would-be kidnapper. The face of evil. Her living nightmare. A chill slithered down her spine.

"Hurry, Tess!" Justin pulled harder on her arm.

The man pushed to his knees and grabbed for the gun he'd dropped when he'd lost his hold on her.

"Justin!"

Justin spun around at her cry. "Get in the truck!"

He ran back toward her assailant, but fear rooted her to the spot. Her cowboy reached the pistol just before the man's fingers could close around the weapon. With a brisk kick, Justin sent the gun sliding across the pavement.

Another swing of his booted foot caught his opponent in the jaw. The man howled with rage, collapsed on the ground again, and held his injured face. Justin fled for the Jimmy. "Tess, get in! Let's go!"

Jolted into action by his shout, she mashed the remote button on the key chain that unlocked the doors. She fumbled with the handle on the driver's door, only to have him reach around her and yank it open.

He shoved her inside then followed, pushing her to the passenger seat. "I'll drive."

Snatching the keys from her, he jammed one in the ignition and threw the truck into reverse. The Jimmy's tires slipped on the wet pavement before finding some traction and squealing as he peeled out of the parking lot.

The crack of a gunshot reverberated through the damp air. Tess screamed.

"Are you hit?" He glanced over, his eyes dark with concern.

Her body convulsed with fright. Her knees and hands stung. She registered these facts on some level, but shock rendered her mute.

"Tess? Are you hurt?" Justin asked again, his voice rising.

She managed a quick head shake then hugged herself to suppress the shudders ravaging her body. "How did he f-find me so f-fast?" Closing her eyes, she moaned. "Oh, God, I knew he'd find me."

"What are you talking about, Tess? Are you saying you knew that guy?" Incredulity filled his voice.

She chewed her lip, remembering the black, evil eyes of her attacker. She rocked slowly, squeezing her arms more tightly around her. "Not him. But . . ."

"But what?" Justin guided the Jimmy on to the interstate, passing cars as he inched their speed up well past that of the other traffic. "What did he want, Tess?"

If the man had gotten her into the car . . .

If Justin hadn't come along when he did . . .

If she'd been alone . . .

When she realized how close she'd come to dying, a whimper escaped her throat. What did it feel like to die? Would the man have let her suffer?

Knowing Randall wanted her dead was a whole different creature than actually experiencing a brush with death.

Drawing a shaky breath, she turned tearful eyes toward Justin. He'd saved her life. The reality of that truth seeped in through the thick veil of her terror.

Should she trust Justin with the truth? Didn't he deserve to know what he'd gotten himself into? If he knew, she could convince him to save himself, to leave while he could. Was that what she wanted?

"Tess?"

With an effort, she forced her tongue to work. "He was going to kill me. Randall sent him."

"Some guy's trying to *kill* you?" His expression said he wouldn't have believed her if he hadn't just witnessed her attack.

She nodded. "I don't understand how he found me so fast. I knew he would come after me, but—"

"Christ." Justin ran a hand through his hair, knocking off his Stetson, which tumbled to the floor of the backseat. "No wonder you were acting so jumpy." He tapped his fist on the steering wheel and expelled a deep breath. "Maybe you should tell me exactly what's going on here. Why is this guy . . . what's his name? Randy?"

Tess fought a wave of nausea. "Randall."

"Who is Randall, and why does he want you dead?"

Several tense seconds ticked by before she answered. "He wants to keep me quiet. He's killed before. I just found out about the other murders, and—"

With an abrupt jerk of the steering wheel, Justin exited the interstate for a small two-lane road. She grabbed the armrest on the door to steady herself. Easing onto the narrow shoulder, he stopped the car and faced her.

"Who is Randall?" His blue gaze bore into hers.

Tears brimmed in her eyes. She thought of the naive girl she'd been when she'd met Randall following the loss of her family. Ironically, she'd needed his protection and the home he'd offered. Now the man who'd vowed all those years ago to help her wanted her dead.

She filled her lungs with a reinforcing breath, fighting a swell of shame. "My husband."

Calling Randall her husband, the role he'd claimed without benefit of making the title legal, was easier than explaining the truth.

A shadow crossed Justin's face, and he closed his eyes. "Shit!"

She jumped at the harsh sound of his curse, and a tear trickled down her cheek. "You should go now. I was wrong to put you in danger when I picked you up."

The rugged features of his face hardened, and he narrowed his eyes. "I'm not going anywhere."

His declaration hit her in the stomach like a fist. "But you can't stay with me. It's too dangerous."

"No way am I leaving you alone with a killer after you." His gaze and the resolve underlying his tone brooked no resistance.

"This isn't your problem, Justin. I can't let you—"

"I'm making it my problem."

When she shook her head, he leaned closer and cupped her jaw in his hand. Strong but gentle, his touch sent a heady sensation spiraling through her.

"I won't turn my back on you. I can't walk away. This is

something I have to do. Not just for you. For me. I made a promise to Rebecca . . ." He ducked his head, and his expression grew stormy. "Look, I don't expect you to understand. But the thing is, you're stuck with me." His thumb swiped at a tear clinging to her chin. "We'll be all right, Tess. I won't let anything happen to you."

His words stirred a warm reassurance inside her that battled with her icy fear of Randall's power. She wanted to believe Justin, wanted to think she might survive this nightmare.

Searching the bright promise in his eyes, she curled her bottom lip in and worried it with her teeth. His blue gaze dropped to watch her abuse her lip. Smoky desire filled his eyes. The muscles in his jaw tightened and flexed, and he slowly lifted a finger and dragged it over the roughened skin. His breath hissed through his teeth as he caressed her chapped lips with his fingertip. When he raised his penetrating stare to meet her eyes, the air stilled in her lungs. He intended to kiss her, she knew.

The simple idea of his kiss sent a tremor racing from her head to her toes.

Sliding his hand from her chin along the line of her jaw, he settled it at the nape of her neck. He drew her nearer, angling his head.

She tensed and pulled away. "No." Raising her hands to his chest, she pushed at him and averted her head. "Don't."

Unable to meet his gaze, she squeezed her eyes shut and pressed a trembling hand to her lips, left tingling from his touch. She heard his tired sigh, and a cool draft swirled around her, telling her he'd backed away.

"Please," she whispered, "we need to keep moving. Can we go?"

She heard the crunch of gravel as Justin pulled back onto the two-lane road. Her head already swam with the lightning speed of events that had changed her life and set her on the road. His attempt to kiss her gave her mind too much to process. She shoved thoughts of it aside so she could think more clearly about her situation and what she must do to shake Randall's henchman.

"I'm sorry," he said. "I know I shouldn't have done that."

She heard self-reproach in his low murmur. Peeking over at him, she found him staring out the windshield with a hard, worried frown darkening his face. The concern and determination reflected in his expression reminded her of his vow to stay with her. She couldn't fathom why he would want to put his life in jeopardy to help her. While his motivation puzzled her, she couldn't deny a twinge of relief. The promise of his protection enticed her to ignore the doubts about his reasons for involving himself in her problems. But how could she justify putting him in danger? He'd already risked his life to save her from Randall's man.

"The first thing we have to do is figure out how he found you." Justin glanced at her. "Have you used a credit card or seen someone he knows? Did you tell anyone your plans?"

"No. Except . . ."

His brow furrowed, and she swallowed hard.

"There was the guy at the car dealership where I traded in my car." Shaking her head, she rubbed her arms, fighting the damp chill that seeped to her bones. "Someone could have followed me, I guess, but I didn't see any one specific car behind me."

Justin dragged a hand down his cheek. "We should go to the cops and—"

"No!" Alarm sharpened her tone. "No police. Randall might have . . . he has contacts everywhere. Probably within the police department. I can't be sure, but I can't risk it either." She bit her lip and shivered. "You don't understand about Randall. He's a powerful man, and he holds a lot of influence over—"

"The phone," Justin said as his gaze swung from the road to Tess. Glancing down at her cellular phone, he slapped the steering wheel. "Of course! They traced the phone. You had it on. It rang earlier."

Tess gaped at him as his assertion sifted through her mind. A knot formed in her stomach, and she groaned. "How could I have been so stupid! I thought I'd been so careful!" Frustration and anger over her slipup churned inside her, and she balled her fists.

In her mind, she heard Randall's scornful laughter. *Dumb bitch! You thought you could get away from me? You don't have the nerve or the brains to outsmart me!*

A rock lodged in her chest, and she sighed. "Stupid, stupid—"

"Hey!" Disapproval colored Justin's voice. "You were scared. You made a mistake. Now let it go."

"But—"

"But nothing." He snatched up the phone, jerking the recharging cord from the cigarette lighter and rolled down his window. In a smooth motion, he flung the phone out of the car. "There. Problem solved. I don't want to hear any more about it."

The tension in her stomach uncoiled a fraction, but she couldn't forgive her screwup easily. Her mistake may have blown her best chance at escaping Randall. Her carelessness endangered Justin, an innocent in her grim situation. Neither was forgivable.

So why did Justin's eyes hold such tenderness and absolution when he glanced to her from watching the road?

"Tess, I meant what I said before. I won't let anyone hurt you. Not Randall. Not his flunkies. Nobody."

43

Her uncertainty must have been written in her expression, because he gave her a half smile, adding, "I know you don't believe me. Things probably look pretty hopeless right now. But you've only lost when you quit fighting. Remember that, okay?"

His attempts to encourage her touched her, though she couldn't quite muster even part of the optimism he had. Justin didn't know Randall.

He didn't know Randall's capacity for cruelty or his relentless and ruthless tactics for getting what he wanted. He didn't understand the scope of Randall's power or the terror his wrath caused. And Tess could only pray that he never did.

"Hello, Randall. How's the golf swing, friend?" Dalton Montgomery said brightly, and Randall grimaced. The insufferable bore probably wanted to play eighteen holes. No matter how valuable his alliance with the banker, he was in no mood to endure the man's company anytime soon. Tess's disappearance had eroded what little patience he had.

"Dalton," he replied coolly. "What can I do for you?"

"Oh, nothing for me. I was calling to see if there was anything else I could do for you and Tess. She didn't say what was wrong, but I got the definite impression she was upset when she stopped by the bank this morning."

Randall gripped the receiver tighter and pushed away the file he'd been perusing. "You saw Tess today?"

"Didn't she tell you? When she came in to make the withdrawal . . ." Montgomery paused. "You know I won't say anything about whatever private business you have that requires such a large cash withdrawal. We pride ourselves at First National on our discretion."

Gritting his teeth, he fought to control the rage flaring inside him. He couldn't let the banker know the sneaky bitch had bested him. "Just how much did Tess withdraw?"

"Uh, about twenty-four thousand, I believe. Do you mean you didn't know?"

"Certainly I knew." He kept his voice even through sheer force of will. "Just making sure she did as I asked. You'll excuse me now. I'm in a meeting." Randall carefully depressed the switchhook to disconnect the call.

Slamming down the receiver, he cursed viciously under his breath. Then again, louder. He didn't bother having his secretary call Morelli. He dialed the number himself.

When Morelli answered, Randall began without preamble. "She stole twenty-four thousand dollars from me. Did you know that? Have you found anything out, or do I have to find her myself?"

"No, boss. We're on her trail. She traded her BMW for a Jimmy. We know that much. I've got men all over the state lookin' for her. But she hasn't used her credit card yet and—"

"Of course she hasn't! The bitch has twenty-four thousand dollars cash of my money!"

"She's a smart broad, boss. Don't look like she wants to be found, and she's sure made it tough."

"Are you telling me she's smarter than you are? That you can't find her?" His barely suppressed rage darkened his tone. "Because if you are—"

"No, sir. Like I said, we're on her trail. One of our boys even had her for a while, but she got away. We're close—"

"What?" When he shot to his feet, his black leather desk chair toppled over. Fury pumped through his veins. "She got away? Who the hell'd you send after her? A damn Boy Scout?"

"No, sir. Dominic's one of the best in the business. But she had help. Some do-gooder jumped him from behind—"

"I don't want excuses. I want my wife. And, Morelli, the stakes have changed. She stole from me. If she gives you any more trouble, use force to bring her back. Understand? The little thief has to pay for what she's done."

"Right, I'm on it."

"And be sure to let Dominic know how *disappointed* I am in his failure." Silence answered him. "Morelli?"

"Yes, sir. I'll see to it myself."

"Good." Randall slammed down the receiver and braced his arms against the side of his long mahogany desk. He tried to cool his anger with deep, slow breaths, but the rage in him had a life of its own. Images of another woman who'd betrayed and manipulated him taunted him, and his fury boiled to a peak.

With a roar and one swipe of his arm, he cleared his desk. Files on multimillion-dollar mergers fluttered in the air like a flock of pigeons startled from their roost. Hoisting a crystal vase filled with dried willow branches, he hurled the arrangement across the room. The crystal shattered against a window offering a panoramic view of San Antonio's Riverwalk, but his anger remained intact.

An image of himself shone from the polished mahogany desktop he'd cleared. Staring at the face of the fifty-two-year-old man reflected in the dark wood, he saw not the successful businessman he'd become, but the scrawny, frightened little boy he'd been. That boy still lived inside him, reminding him daily of how it felt to be helpless and under someone else's control. Never again, that boy swore.

In his dark brown eyes and graying chestnut hair, Randall saw the man his father would have become . . . if he had lived to fifty-two. Of course, his father's hair would have been shaggy and needing a wash rather than neatly groomed by the best barber in San Antonio, as befitted a businessman of

Randall's stature. The tailored shoulders of his Armani suit emphasized the wide span of strong shoulders, but he saw the thin frame of a boy starving as much for his father's acceptance as for food. The only recognition of his existence he'd ever received came in the form of beatings from a worn leather belt.

I'll teach you not to run from me, you little snot! Who do you think you are? You're nothing! You'll never be anything but a burden to me!

He'd proven his old man wrong a million times. Every dollar in his bank account showed George Sinclair that his son was somebody. Money was power.

Randall had surrounded himself with people who jumped when he snapped his fingers. He'd scraped and clawed to build a business empire that stunned the competition. For years, his life had been filled with the best of everything. Even his wife drew the envy of his peers. Bending the young girl he'd taken in to his specifications had been simple, using the technique he'd learned well from his father.

He'd have never imagined his mouse of a wife would have the balls to defy him like this. Yet she'd proven herself disloyal and ungrateful for his generosity. A fire smoldered in his gut, and he dug his fingers into the edge of his desk, struggling to regain control.

"When I'm finished with you, Tess, you won't make the mistake of betraying me again."

Tess remained silent and withdrawn as the miles ticked off on the odometer. Justin used the time to do his own thinking. His journey to Nashville had taken a giant detour, and he couldn't help but think God had thrown Tess in his path as a test.

When he'd finally quit talking about his aspirations in the

music business and dedicated his life to making his dreams a reality, his past returned to haunt him. God couldn't have given him a clearer message if he'd written it in gold across the sky.

You can't have your dream until you make amends for your failure. Before I give you the future, you must pay for the past.

He glanced at the woman riding beside him, her hazel eyes still wide with fright and unwilling to close for much-needed rest. Beneath the fear, however, he sensed a fighting spirit. She'd had the courage, the good sense to get out of Dodge, away from her husband. Granted, layers of self-doubt, intimidation, and pessimism still choked out the spark inside her, but he intended to nourish that spark, fan it to life and help her find her inner strength. Rebecca would have accepted no less.

They'd outrun the worst of the rain. Only a light sprinkling remained, and the sun managed to peek out through tiny breaks in the clouds. He took the change in the weather as a good omen.

The silence in the car dragged on for several more minutes, until Tess spoke. "Why?"

Without asking for clarification, he understood her terse question. She needed more than platitudes, more than the *because I have to* that sprang to mind. She wanted to understand what compelled him to force his way into her life, and she deserved to know the truth.

"I promise I'll tell you everything later. Right now, why don't you try to get some sleep."

She gave him a tiny, humorless laugh. "Sleep. I've almost forgotten what that is."

Massaging the stiffness out of his neck muscles with one hand, he blinked his gritty-feeling eyes. "Well, I could use a good night's sleep. There's a town in about another forty miles. What's say we stop there and get a room for the night?"

Her head whipped around, and the apprehension in her eyes now focused on him. "Get a room?"

"Yeah. We have to stop sometime." Tugging up one corner of his mouth, he flashed her a gentle grin. "You do plan to stop for food and sleep, don't you?"

Her hands moved restlessly in her lap. "I . . . I . . . ."

"Is it stopping that bothers you, or sharing a room with me?"

She turned away and watched the passing scenery for a moment before answering. "Either. Both."

"Tess, we tossed the phone, so he's not tracking us anymore." Justin rubbed his chin and returned his attention to the highway. "He won't know where you are. It's safe to stop." With a sideways glance, he found her chewing her bottom lip again. "Will you stop that? You're going to make it bleed." When she cast him a startled frown, he grinned. "Your mouth is too pretty for you to go around mistreating your lip that way."

Dumbfounded silence was her only response.

"As far as the room goes, just get used to the idea. I'm not letting you out of my sight. Not after what happened back there." He paused and tapped the steering wheel with his fingers. "I've been thinking. If we register as Mr. and Mrs. Justin Boyd, your name doesn't appear in the hotel records. That's added protection for you, right?"

She blinked, her eyes still full of distrust, but she nodded.

"I'll ask for two beds, of course. And I won't try to jump your bones, if that's what you're thinking."

Her eyes grew even wider. Then she turned away with a swift, jerky motion. She raised a neatly manicured fingernail to her teeth, and he reached over to catch her hand.

"Same goes for the fingernails. No biting allowed. I'm not going to let anyone hurt you." He wrapped his fingers around her shoulder and squeezed gently. "Try to relax."

She shivered. "Easy for you to say." Lifting her chin, she faced him, irritation blazing in her eyes. "Look, I don't know why you've decided I'm your charity case or your personal damsel to save, but I didn't ask for a bodyguard. Not that I don't appreciate the help you gave me back at the restaurant, but the thing is, I'd rather do this alone. I don't want to be responsible for putting you at risk. I don't want a roommate. And I don't need a nag telling me not to bite my nails if I feel like it!"

Try as he might, he couldn't suppress a grin.

"Now what are you laughing at?" Her wrinkled brow and chiding tone reflected her pique.

"I knew there was a spark buried in you."

"Excuse me?" She tipped her head, pinning him with a baffled stare.

"Never forget the fact that you took action, Tess. No matter what else happens, you had the courage to get away from a bad situation. That in itself is a victory."

Clearly, his directness caught her off guard. She sank back against her seat and seemed to wilt. "It wasn't courage that made me leave. It was fear. I'm not nearly as heroic as you want to paint me." Dropping her chin, she stared down at her hands.

"I know what I see. Besides, courage isn't the absence of fear, it's the ability to act despite the fear."

She gave him a brief glance then seemed to be considering his point. Silence returned for the next several miles, but now the quiet felt more companionable than tense. When he pulled the Jimmy into the parking lot of an independently owned motel, he sensed the tension filling her again.

Taking her hand, he brushed a kiss on her knuckles. "Shall we check in, Mrs. Boyd?"

Her gaze lingered on their linked hands for a moment before lifting to meet his. The misgivings he read in her expression as she weighed her options faded, and with a light squeeze of his hand, she relayed the faith she put in him. He accepted her trust as the precious gift it was. Warmth spread through him and seeped into the dark crevices where guilt and despair had lived for long years.

When her mouth curved in a small smile, her face glowed. Tess had an undeniable beauty, inside and out. His thoughts leaped to his impulsive attempt to kiss her. Even stroking her lush mouth with his fingers had fueled a desire he knew he had to control. He'd promised her safety, and she'd offered her trust.

Now they would be sharing a room, posing as man and wife, sleeping within the same walls. He'd sworn not to touch her, and his conscience wouldn't let him break that oath.

But if she made the first move, all bets were off.

Chapter Four

His men were waiting when he strode into the dim warehouse. Tony Morelli gave them a grim look as he approached, relaying his disgust with their piss-poor work. Dominic seemed particularly edgy, despite his dark glower. And so he should be. He'd not done his job, made Morelli look bad to Sinclair. By all rights, Dominic should be quaking in his snakeskin boots.

"Let's have it. What do we know? Where is she?" Morelli barked.

Henry Granger, a tall, burly man Sinclair had handpicked, spoke first. "We know she went north since Dom tracked her to outside Waco. We've focused our efforts in that region, put more men there."

"That was hours ago," Morelli growled and stepped closer to Henry. "She could be anywhere in a two-hundred-mile radius by now."

Henry squared his shoulders. "We've got the area covered. Got the whole damn state covered for that matter. She won't be hard to find. A woman as hot as Tess Sinclair is gonna get noticed, whether she wants it or not."

Dominic shifted his weight, drawing Morelli's attention. "We've got ears on 'bout any number she might call. Her secretary, their house . . . everyone right down to her hairdresser. If she calls anyone for help, we'll trace it."

"If." Morelli faced Dominic fully. "If she calls. And what

if she don't? Sinclair's frothin' at the mouth. He wants her back yesterday!" He stepped closer to Dominic and shoved his face close to the shorter man's. Close enough to smell the man's sweat. "Do you understand what I'm sayin'?"

"Our men have given pictures of her to places along the highways where she might stop. Motels, restaurants, gas stations and the like. Put a real sweet price on any lead that pays off. We've already got tips comin' in." Dominic gave him a satisfied grin. "We've got eyes everywhere."

Morelli stepped back and rubbed the bristly stubble on his jaw. "Sinclair says she stole his money. When you find her, if she makes trouble, no need to be gentle with her."

He glanced from Henry to Dominic to make sure they'd understood. Like 'em or not, those were Sinclair's orders. His job was not to second guess, just to comply. Still, hurting a woman wasn't Morelli's style. He'd slit his share of men's throats in his day, but with women, well . . . women were good for so many nicer things. Speaking of which . . .

He glanced at his watch, eager to finish his business and get back to Maria. If this morning was any indication, his wife had some nice things planned for him when he got home. His blood heated at the thought.

"All right. I want another report tonight. You get anything promisin' on her, I want to hear. Got it?"

"Got it."

Dominic turned to leave, and Morelli sent Henry a silent signal.

"Not so fast, Dom. Sinclair wanted you to know how disappointed he was that you let his wife get away."

Dominic stopped and cast a wary glance over his shoulder. Henry grabbed him in a wrestler's hold, pinning the stocky man's arms to his sides. Panic filled Dominic's eyes, and Morelli snarled in disgust.

Whipping a switchblade from under his jacket, Morelli seized Dominic's right hand.

"Noooo!"

Dominic's pinkie came off with a quick, clean swipe of the switchblade, and the man crumpled to the floor, howling in pain.

"Don't fail Randall Sinclair or me again, Dom. He's not likely to give you a third chance."

Tess stood in the middle of the floor, rubbing the goose bumps on her arms and moving her gaze around the dark motel room. The dark green and blue patterned bedspreads had been chosen to hide dirt, she supposed, and not to dispel the gloomy ambience.

Justin's backpack bumped her fanny when he scooted past her, attesting to the narrow confines. She stepped out of his way, rubbing her bottom.

As he dumped his possessions in the corner by one of the sagging beds, he grinned at her. "Sorry."

With a click, he snapped on the wall light, and a golden glow spilled from behind the scalloped, plastic lampshade. The soft light brightened the room some, but Tess remained uneasy.

Eyeing Justin as he settled in, she acknowledged that her discomfort came from her circumstances and not her environment. The small motel room seemed even smaller because of the man hanging his cowboy hat on the top end of his guitar case.

She also acknowledged that her discomfort could not be called fear. Although fear had been a living thing inside her for most of the day, she trusted Justin. Her uncertainty sprang from the way he'd thrust himself into her life, appointed himself her protector. Even after his first-hand taste of the danger she faced, he chose to stay with her, flatly refused to leave when she begged him to get himself out of harm's way. But why? He was hiding something from her, and that missing piece of the puzzle gnawed at her.

She intended to draw the truth from him. Somehow.

Justin turned down the window unit air conditioner, which blew musty-smelling, damp air. The elimination of the cool draft eased the chill that prickled her arms, burrowed to her bones, and even made her nose run. She longed for a chance to change into warm, dry clothes after spending the afternoon wet and shivering.

Apparently, her roommate had similar ideas, because he stripped his damp T-shirt over his head and began rummaging in his backpack. "Draw straws for first dibs on the shower?"

Tess stared at his wide, taut chest and tan nipples with a nervous fluttering in her stomach. Why had she agreed to share a room with him? Surely there'd been a suitable compromise if she'd taken the time to think it through.

"Tess?"

Then again, he hadn't given her much choice.

His high-handedness nettled her, but she kept silent. Experience had taught her that the less she argued or provoked, the better. When he bent to dig in his pack again, she followed the bumpy path of his spine down his muscled back to the point it disappeared into his jeans.

"I don't mind waiting, if you want to go first," he said. "Just save me a little hot water. Okay?"

Sharing close quarters would be awkward at best. She knew next to nothing about this man. Except that he had a charm, a reassuring manner, a presence about him that managed to lull her despite the circumstances. His sense of fairness led him to pay for half of a motel room she'd guess he couldn't afford. He had a stubborn streak that made reasoning with him an exercise in futility.

And he was as handsome as the devil.

The unbidden thought popped into her mind, rattling her senses, much the way his near-kiss had startled her. She raised a hand to touch her lips, remembering the soft pressure of his fingers there.

He'd said her mouth was pretty. Warmth gathered in her chest and radiated outward, tingling in her limbs, muddling her brain. She should know better than to take his offhand compliment seriously, but his kindness touched a raw nerve, soothed her bruised spirit.

Echoes of Randall's rage, just one night before, filtered through her mind. In recent years, all she'd known from Randall was humiliation. She suppressed a shudder and chased the ugly memories away by focusing on Justin's activity. He pulled a pair of white briefs out of his backpack and tucked them under his arm with the fresh jeans and T-shirt he'd already extracted.

The corners of his eyes crinkled when he faced her. "Yo, Tess? You in there?"

"Hm?" Snapped from her dazed examination of him, she met the amusement in his blue eyes.

"And women accuse men of not listening." He shook his head. "Do. You. Want. The. Shower. First?" He pinned her with a pointed gaze and curled his lips in a wry smile.

"Oh. Uh . . . no, you go ahead." She stepped over to the bed farthest from him and sank wearily on the edge. "You never did eat before. You must be starving."

Rubbing his lean stomach, he came around the end of his bed and headed for the shower. "You're right about that."

Drawn by the motion of his hand, her attention lingered

on the dark hair sprinkled across his abdomen. "I could order room service if you—"

His laughter interrupted her. "We're not in the Marriott, Tess. I don't think room service is an option."

Frowning at him, she scrunched the ugly bedspread in her hands. "I know that. I'm just tired. My brain is kind of numb, and I—"

"Don't sweat it. I'll get something from the vending machine later." He waved a dismissive hand as he sauntered toward the bathroom.

"Nothing nutritious ever came out of a vending machine, Justin."

He paused and cast her an odd look. She caught her breath, realizing her comment could have been construed as a challenge rather than concern.

"Junk food got me where I am today. Something nutritious would probably send my body into shock." With a wink, he disappeared into the bathroom.

After a moment to release the air from her lungs, Tess found herself grinning. Justin's easy-going demeanor and sense of humor were foreign to her. Randall had little patience with her occasional attempts at levity, and his overbearing nature soon quashed her desire to try to lighten his mood. Peaceful coexistence quickly proved her best tactic with her common-law husband.

Compelled to feed Justin, to repay him for saving her life if nothing else, she mulled over the options for food. Having something delivered seemed the best bet since it wouldn't require her leaving the safety of the room and Justin's proximity.

She paused, mulling over the idea that his presence gave her a vague sense of security. Maybe she'd had selfish motives for not fighting his decision to stay with her. As crazy as it seemed, she felt safer with this man she'd known for a few hours than she did around the man she'd moved in with twelve years ago when she needed a different kind of security.

Yet she knew better than to let her guard down. If nothing else, the kidnapping attempt showed her Randall's men could strike at any time, anywhere. That thought sent a fresh wave of chills prickling over her skin.

With a weary sigh, she opened the phone book and found the number of a pizza store that delivered. She reached for the phone but paused with her hand suspended over the receiver, a haunting memory seeping through her mind.

She'd been in her kitchen, cutting up raw chicken for a casserole just two days ago when the phone rang . . .

If only she'd never heard that incriminating call. She shook her head. No, that call and the events that followed, all the wretched things she'd discovered about Randall, had been the catalysts to make her act. She'd finally screwed up the nerve to walk away from a miserable existence, and she would never look back. Now she could only pray she lived long enough to find the new life she craved.

A loud thump from the bathroom jolted Tess from her reverie, and adrenaline spiked her pulse.

"Ow!" Justin yelped. "Damn that hurt!"

She glanced toward the bathroom door. "Justin?"

"I'm all right. Just clumsy is all."

She put a hand over her racing heart and dragged in a calming breath.

When she called the pizza store, she ordered by rote the same sausage pizza Randall liked but she'd learned to hate over the years. Just before she hung up, she caught herself.

"Wait!" she called to the woman on the line. "Change that to a vegetarian pizza with whole wheat crust."

The freedom to do as she chose, without Randall's censure, caused a ripple of joy to flow through her. For tonight at least, she could breathe easier, do whatever she wanted. A small victory.

She sighed and lay back on a pillow, stacking her hands under her head to stare at the ceiling. She listened to the voices that passed outside their door, the rumble of traffic on the highway, the distant wail of a siren. Somewhere out there, Randall's men were looking for her. Closing in on her. She had to remember that, had to stay alert and be cautious. Her life depended on it.

A moment later, Justin's voice carried loud and strong over the sound of the shower. His singing was so incongruously lighthearted in contrast to the ominous track of her thoughts that she started at the sound. After a moment, Tess cracked a grin as she listened to him croon. His rich, mellifluous tenor voice gave her a measure of comfort, and she closed her eyes. His cheerfulness helped her keep her mind from dwelling on her frightening past and uncertain future. The familial ease that he displayed with his shower concert took the rough edge off her nerves.

An image of Justin naked, rivers of water streaming down his lean body as he showered, flashed in her mind's eye. Startled by the sensual picture, she quickly opened her eyes again. Her heartbeat accelerated. Still, his voice skimmed over her like a lover's hand, leaving a tingle on her skin. She wrapped her arms around herself, dismayed by the path her thoughts had taken. Allowing herself to feel any attraction to her rescuer would only complicate things for her. She needed to keep her association with him as emotionally detached as possible. Objectivity would make freeing herself from him easier.

The water cut off, and Justin whistled now.

Tess stared at the ceiling with wide eyes, afraid to close them again because of the graphic vision she'd conjured before.

When the bathroom door opened, she refused to look at Justin, uncertain what she'd find or what he might read in her eyes, but her peripheral vision followed his movement around the room.

"No TV, huh?" he asked.

"No."

"I never watch much, anyway. How about you?"

"No." Listening to the whisper of cloth, his soft tenor humming, and the thud of her heartbeat, she searched for a distraction. "I ordered us a pizza."

"Oh, yeah? Cool. What kind?"

"A large vegetarian with whole wheat crust."

The rustle of clothing stopped, and the shadows on the ceiling stilled.

"You're joking, right? You didn't really ruin a perfectly good pizza with vegetables and whole wheat, did you?"

Teasing laced his tone, yet she tensed.

"Yes."

She heard a snort-like sigh then a low chuckling, and she relaxed her muscles again.

"At this point, even vegetables sound good. I'm starved."

When the shifting shadows told her he'd moved across the room toward his backpack, she pushed off the bed. Keeping her eyes averted, she ran for the bathroom.

Her hot shower relieved the physical chill, but she doubted anything could ever remove the icy horror of the past few days from her memory. As she emerged from her bath, her own stomach rumbled for food.

Once dressed, she headed out of the bathroom and found

Justin sitting on the bed with his back against the wall. His long legs stretched in front of him, and he held his guitar on his lap. He'd donned a dry pair of jeans and a blue T-shirt, but his feet were bare. His longish hair had been brushed away from his face and curled damply around his ears and nape. The fantasy image of him in the shower she'd conjured moments ago wasn't nearly as breathtaking as the reality she gaped at now.

"How long did they say delivery on the pizza would be?" He plucked at the strings of his guitar, tuning it.

"I didn't ask." Studying him, she found nothing, from his wavy black hair to his narrow, bare feet, that wasn't beautifully masculine, relaxed and . . . sexy. The moment the word entered her mind, Justin raised his gaze to hers, and her heart leaped. The air crackled with the electricity in his knowing blue eyes, as if he'd read her thoughts. Her body grew warm from the heat in his gaze.

What if she had allowed him to kiss her? She looked at his lips and imagined their sweet caress against hers, the gently coaxing suction—

A staccato knock on the door reverberated through the room like gunfire. Tess jerked, tension thrumming through her as her attention darted to the door.

"Hang tight. I'll get it." Justin swung his legs off the bed and shoved to his feet.

Tess shrank back out of view and listened, her heart drumming.

"Evenin'," Justin drawled.

"Twenty-one sixty-five," the delivery boy said.

Tess released the breath she'd been holding. The pizza. Not a hit man.

Justin took the pizza and brought it inside as Tess got her purse. She opened it only a crack, careful to conceal the bundles of bills she'd gotten that morning at the bank. Keeping the huge amount of cash in her purse made her nervous, but what option did she have?

She fished a bill out and thrust it at Justin. He handed her the pizza as he took the money, mumbling under his breath, "Expensive vegetables."

When his gaze dropped to the bill she'd handed him, he gave a low whistle. "I hope he's got enough change."

Her gaze flickered to the one-hundred-dollar bill she'd drawn out. Snatching it back, she traded it for a twenty and a five. "Tell him to keep the change."

While she put the pizza box on the bed and knelt on the floor, he paid the delivery boy and locked the door.

"How is it? It smells fantastic." He tucked a long leg under him as he sat on the floor beside her, bending his other leg in front of him.

Tess handed him a large slice with cheese strings dripping from the sides. "It's hot. Be careful."

They ate in silence for several minutes, demolishing half the pizza in record time.

"So, which way are you thinking of heading tomorrow?" Justin picked up his fourth slice and peered at her over the gooey cheese. "Do you have a destination in mind? A friend somewhere you can stay with?"

She chewed her pizza thoughtfully, shaking her head. "No. I'll go wherever the road leads, I guess."

Her response earned her a lopsided grin from Justin. "I like a woman with a sense of adventure."

Tess scoffed. "Adventure never factored into this trip. A sense of panic is more like it. Now I'm just drifting . . . sorting through things. I've got a lot of decisions to make."

He cocked an eyebrow. Before he could ask more questions, she grabbed for the first topic she could think of to redirect the conversation. "Tell me about the rest of your family. Are they all in Wallerton?"

Chuckling, he wiped his mouth on a napkin. "Wellerton."

"Whatever."

"My parents are in Wellerton, but I have an older brother who's an attorney in Austin. A real hotshot, that Brian. I'm a bit of a disappointment to my parents compared to my brother."

"Don't say that!"

Justin shrugged. "It's the truth, and I'm used to it. Every time I got into trouble growing up, they gave me the 'why can't you be responsible like Brian' lecture. I never finished college and didn't have a white-collar job like Brian. Instead, I framed houses for a construction company by day and played at a honky-tonk by night. That is, until last week, when I decided to ditch everything for a shot at the brass ring. My parents hated that decision. They thought I should be more settled, more 'practical about life.' " He said the last phrase in a deeper voice, apparently mimicking his father.

Pausing long enough to take another bite, he glanced at her as he continued. "But I can't settle for something else. I love music. It's what I was meant to do. I know it is."

Blue fire sparked to life in his eyes, and Tess grinned.

"I like a man with faith in his dreams."

Justin flashed a wry grin. "Thanks for the vote of confidence. Amy, my ex-girlfriend, thought I was crazy to insist on going to Nashville. We parted friends, but her lack of faith hurt. I'm as determined to prove them all wrong as I am to succeed for my own sake." He cast her a sideways glance, twisting his mouth. "Petty of me, huh?"

In answer, Tess reached for his hand and curled her fingers around his. The gesture felt right, felt good. Justin squeezed back. "I don't know," she said. "Didn't anyone support you? Encourage you? Respect your talent and your courage to pursue your dream?"

Somber shadows stole over his face, and he slipped his hand out of hers to rake his fingers through his hair. "Rebecca did."

"Rebecca? Your angel?"

Turning away from her, he locked his gaze on the opposite wall. His expression remained dark, and the muscles in his square jaw flexed as he clenched his teeth. The shift in his mood piqued her curiosity.

"That is one butt-ugly picture," he mumbled.

Tess turned to glance at the painting across the room. "Fits the decor though. The whole room is ugly."

He swept his gaze around the room, as if seeing it for the first time, and grunted. "You're right."

When he fell silent again, brooding, Tess started cleaning up the pizza. He was clearly reluctant to discuss Rebecca, so she let the subject drop. He'd respected her right to have secrets, and she'd give him the same privilege. Rising from the floor with the pizza box in her hand, she moved to put the leftover pizza in the trash.

"She was my sister."

His admission replayed in her head a couple times before the oddity of his phrasing finally sank in. "Was?"

"She died a couple years ago. Rather, she was murdered."

Tess numbly set the pizza box on the edge of the sink and stared at him. She swallowed hard before she found her voice. "Oh, my God. Justin, I'm so sorry."

Lifting a hard gaze to meet hers, he squinted at her. "Why? You have no reason to be sorry. Her death wasn't your fault."

She blinked at him. "I just meant I—"

"If anyone's to blame, it's me. I let her die."

Chapter Five

Tess stared at Justin mutely for the space of several stumbling heartbeats. Pain filled his eyes, and the back of her neck prickled with apprehension. "What do you mean?"

He looked away and ran a hand over his face, sighing heavily. "It's not pretty. You sure you want to hear it?"

A dark foreboding crept through her, and she trembled. Wrapping her arms around her chest, she sank on the edge of the bed. She'd thought she needed to know his motivation for helping her, but now she wasn't sure. Did she want to hear the truth? She had enough horror in her life without hearing the ugliness in Justin's life as well. Still, she heard her voice, weak and raspy, whisper, "Go on."

He stared at her with a spooky intensity before he spoke. "Rebecca was three years older than me. She met Mac in college, and they got married after dating for just four months. He was an engineering student and kind of conservative. Rebecca was the exact opposite of him in so many ways. I couldn't understand the attraction between them, but since Rebecca seemed happy, I kept my mouth shut."

He rubbed his hands on his jeans, and his breathing grew shallow and quick. He stared at the painting across from him, though she knew from his expression he saw nothing. He shuddered, lost in his memories. Clearing his throat, he forged on. "One night she came by my apartment. She'd had a fight with Mac and . . ." Justin gritted his teeth, scrunching his face with the emotion that tortured him. "The bastard had given my sister a bloody lip and a black eye."

Nausea gripped Tess. She knew too well where his story was going. "Oh, God." Pressing a shaky hand to her mouth, she watched Justin wrestle with the past, her heart breaking for him. Her mind reeled with the implications of what he told her. After a heavy silence, she asked, "What did you do?"

Justin scoffed. "Not jack shit." He squeezed his eyes shut and shook his head in regret. "Not that night, anyway. I wanted to rip Mac apart. I was on my way out the door to give the jerk a taste of his own medicine, but Rebecca begged me not to. She swore it wouldn't happen again. She defended the creep and went on and on about how he loved her and how she'd provoked him."

A weary sigh hissed through his teeth. "She made me swear not to tell our parents or Brian. She made me promise not to say or do anything, telling me she could handle him, swearing she would be all right. But she wasn't all right. It happened again. This time I didn't listen to her pleas not to hurt Mac. I tracked him down at a local bar and beat the snot out of him. Got arrested for my efforts, too. You can imagine how my parents loved that!"

"Didn't you explain why—"

"Naw. I'd promised Becca not to say anything, and a man's only as good as his word. They already thought I was a screwup, so what difference would it have made?" He looked down at his hands, which he'd clenched in tight fists. "All I did by pounding Mac was give Becca one more thing to worry about. Mac's abuse didn't stop. I quit college so I could be nearby and keep an eye on the situation, for all the good that did. I begged her to leave him. I threatened her. I nagged her. But I never told anyone. I never called the police. And she always went back to him." Justin's tone held years of self-reproach and guilt. "He hit her in the head with a golf club one night and killed her."

Compassion for his pain flooded Tess, crimping her throat. She ached for some way to relieve his suffering, but his story left her too stunned, too shaken to move. "Justin, you tried—"

"I didn't try hard enough!" His blue eyes flashed, cutting through her like lasers. With a scorching curse, he kicked the legs of a nearby chair with his bare heel. The chair rocked then tipped over. "I knew she was in danger, and I didn't do enough!"

The anger in his voice warned her to back off. Common sense told her his frustration had nothing to do with her. But Randall had never needed a reason to take his rancor out on her.

Tess pulled her knees to her chest and huddled on the bed, watching Justin warily. While an inner voice reasoned that any man who'd fought to free his sister from a violent man would never use violence on a woman himself, her survival instinct still went on full alert.

Burying his face in his hands, he sucked in several deep breaths. When he lifted his head and met her gaze, the tension in his expression had eased, though his eyes were still bright with emotion. He pushed himself off the floor and started toward her.

Tess lifted her chin and fixed a leery gaze on him. A knot of anxiety twisted inside her, and she scooted backward across the bed, ready to flee. When he raised a hand toward her, Tess forgot to breathe. Instinctively, she drew back, and her head bumped the wall.

Furrowing his black eyebrows, Justin brushed her cheek with his palm. "You don't get it, do you?" He shook his head.

"I'd die before I let anyone hurt you. I turned my back once, but I will never make that mistake again."

The low, husky timbre of his voice wrapped around her like a hug. She filled her lungs as relief washed over her, leaving her body weak and shaking. "Then this is about your sister. You can't forgive yourself until you save another woman in her place."

His hand fell away from her cheek, and he pressed his mouth in a thin line. "No. I'll never forgive myself for letting Becca die. But I can damn well make sure it doesn't happen to you."

With a sigh, she rolled off the bed, away from him. She was getting far too involved with this man for anybody's good. She had to stay detached in order to make a clean break from him. Soon. "Go to Nashville, Justin. Forget about me. If I can find a quiet town where no one knows me, the chances of Randall finding me are remote. I'll be fine." She worked to infuse the statement with a credibility she didn't feel.

Squaring her shoulders, she met his dubious expression with her own determination. She had to convince him to go his own way. He would get himself in too deep, if she didn't extricate herself as soon as possible. "I don't *want* you involved in my problems."

Justin sat in the middle of the bed with his arms propped on his bent knees, his expression melancholy. "You haven't listened to me, have you? I won't leave you. Not until I'm sure you're safe. I couldn't live with myself if I walked away now, without doing anything to help you free yourself."

"But I am free. I got away, thanks to you. Your work is done. You're free to go." With a wide sweep of her arm, she motioned toward the door. "Mission accomplished."

He rolled his head from side to side, stretching the muscles in his neck, and he groaned. "Tell me something, Tess.

Do you really believe he's given up? Your husband sent a man after you with a gun, and now he's just given up? Earlier today, you said—"

"I know what I said." Tess closed her eyes, and her shoulders drooped. "You're like an aggravating stray dog that won't take a hint, you know?" She looked at him squarely and shouted, "Shoo! I don't want you. Go away!"

His face brightened. "Nope. You messed up when you fed me. Now, I'm gonna hang around forever."

"I wanted to repay you," she said, splaying her hands in exasperation. "I figured food was the least I could do after you saved my life."

"True." A smart-alecky grin lit his face, and she gave up. The teasing, laid-back Justin she'd traveled with today had returned. Having buried the pain and frustration deep inside once more, he resumed his role as the jovial companion. But she saw his humor and teasing in a new light. People dealt with pain in different ways. Was Justin's ready grin just a mask? His laid-back joking a shield?

A sharp stab of sympathy pierced her heart. Her carefree and cocky cowboy proved a more complex man than she'd guessed.

Sighing, she crossed the room to her suitcase and worked to tamp down the swell of emotion her new understanding of Justin triggered. She couldn't afford to peel back the layers of this man and invest any of herself learning what made him tick. If she started to care about him, she'd create a bond she had no right building. She meant to get Justin out of her life as soon as she could figure out how. No point complicating her task with attachments that would hurt her when broken.

A heaviness settled in her chest. She'd likely spend her life alone, holding herself apart from real affection or commitment or emotional connection. The hope she'd had as a young woman for the kind of love her parents had shared had been shattered in the first year of her life with Randall. Although Randall had refused to marry her legally and had tainted her view of matrimony, she clung to the memory of her parents' happiness.

Though she'd never vowed "till death do us part," she hadn't realized how ominous the truth was. Not only would she never have the chance to feel the special bond her parents had shared, she doubted she could ever truly free herself from the man who'd stolen her hopes and dreams.

The weight in her chest tightened, rose to her throat, and Tess struggled to contain the tears that would serve no purpose. She had learned long ago to accept her lot in life. So why did she belabor the facts and torture herself now?

Clearing her throat, she faced Justin again and scowled at him. "You're on my bed, and I'm tired. Please move."

Instantly, she regretted the sharpness of her tone. She was mad at herself, not him. Discouraged by her emotional weakness, weary from the strain of the day, and pessimistic about her future, she unfairly took her frustrations out on the most convenient target.

Such transference was unlike her. Around Randall, she had learned to bottle up her feelings and stoically bear the brunt of his temper. What had happened to her?

Justin cocked an eyebrow and scooted off the bed. "All yours."

Her body and spirit sagged as she watched him meander toward his bed, where he restored his guitar to its case.

"Justin."

His gaze rose to hers as he snapped the case shut. "Hm?"

"I'm sorry. I've been rude to you all day, and it's not right." Guilt sapped her strength, and she wrinkled her brow. "Forgive me?"

Bracing a hand on his hip, he regarded her with a placid expression. "Forget it. We've been on something of an emotional roller coaster today. What we both need is a good night's sleep. Things will look better in the morning."

Despite her fatigue, a soft smile found her lips. "The eternal optimist. You're amazing."

"Attitude is everything, Tess."

She mustered the energy to brush her teeth before crawling into bed, but sleep eluded her. A parade of worries marched through her head. She stared into the darkness, listening to the creaking of the next bed as Justin made himself comfortable and flapped the sheets.

"Justin?"

"Yeah?" A sleepy rasp thickened his voice.

"What happened to her husband? Rebecca's husband."

She heard him heave a deep sigh. "After tying up the courts and fighting the charges against him for two years, he was convicted of involuntary manslaughter last month." Bitterness colored his tone. "He'll get out after serving just two years."

"Two years?"

"Yeah."

"That's not right."

He remained silent for a long time before whispering, "No, it's not. Rebecca lost probably sixty years of her life, and Mac will only lose two." He paused. "Good night, Tess." His bed creaked again as he rolled over.

Two years. Fury swirled inside her at the injustice.

The same thing would happen with Randall, she knew. With all his connections, his ruthless power, his lethal procedures, Randall would never pay for his crimes. He'd built a business empire, a legion of minions, and an intimidating reputation by sheer will—and cutthroat tactics. Randall was a steamroller who would take down anyone or anything in his path.

Justin had unwittingly stepped in front of a speeding locomotive.

She accepted the fact that she would always be at risk, would always have to look over her shoulder. But she couldn't let Justin die for her mistakes.

She knew what she had to do.

Her decision made, she rolled over in search of sleep.

"We've got men at the airport, the bus and train stations all over the area, in case she ditches the Jimmy. We're doin' everything we can, but . . ." Tony Morelli rubbed the side of his nose and floundered for the best way to explain the poor results he'd had finding Sinclair's wife.

Randall Sinclair's face remained impassive as he leaned back in the leather-upholstered armchair behind his desk. "But?"

Morelli cleared his throat. Sinclair's calm unnerved him more than if he yelled. Unseen, unheard dangers were always the most deadly, he'd learned.

"I really hate the word 'but,' Morelli." Sinclair drew a slow, measured breath and glanced away before returning his dark, placid gaze. "It's usually followed by all sorts of lame excuses why someone's not obeying a direct order."

Morelli straightened his back. "We've covered all the bases. We'll have her soon enough."

"I'll decide what is soon enough." Sinclair leaned forward and narrowed a feral glare on Morelli. "I want my wife back. Expand your search. Up the reward for information. It's not like I'm really going to part with any cash once we have the info we need. She could be out of the state by now. Even out of the country. You realize that, don't you?"

"Yes, sir. Though it's not likely. If she'd gone to an airport, my men—"

"Your men let her get away once already. Your men had better come up with something, or I'm going to hold you personally responsible."

Swallowing the acid that rose in his throat, Morelli nodded. "Yes, boss."

"It seems to me you don't appreciate how upsetting it can be for your wife to go missing. I'd hate for you to find out the hard way, Tony. Maria is such a pretty thing."

Morelli's eyes widened at the implied threat.

"You have until tomorrow morning."

Morelli nodded and turned to leave the office. He understood, perhaps better than anyone, how Sinclair worked. Ever since Sinclair had helped pay off his gambling debt to a loan shark with a mean streak, Morelli had worked for the business tycoon. His methods were more subtle than the loan shark's, but no less lethal. But Morelli had always been on the trigger end of the gun, meting out Sinclair's version of debt repayment. Morelli knew Sinclair's cold-hearted capacity to bend people to his will, and the extent of the danger Maria was in, if he couldn't produce Tess Sinclair by morning.

"Tess?" Justin propped on one elbow and peered through the blackness to the second bed.

"Angie," Tess whimpered. Her head tossed restlessly from side to side. "Not Angie."

"Tess, wake up."

"Don't!" Her voice sounded tense, tormented by the nightmare that haunted her. "No . . . no!" She thrashed her arms as if fighting someone off.

Justin debated shaking her. His heart wrenched for her anguish, but she might be more frightened if he woke her.

She kicked at the sheets that trapped her legs, and sweat popped out on her brow, despite the chill from the powerful motel air conditioner. She whimpered then became still except for the near-convulsive shivers that wracked her body.

He watched her sleep. Sympathy knotted his gut. Her hair, an unusual shade of light brown, spread in a tangle on the starched white pillowcase. Her long dark eyelashes fanned in a similar fashion on her dewy, ivory skin. Having kicked off her sheets, a generous amount of her slender thighs was exposed. The wind suit pants that she'd removed, once under her sheet, lay crumpled near the foot of the bed.

His gaze slid over her feminine curves and the smooth skin of her legs. He swallowed hard when his groin tightened.

Again, he suppressed the urge to touch her he'd fought all day. She was off limits. She'd made that clear when she'd rebuffed his kiss. He wouldn't test her. At least, not until she gave her consent. Instead, he settled for watching her sleep, pondering how in a matter of hours he'd become so enthralled by her beauty, so involved in her plight, so captivated by her lovely smile.

In her, he recognized the skittishness and self-doubt that the counselors he'd consulted after Becca's death had described as common for a victim of abuse. A *survivor* of abuse, he corrected. The counselors emphatically referred to women like Tess with the accent on the positive. "Attitude is everything," he mumbled softly.

His need to understand what had compelled his fiery, confident sister to stay with her husband had led him to numerous experts. He'd learned plenty, but more questions *and* his guilt remained.

He scanned Tess's body again, this time looking for telltale bruises or scars. He saw none but knew better than to assume anything from the lack of visible evidence.

Plowing his fingers through his hair, he watched her vigilantly for another minute. When he felt certain that her nightmare had passed, he straightened her sheet and re-covered her.

As he placed a light kiss on her brow, an ache filled his chest that he recognized from the days he'd watched Rebecca go back to her abusive husband time and again. His protective, possessive machismo had done Rebecca no good when she'd needed it most. Why should he think he could do any better for Tess? He'd screwed up the most important job he'd ever faced, and Rebecca had died.

He'd let her down.

But he'd been given another chance, and he damn well wouldn't blow it again.

Chapter Six

A loud squeak woke Justin the next morning. He opened his eyes, squinting against the early morning sunlight that flowed in through the open motel room door.

The door closed, throwing the room into darkness. He sat up, rubbing his eyes and shaking off the cobwebs of sleep. When what he'd witnessed registered, he jolted awake faster than if he'd downed a double shot of espresso.

With a glance to the other bed, he confirmed that Tess was gone. Across the room, her suitcases had disappeared.

"Aw, hell," he grumbled. He threw back his covers and snatched his jeans from the foot of the bed. Jamming his legs into his pants, he stumbled out the door.

He heard Tess crank the truck engine and watched in stunned disbelief as she backed out of her parking place. She was ditching him.

"Tess!"

His shout drew a startled look from her. Biting her lip, she turned away.

Barefooted, he hurried across the pavement to her truck door and slapped the window with his palm. "Where are you going?"

She didn't even spare him a second glance. Engine roaring, her Jimmy rocketed toward the parking lot exit.

Justin gave chase. He bolted across the lot with an athlete's speed. His bare feet pounded the rough asphalt. "Tess!"

Traffic on the main road required that she stop and wait for an opening to pull out. He caught up to her and grabbed the driver's door handle. Yanking the door open, he braced a hand against the edge, blocking her from closing it again. "What the hell are you doing?"

Tess planted a hand in the center of his chest and shoved. He didn't budge.

"Get out of my way, Justin. I'm leaving, so don't try to stop me."

"Not without me, you aren't. Have you forgotten about the guy with the gun who grabbed you yesterday?" He wrapped his fingers around her upper arm, and irritation flashed in her hazel eyes.

"The man with the gun is exactly why I have to do this by myself. If you stay with me, you'll be in as much danger as I am. I can't live with that."

Her chapped, worry-abused lips pressed into a thin line of determination, while a bleak vulnerability dimmed her eyes. The contrast of stubborn resolve and fear in her expression made his heart turn over.

"Nice try, sweetheart, but no dice. Out of the truck. Now." When he tugged on her arm, she pulled it back. She flattened her hands on his chest again and shoved. The warmth of her fingers on his skin didn't escape his notice, but he had more immediate concerns that kept him from savoring the contact.

"Justin, please! Let me go!"

Tears puddled in her eyes, wrenching his gut. "No can do, babe."

He stretched in front of her, reaching for the keys in the ignition while she battled him, swatting and grabbing to impede his progress. One of her fingernails caught him in the eye.

"Yeow! Watch it! That hurt!" He clapped a hand to his injured eye and scowled.

"Justin, I'm sor—" She swallowed the rest of her apology as his arm wound around her waist, and he hauled her from the front seat. "No! Stop it!" Her fingers clung fiercely to the steering wheel. "Justin, I'll scream if you don't let go right now!"

He began prying her fingers off the steering wheel.

"Justin, I mean it!"

"Then let it rip. But when you wake the rest of the motel with your hollering, I'll tell them you were stealing my truck."

Tess growled her frustration. His perseverance, or perhaps her dismay over his threat, finally allowed him to take control of the steering wheel and pull her from the Jimmy. The truck rolled when her foot came off the brake, and he quickly slid in and mashed the pedal again.

"But it's my car!" Her hands balled into fists, and she stomped her sandal-shod foot.

Shifting into reverse, Justin flashed her a smug grin. "Technically it's a SUV or a truck, not a car, and if you'll just step away, I'll put it into the parking place." With a hand on her shoulder, he nudged her away from the Jimmy. She narrowed a glare of indignation and disbelief on him. He could feel the quiver of unexpressed anger roiling in her body. He backed her away from the vehicle and closed the door.

Once he'd parked the Jimmy, he glanced in the rearview mirror to find her still standing beside the road, her face buried in her hands. Her wilted posture reflected a sense of defeat. Contrition for his bully-like tactics tightened his chest. He deserved her fury and fully expected to get an earful of her displeasure for his overbearing treatment. Under the circumstances, forcefulness seemed his only option, but he hadn't considered how his bossiness might wound her spirit.

Bouncing the keys in his hand, he stepped out and locked the Jimmy. He waited for her to walk back across the parking lot. But she didn't.

"Tess," he called to her, but she made no move to join him.

Fastening his jeans as he walked, making his way toward her, he watched her flex her fingers and draw slow breaths. "Hey, aren't you coming?"

She lifted her chin and gave him a look of cool control, devoid of emotion. Pivoting on her toe, she brushed past him without a word. As she stalked back to the room, he followed. The stiff jerky movement of her body belied the calm in her expression.

"I know you want to yell," he said, "so go ahead. Let me have it."

Silence answered him. She turned the doorknob to their room and found it locked. "Do you have a room key?" she asked without facing him.

Sighing, he shook his head. "You mean you don't either?"

"I hadn't planned to be back. I didn't need one."

"Wait here. I'll go get one from the office."

She angled her head, casting him a blank stare, and he frowned.

"Come on, Tess. I know I ticked you off, but I told you I couldn't turn my back on your situation."

She didn't even blink. For a moment, he had the sensation she'd left her body and he talked to a shell. Clearly, she'd withdrawn. His chest wrenched tighter.

With an eerie, dark certainty that caused a chill to spiral inside him, he understood that he witnessed her defense mechanism. Shut down, show no emotion, avoid confrontation.

When he stepped closer to her, she backed against the

brick wall of the motel and eyed him warily. Justin held up his hands, palms toward her. "Easy. I'm not going to hurt you."

He propped his hands on his hips and cocked his head. "It's okay to yell at me, Tess. I suppose I deserve it." He paused and grinned. "But would you have turned the truck around and waited for me if I'd simply smiled and said please?"

Nothing.

Blowing a gush of air through pursed lips, he shook his head and turned his gaze toward the road. "I'm not your husband, Tess. You can get mad at me without worrying that I'll strike back." Facing her again, he found her eyes wide and her lips parted in surprise. He flattened his hands on his chest and bent his knees to bring his head eye-level with hers. "Tell me what you're thinking, Tess. Scream at me. Give me hell for acting like a bully."

When she turned away, he dropped his hands to his sides and straightened. "Okay. Whatever. I'm sorry, though, for scaring you and overpowering you to get my way. I apologize. I was desperate and didn't have a lot of time to think it through." He wedged his fingers into his pockets and hunched his shoulders. "But that's not a good excuse, and I'll try to do better next time. Okay?"

She crossed her arms over her chest, still giving him the silent treatment.

Turning, he headed toward the office. "I'll be right back as soon as I get the key."

He scowled as he walked past the row of motel room doors toward the front building, wondering what he could do to bring Tess out of her isolation.

Humor had worked well the day before. Music had always been healing for him. But he could imagine Tess's wounds were deep. From what he'd learned after Becca's death, women with abusive partners coped in whatever way they could. Sometimes that meant detaching themselves from their situation, losing a part of themselves.

Becca had blinded herself to the truth. She'd been so stubbornly optimistic that her love would change Mac.

Tess hadn't said much about her husband, but Justin would give her time. When she was ready to talk, he'd give his support.

After retrieving a room key and opening their locked door, he gathered his possessions and threw them in the back of Tess's Jimmy. "Okay. Now we leave. Want me to drive first?"

"I have a choice?"

He didn't miss her sarcasm, and he grinned. Sarcasm was good. Sarcasm showed spunk. The spark he'd seen yesterday had returned.

"Sure you have a choice. But . . ." He aimed a finger at her. "The driver picks the radio station."

She arched an eyebrow. "In that case, I'm driving." Climbing into the driver's seat, she haughtily tossed her ashen hair. "All day!"

Justin chuckled. "Yes, ma'am."

"Would you stop calling me ma'am?" Tess cranked the engine, while he buckled the belt in the passenger seat. "I'm only thirty-one. I don't think that makes me a ma'am."

"Thirty-one, huh?" He raked her with an appraising gaze. "I'd have guessed more like twenty-five."

She responded with a short, humorless laugh. "Nice try, but I own a mirror. I look every day of thirty-one." She glanced over her shoulder to back out of the parking space. "Maybe more."

As she turned back to the front, he caught her chin. She lifted startled eyes to meet his. "Then buy a new mirror.

81

Yours is broken. You're a beautiful, vibrant woman, Tess, and don't you forget it."

Her mouth worked as if she were trying to speak, but no sound came out. She blinked then pulled her chin from his grasp. She drove to the front door of the motel office and stopped the car. Her hands dropped to her lap, and she whispered, "But I feel a hundred years old."

He watched her go inside to check out, a sympathetic ache in his heart. He had his mission for the day cut out for him: Help Tess enjoy her life. Fan the spark inside her to a blaze. Give her back some of the joy her husband had stolen.

He thought of his promise to Rebecca to not turn away from abuse again, and for the first time in the two years since her death, the stinging guilt loosened its grip.

"Why did the chicken cross the road?"

Tess sighed, though she smiled indulgently across the front seat at Justin. "Why?"

His trademark impish grin spread across his face. "To show the armadillo it could be done."

She giggled, more because of his devilish expression, the light dancing in his eyes, than because of the lame joke.

And because laughing with Justin felt good. She'd forgotten how good laughter could be. Once he'd gotten her giggling like a school girl, she couldn't stop, as if he'd pulled the cork on years of bottled-up mirth.

She could remember laughing a lot with Angie when they were young. They giggled and whispered in bed at night until their parents had come to the bedroom with a semi-stern reminder that it was time to sleep. She'd snuggled close to her big sister, and the world had been a happy, safe place.

The warm memory brought a satisfied smile to her lips.

Until she remembered the rest.

Along with laughter, Randall had stolen Angie from her. If she had known the truth sooner, she could never have stayed with him for all those years. Nausea swept through her now at the thought of the months she'd lived with the man who'd ordered her sister's murder. She clutched the steering wheel tighter.

"Tess? You okay?" Justin's voice sounded as if it came from a deep well, while Randall's voice rang harsh and real in her mind.

When she got a notion to hold my business dealings against me, she, like Fannin, learned how I deal with traitors. . . . Her pimp owed me money. . . . A simple business transaction.

"Tess!" Justin grabbed the steering wheel and righted the path of the Jimmy, guiding them off the shoulder in a spray of gravel. "Jesus! Watch where you're going!"

Tess shuddered. "I—"

"Where did you go just then? Are you all right? God, you're white as a sheet!"

"I'm sorry."

He wrapped long, strong fingers around her hand as she gripped the steering wheel tighter. When his thumb brushed her wrist, rhythmically stroking, a calming warmth spread through her. His hand moved up her arm, his calloused palm gently abrading her skin. His soft touch chased the lurking shadows from her mind.

"Want to talk about it?" The husky rasp of his voice took the edge off the anxious quiver inside her. But she'd never be able to put Randall's evil totally out of her mind. Could never completely relax. To do so could mean getting caught.

"I'm okay. I was just thinking about . . . just remembering—"

"Don't. It's behind you now. Focus on the future. You're safe now. I won't let anything happen to you."

His reassurances and kind smile filled an empty place in her soul. She'd almost given up her childhood belief that men like her father really existed. Maybe she'd only imagined her father was good and kind and protective to fill a youthful fantasy. She'd dreamed, like other little girls, of a handsome and brave prince whom she could trust and love and have faith in.

When Randall had entered her life, she had seen him as her rescuer. A dashing, confident man who'd saved her from the dire poverty and isolation she'd been facing. She'd still been consumed with grief over Angie's death, and he'd seemed the answer to a prayer.

How wrong she had been.

Now, Justin offered her comfort, hope. Did she dare allow herself to trust in the promises he made? He made it easy to believe in a bright future. She had to remind herself she had no future with him. Their association would end in a matter of hours, a few more miles, as soon as she found the nerve to separate herself from the lifeline of encouragement and joy he gave her. A hollow pit settled inside her, considering that bleak moment she had to face.

"So . . ." She cleared her throat to quiet the nervous tremble in her voice. "Tell me another corny joke." The smile she gave him fell short of its mark, but he apparently gave her credit for trying. His own smile brightened his face and pierced the chill around her heart.

Tess rolled her shoulders, working loose the knots of tension. She savored the moment, knowing how few like that one she'd likely have in her future. And she silently thanked Justin for the precious gift he'd brought her. He'd given her a reason to smile, a reason to hope. Yet, all too soon, she'd have to find a way to leave him. No matter how much it hurt.

★ ★ ★ ★ ★

Tony Morelli cursed and slammed down the phone. Another bum lead. He knew that, sooner or later, Tess would make a slip and leave a trail that his men would find. But time was his enemy. Morning had dawned hours ago, and he couldn't quit worrying about Maria. She'd been fine when he left this morning, and he'd warned her to stay inside, keep the doors locked. But still . . .

Damn! Where could the Sinclair broad be hiding? She'd never struck him as the smart type. How had she dodged his men for so long? Along with a respect for her resourcefulness, Tess Sinclair had earned his wrath. It would be her fault if anything happened to Maria . . .

His cell phone trilled, and he snatched it up. "Yeah?"

"Tony, help!"

Morelli sucked in a sharp breath. "Maria?"

Another voice, deep and deadly, came on the line. "Time's up, Morelli. You want your woman back, you gotta find Tess Sinclair."

Morelli didn't recognize the voice, but he didn't need to know who had Maria to know they meant business.

"You sonofabitch, don't you hurt her!" He knew he sounded scared, had known his love for Maria made him vulnerable. But what choice did he have? No way would he give Maria up, and he was in too thick with Sinclair to walk away and live to tell about it. "If you so much as touch her—"

The line went dead, and with a growl of frustration, he threw the phone across the room. "Shit!"

The phone rang again, almost immediately, and he hurried to grab it with his heart in his throat. "Maria?"

"No, it's Dominic. We got a lead."

Consumed with thoughts of his wife in some Sinclair

thug's grasp, Morelli hesitated a moment before the news clicked. "A lead?"

"You said to let you know if we got somethin' solid. Well, we've got two confirmed reports that she spent the night at a motel near Lubbock. The morning desk clerk recognized her from the picture we sent out, and another guest saw her last night."

"Who do you have in the area?" Morelli waited impatiently while Dominic coughed.

"Harrington called in the tip. Grossman has put his guys on it, and I'm on my way there now. If she's still in the area, we'll find her."

"Move fast. And no more screwups."

He jabbed off the phone and headed out to his car. He'd go to Lubbock and find Tess himself. Sinclair had said he could use force to bring Tess back if needed. Morelli relished the thought of putting the bitch through the same torture he suffered over Maria. Oh, yes. When he did find Tess Sinclair, he would use a great deal of force to bring her home. Nothing and no one would stand in his way.

Chapter Seven

"A king-sized bed or two doubles?" The man behind the motel desk looked bored. He turned his attention back to the basketball game on his small TV where, according to the graphic that flashed on the screen, the Chicago Bulls and Utah Jazz were playing.

"We have a choice?" Justin whispered to Tess. She grinned at his facetious question.

The motel, a decrepit, unpopulated brick structure, represented the first civilization they'd seen in miles, after Justin grew restless driving the interstate and ventured off on a side road. And even that fact barely persuaded Tess to stop.

The exterior of the establishment didn't bode well for the accommodations. Tess prayed for clean bed sheets at the very least. Paint peeled in large flakes from the room doors, and the roofing shingles hung askew in places, suggesting interior leaks. Weeds sprouted in the cracks of the sidewalk, attesting to a general lack of upkeep.

The ramshackle front office reeked of cigarette smoke and mildew. She didn't hold out much hope for the sheets.

"Two doubles," Tess told the man watching the basketball game.

"Huh?"

"Two double beds, please." She handed the desk clerk a twenty-dollar bill, which, according to the neon sign sputtering out front, would cover the cost of a room. She cut a sideways glance to Justin, whose grim expression spoke for his discomfort with relying on Tess to finance their room for the night. He'd argued that he should pay half, as he had last night's bill, but she refused. All day he'd counted his money carefully and spent it judiciously. She respected his desire to pay his way but understood his tight reserves, the seed money for his dreams of Nashville. No way would she deplete his cash store when she carried a small fortune of Randall's money in her purse.

Her money, she corrected. Her income had been deposited to that account, too. She'd only taken half of what the balance showed. She owed Randall nothing for the money she withdrew.

While she waited on the man to find a key for them, she glanced around the motel office again, until her gaze snagged on a familiar picture.

Of her.

Icy horror froze her blood, and she gaped in disbelief.

Reproduced in grainy black and white, her picture headed a flier boasting an outrageous reward for information regarding her whereabouts. The contact phone numbers were unfamiliar to her. No doubt, Randall's men were at the other end of those phone numbers.

If Randall's thugs had spread her picture far enough around the state to have reached this seedy motel, was there anyplace she could go and not be recognized?

Dear God. She'd come too far to be caught now. She couldn't go back to Randall. She'd rather die than be caught.

Forcing enough spit into her dry mouth to swallow, she willed herself not to panic. With tense, jerky movements, she sidled over to the poster and scrunched it in her hand. Glancing toward Justin, who seemed as absorbed in the basketball game on the TV as the desk clerk, she balled the flier in her hand and slipped it into her pocket.

"Room three."

She flinched when the desk clerk unceremoniously tossed a key toward her. He turned his back then did a double take.

"Hey, you look familiar." The desk clerk scratched his chest and eyed her with a wrinkled nose.

Her breath hung in her lungs. *No, no, no!*

"Are you somebody famous? A model maybe?"

She cleared her throat and shook her head. She peeked up to find Justin watching her. Silently, she pleaded for his help.

"I know you from somewhere—"

"Miss Texas," Justin said, and Tess blinked her surprise. "Three years ago she was Miss Texas. I bet that's where you remember her from."

The man's eyes widened, then he furrowed his brow. "Maybe. I don't know."

"I'm sure that's it." Justin stepped over to scoop up the key. "Thank you." He put a hand on her back to hustle her out of the grungy front office.

Tess didn't release her breath until they were well away from the desk clerk's scrutiny. She trembled from head to toe, her heart thundering.

Justin said nothing about the incident, but she felt his gaze as he followed her inside the tiny motel room. What would he do if he knew the exorbitant reward Randall was offering for information on her whereabouts? Greed was a powerful motivator, eclipsing even the most well-meaning intentions sometimes. For now, she'd keep the flier as her secret and pray Justin hadn't seen it before she stuffed it in her pocket.

Sighing her fatigue, she scanned the accommodations. As expected, room three was no better than it promised. She walked to a bed and threw back the covers to inspect the sheets. "Well, it's just for one night."

Justin closed the door and tried to lock it, but the security chain had no matching plate on which to attach it. The door latch popped up when he rattled the knob. He glanced at her with a wry grin. "Looks like I'm the security system tonight."

"Are you a heavy sleeper?" She watched Justin tug off his hiking boots.

"Tonight I won't be." He stripped off his shirt and tossed it at his backpack. When he missed his target and the shirt dropped to the floor, he ignored it. Tess rolled her eyes. Apparently, some male traits were universal.

Justin sighed as he flopped on a bed and stacked his hands behind his head. "It's stuffy as hell in here. Is there an air conditioner over there, Tess?"

His gaze and a nod of his head toward the window directed her attention away from the expanse of his bare chest. She moved around her bed and checked the rusty protrusion beneath the front window. Clicking a small knob, Tess felt a steamy blast of air blow from the unit. "There. At least it will move the air a little."

"Mind if I hit the shower?" Justin asked as Tess, out of habit, picked up Justin's shirt and folded it before laying it across the top of his backpack.

"No, go ahead. I don't think I'll bother with a shower tonight. I'm not that brave."

Justin chuckled as he rolled off the bed and headed to the bathroom.

Opening her suitcase, she rummaged through it for a clean shirt. She could at least change clothes and feel somewhat fresher. When Justin returned from the bathroom, her hand stopped, poised on the top button of her blouse.

"On second thought, I'll skip the shower too. I don't enjoy bathing in brown water."

"The water is brown?" Tess wrinkled her nose in disgust.

"And thick."

"Eww!" She covered her mouth with a hand and shuddered. Yet for all the grime and dilapidation of the tiny motel room, she'd rather be there with Justin than in luxury with Randall.

Justin flipped on a lamp between the beds and walked over to his guitar case. Taking out the instrument, he sat in one of two mismatched armchairs. It rocked unsteadily as he settled in it.

Tess chafed her arms and paced, still not able to shake the uneasy chill of having seen her face on the flier. Randall's men were close. She knew they were, sensed it instinctively. Her stomach rioted at the prospect, and she drew a deep breath for composure. What good would it do her now if she lost her cool? She had to try to stay calm.

From the side pocket of her purse, she pulled a women's magazine she'd bought earlier when they'd stopped for gasoline and drinks. She settled on one of the beds and flipped to the front page. Justin plucked idly while she tried futilely to read. After a few moments, she gave up the illusion and turned her attention to Justin and his guitar.

She watched him play, his face the picture of contentment, and she reflected on the day they'd spent together. Their conversation had covered his sweet tooth, his childhood crush on his third-grade teacher, and his preference for the Braves over the Astros. He'd had to tell her the teams played baseball.

She'd told him how she and Angela had dodged and lied to Children's Services to avoid being put in foster homes after their parents' deaths in a car accident when she was fourteen.

She'd carefully avoided mention of how Angela had eked out a living for them in the months that followed.

She'd forgiven him for his dictatorial thwarting of her attempt to flee that morning. He doggedly insisted that he had to protect her, had to see her safely freed from Randall's threat. His determination and conviction made him more admirable in her eyes.

Observing Justin through the day, she learned that fiery passion lit his eyes whenever he talked about his music, that a dimple dented his cheek when he flashed the lopsided grin that said he was teasing, and that he tended to touch her—frequently.

He often squeezed her shoulder or patted her arm or rested his hand at her back as they walked into a gas station to buy a snack. The frequent contact proved maddening and wholly unlike the cold, possessive way Randall touched her. She craved Justin's touch and missed it when he took his hand away.

Through the course of the day, sharing snippets of her life with Justin, hearing about his youth and family, giggling over nothing, and teasing about everything, she'd found a closeness to him that surprised her. The freedom to express her opinion and joke with him refreshed her. With him, she blossomed to life like a flower receiving rain after lacking water for too long.

How was it possible that she could feel more connected to a man she'd known for two days than to the man she'd known for thirteen years?

But allowing herself to form any expectations from him meant trouble. He'd go his own way soon and pursue his dream in Nashville while she hid herself in Anytown, USA. They had no future together. She repeated that fact to herself over and again. And still she longed for his tenderness, hungered for it after years in a stark relationship.

"I've been thinking," he said, still playing softly and interrupting her musings. "I think you'd like John Michael Montgomery."

"Oh? Is he a friend of yours?"

He chuckled warmly. "No."

Justin began playing a new melody then sang about a girl who thought he could rope the moon. He paused in the middle of the ballad and smiled at Tess. "That is John Michael Montgomery."

"I like him." She returned a grin. "More."

He finished the song then sang about a love he swore would always be there.

"You also might like Ty Herndon." Justin sang another ballad then listed a half dozen other country balladeers and introduced her to *their* music.

She listened with a rapt fascination to his voice, studied the flicker of light in his eyes, and watched the way his fingers caressed and plucked the guitar strings. She remembered how those fingers felt when he touched her. Strong but gentle. Warm.

Heat collected inside her at the thought.

Her gaze drank in his rugged, square jaw, straight nose and seductive lips. "You know, Mr. Boyd, speaking as an experienced marketing professional, your promotional staff is going to love you when you sign your first recording contract."

Raising his gaze, he arched an eyebrow. "Oh?"

"With that face, those eyes, your smile, you're an easy sell. You're going to have legions of female fans, dying to get their hands on you."

He ducked his head for a moment then gave her a flirtatious wink. "Thanks, doll. But what about you? Will you be one of my fans?"

"I already am." Her answer rolled off her tongue before she stopped to realize what she'd said. The smile that blossomed on his face reflected his appreciation of her support, her compliment of his appearance, and . . . something more. A tingle skittered over her skin, and she tried to refocus her thoughts.

But something in the way Justin looked at her while he sang the lyrics about love and lovers mesmerized her, almost made her believe he meant the things he was singing to her.

Her brain said the notion was ridiculous. Justin was a performer who'd mastered the technique of engaging his audience. Period. Perhaps, because her life with Randall had lacked tenderness and affection, her soul thirsted for it and imagined it where nothing existed.

She'd never heard an endearment or expression of love from Randall and had learned not to expect any. And sex had been something to endure while Randall groped and satisfied himself with no consideration for her pain or pleasure. With Randall, sex had been rough, fast and crude, and he'd often turned the experience into a form of humiliation or punishment for her. Yet she had numbed herself to what was happening, to the suffering she endured, fearing retribution. As long as she gave Randall no reason to be upset, she could actually believe at times that her life wasn't so bad after all. She could convince herself that the empty existence, the bleak days and long nights, were better than any other options.

She'd lied to herself.

With a shudder, she conjured up an image of her last night with Randall and the brutal way he'd forced himself on her. The memory made her skin crawl.

"Nobody writes a ballad like a country ballad," Justin

said, drawing her mind back to the present. She forced the horrid picture of Randall's leering face out of her mind and tried to infuse humor in her voice.

"Mr. Boyd, are you trying to convert me to a country fan?"

"Yes, ma'am. Tryin' my darnedest. How am I doing so far?" His devilish grin made Tess's heart patter.

Randall would be livid to know she was alone in a cheap motel room with another man. He'd be out of his mind with jealousy and possessive rage to think of Tess anywhere near a man of Justin's appeal, especially if he knew how often she pictured Justin as her lover.

The idea of spiting Randall, of flaunting her freedom from his tenacious hold over her, swam with heady and potent effects in her mind. She rejected vengefulness under most circumstances. But she couldn't deny the powerful lure of the notion that she could rebel against Randall's cruelty, his sexual dominance, his perverse pleasure in her humiliation. The ghost of an idea began to form in her mind.

"You're doing fine," Tess said. "I'm enjoying my concert."

"Good." Justin's eyes sparkled as he began playing again. His gaze held Tess's. The romantic lyrics, the golden glow of the lamp, and the hypnotizing blue in Justin's eyes toyed with her emotions. Her heart thumped heavily in her chest, and her blood seemed to thicken and slow, making her body grow oddly numb.

"Don't move," Justin said abruptly, his expression becoming serious, intent. Tess's chest constricted as he set his guitar aside and crossed the room without moving his gaze from a point near her head.

When he reached the side of the bed, he picked up her magazine from the nightstand. Putting his knee on the mattress by her hip, he stretched across her. His body pressed warmly against her as he thwacked the magazine against the wall.

Justin cursed under his breath. "He got away."

"Who?"

He levered back enough to peer down at her. "A large roach."

Tess wrinkled her nose in disgust. "Oh."

A low, sexy chuckle rumbled from his chest. "Not big enough to carry you off, but I wasn't taking any chances on losing my audience." His eyes glowed with mischief.

She frowned at him as he levered away. "Where did it go?"

Justin's mouth twisted in a wry grimace. "Probably to join some friends under the bed."

She shivered visibly, and he ruffled her hair. "Don't worry. They don't eat much."

As Justin turned to walk away, she bolted upright and grabbed the waist of his jeans. The decision wasn't so much a conscious one as an impulse that seized her so suddenly, so strongly, she couldn't ignore it, didn't stop to analyze it.

When he came up short from her hold on his waistband, he twisted to glance back at her with a puzzled arc in his brow. She slid her hand along the denim as he faced her, meeting her reluctant gaze. Tess dropped her chin, avoiding the question in his eyes.

Rising on her knees, she slid her hand up his chest. The crinkly dark hairs sprinkled across his skin tickled her palms, but nervous tension numbed her head too much to enjoy the sensation. With a boldness that belied the quivering in her stomach, she framed his face with a hand on each cheek and closed her eyes. She seized his mouth with hers so swiftly their teeth clicked against each other. Pressing her body to his, she felt the quick, startled tensing of his muscles before he relaxed and absorbed her weight with his strength. His wide, warm hands settled at her waist, and his mouth responded to her kiss with skillful strokes and gentle suction.

The sweet, hypnotic caress of his lips distracted her momentarily from her intent, from the hastily decided rules for her actions.

Don't feel. Stay in control. Get it over with quickly.

She would have her revenge against Randall, flaunt her freedom from his sexual dominance, and hold herself emotionally apart from what she was doing.

Recalled to her plan, she took Justin's hand in hers and guided it under her blouse, under her bra. She pressed his hand to her breast. A soft moan rumbled from his throat. Her traitorous nipple puckered, an outward indication of the prickling heat that collected where his hand cupped her.

Without stopping to consider her actions, lest she lose her resolve, she sought the bulge at his groin and rubbed him. She heard his breath catch, and he angled his head to recapture her mouth, nipping at her lips with an enticing playfulness. His kiss enchanted her too much, made her want what she couldn't have. Reluctantly, she ducked her head, removing her mouth from his.

His hand stirred on her breast, kneading her carefully, massaging her until she could barely think. Needing to regain control, she grappled with the zipper on his jeans, tugging it down. With trembling hands, she fought the fabric of his briefs out of her way and wrapped her fingers around the swollen proof of his arousal.

"Oh, Tess." His words mingled with a low growl, and she heard him suck in a deep breath. As she bent her head toward her new target, his hand slipped from her breast. He sank his fingers in her hair, and she waited for the stinging pull at her roots that Randall employed. But Justin's fingers massaged her scalp with a controlled tenderness.

She kissed the masculine heat in her hands once then licked him, her stomach bunching in anxious knots.

"Oh, God," he groaned, and his fingers tightened in her hair. She put him in her mouth, and he jerked.

"Wait." His voice sounded tight, strangled. Grabbing her shoulders, he shoved her away. "Stop, Tess. Just . . . slow down."

Cold fingers of shame clutched her heart in a vise grip. *Oh, God! What had she done?*

On his way in from the garage, Randall dropped his keys on the Italian marble kitchen counter and strolled into his living room. The silence mocked him. The stillness in the house laughed at him, flaunting Tess's continued absence. An unfamiliar ache he refused to identify settled in his chest.

Loosening his tie with a vicious tug, he stalked to the bar and uncapped the crystal decanter on top. Without Tess to fetch his scotch, the task of pouring his evening drink fell to him. If Tess weren't found soon, he'd have to reconsider hiring a household staff. Tess's reliability had made that expense and risk to his privacy unnecessary until now.

After pouring two fingers of the amber liquid, he downed the drink in three gulps. The scotch burned his throat and fueled the fire already blazing in his gut. Restless energy made him feel like a caged tiger needing to pace. Randall refilled his glass and headed upstairs to the master bedroom.

The lingering scent of Tess's perfume hung in the air. She preferred an inexpensive fragrance from the department store, available even to common factory workers. The flowery scent matched his opinion of her: sissy-sweet, no substance, and maddeningly sexy. Just a few whiffs of the perfumed air made him hard. He thought of her ripe body, and his blood became hot and thick. His body ached for sexual release. And something more.

But Tess was gone.

He could, of course, have one of his other women at the house in minutes with a phone call. But tonight, none of the others would do. He wanted Tess. Only with Tess could he relax his guard enough to fully appreciate the pleasures of sex and satisfy his restless cravings. He was loath to examine why this was so. Once again, he shoved the troublesome vulnerability aside.

But the fact remained that he felt something for Tess he'd never felt for another woman. He tried to deny the feeling was love. Love crumbled one's defenses. Above all else, he had to stay in control. So how did he control the hollow ache in his chest in the wake of her disappearance?

Gripping his glass of scotch tighter, he clenched his jaw at the injustice of her flight. How could she do this to him? He'd given her everything a woman could want. She owned a closet full of fine clothes, a trove of the best jewels, and a sporty foreign car. He gave her far more than she'd have ever had without his generosity. With her disappearance, she'd thrown his lavishness back in his face. The ungrateful bitch!

Balling his free hand, he spun toward the door and stomped out. Damn her!

He'd even permitted her to attend college when she'd asked. Then he'd allowed her to work in the marketing department of his corporation when she'd wanted a career. Hell, he'd recognized her talent and known the benefit her skills could provide his growing business. As long as she met all his demands at home, what did he care if she played businesswoman by day? Having her office in the same building with his certainly made keeping tabs on her activity easier. Of course, she knew better than to step out of line at work, just as she did at home.

Or so he'd thought.

She had managed to run from him, despite all his precautions. Ironically, Tess had done the very thing he'd hated his mother for *not* doing. Why hadn't his mother gotten him and herself away from his bastard of a father? She'd loved her booze and that sorry old man more than she'd loved her own son. She'd let him suffer, and he'd hated her for it.

Tess had soothed the sting of his mother's betrayal. Tess had seemed so loyal, so willing to please . . .

With an angry growl, Randall took another swig of his drink as he marched back downstairs to the living room. The smooth liquor took the edge off his frustration.

Control. Stay in control.

As best he could tell, she hadn't gone to the cops with her accusations. Not that anyone could connect him with Fannin . . . or her slut sister. Or any of the others. Morelli was careful, discreet. Randall paid his men well, so he felt safe.

But Tess could prove a wild cannon. If she had the gall, the guts to run from him this way, what else might she do?

She'd taken half of their joint account, he remembered, and his fury blazed hotter. Having both of their names on the account had been a necessary concession in order to have her paychecks deposited directly. His mistake had been leaving so much in that account, instead of transferring the money to the accounts he controlled. Now Tess had $24,000 to finance her little escapade. He'd see that she repaid every penny—in one form or another.

Making his way back through the living room to his office, he unlocked the massive door that ensured only he ever entered this room off of the main living quarters. He strode across the Persian rug to his desk, where he slammed his glass down.

Sinking into the deep cushions of the leather chair behind the antique desk, he settled in to brood. Though he'd spent many hours in solitude in this room, tonight the book-lined walls seemed suffocating. He refused to think he could be suffering from anything as weak as loneliness. He didn't miss Tess. The very notion made him scoff in denial.

Yet the empty ache remained. Had he fallen in love with her after all these years?

His thoughts drifted back to the day he had walked into the godforsaken tenement where she and her sister lived. He recalled the wariness in her keen eyes as he introduced himself as a friend of Angie's. He'd seen her potential immediately. Even at sixteen, she'd had a woman's body. The certainty that no man had tested her bedroom skills sweetened the deal for him. He liked knowing he would be the sole proprietor of such fine female real estate. Throughout their years together, his exclusive rights to her body gave him a certain peace of mind nothing else could.

Angela had been a looker, too, but she'd ruined herself, selling her wares to any dick with fifty bucks to spend for a tumble. Randall remembered the rush of excitement he'd known the day Morelli had informed him his favorite hooker had a sister who might take up where Angie had left off. Instead, Tess had proven the perfect material to become the envy of his colleagues and the answer to his need for a classy woman at his side.

He'd earned her trust, groomed her to be his "wife," and staked his claim as soon as she turned eighteen. In thirteen years, after he'd set her straight about who would be in charge, she'd never disappointed him. He'd never seen the need to make her position as his wife official. Until three days ago.

She'd confronted him about Fannin with an impertinence that surprised him. He should have taken stronger action right then. He should have realized how knowledge of his side business would chafe Tess's rigid sense of morality.

He drummed his fingers on the desk and scowled. His silly, naive Tess, who returned change if a cashier overpaid her, had clearly been appalled at the idea that he controlled the fate of another man's life. And death.

Watching her face grow white as he described having her sister killed had been comical. The woman had been so clueless.

Randall slid open the top drawer of the desk and removed the .357 Magnum stashed there for security purposes. With a flick, he opened the cylinder. He kept the revolver ready with one cartridge. His aim had been honed at the firing range, and he felt confident he could take out an intruder with one shot. The empty chambers ensured the revolver held no threat for him after being fired once, should his one shot fail to stop his opponent.

Tonight, one cartridge didn't give him peace of mind. Shuffling through the drawer, he wrapped his fingers around five more bullets and slid them in the waiting chambers. The cylinder made a satisfying click as he snapped it back in place. Now he was ready.

Randall stroked the grip like a lover fondling his mate. He couldn't pinpoint the source of his intuition, but something about Tess's disappearance left him on edge. He didn't intend to be caught unprepared.

Chapter Eight

Tess backed away from Justin. She kept her eyes cast down, and her throat closed as tears swelled. She heard him rezip his jeans, and the rasping sound chafed her nerves. With a horrifying clarity, she saw her advances through Justin's eyes. Revulsion twisted inside her. Sweet, honorable Justin. She'd used him to hurt Randall.

Nausea, mortification and fear washed over her like a tidal wave, and a shudder shook her body.

He panted, drawing in deep gulps of air, while she wished for the power to disappear, to dissolve into nothingness and not have to face his incrimination, his disgust.

"Tess?" His voice held some of its normal calm but not nearly all of it. "What was that about?"

Several seconds ticked by with only the lonely hum of the inefficient motel air conditioner filling the quiet.

"I know it wasn't about sex, and it wasn't about you and me . . ." He paused. "Was it?" But his tone said he knew the answer. "You don't have to prove anything, honey. Not to me. Not to him."

Honey. The endearment resounded like a bittersweet melody and left her with a hollow ache.

He cupped her chin and tipped her face up. Still she dodged his gaze. She couldn't bear to let him see the regret and humiliation in her eyes.

"If it was for you, there are better ways. Talk to me,

sweetheart. I want to help."

"It was nothing, Justin. Just go away. I'm sorry." A shiver raced through her.

"Tess."

She hated the sympathy lacing his voice. She didn't deserve his sympathy, only his contempt. His hand stroked her hair with a tenderness she couldn't comprehend.

"Tess? I'm not saying no, but I only—"

"Please," she croaked, "just go."

Sighing heavily, he moved away. "All right. I can't make you open up to me if you don't want to." He headed to the sink, where he splashed water on his face, and Tess curled into the fetal position on the bed.

Whore! Randall's voice screamed at her, and she tucked her knees tighter against her chest. *Slut!* Tears of shame rushed to her eyes, and she choked on a sob that wrenched from her throat.

"Tess?"

She heard the concern in Justin's voice and regretted the guilt she knew he'd feel, the responsibility for her tears, though none of it belonged to him. Randall had done this to her. He'd robbed her of her dignity, turned her into a vengeful, hate-driven slut.

A warm hand brushed her back. "Tess, honey, what's wrong? Please tell me. I want to help, if I can."

"Randall was right," she muttered through her tears. "I hated him for calling me a whore, but I just proved he was right. Despite everything I did to avoid becoming one, that's what I am. Oh, God!"

"Randall called you that?"

"And I am, too. I just proved it. Only a hooker would do what I just did to you. I'm so sorry."

She buried her face in the musty bedspread and sobbed.

The bed sank as Justin sat down beside her. "Come on, Tess. Don't cry, sweetheart. Please." He stroked her head and back, and his voice reflected his discomfort and uncertainty. "Tell me what he did to you, Tess. Tell me why you believe what just happened was so bad. What made you do it?"

"Revenge," Tess cried. "I hate him."

Justin deserved answers. After what she'd put him through, after all the patience and kind understanding he'd shown her, he deserved some answers. But talking about it hurt. Dredging up what she'd buried so deep frightened her.

Yet like a lanced wound, the poison bubbled up and poured from her. "I hated what he made me do. But every time he wanted sex, *any* time he wanted it, I gave it to him. To keep the peace. Like the whore he said I was." She trembled and felt him slide an arm under her to pull her up and into his embrace. He folded her in his arms, and she covered her face with her hands, mortified.

"I was afraid to say no to him. So I always . . . I sold my soul to him . . . because I needed . . . because I—"

"Ssh. Easy. You're okay now. He can't hurt you anymore." Justin's hold on her tightened. "Don't cry, Tess. Please. If I were a gentleman, I would have stopped you sooner. Hell, I knew something didn't add up, but I didn't stop you sooner. I wanted to believe it meant more than . . . revenge."

She peeked up at him timidly, bewildered by what Justin was telling her. "You did?"

He nodded.

Drawing a shaky breath, she opened her mouth to speak, but Justin placed his finger across her lips.

"You are not a whore for having sex with your husband, no matter how badly he treated you or how selfish he was about taking it from you." He leaned her back and nailed her with a hard gaze. A fierce conviction burned in his eyes. "And you are not a whore for what just happened between us. Do you hear me? I didn't pay you anything, nor will I. A woman isn't a whore because she kisses a man she cares about. You hear me, Tess?"

"But—"

"But nothing. Call what you just did foreplay. Call it a mistake if you must, but do not call yourself a whore. Your husband was wrong, Tess. Wrong to hurt you, wrong to make you think so little of yourself, wrong to make sex something other than beautiful for you." Justin sighed with frustration. "Please, Tess. Please believe that much is true."

She held his gaze for a moment, trembling. "He wasn't my husband."

Justin knitted his brow in confusion. "I thought you said—"

"He always called me his wife. Probably believed I was somehow, but we were never legally married. He took me in at a time when I had nowhere else to go."

Justin's expression mellowed. He brushed a hand along her cheek, while he squeezed his eyes shut. "Tess . . ."

She held her breath, knowing somehow what he was about to say and uncertain how to respond.

"I want to make love to you," he whispered, confirming her instinct.

Her chest tightened, making it hard to breathe, impossible to speak. As he opened his eyes to look at her again, the tenderness and understanding in his gaze made her soul cry with longing. She needed what he was offering. She wanted him to fill the void Randall had left inside her, wished with every fiber of her being that she could feel whole just once. But what would it cost her in the long run if she opened herself to Justin's affection?

"I'm scared, Justin."

"Of what? Not of me? Please, Tess. Don't be ever scared of me." He sank his fingers into her hair and cradled her head between his palms.

She shook her head in denial. "No. Not of you."

"Tell me to go to hell, Tess, and I'll walk away right now. I won't touch you."

What went unspoken was the promise that if she said nothing, if she didn't send him away, he would make good his desire. That possibility captivated Tess. The sound of her own heartbeat drummed in her ears when she thought of making love to this man. For the past two days, she'd laughed with him, shared confidences with him, found inspiration from him. In some ways, she'd already been more intimate with Justin than she'd ever been with Randall.

"Justin, I . . ." She searched for a way to tell him what was in her heart, a way to understand it herself, but what she felt defied explanation.

He waited a beat, then another, for her objection before lowering his lips to hers. His kiss whispered across her lips, soft, patient, tentative. Sparks shot through her veins. When he withdrew, no more than a fraction of an inch, she gasped at her body's dramatic reaction.

"Tess?"

"I'm all right. I . . ." She met his gaze, and the rest of her sentence lodged in her throat. Eyes that she thought she'd memorized looked into hers, smoky with desire, dark with passion.

When he kissed her again, his mouth conducted a seductive exploration, testing, searching for just the right angle to fit more fully on hers. She moved her lips against his in return, matching the gentle suction and caress of his mouth with her own. A flutter stirred deep inside her.

Justin didn't rush her. The taut muscles in his arms, his

shallow, uneven breathing, and the heavy thumping of his heart under her hand gave evidence to his restraint.

Finding the throbbing pulse in his neck with her lips, she trailed soft kisses across his jaw until she found his lips again. A rumble of pleasure vibrated from his throat as he lowered her to the mattress, following her down. He raked fingers through her hair while he nipped and teased her lips. He deepened his kiss with a possessiveness that stole her breath. A foreign thrill spiraled through her, leaving her dizzy in its wake.

He broke the kiss briefly, finding her eyes with a piecing blue gaze. "Tess, honey, you are a lady in the truest sense of the word. Please believe that. Don't ever doubt it. And don't be scared anymore. Not tonight. Not ever. Not with me."

She searched the pleading, earnest appeal in his eyes and lost herself in the promise of sweet comfort he offered. He caressed her cheek and pressed his warm lips to the side of her throat.

"You have two freckles." He nuzzled her skin. "Right here. I've wanted to taste them since the first moment I saw them, for what feels like forever." He kissed her neck with a hot, wet, open-mouthed fervor, and a long-forgotten ardor unfurled in her and raced through her blood.

Slowly he released one then another button on her blouse. His lips followed his fingers down the valley between her breasts as he parted the fabric. The scratch of his stubbled cheeks on the swell of her breasts and the sweep of his thumbs across her nipples electrified her every nerve ending. He opened her blouse and trailed soft kisses and feathered strokes across her belly. Losing herself in his tender touch involved no more than closing her eyes and letting the sound of his voice lull her.

"So lovely," he murmured.

She trembled when he pushed the lacy demicup of her bra away. He bared the rosy bud of her nipple then grazed it with his tongue.

Everything Justin did stood in stark contrast to the way Randall had treated her. Where Randall grabbed, Justin caressed. Where Randall ripped, Justin showed care. Where Randall ravaged, Justin soothed. Justin was loving, tender, coaxing. Randall had been thoughtless, rough, demanding.

The sweetness of Justin's careful, gentle ministrations made her body hum with bliss and gratitude. He made her feel wanted, cherished, feminine in a way she'd never felt in her life. He made her happy. Arching her back, she allowed him access to unhook her bra, then helped him slide it off with her blouse. Discarding her clothes on the floor, he raked his gaze over her with an open appreciation, his pupils dilating with desire. Tess gave him the same scrutiny and felt her blood heat.

Reaching for him, drawing her hand down the wide, firm plane of his chest, she savored the tickle of the crisp, dark hair and the heat of his skin, which she'd disregarded earlier. Justin sighed his satisfaction when she added her kisses to the wandering of her hands.

Twisting his leg around hers and sliding his arm around her waist, he rolled to his back and pulled her on top of his long, hard body. Cupping the back of her head with one hand and a breast with the other, he took her mouth again with a hungry, heated kiss. His lips claimed and plundered then slowed and soothed, building a need in her for his total possession.

The sensations that he brought alive in her were new. Never before had she imagined her body could respond to a man's touch and kisses with the powerful surges of craving and emotion that swirled in her, leaving her head swimming. An escalating longing for release coiled in her womb.

He moved his hands to pull her hips down against his groin and rubbed the steely length of himself along the juncture of her thighs. Her breathing grew quick and choppy. She heard Justin's answering moan when he rolled on top of her again. He tugged on her shorts and panties until she could kick them off. Then turning on his back at her side, he freed his legs of his jeans and briefs in one swift, efficient motion. He gathered her against his nakedness and pulled the sheet over them.

Her curves molded to his contours. His rigid, muscled body absorbed her yielding softness as if they were made to fit together.

"You feel wonderful," he mumbled as he nuzzled her neck, her ear, her hair.

She slid her fingers up the curve of his spine and across his broad shoulders. His hands skimmed over her skin, arousing, adoring, and she reveled in the heavenly tenderness. The warmth from his body enveloped her in their cocoon under the sheet, and Tess savored the security in his nearness. Yearning numbed her mind to everything except the sweet sensations Justin elicited with his touch. Need replaced logic. Hunger obliterated reality. When he wedged a leg between her thighs, she opened herself to him, and he nudged her with his erection.

"Look at me, Tess," he whispered.

She obeyed, though her eyelids were heavy. As he entered her, his blue gaze penetrated her, reached for her soul, and branded her heart. Once he was buried deep inside her body, he kissed her softly and whispered, "You're free of him. Don't ever look back. You belong with me now."

He withdrew then slid back inside, moving slowly, stroking her, encouraging the pulsing beat that promised her the height of ecstasy. She lifted her hips and joined him in a motion that bound their bodies in an age-old rhythm.

"Oh, Tess. Sweet Tess." Increasing the tempo, he boosted the sweet harmony of their fusion.

She clutched his shoulders and closed her eyes as he carried her higher, further into a state of unbelievable bliss until oblivion enfolded her. When she opened her eyes and lifted a stunned and dreamy-eyed gaze to his, Justin's eyes still held her with a loving warmth and encouragement. He flashed her a sultry grin, then with a final deep thrust, he joined her in a shuddering release. His body shook, and he drew her tightly against his chest as he sucked in deep breaths in the aftermath of his climax. He pressed his lips to the top of her head then tipped her chin up so that he could cover her face with tiny, butterfly kisses.

"Sweet Tess. My Tess," he murmured as he held her.

That should have been the end of it according to Tess's experience. But Justin's gentle caresses, the soft, warm press of his lips, the whispered endearments didn't cease. He continued to lull, to comfort, to thrill her well into the night. He made love to her again, brought her to the heights of ecstasy and always, always treated her to the loving tenderness and respect that shone in his eyes. As Tess fell asleep that night, her body was sated, and she was wrapped in the safety and heat of Justin's protective arms.

But her heart ached with a searing regret. While Justin had given her a memory she would cherish for the rest of her life, she had put a price on his head. As her lover, Justin became Randall's enemy number one. She could delay the inevitable no longer. One way or another, she had to break free of Justin.

Tomorrow.

Chapter Nine

The room was warm. Actually, stifling better described it. Justin had guessed the run-down, rat-hole motel wouldn't have a decent air conditioner, but considering he'd imposed on Tess's good will and generosity, he had no right to gripe. At least he'd had a bed to sleep in last night.

The stirring of the soft body beside him brought his gaze down to the face, flushed pink from the heat, that rested on his shoulder. Pressing a light kiss to Tess's clammy forehead, he sighed.

He wondered how she would feel this morning about what had happened between them last night. Although he hadn't regretted a minute of it, he wasn't the one fleeing an abusive jerk. He wasn't the one whose self-esteem had been so pounded by a thoughtless bastard that she believed herself a whore.

Their lovemaking could prove to reinforce that idea in her mind. He'd have to be certain that by morning's light, she didn't beat herself up over what, to him, had been an exquisite and moving experience. As he reflected on the evening they'd spent together, one thing stood out, one thing besides the earth-shaking sensation of completion he'd felt when he joined their bodies. Even before he'd touched her, even before she'd caught his jeans and stopped him from walking back to his guitar, he'd sensed a unique connection with her. Her unconditional belief in his eventual success in Nashville, her unfailing support and faith in his ability to see his dream to fruition, fed a hunger inside him. She alone shared his vision, his confidence in his talent.

Except for Becca.

He'd wanted success to cover some part of his liability for letting Rebecca down with Mac. Guilt and a determination to make Becca proud fueled his mission, his goal of recognition in Nashville. Tess made him believe, really believe, it was possible. Her eyes had glowed with admiration while she watched him play his guitar.

When she let down the protective guard that held her at bay, he glimpsed the depth of her trust and confidence in his promise to protect her, too. Her unspoken faith in his capabilities as her guardian chipped away at his doubts and his compunction over his failure with Becca. His heart filled with affection for the woman who'd encouraged him and renewed his conviction to make up for his past mistakes.

And then they'd shared a night of unbelievable passion and mind-blowing sex. Had he ever really loved Amy the way he thought he had? She'd never given him the same feeling of wholeness, the inspiring support or unqualified faith that Tess did.

But whatever it was he felt for Tess, one inescapable fact remained. He couldn't get emotionally involved with her. As easy as it would be to convince himself he was falling in love with her, he could never give her what she needed or deserved in a relationship. He was bound to break her heart, and he couldn't live with that fact.

She needed someone who could provide her the security and peace of mind her life with her husband had lacked. He lived life by the seat of his pants. In the past, when he did accept responsibility in some form, he had never followed through. Rebecca had suffered from his failure. Amy had drifted away from him due to his lack of commitment. He'd left college to help Rebecca, quit his construction job to chase a dream, and had barely enough money to make it to Nashville.

No, he was not the kind of man Tess needed complicating her life. Once he saw her safely hidden away where her husband couldn't hurt her, his sense of honor dictated that he part company with Tess. She needed someone she could depend on for the long haul. His track record proved him unreliable. Stubborn, yes. Determined, definitely. But more often than not, a disappointment in the long term.

Tess's hair tickled his arm, drawing him out of his musings. When he brushed it back behind her ear, her eyelids fluttered, and she peered up at him with sleepy, hazel eyes.

"Mornin'," he drawled, tugging one side of his mouth up in a lazy grin.

The pink in her cheeks darkened, and her eyes widened a fraction. Shutting her eyes again with a wince, she rolled away from him and tugged the sheet up around her, despite the humid heat in the room.

He turned on his side, propping himself on his elbow and running a finger down Tess's spine. She shivered.

"Tess?" He lifted her hair and kissed the side of her neck. "Talk to me, sweetheart."

"It's hot in here."

"You noticed that too, huh? I was hoping it wasn't just me."

"What time is it?"

"Why?" He leaned over her to nuzzle her cheek. "You have somewhere to go?"

Tess angled her head to look at him. "No, I—"

Justin's kiss cut her off.

"Good. Then we have time to play some more before we get up." Though he playfully tweaked her nose, he monitored her expression carefully.

"Justin . . ." Her eyes grew serious and dark.

"Tess," he returned and laid a finger across her lips. "Please don't feel bad about what happened last night."

"I don't. Not really, but Randall—"

"Is in the past. You left the sonofabitch, remember?"

"It's not as simple as that. If he found out about you, he'd be so angry. He's very possessive."

"Last night you said you two had never married. He holds no claim on you. Unless you still love him."

Tess sat up, hugging the sheet to her chest. "No. I've never loved him. That's not the point."

Raking his hair away from his face, he sat up as well and faced Tess. "What is your point? What's wrong?"

When she looked at him, tears puddled in her eyes, and Justin's heart wrenched.

"You don't understand about Randall. He has a lot of power. If he found out what we did last night, he'd . . ." Tess shuddered. "Last night was a mistake. A big mistake. You should leave. Forget you met me, and don't tell anyone about—"

"What?" He blinked his disbelief then laughed. "Are you serious? I'm not going anywhere, babe."

"Justin, he'll kill you!"

"I'm not scared of Randall, Tess. Not that I plan on meeting him. I mean, isn't that the point? Getting you away from him?"

"He's looking for me, though. And if he finds me, if he knew about you, if—"

"If, if, if. Tess, honey, if he does find you, I'm gonna be right by your side. I won't let anything happen to you."

Her face wrinkled with distress. "Justin, Randall is evil. He'll kill you. He already wants me dead."

Drawing her into his arms, he lay back on the bed, holding her close. "I know you're frightened, honey. But *I promise* I won't let him hurt you ever again." With a finger under her chin, he tilted her face up and kissed her damp cheeks. "Okay?"

Taking her silence as acquiescence, he hugged her tighter. "Now, do you want to make love again and then find something for breakfast, or do you want to eat first and then come back to the room to make love again?"

She pushed up on an arm and regarded him with an incredulous expression.

He flashed her a mischievous grin and wiggled his eyebrows. "I don't know about you, but I vote for before and after breakfast."

Tess's brows knitted in a mask of concern and heartbreaking sorrow that wiped the smile from his face.

"Tess, he's not going to get near you. I swear. You trust me, don't you?"

Her eyes closed slowly, and she nodded. Once again, her confidence in him caused a star-burst of warmth to explode in his chest. Justin plowed his fingers into her hair and captured her face between his hands. The kiss he placed on her mouth merely brushed her lips, but she answered with a soft whimper as she fell against him and wrapped her arms around his neck. He kissed her again, more fully, intending to reassure her with his slow and gentle patience. Even if he couldn't stay with her once she was finally safe, he could spend the time until that day giving her the tenderness and pleasures that her husband had denied her.

But having her pliant body pressing against his made restraint difficult. When he parted her lips with his tongue, her tongue greeted his and tangled with it. From there, patience was forgotten. She made love to him with desperation and urgency, and he lost himself in the sweetness of her kiss, her lush body, her welcoming warmth.

Later, they languished in each other's arms, the sheet tangled around their legs. Sweat rolled from their skin.

Justin breathlessly sang the refrain of a recent country hit that compared being in love to eating melting ice cream and the rush of swerving around a cow in the road.

Tess peeked up at him and chuckled. "What?"

" 'Diamond Rio.' " He chucked her under the chin. "Great song."

Tess looked skeptical.

"Ah, darlin', if you give me half a chance, I'd open the doors for you to a world of steel guitars and honky-tonks."

"Sorry, I didn't bring my passport. You'll have to make that trip alone." She cracked a grin.

Instead of answering her quip, he ran his gaze over her perspiration-slick body. "Do you realize that as sweaty as we are, we have no way to bathe? Unless you want to take your chances with the muddy water."

She grimaced. "Ugh." Catching a bead of his sweat as it trickled across his chest, Tess sighed. "Oh, well. At least we'll stink together."

"I'm starved. Let's go rustle up some grub, pilgrim," he said in his best John Wayne voice.

"I knew you were a cowboy!" Tess giggled, and the happy sound resounded in his heart.

He swatted at her bottom as he kicked free of the sheets and strolled over to his backpack to find a clean pair of briefs. After putting on his underwear, he paused by the pitiful excuse for an air conditioner and flipped open the control panel.

"Tess!" He scoffed. "We've been sweltering all night because all you turned on was the fan!" Jabbing the button marked "cool," he sighed when chilly air rushed out of the vent at his feet. "If I had known that you . . ."

He swallowed the rest of his admonition when he faced her and saw the color drain from her cheeks. His gut knotted when he realized what he'd said and the tone he'd used.

"Oh, man, Tess, I'm sorry! I didn't mean . . ." He huffed in self-disgust and pinched the bridge of his nose. He'd screwed up again, proof positive why he could never make Tess happy over the long haul. Raising his eyes to her, he saw the tint returning to her face. "Forgive me, please."

He stepped over to her and folded her in his arms. "Tess, I'm so sorry for yelling. You made a simple mistake. Don't worry about it."

She pulled away from him, giving him a leery, appraising once-over. A flare of anger burned in his chest for the man who'd intimidated Tess until she learned to suppress her emotions. But more than anything, he swam a flood tide of frustration with his own thoughtless mouth. He'd always been too quick to speak, prone to trigger responses that drove his family nuts.

"Don't withdraw again." He held his hand out to her, and his tone pleaded softly. "Please. You don't have to hide your feelings from me. I want to hear you yell back if that's what you feel like. Come on, I can take it."

She shook her head. "It's okay. Forget it."

"Tess . . ."

"Just forget it. It doesn't matter." Turning her back, she walked away.

"It *does* matter. Retreating won't solve anything. I don't want you storing up resentment against me. Let it out, and let's clear the air. I can't promise I'll never lose my temper, but if I do, I want you to hold your ground and yell back."

Silently she dug through her suitcase, ignoring him.

He sighed wearily. "Don't let him win, Tess."

Her movements stilled.

"I've seen a spark in you, and I want to help you nourish it. I know you don't believe it, you don't see your potential, but it's there. You have a core of strength and courage that's admirable, Tess. Draw on it. Build on it. You've come a long way just by breaking free from him. Don't retreat now."

She turned a haunted expression toward him. "I may have been strong once." Biting her lip, she dropped her gaze. "But any spark I had is gone. I traded it with the rest of my dignity when I gave myself to Randall. I bartered myself for survival." Her hands plowed restlessly through her possessions, and her face grew rigid and unforgiving.

"Look again. I can see it. Trust yourself. But for God's sake, don't let him win." He crossed the floor to her and lifted her chin with his palm. Meeting her gaze head on, he said emphatically, "I believe in you, Tess. Don't give up."

Doubt still filled her eyes, but the twitch of her lips and her weak smile of acknowledgment said she'd heard what he said and had planted it somewhere deep inside. For now, that was enough.

"What did you say the name of this town is?" As Justin drove the Jimmy out of the motel parking lot, Tess squinted in the bright sunlight at the map she'd picked up at a gas station the day before.

"Vernon."

"Justin?" She shook her head and wrinkled her nose. "How can that be? We were nearly in Amarillo before you started driving yesterday."

"I know. But Nashville is east. I drove east."

"You backtracked."

"Yep, 'cause you went the wrong way."

"The wrong . . ." She stopped and took a breath to calm the irritation in her voice. "There is no wrong way except anything that takes me back toward San Antonio. I need distance. I need to get far away from south Texas. Your change of course means that I wasted a whole day driving—"

"The wrong way. Nashville is east." He sported a cocky grin, and the protest on her lips died. She didn't want an argument, knew fighting wouldn't change what had been done.

Justin didn't know about the flier with her picture, didn't understand how close Randall's men were. But she did. She imagined them breathing down her neck, and her spine tingled with dread.

Distance. They had to put more distance between her and Randall's realm of power.

Taking a slow breath, she explained what she thought was obvious. "I can't go to Nashville with you, Justin. Randall could easily have contacts there. Besides, you want to make your presence known, and I have to hide out. I need obscurity."

His smile faded, and his expression became unreadable.

She sighed. "We can drive toward Nashville for you, and I'll let you out there. But I have to keep moving. The farther, the better."

"Then I'll keep moving with you. Nashville's not going anywhere. My first priority right now is seeing you're safe."

A pang of gratitude plucked her heart, along with the bitter irony that her priority today had to be ditching Justin somehow. For his safety.

But maybe, just maybe, they could drive toward Nashville together a while longer. She could store up a few more treasured memories, he could get that much closer to his destination, and then . . .

She hated to think beyond the here and now. Before she'd met Justin, building a life away from Randall had been a blissful goal to strive for. Now, starting a new life by herself seemed lonely. Still, her selfish desire for his company and the safety she gained from his presence didn't outweigh her moral obligation to shield him.

She huffed her frustration and turned toward the window. How long did she dare stay with him? Randall's men could be anywhere. They could strike in a split second, as the man at the fast food restaurant had. *With no warning.* She leaned her head against the window to brood.

Then she spotted the first of the buildings.

Tess and Justin looked at each other across the front seat of the Jimmy and gave a mutual groan of disgust and disbelief.

"Two more miles! Not more than a few blocks!" She waved her hand at the line of buildings, including a large hotel belonging to a national chain and a series of fast food restaurants. "If we'd just driven a little further last night, we could have had a decent room, a decent meal, a decent—"

"But we wouldn't have had as much fun." Justin gave her a lopsided grin. "So we roughed it a little because we stopped too soon. So what?"

She studied the nonchalance in Justin's indifferent shrug and marveled again at his easy-going nature.

"I'm kinda partial to the ole Catch-a-Wink today for sentimental reasons," he added with a puckish expression.

Turning her attention back to the line of buildings, she spotted the black and yellow sign at the same time Justin did.

"Bingo. Waffle House!" He turned in at the restaurant, and her stomach rumbled at the thought of food.

Remembering the flier with her picture, Tess turned to the

backseat and retrieved Justin's Stetson. She twisted her hair up and tucked it inside the hat and reached in her purse for her sunglasses, despite the overcast day. It wasn't much of a disguise, but she prayed it would be enough.

After breakfast, Tess convinced Justin to check into another hotel long enough for them each to shower. While she hated the three-hour delay it cost them, the shower went a long way toward reviving her spirits. Once back on the road, Justin took the wheel and headed down a two-lane state highway, citing a need for a change of scenery. As they settled in, he found a country station on the radio. Tess arched an eyebrow and gave him a teasing scowl.

He grinned smugly. "Remember? The driver gets to pick the entertainment."

With a groan, she settled back in her seat. Her body ached with a stiffness that reminded her of the night and the feel of Justin's body entwined with hers. The memory sent a warm tingle skittering over her skin, and she smiled.

Tilting her head, she watched the raven-haired man behind the wheel. A day's growth of beard shadowed his handsome profile, as it had the day she picked him up along the rain-drenched highway in south Texas.

His lips puckered, and he whistled with the tune on the radio. She turned her thoughts to his entreaty that morning. *For God's sake, don't let him win. Don't give up.*

When her parents were alive, before Angela had sold her body to keep them alive, she'd known the kind of hope Justin encouraged in her. Did she still have the strength Justin said he saw? Could she ever forgive herself for letting parts of herself die when she gave herself to Randall? She'd been so young and alone, so frightened of the dead-end life she faced. She'd believed Randall loved her. How could she have known she was only trading one form of misery for another? How could she have known that instead of selling her body to survive as Angela had, she'd sell her soul?

Perhaps she could forgive herself for her youthful ignorance, but when Randall had shown his true nature, why had she stayed? For thirteen years, she'd given to Randall until she had nothing left, and still he'd demanded more from her. He'd killed the spirit of the young woman who'd dreamed of happily ever after. He'd sapped the energy from the girl who'd giggled with her sister and bubbled with life in the innocent days of childhood.

Reaching out, she stroked the unshaven cheek of the man who'd challenged her to find that girl again and draw on her strength. Was part of the old Tess still buried inside her?

Justin cut a sideways glance at her and smiled. His peaceful optimism warmed her, and she closed her eyes. Lulled by the hum of the tires and her full stomach, she fell asleep.

She didn't wake again until Justin stopped the car, and she sat up blinking to see where they were.

"Pit stop," he said. "We need gas, and I need chocolate."

"And it's my turn to drive," she added, reaching into the backseat for Justin's hat as she had at breakfast.

Tess tugged the brim of the hat low, and Justin took her hand as they walked into the gas station.

The idea that he viewed them as a couple needled her conscience. Did he think their lovemaking was the beginning of something lasting? She'd fallen into a trap of her own making. She'd known better than to start caring for Justin. Her affection for him already complicated an untenable situation.

Whether or not Justin realized it, she knew chances were good that Randall would find her sooner or later. When he did, she would die.

It was her duty to ensure that Justin didn't.

★ ★ ★ ★ ★

Tess sat in the driver's seat of the Jimmy and wrapped sweaty hands around the steering wheel. Justin was still inside, using the restroom of the gas station/minimart where they'd stopped. This was her chance. All she had to do was press the accelerator and drive off without him.

For his own good. For his own good! Yet no matter how many times she repeated the phrase to herself, she couldn't drive away. Conflicting emotions warred inside her and brought tears to her eyes. How could she leave him stranded? He could, of course, fend for himself if he had his pack and his guitar. That thought gave her the courage she needed. If she unloaded his belongings and left them on the curb for him to find . . .

She climbed out of the truck and circled to the passenger side. She had to leave him. She had to do it. He'd have everything he needed to get by, along with the safety of his anonymity. Her mind set, she opened the back door to pull out his pack.

The pack weighed a ton. She struggled with it, then groaned when one strap caught on a lever just under the seat. She pushed it back in, unsnagged the strap, and tried again. She was losing time. Justin would be back soon, and her opportunity would be gone. Her fingers trembled as she hurried.

"Hey, buddy, you seen this woman around here?"

Justin turned to the stocky, pug-nosed man who stopped him on his way out of the men's room. Dropping his gaze to the photograph the man poked at him, Justin's heart slammed against his ribs. Yeah, he'd seen the woman in the picture.

But he didn't know her by the name under the black and

white head shot. "Sinclair," the caption read. Not "Carpenter."

He worked to show no recognition or alarm. Tess had warned him not to underestimate Randall's scope of power and ability to find her. He recalled her few efforts that morning to disguise herself and her reaction to the desk clerk who thought he recognized her.

Justin shook his head and shrugged. "Tess Sinclair? Never heard of her. Why do you ask?"

"You haven't seen her around here then?" the stocky man asked, ignoring Justin's question.

"Naw. Sorry." He thought about Tess, sitting out in the truck while this creep flashed her picture around inside. How the guy had missed seeing her when she came in to use the restroom was anybody's guess.

As calmly as he could, as fast as he could, Justin returned to the Jimmy. He scanned the parking lot as he left and watched the stocky guy show Tess's picture to another couple that had just left the store. Without taking his eyes off the suspicious man, he jogged to the truck.

Tess was leaning in the backseat, fumbling with something.

"You ready to go?" He climbed into the driver's side and cranked the engine.

She looked at him with wide, startled eyes, and her shoulders drooped. Giving him a reluctant nod, she closed the back door and climbed in the front. "Yeah, I guess. Unless—"

Before she could finish her sentence, he tore out of the parking lot and hightailed it for the interstate.

Chapter Ten

As Justin took a corner too fast, Tess grabbed the edge of her seat and cast a curious glance at him. "Where's the fire?"

He checked the rearview mirror to see if anyone had followed them from the gas station. When he felt sure no one had, he backed off the gas. Only then did he draw an easy breath. Tess stared at him like he'd lost his mind, and he gave her what he hoped was a reassuring smile.

"Sorry. I didn't mean to scare you, but there was some creep at the gas station who . . ." He decided telling her the truth might cause her to panic.

"Who what?" Her gaze narrowed, and worry wrinkled her brow.

"Who, uh, propositioned me."

Tess's eyes widened, and a giggle bubbled from her. "He what?"

"You heard me. He gave me the willies, so I got the hell outta there."

Now Tess laughed without mercy. "What did he say?"

Justin scowled. "Nothing a lady should hear. Would you stop laughing? It's not funny!" *Or at least the truth wasn't funny.*

"Can't say that I blame him for trying." She leaned toward him and dragged a finger down his cheek. "You studpuppy."

Her laughter filled the truck with an effervescence that

lightened his mood and stirred new emotions deep inside him. He recognized that he'd begun to feel more for this woman than lust, concern and friendship.

And it scared him. He had no place in her life. The close call with the dude at the gas station only made clearer his need to find her a safe hideout quickly. The sooner the better. He couldn't afford to grow any closer to her. He was too likely to let his emotions cloud his judgment. He would never forgive himself if he let his feelings get in the way of doing what was best, what was right for Tess.

Glancing at her, he wondered about the name on the picture. Sinclair.

"What is Randall's last name?" he asked without preamble, and Tess sobered.

She cast him a dubious gaze. "Why?"

"It can't hurt for me to know who and what we're dealing with, can it?"

Swinging her gaze to the passenger-side window, she fell silent.

"Sinclair," she whispered finally, almost too softly to be heard.

He nodded, grateful that she'd trusted him with the truth. Having her faith, her honesty, sharpened his sense of responsibility for her. He'd do anything to see that he didn't betray that trust or let her down.

That night when they stopped outside of Shreveport, Louisiana, Justin suggested they drive away from the interstate and find a motel in town. Tess gave him a concerned look that said she wondered what he wasn't telling her, but she nodded her agreement.

"You certainly have a lot of freckles on your back, Mr. Boyd. Did you know that?" Tess dragged a finger across

Justin's broad, muscled back as he lay on his stomach with his hands stacked under his cheek.

"Not only do I know about those freckles, I know that if you connect all of them in the right order, they make a picture of a teddy bear." His voice held the craggy, lazy rasp of a drowsy man languishing in the aftermath of satisfying sex.

Tess snorted. "Yeah, right."

While Justin lolled about, she crackled with energy. The sensual delights he introduced her to excited and invigorated her. Try as she might to regret her second thwarted attempt to leave Justin behind, she enjoyed his company, his friendship and their sex too much to tarnish it with second thoughts. A world of sweet sensation and discovery, a new appreciation and acceptance of her body, and the freedom to dabble and play lay spread at her feet. She intended to savor it all. She knew this nirvana would not last.

He levered up and turned a disappointed gaze on her. "You don't believe me? Are you calling me a liar?"

"I'm saying you're not going to trick me into believing something as silly as that."

"Get a pen," he challenged. "I'll prove it."

She furrowed her brow and frowned at him. "Justin—"

"Get a pen."

With a sigh, she got up from the bed, already well mussed from their lovemaking, and dug in her purse until she found a pen. "All right, wise guy. Prove it."

"Start with the one closest to my right shoulder blade, and then, well, you'll figure it out. I can't see my own back, so you're on your own."

Studying his expression for any evidence of insincerity, but not detecting any, she put the pen down on a mole near his right shoulder blade and began a trial run. Obviously, she had the wrong combination. The shape she made looked nothing like a bear. She tried again. And again. Justin's back looked like a road map, but no teddy bear emerged.

"That's not permanent ink, is it?" he asked after a few minutes.

"I wish it were," she returned grumpily, as his deception became more and more obvious.

"Why do you say that?"

"Because there is no damn teddy bear or any other animal on your back, and you're a dirty dog for playing on my gullibility like that!"

He laughed and twisted around to catch her hand in his. "Maybe you're not connecting the dots right."

"Maybe you need a few more dots on your face!" She swiped at his nose and left a satisfyingly long stripe on its tip. The grin that blossomed on her lips sprang from her soul. Not since Angela's death had she known this freedom to laugh and tease. Her happiness fed her hungry spirit.

"Gimme that pen!" He grabbed for the pen, chuckling, but she stretched her arm to hold it out of his reach. He tickled her side. With a yelp, she drew her arm in to protect her ticklish underarm. The pen now within reach, he snatched it from her, and his eyes lit with a mischievous gleam.

Tess wagged a finger at him. "Oh, no, you don't!"

She tried to scamper off the bed, but he hooked an arm around her waist and dragged her back. Climbing on top of her, he pinned her hands down as he straddled her, a task made easy since her laughter left her weaker than a kitten.

Justin raised his T-shirt, which she wore, and drew on her stomach. "Stop laughing, your jiggling is ruining my artwork," he complained.

She bit the inside of her cheek to quell her giggles and tried to be still. But the pen tickled, and she squirmed. The heat of his thighs, trapping her hips, and the juxtaposition of his sex so close to hers started a prickle of anticipation.

"There." He capped the pen and swung his leg back over her as he stretched out at her side. Nestled against her, he stroked the length of her leg with his foot.

Propping up, she peered down at her belly to see what he'd drawn. The figure was unrecognizable. "What is that?"

"A teddy bear."

Tess's giggles erupted again. "A musician you may be, but an artist you're not."

"You kept moving. Besides, it probably looks more like a bear than those scribbles you were putting on my back."

She shook her head and gazed with a full heart at his shining eyes and the rugged lines of his handsome face. "You're crazy. You know that?"

"Better crazy than gullible."

Tess slugged his arm in jest.

"Watch it. I still have the pen." Holding the pen out of her reach, Justin rolled to her so that his body covered half of hers, then pressed a kiss on her lips. The touch of his warm mouth electrified her. Her body tingled, and her nipples peaked.

"Now what do you want to do?" A sultry smile curved her lips, and she ran her fingers through the unruly waves of his hair. Playing the vamp gave her a heady sense of power and control she'd never had before. With Justin, she felt free to experience new possibilities.

"We could channel surf." He strummed her spine idly, his face the picture of lazy contentment, while he sent ribbons of desire spiraling inside her.

"Channel surf? What do you mean?" Her voice sounded as thick and relaxed as his.

"On the TV, you know, when you keep flipping from one station to another."

"Why would you do that?" She blinked her bewilderment.

"Because I'm a man, and that's what men do," he answered in an unusually deep voice.

Tess grinned. "I don't like TV much. Never watch."

"Well, I do have another idea, but . . ."

His singsong tone piqued her suspicion. "But what?"

"It would mean getting dressed and going out."

A pang of disappointment and alarm pricked her bubble of bliss. "Out? Out where?"

"I saw a little place back up the road that I thought . . . maybe . . ."

"Spit it out, Boyd. What kind of place?"

"A honky-tonk."

She wrinkled her nose and gave him her low, you-gotta-be-kidding laugh. "I'll pass."

Justin scowled. "Damn it, Tess, why? You keep saying you hate country music so much, but you like the stuff I've played for you. Go with me tonight, and give it a try. Please?"

He looked truly offended, even crushed by her refusal, and Tess's heart turned over. How could she refuse him anything, after all he'd done for her?

"It's what I do, Tess. Country music is my life, my dream. Can't you just—"

She muffled his argument with a hand over his mouth. "All right. I'll go with you."

Grinning his satisfaction, he scooted off the bed to dress, and his words rang in her ears. *Country music is my life, my dream.*

His comment reminded her that their goals were incompatible. He wanted, deserved to have the music spotlight on him. She had no option but to hide. Any inkling of trying to stay with him dissolved with that fact.

She hadn't decided when or how she would try again to

leave him, but they'd reach Nashville in one more long day of driving. Nashville had to mark the end of their association. She couldn't let Justin give up his dream.

But just for now, she wanted to pretend they could have a future together, a life as happy as the past three days had been. She wouldn't spoil the night worrying about what would happen when they reached Music City.

Justin drove them to a small, nondescript brick building. The lighted sign out front read: "The Watering Hole. Tonight Hank Jones and the Cattlemen."

Justin patted her leg. "Remember, you promised to keep an open mind and to try to have fun."

With a groan, Tess put on his cowboy hat. "Yes, sir."

He led her inside a dimly lit room where music blared. A thin haze of cigarette smoke swirled around the overworked ceiling fans. Jean-clad men and women in short skirts and cowboy boots danced in a crowded space in front of a tiny stage. Wood planking on the floor and exposed beams on the ceiling added to the barn-like, relaxed atmosphere.

Moving a full ashtray off a table, Justin pulled out a ladder-back chair for Tess. "Want anything from the bar?" he yelled over the din of drums and guitars from the band playing on the small stage.

"White wine spritzer."

Justin stared at her blankly for a minute. "Are you trying to get me beaten up?"

"What?"

"I can't order a white wine spritzer in a place like this. Have you ever drunk a beer in your life?"

Tess raised her chin a notch, insulted by the implication that she was a snob. "Yes."

"Will a beer do?"

Tess rolled her eyes. "Why'd you ask what I wanted if my only choice is a beer?"

"I didn't ask what you wanted. I asked if you wanted anything from the bar. At a place called 'The Watering Hole' that usually means beer or whiskey."

Tess tried to frown at him, but his blue eyes twinkled devilishly. "I'll have a beer."

As he crossed the room with his long-legged gait, Tess admired the rear view of jeans over firm tush. She noticed several other female heads turning to stare at her dark-haired cowboy, and she gritted her teeth.

Eat your hearts out, ladies. He's with me.

When Justin returned, he carried two tall, brown bottles of beer. He gave the band his full attention for a few minutes then turned to Tess. "They're not half bad."

She had just reached a similar conclusion about the beer. The bitter twang grew on her, and the cold brew made her blood warm and her head woozy.

"Does that mean they're only half good?" she teased.

"Come here." Rising to his feet, he held out his hand.

She gave his hand a dubious glance. "Why?"

"I want to dance."

"Uh-uh." She shook her head, and Justin raised an eyebrow.

"You promised."

"I promised to try to have fun, and I'm having a blast right here in my seat." She smiled to punctuate that fact.

"I'm not above causing a scene, Tess."

That got her attention. She believed he would. The glitter in his eyes confirmed it. The last thing she needed was extra attention drawn to her, no matter how remote the possibility Randall's men would look for her in this dive.

With a glower, she gave him her hand. "One dance. That's all."

A cocky grin curved his lips as he slid a hand to the small of her back and led her across the room. The warmth of his hand burned her skin through the thin fabric of her sundress. The gentlemanly possessiveness of the gesture wound around her heart like a vine, rooting itself.

When they reached the dance floor, a slow song was playing, and he pulled her into his arms. A little light-headed from the beer she'd drunk too fast, Tess closed her eyes and leaned against his solid strength. She moved with him as he swayed and hummed in her ear then sang softly with the love song's refrain.

He moved his hand up and down her spine as they danced, and her head buzzed with the dizzying effect of his slow caress. His hard thighs brushed hers as they shuffled around the floor. When she circled his neck with her arms, he smiled down at her.

If she tried, Tess could forget at that moment that the rest of the world existed. Her heart seemed to swell to twice its normal size, and she blamed the beer for the heady rush of emotions. To properly identify the source of the tender ache that flowered inside her would mean setting herself up for a painful loss when they went their separate ways.

But for now, she could pretend that day wasn't coming. Just for a little while, she wanted to forget what she ran from, wanted to forget that anything mattered except the blue eyes and lazy grin that beamed at her. When the song ended, Justin pressed a sweet kiss on her lips.

The lead singer of the little band wailed the opening line of a rowdy song, startling Tess out of the dreamy moment of bliss.

"Hey, they're playing our song," Justin said with a sly grin.

"Our song?"

Justin sang with the band, and recognition dawned on

Tess. "That silly song you made me listen to in the car the other day!"

She chuckled and started off the dance floor, but Justin caught her hand. Spinning her around, he twirled her so that her arm crossed over her chest and her back came up against his chest. He began a shuffling step then spun her out again, leading her in a dance that reminded her of the shag that she'd learned from Angela in more carefree days.

Staring at Justin, somewhat stunned, she stumbled clumsily as he scooted and twirled her around the dance floor. Her gaze dropped to watch his feet, and she tried to mimic the heel-toe-stomp pattern that he demonstrated. His hands captured her hips and encouraged them to sway as he pulled her along with her back up against his chest again. The heel-toe-stomp pattern repeated, and Tess picked up a few of the steps.

"That's it!" Justin shouted over the loud music.

She concentrated on keeping up and not losing a step. Glancing up at the approval on Justin's face, she realized she was having fun. A lot of fun. A smile burgeoned on her lips then spilled over in a laugh. Another fast, bouncy tune followed, and they stayed out on the floor to dance some more.

Her grin stayed in place simply because she was happy and having the good time Justin had promised. But Justin had a way of making even the mundane enjoyable. Whether he serenaded her with his guitar, teased her about freckles, or merely filled the long hours on the road with conversation, he had a way of making her smile, of making her enjoy life.

Dear God, how she would miss him.

When they finally left the honky-tonk and returned to their motel room, she brushed her teeth and tumbled wearily into bed. Justin joined her a few minutes later, cuddling up to her like a spoon. His arm slid around her, and he kissed her hair, murmuring his good night wishes, as if it were something he'd done a hundred times before. Tess squeezed her eyes closed, savoring the natural comfort of the moment—the kind of moment that husbands and wives were supposed to share, but she'd never had.

As she drifted to sleep, her heart filled with a bittersweet longing for a lifetime of nights like this one. With this man.

A loud pounding woke Tess and Justin the next morning. Tess bolted upright, tensing, while Justin fought to clear the cobwebs of sleep and remember where he was. One look at the terror in Tess's eyes triggered a flood of memory. The cold slap of reality brought him fully awake.

"Stay here," he told her as he tossed back the sheets and grabbed his jeans from the floor.

"Who is it?" he called but received no answer.

Recollection of the goon who'd been showing Tess's picture at the gas station flashed with vivid clarity in his mind.

"Who's there?" This time his voice held a note of irritation that raised his volume.

"Room service."

He squinted to look through the peep hole in the door and found a uniformed motel employee with a tray of food.

"We didn't order anything." He barked his reply, partly in annoyance for his disturbed sleep and partly because of the scare the inept employee had given them.

The young man with the tray of food looked at his order ticket then the number on the door. "Oh, yeah, sorry."

Justin scoffed as he turned back to Tess. "False alarm." Stripping off his jeans again, he climbed back under the covers and pulled Tess into his arms. Her body trembled. "It's okay, baby. There's nothing to be scared of."

"This time," she said morosely, sagging against him.

He kissed her cheek and remained quiet for a minute as he calmed her with soothing strokes on her back. His mind strayed to all the implications and contingencies he'd blindly avoided up to this point. He didn't want to consider that Tess could be involved in something more sinister than straight domestic abuse. But she had men after her, and she jumped at her own shadow. He couldn't ignore the simple fact that Tess's circumstances rang with an ominous note. Ignorance of what they faced put him at a disadvantage. Whether he wanted to face the truth or not, he needed to know what Tess knew.

He sucked in a deep breath, trying to dispel his disquiet. "Tess, don't you think it's time you told me what happened with Randall? After living with him for years, what made you leave now?"

Chapter Eleven

"You said Randall was evil. What did you mean by that?" Justin kept his voice gently coaxing, but she still stiffened at the mention of Randall.

She didn't answer right away. He waited patiently for her to sort her thoughts and decide what and how to tell him. When she spoke, her hushed voice trembled. "I hadn't been happy with him for a long time. I never loved him, but when he took me in years ago, I was so young and scared I didn't look to see what I was getting into. I was so grateful to him for providing me a way out of a bad situation that I didn't realize how much worse my life could be with him. I was blind then to what kind of man he was."

"What kind of situation did he get you out of?" Justin brushed a wisp of ash-brown hair away from her eyes and tucked it behind her ear.

"Dismal poverty. My sister, Angie, took care of us as best she could, but when she was killed, I had nowhere to turn. Or so I thought."

"This was after your parents died in the car wreck?"

She nodded. "We didn't want to be separated or get sent to foster homes. Angie quit school and started working to support us. We hid the truth about our situation pretty well, but we were so poor . . ."

Tess paused and sighed, and the emotion that flickered across her face twisted his heart.

"Angie worked a minimum wage job for a while, and then . . ." Her face crumpled, and tears welled in her eyes.

Apprehension tightened his gut. Instinctively, he reached for her hand and gave it a gentle squeeze.

"One night Angie came home really late. She was crying and . . ." A shudder raced through Tess. "She'd sold herself to a guy at the diner where she worked. She could earn more money hooking than any other way, she said. I argued with her about it, but she said it was the best way. She wanted me to have money for college."

"Your sister prostituted?" Disbelief made his voice hoarse. Squeezing her hand harder, he tried to absorb the revelation. He tried to picture Tess as a frightened teen, struggling to make ends meet and watching her sister turn to prostitution to support them. A heavy sorrow weighted his chest.

"Her pimp killed her when I was sixteen. Randall showed up right after Angie died, and he said he was a friend of Angie's . . ." Tess bit her lip, and when she closed her eyes, fat tears spilled down her cheeks. "I trusted him. Blindly trusted him. He paid the rent and groceries until I turned eighteen. Then he offered to marry me. I jumped at the chance to marry a rich man. Until then, he'd been nothing but kind and generous to me."

"When did you realize he wasn't what he seemed?" Justin brushed his thumb on the underside of her wrist, hoping to comfort her.

"In the first couple of months, after I moved in with him. He never married me like he said he would and . . ." Her eyes held a distant look, her thoughts clearly lost in painful memories. "Once we were in his house and I was under his control, he showed his true colors. He set out in no uncertain terms how he expected me to behave. I was to obey his every command like a trained dog . . . and perform for him sexually whenever he wanted it. And if I showed any resistance, he . . ."

When she paused, Justin's breath stilled. "He what?"

His throat tightened. The wrenching pain he'd experienced when he learned about Rebecca's suffering returned in force, bolstered now by the anger and guilt that were the legacy of Rebecca's death.

"He hurt me." Tess glanced up at him with a hollow, haunted expression. "Not brutal beatings like you said your sister's husband gave her. He slapped me around a little. It was nothing really. Not compared to—"

"Nothing?" Incredulity and frustration sharpened his tone. "Nothing, Tess? God!"

He slammed his fist down on the mattress with a bitter curse, and Tess tensed. Turning a pointed gaze on her, he pled his case. "No man has a right to hit a woman. Ever. A slap is not 'nothing'! Do you hear me?"

How many times had he argued with Becca over this issue? Why hadn't she listened to him? His sense of helplessness, battling his sister's stubborn pride and her blind loyalty to Mac, had nearly killed him. In the end, his failure to take decisive action had killed her.

Tess's eyes widened, and she searched his face with a stunned and uncertain expression.

Drawing a calming breath, he softened his tone. "Do you understand, Tess?"

She nodded weakly.

"Okay. Finish what you were saying, please." Brushing her cheek with his knuckles, he quirked a smile of encouragement.

As Tess continued in a voice barely above a whisper, she turned away. He recognized the gesture. Rebecca had been ashamed when she talked of her abuse.

He muttered a nasty epithet under his breath and ached

for the opportunity to wrap his hands around Randall's neck. For Tess's sake, he tamped down his anger and pulled her into his embrace.

"You're safe now, baby. Don't feel bad about it. He did it. He's the sick one. Don't blame yourself."

Tess shivered. "He didn't always hit me, only sometimes when he was really mad. I learned how to appease him, how to avoid his tantrums, but he kept me under his thumb. He made sure I was afraid of him. And I was. I am."

"So what happened that finally made you leave him?"

"I found out how truly evil he is. He's a powerful man. He has so many people who work for him, who'll do his bidding because they fear him or because they have no conscience or . . ." Tess ground the heels of her hands into her eyes and released a shuddering sigh. "I found out by accident. I overheard a phone call. He had a man murdered. He made sure it looked like a suicide to cover his tracks. He hired a hit man to kill a business associate. I don't know why or what Fannin did to upset him, but . . ."

Justin's blood went cold. Involuntarily, he tightened his hold on Tess. "He had a man murdered? Are you sure?"

She nodded, and her voice cracked as she began to cry. "He killed Angie, too." Turning to bury her face in his chest, she sobbed bitterly. "My sister. He killed my sister."

"I thought you said her pimp—"

"Randall ordered her murder. He told me so the night I found out about Fannin. Oh, Justin, I couldn't stay. I'd lived with him for years but never really knew him . . . never knew how evil . . . I couldn't stay and live with a murderer."

He kissed her forehead. "I understand, babe." He stroked her hair and rocked her in his arms, a million questions running through his head. "Was Randall one of Angie's johns?"

"Apparently."

Justin hugged Tess closer. "Why did he have her killed?"

Tess raised damp, red eyes to him, tears spilling down her cheeks. "I don't know, exactly. She upset him somehow. She resisted him, defied him. Randall hates to have his authority challenged."

"His *imagined* authority." Justin tipped Tess's chin up to make sure she listened. "The guy sounds like a real control freak. But in truth he has no power over anyone. You can't give him the power, Tess. You have to take control, stand up to him."

"And get killed like Angie did?" Stress made her voice shrill. She shook her head. "No, Justin. You can't fight Randall. He doesn't allow—"

"He only has power if you give it to him, Tess." Justin furrowed his brow and narrowed a gaze of concern on her. "You have to take back the power when he tries to control you."

She made a soft scoffing noise and shook her head. "You don't understand how he is."

"What I do understand is that the minute you give up, he's won." He ran a loving finger from the hollow of her throat, between her breasts, and tapped a finger over her heart. "Draw on what's in here. You had the strength to leave him, and I'm betting that's only a hint of what's inside you if you look good and hard. He's held you down long enough. Time to fight back, Tess."

She stared into his eyes with an almost awestruck look on her face.

"Promise me you won't give up. Will you use that strength that's inside you and fight back for me, Tess?" Justin searched her eyes for the spark of life he'd seen before, the evidence of the vital, determined woman he knew she was. What he saw warming her hazel gaze went beyond his expectations, and his heart thudded a slow, heavy beat in response. What he saw shining back at him looked a lot like love.

Regret squeezed his chest. He had never intended for things between them to go so far, but a deep bond had developed. All too soon Tess would see him for the man he really was, a man with nothing more than smoke and mirrors. He could say the right words of encouragement, offer the compassion she craved, even provide her the protection and safety she needed. But that was all he could promise. Beyond that, his track record had proven dismal. If Tess was falling in love with him, she was doomed to have her heart broken. Once again, it seemed, in trying to help, he would hurt someone dear to him.

Justin seemed somber. Not that Tess could blame him. If she'd had everything spilled at her feet the way he had this morning, she'd be somber too.

She put a hand on his leg. When he glanced at her from the driver's seat, she gave him a tremulous smile. Scooping her hand in his, he carried it up to his lips for a kiss. "You okay?"

She nodded. They'd been driving for two hours in almost complete silence. Although she'd grown thoroughly sick of being in the Jimmy, telling Justin about Randall had renewed her fears and the need to keep moving. Justin, it seemed, shared her sense of urgency now, and although it did little to calm her, she felt marginally better knowing he understood the danger she was in.

The danger he was in.

Tess sighed at the thought. She'd never wanted to involve Justin in her problems. Yet somehow, because of her inept attempts to leave him, her susceptibility to his charms, and her hunger for the friendship and affection he offered, she'd selfishly allowed him to weave himself into the tapestry of her horrible ordeal.

At this point, just one day of driving away from Nashville, she figured she owed it to Justin to take him that far. For all his consideration and kindness, she could do that much to help him achieve his dreams. Then she would have to cut him out of her life. For good. She would have to make it clear he couldn't contact her, couldn't put himself in jeopardy.

Silently, she prayed she wasn't being foolish, taking an unnecessary risk by delaying their parting until Nashville. How close was Randall to finding her? God only knew.

She was so lost in thought, she didn't notice Justin pull off the Mississippi highway until he stopped the car in the shade behind a large tree at the side of the road. Scanning the isolated stretch of road, Tess knitted her brow with a curious frown. "Why are we stopping here?"

"Because it's secluded."

"Why do we want seclusion?"

"Because I'm not an exhibitionist."

Before she could respond, Justin pulled his T-shirt over his head. Tess's heart drummed with nervous and expectant adrenaline. "Mr. Boyd?" She tried to sound lighthearted. "What do you think you're doing?"

"I think I'm hoping to seduce you. I can't keep my mind on my driving for wanting you. I'm like an addict. I can't get enough of you, now that I've had a taste."

Tess giggled awkwardly as he leaned across the bucket seat toward her. "You mean here? Now?"

"That was the idea." He cupped her chin with a warm hand. "Kiss me, Tess."

"But—"

He smothered her feeble protest with a kiss that melted any reservations she might have had, while stirring a bittersweet ache in her chest. She would miss his kiss so much when he was gone.

His mouth had the persuasive power to awaken the tingling response of her body in seconds. His greedy kiss consumed her, and she returned his fervor. Their tongues mated and danced while he freed her from her shirt and pushed aside her bra.

When he moved his attention to the breasts he'd bared, she wound her fingers in the thick black waves of his hair. Arching her back in response to the tug of his lips on her nipple, she gasped at the rush of pure, sweet pleasure that spiraled through her. She mewled her enjoyment of the light teasing of his tongue on the sensitive swell of her breast and the hollow of her throat. Her hands roamed restlessly across his bare back, and she dug her fingers into his shoulders. After trailing nibbling kisses from her throat to her earlobe, he reclaimed her mouth with an even greater need and eagerness.

Her fingers moved down the path of dark hair on his stomach. Justin caught his breath and raised his head to gaze at her with eyes made bleary with passion. "Sweet mercy, Tess. What have you done to me? I used to be a patient man."

He rolled away to undo his jeans, and she stripped out of her shorts and panties, mindful only of how much she wanted Justin and the blissful climax her body ached for. He pulled her across the front seat to straddle his lap. While he leaned the seat as far back as it would go, she settled over him.

"Oh, Tess."

Justin sank into her. He held her hips in place as he thrust upward, and fiery sparks shot through her. Together, they raced toward fulfillment.

Mouthing his name, her laud became a begging for release. Tears of joy puddled in her eyes when the pulsing, shattering sensation of completion rocked her.

She tucked the memory, the precious feeling of completeness, in the corner of her mind. These stolen moments of sweetness would have to tide her through the days and weeks to come.

Justin bucked harder as he came, and she grabbed for a hand-hold to steady herself on top of him. The car horn blasted when she clutched the steering wheel, and she gasped, startled.

Justin shuddered and went limp then grinned at her.

"I've heard of women screaming during orgasm, but horn honking . . . that's a new one for me." He sat up enough to kiss her soundly then added, "I kinda like your enthusiasm. How about seconds?"

"You're insatiable," she whispered, her throat tight with emotion.

Justin captured her face between his hands and met her eyes with a penetrating blue gaze. "I could easily fall in love with you, Tess."

Her heart lurched. "Don't say that."

"Why not, for God's sake? It's the truth. You're an incredible woman."

"I'm a marked woman. I'm a noose around the neck of anyone who is close to me." She didn't bother to mention the other thoughts that filtered through her mind—that Justin deserved better than the woman Randall had created, that even if she didn't have a killer after her, her history made her a poor choice for a girlfriend, much less a wife. She was tainted by Randall's evil, and she could never let her baggage weigh Justin down. He had a bright future. She had only the determination to survive, despite her past.

She tried to move off him, battling the tears that welled in her eyes and burned her throat, but he held her arms and pulled her back.

"Look at me, Tess." She refused with a shake of her head, and he caught her chin. "I can call my brother. Remember, I told you he was a lawyer? He can help us get a restraining order against Randall. You can be free of him and his threat."

Sweet, optimistic Justin, she thought sadly and shook her head again. Her tears streamed down her cheeks, and she swiped at them. "A restraining order isn't going to stop Randall. He'd send one of his henchmen to do his dirty work. Don't you understand? I can run from him, but I'll never really be free of him."

"We'll find a way, Tess. Trust me to take care of you. Trust me to get you out of this somehow. I promised to protect you and can't give up until I know you are safe. Not just for you, but for Rebecca too. It's something I have to do."

Tess crumpled against Justin's wide, warm chest and wept for all that she would lose when she left him.

"If we have to, we'll go back to San Antonio and face Randall. We'll hire a lawyer, go to the police, and have the law on our side. We can't let him get away with this. We won't give him any choice in the matter. We'll tell the cops everything we know. We can do this, Tess. Don't give up on me."

His pep talk only cut her deeper. His idealism was one of the things she loved most about him, and she wouldn't taint his optimism with denials. Soon enough, he'd understand their futures were on separate roads.

He held her for precious minutes, until the sound of another car's motor brought their attention back to the country road.

Tess peeked out the window and gasped. "Oh no! It's a cop!"

Clambering off Justin's lap, she snatched for her shorts while Justin struggled to zip his jeans. She pulled Justin's T-shirt over her head, finding it before she found her own, and tugged her bra into place as the policeman tapped on the driver's window.

"You folks all right? Is there a problem with the car?" The officer cast a curious glance at Tess. Her heart thundered in her chest.

"No, sir," Justin said. "No problem. Just taking a short break from driving."

"Well, you can't park here. You need to move the car."

Justin bobbed his head. "Yes, sir. Thanks."

As Justin rolled the window up, Tess watched the officer walk away. "Do you think he knew we were—"

"Oh, hell, yeah. Look at us! Half dressed, hair rumpled. He knew." Justin raked his fingers through his hair as he chuckled. "He knew."

Her cheeks heated. "How embarrassing."

Brushing her cheek with the back of his hand, he cranked the engine. "Can I have my shirt back?"

With a glance to make sure the policeman wasn't watching, she gave him his shirt. "Ready for me to drive?"

"Sure." He climbed out and circled the vehicle while she struggled over the gearshift to slide behind the wheel. She headed out to the highway, knowing all too well that in a few hundred miles she would have to leave the man she couldn't let herself love.

"I'm ready for another pit stop to stretch my legs," Tess told Justin, who'd been scribbling in a small notebook for the last two hours or so. "I'm gonna take the next exit."

"Hm? Oh, okay." He flipped the notebook closed and twisted around to stick it in his backpack.

"What were you doing?" she asked.

"Working on a song. For you."

He smiled, and her insides melted. She stopped at a small gas station at the edge of a town south of Memphis. Except for a rusted-out Dodge Dart, parked near the door to the building, theirs was the only vehicle in sight.

"Are they open?" She craned her neck to look for people inside.

"I think so. I'll pump." Justin hopped out and circled the Jimmy to fill the tank while Tess fished on the floor for her purse.

She climbed out and stretched her back. "I'll go pay. Want anything to drink?"

"A Coke sounds good. Thanks." As she started across the pavement, Justin called to her, "And some M&M's."

She waved to say she'd heard him and smiled to herself over Justin's penchant for sweets. Inside the gas station, she stopped at the glass doors of the refrigerated display and took out two cans of Coke. As she wandered back up the candy aisle to get Justin's M&M's, she passed a man wearing ripped, oil-stained jeans and dark sunglasses. At the checkout, she deposited her purchases on the counter.

A moment later, the man in dirty jeans brought his selections up front to pay. A second man, with a scruffy beard and a black, sleeveless denim jacket, joined the first man. Tess shivered when the bearded man gave her a leer.

"Will that be all?" the woman at the checkout asked.

"Yes," Tess answered quickly, eager to get away from the bearded man's gaze. "Uh, I mean, no. I'm paying for the gas too. For the Jimmy." She pointed out at the car with a nervous flick of her hand and saw the bearded man move up close behind her. His hand bumped her buttocks and lingered there. Recoiling from his touch with a jerk, Tess

149

tipped over her purse, spilling her bundled stacks of cash on the counter.

"Oh, my God!" the checkout woman cried. "Is that money real? That must be thousands! What'd you do? Rob a bank?"

Tess glanced over her shoulder at the men as she scooped the money back into her purse as fast as she could, her heart hammering. "No. Nothing like that."

Her money had the bearded man's attention, along with his buddy's. Pulling out a bill at random, she thrust it at the clerk. "Keep the change."

With that, she ran out of the shop and hurried back to the truck, where Justin waited for her in the passenger seat. She opened his door and dropped the Cokes and candy in his lap before tossing her purse on the floor as if it were something vile.

Justin caught her hand. "Are you all right, Tess? You're white as a sheet."

"I will be. Some creepy guy in there was ogling me, and then I spilled my purse, and—"

"Have you seen the guy before?" he interrupted, his expression alarmed. "Did he say anything to you?"

"No. But he saw my money. They all did."

Justin wrinkled his brow. "So?"

She sighed. "Look in my purse."

He did, and his face blanched. "Holy shit, Tess! How much is this? Where did you get it?"

"It's my money. Mine and Randall's from our bank account. I didn't want to use a credit card that he could trace."

"You've been carrying all this money around the whole time?"

"Yes."

"Dear God, Tess." Expelling a long, slow breath through

pursed lips, Justin rubbed his temple. He stared at her, his face unreadable, and Tess fretted over his reaction.

What difference did it make? The money was rightfully hers.

"I still have to use the restroom," she said. "Will you watch things at the car till I get back?"

Justin gave her a short, not altogether humored laugh. "Damn straight I will."

He turned to push the purse under the backseat. She spun away and hurried to the restroom at the side of the building. She puzzled over Justin's reaction while she used the bathroom and washed her hands. Was he mad at her or just shocked at the sum she was carrying?

She squared her shoulders then studied her reflection in the cracked mirror over the sink. She looked like hell. Combing her hair back from her face with her fingers did little to help. But what did it really matter? With a sigh, she pulled open the bathroom door and started back toward the truck.

Halfway across the parking lot, she stopped short. Her chest tightened, and she swung around, scanning the parking lot once. Twice.

"No," she whispered. "No!"

Justin and the Jimmy were gone.

Chapter Twelve

Justin struggled to draw a breath. A beefy arm clamped his neck, cutting off his airflow. The goon who'd jumped into the truck behind him aimed a blade at Justin's jugular vein. As if to demonstrate his readiness to use the knife, the goon pricked Justin's neck with the sharp tip. The warm trickle on his skin told Justin the knife had drawn blood.

"Just do what we say, and you'll live to see tomorrow," his captor growled.

Without moving his head, Justin cut his gaze to the bearded man who'd slid into the driver's seat and cranked the car before Justin could finish rasping, "What the hell do you think you're doing?"

Before Justin could assimilate what was happening, the bearded man had sent the Jimmy screeching out of the parking lot.

Breathing became Justin's first priority. He tried to turn his head slowly to the side to lessen the pressure of the ape's arm on his windpipe. He filled his burning lungs and focused on his second priority, figuring out how to escape.

Cautiously, he eyed the keys that jangled from the ignition. Why had Tess left the keys?

Simple. Because he was staying with the car. Why not leave them? *Sonofabitch! He'd screwed up again.*

The man driving looked over at him with a leering grin. "That hot little brunette your wife?"

Justin glared back.

"Too bad we couldn'ta waited on her. I wouldn'ta minded having a piece of her." The bearded man smirked and licked his lips. Justin would have traded his soul for one good shot at the bastard.

The bearded driver chortled as he cast sidelong glances at Justin. Finally, the driver took his gaze off the road a second too long. A truck pulled out in front of the Jimmy. As the bearded man swerved hard to avoid a collision, he let a string of obscenities fly. The Jimmy careened left then hard to the right, and the goon in the backseat lost his balance. The arm around Justin's neck fell away, and Justin grabbed for the keys.

"Not a chance, asshole!" The driver knocked Justin's hand away as his partner lunged over the front seat and grabbed Justin by the shirt.

Justin had never been much of a fighter. He'd gotten by on wits and his low-key attitude. But he let it fly with both barrels now. He sent an elbow crashing hard into the driver's ribs. When the backseat goon grabbed a fistful of his hair, Justin dove toward the backseat. He swung his fist at the ape's face. He landed one good shot before the man's knife struck Justin's gut with a force that knocked the wind from his lungs.

"Pull over!" the man with the knife shouted. "Time to dump some dead weight."

His assailant opened the passenger-side door and shoved Justin out of the car before it even stopped. Excruciating pain ripped through Justin's stomach and chest as he hit the pavement and rolled into the tall grass at the side of the desolate road. He clutched the bleeding wound and raised his head in time to see the Jimmy race down the country road and out of sight.

Stranded and bleeding, he thought of Tess. Thanks to his screwup, she was alone. If he'd been paying more attention . . .

Guilt and self-censure riddled him with a pain greater than the gash in his side.

Tess was vulnerable. Penniless. A sitting duck for Randall's henchmen.

He had to find a way to get back to her.

Tess's knees buckled, and she slumped to the pavement. Justin had abandoned her.

He'd stolen her car, her money, all her possessions and left her stranded in the middle of nowhere. He'd seen her stash of cash, and greed had gotten the best of him.

Unless he'd been conning her all along.

She'd heard of con men who preyed on women by seducing them then stealing their money. Why hadn't she seen through Justin's act? Of course, she hadn't seen through Randall until it was too late. Why should she think she'd be any smarter with Justin?

Bitter pain assailed her heart, but she choked down her grief and assessed her situation. She couldn't panic, couldn't afford to wallow in self-pity. She had to think.

Justin had all her money, her only transportation, all of her clothes. Damn him! She had to figure out how to get enough money to survive until—when? She'd have to get some kind of job.

She rubbed her temple. Suddenly she had a ferocious headache. Whom could she call? Who wouldn't betray her to Randall? Only one person came to mind. The secretary in the marketing department where she'd worked for Randall was the closet thing she had to a friend. Randall had seen to it that her social relationships never developed. Although she didn't know Nancy Hindridge well, the woman might be her only hope.

Tess knew her office phone number from memory but didn't have money to place the call. Did a collect call cost anything? Tess didn't know. She'd never had a reason to know. But she was about to find out.

Justin tried to stand, but moving caused blood to gush from his wound faster. He grew increasingly light-headed. If he didn't get help soon, he could die, and then what would happen to Tess?

The rumble of a car engine filtered through the buzzing in his ears, and he struggled to his knees to flag down the passing vehicle.

A man in a sport coat jumped from his car and hurried over. "What happened to you, man? You're bleeding."

"My truck was stolen," Justin gasped. The effort it took to speak surprised him. "I've been stabbed. Tess—"

"Hang on, man. I'll call 9-1-1. Lie down!"

Justin must have passed out then, because the next thing he was aware of were mumbling voices and jostling as two men loaded him in the back of an ambulance. He searched the faces leaning over him. Tried to talk. Tess. Someone had to help Tess.

His eyes drooped heavily. He struggled to stay conscious. Maybe if he closed his eyes for just a second . . .

Then he saw a beautiful face, a face he loved, above him. She was there. Like a dream but more real. He whispered her name, reached for her.

"Easy, buddy. Lie still," one EMT said.

He whispered her name, tried to call her back so she wouldn't leave him.

"What'd he say?" the EMT asked his partner.

As Justin closed his eyes, succumbing to the numbing blackness, he heard the second EMT answer, "It sounded like he said 'Rebecca.'"

The tape machine began rolling when the secretary picked up the incoming call. "Sinclair Industries. Marketing."

"I have a collect call from Tess. Will you accept the charges?" an operator said.

The man in a basement room sat up in his chair and stubbed out his cigarette. "Get Morelli! We got her! She's on the secretary's line!" He held the headphone tighter to his ear and listened.

"Nancy?"

"Tess? My God, what happened to you? Word around the office is that you were kidnapped!"

"I can't explain right now. I need your help though."

"What? Tess, does Mr. Sinclair know you're okay?"

"No! You can't tell Randall anything about this call or what I'm about to ask you to do. Do you understand that? Please, Nancy, it's crucial!"

"Tess, you're scaring me! What's wrong?"

"I'm in a little town outside Memphis. At a gas station. In a minute I'll give you an address. I need you to wire me some money . . . as much as you can afford. I swear I'll pay it back with interest as soon as possible. I have no money, no car, no place to stay. I'm desperate, Nancy, or I wouldn't ask."

"Why can't you call Randall?"

"I just can't. Swear to me you won't tell him or anyone else where I am."

"Tess, I want to help you, but I don't have much money. The best I could do is maybe two hundred dollars."

"Nancy, you're a godsend! Thank you!"

"Where should I wire the money?"

"Have you got a pen?"

The man listening on the headset wrote down the address, too—just in case there was a problem with the tape.

"Got it?" Tess asked Nancy.

"Got it," she replied.

"Got it," the man said, grinning smugly. "Wait till Sinclair hears this."

Chapter Thirteen

Tess waited at the gas station for almost two hours, hoping that Justin might change his mind and come back for her. Then, giving up that ludicrous hope, she walked down the street to the bank where the young woman at the gas station said she could receive a wire. When the money Nancy promised to send came, she walked another block to a cheap motel to get a room.

She spent the first hour in the room crying, then she went out for a newspaper so she could begin searching the want ads for a job. Later in the evening, having used what was left in the only box of facial tissues she found, she called the front desk of the motel to ask for more. While she waited for the tissues to be delivered to her room, she showered, cried some more, put her dirty clothes back on, then flopped on the bed. When the knock finally came on her door, she dragged herself off the bed and pulled the door open. And her heart leaped to her throat.

"Maria?" Tony Morelli called into the dark room at the address he was given to find his wife.

"Tony?" a weak voice answered.

"Maria, is that you? Where's the freaking light switch?" Tony groped in front of him as he fumbled for the light switch and kicked a chair in the process. When he finally found the control, he flooded the room with light and turned to find his wife.

"Holy mother of God! Maria!"

He stared with dismay at his wife's naked and battered body. Her wrists had been handcuffed over her head to an old bed frame.

"Tony," she whimpered. "Why'd they do this to me? What did I do?"

A white-hot Italian rage flared in Morelli's gut. Damn that bastard Sinclair to everlasting hell! How dare he do this to his wife? Especially after he'd busted his ass finding Sinclair's unfaithful bitch of a wife.

Rushing to Maria, Morelli searched for a way to free her hands from the cuffs.

"Ah, *cara mia*," he crooned softly, his hands trembling as he stroked her cheeks. The pain in Maria's dark eyes cut him to the quick.

Sinclair had found Tony's weak point, the only thing in life that mattered to him. But Sinclair would pay. Tony would find Sinclair's vulnerable spot and exact his revenge, if it was the last thing he did on God's earth.

Randall Sinclair would pay for hurting his Maria.

"Hello, Tess. Have you enjoyed your little adventure?" Randall asked with a deceptively serene façade.

"Randall." Tess's legs became rubbery, and her lungs felt as if they'd collapsed. Terror in its purest form raced through her blood and closed icy fingers around her heart.

He stepped into the room, brushing her aside, and for a fleeting moment she entertained the notion of running out the door and screaming for help. But she doubted that would do any good.

As she closed the door, her legs seemed rooted to the spot.

Randall wouldn't kill her here. He might have been seen

entering the room. He'd wait until one of his men could do the job and make it look like an accident. Or suicide.

When she finally turned to face Randall, a stinging blow found her cheek. Pain skittered from the point of impact through her head, and she crumpled to the floor.

"Get up, Tess. We're going home." Randall tugged on the cuff of his tailor-made dress shirt, straightening the sleeve. "My plane is waiting at the airport. Get your things together quickly."

"Randall, I can explain. I just needed some time to think and to get my head straight. I was upset when you told me about Angie and I—"

"There will be time for explanations later." He reached out and stroked her cheek, though the gesture and his expression lacked any affection. "I do hope you have answers concerning your behavior."

His voice sounded calm, forgiving, but Tess wasn't fooled for a minute. His composure frightened her more than his anger. She knew his rage boiled just beneath the surface.

"Right now, the important thing is that I've found you. We need to get back to the plane." He consulted his gold Rolex watch. "I'm a busy man, Tess. This side trip to pick you up has cost me a great deal of valuable time. I hope you appreciate the significance of that."

She met Randall's gaze. Would it do any good to beg for mercy? Did she want mercy? At this point, she was ready to die. She didn't want to go back to the existence she'd known with Randall. She couldn't stand the idea of facing life without Justin, knowing how he'd betrayed her. Life held nothing for her.

"I'm sorry, Randall. Truly I am."

"Trust me, Tess. You *will* be sorry."

The fire in Randall's eyes made her tremble.

An hour and a half later, she sat in a cushioned chair that, despite being designed for comfort, might as well have been made of jagged rock. To Tess, it felt more like an electric chair. Randall had hired a private jet to come after her, an expense he'd no doubt add to the list of grievances he held against her. For the first several minutes of the flight back to San Antonio, he'd glared at her silently, making her wonder how he'd make her suffer.

Then he shot out of his seat to tower over her, and the grilling began. She understood that the severity of her punishment hinged on the answers she gave.

She carefully avoided any mention of Justin. She answered Randall's questions about trading the BMW for the Jimmy, bribing the salesman to forge Randall's signature to complete the trade, using the cash from the bank withdrawal to pay for food, gas and motels. He asked how far she'd driven each day, what she'd eaten, how often she'd stopped, how fast she'd driven, and on and on. Randall worded his relentless questions in tricky ways, clearly trying to trip her up, to catch her in a lie, which Tess knew was the worst offense she could commit at this point.

"How much money had you spent of the twenty-four thousand by yesterday afternoon?"

"About four to five hundred, maybe. I'm not sure exactly."

"And what happened to the rest?" Randall braced his arms on Tess's chair and leaned over her, fixing her with a pointed gaze.

"Like I said, it was stolen."

"Be specific. How was it stolen?"

She drew a deep breath, and pain sliced her heart at the memory of Justin's abandonment, his theft. "I left the money in the car while I went to use the restroom at a gas station. That's when the car was stolen."

"How'd the thief get the car key? Or did they hotwire it?"

Clearing her throat, she whispered, "The key was inside."

Randall's face reddened, and his eyes burned with rage. "How stupid are you?" His tone held a deadly calm. "Are you telling me that you left more than twenty-three thousand dollars and the keys in a brand-new Jimmy while you took a piss?"

She searched for an answer to placate him.

"Are you?" he screamed in her face, slamming his hands down on the arms of the cushioned chair.

Tess jumped. "No!"

"No? Then there was someone with the car and the money?"

A sick, sinking feeling washed over Tess as she realized her slip. Randall must have read terror or panic in her eyes, because he moved in for the kill.

"You weren't alone. Were you, slut?"

She knew the trap she faced. If she lied, Randall would see her deception in her expression. She'd always been a terrible liar. She was almost certain he had ways to find out the truth, to verify what she said.

"Who was with you, Tess? A lover?"

"A friend."

"A friend?" Randall smiled with a sickening sweetness, then his face became hard again. "You don't have any friends, Tess. Who was with you?"

"Someone I met. I was just giving h-her a ride." Tess's voice caught as she made the decision at the last second to try to pacify Randall's suspicions. Randall honed in on the pronoun.

"Her?"

Tess nodded.

"What was her name?"

Tess swallowed hard. *Please, God, help me.*

"Rebecca." The name came like an answer to a prayer.

"Rebecca what?"

"Rebecca Boyd. She was on her way to Nashville and needed a ride."

"I see. And where did you meet Rebecca Boyd?"

"I picked her up along the interstate one day, when it was raining."

"Where?"

"Just outside of Waco."

"Where was she from?"

"Wellerton, Texas." By giving Randall a facsimile of the truth, she hoped her face would give nothing away. He seemed to believe her. The speed and confidence of her replies impressed him, she could tell.

"How old was she?"

"I didn't ask. I'd guess she was about my age."

"What did she look like?"

She wanted to ask why it mattered, but she knew why. He would verify everything she told him. Tess's heart thudded. If he checked on Rebecca, he'd discover the woman was dead. But she'd come too far with the lie to turn back now. She prayed now that Rebecca and Justin had shared a family resemblance.

"Black wavy hair, blue eyes, tall, slim."

"Pretty?"

Tess nodded. "I guess."

He stared at her for a minute. "This woman, this Rebecca Boyd, stole the car and money, didn't she?"

Tess shivered, and unbidden tears filled her eyes. "I don't know. Probably."

Randall's lips compressed to a thin, stern line. "Still believe she was your friend, Tess?"

His remark hit its target. Tears spilled from Tess's eyes. "No."

"Mr. Sinclair, we've been cleared to land in San Antonio," the pilot announced over the intercom.

With one last dark glare, Randall returned to his seat.

Tess turned to stare out at the twinkling lights of the city below them, the city she'd fled four days before. In four days, she'd lived a lifetime. In the past few hours, she'd aged fifty years. And she knew the worst was still to come.

Chapter Fourteen

Returning to her house should have felt like a homecoming, but Tess could muster no such sentimentality for the walls and roof she shared with Randall. She numbed her mind to any thoughts of sorrow or loss. Remembering Justin and the laughter they'd shared promised to shatter the last of her composure. Dwelling on how close she'd come to winning her freedom from Randall served no purpose. She swore to herself she wouldn't let him see her fear and defeat, but her body sagged like a punctured balloon and her spirit drained from her. He escorted her upstairs, and she waited with trepidation for what she knew would come.

She didn't have to wait long. Though he remained eerily serene, his placid demeanor caused an apprehensive prickle on her neck. She didn't trust his outward calm. The tight muscles in his arms and face showed the tension he barely held in check. They'd no more stepped into their bedroom than he grabbed her arm and turned her toward him.

"There. Now you are back where you belong. My bedroom." His hand squeezed her arm, and he tugged her closer. "You're my wife, Tess. Did you really think I wouldn't come after you? That I wouldn't find you?" He ran a hand down the side of her face, and when she met his gaze, his dark eyes smoldered with anger, lust, and a righteous sense of power.

A tremor rippled through her.

"I've given you everything money can buy," he said. "What more do you want?"

His tone had a hard edge, yet she also detected a grief, a genuine puzzlement that shocked and disturbed her. She raised her chin a notch.

"Nothing," she replied with a boldness that surprised her. "I want nothing from you."

His gaze narrowed. She saw a combination of ire and rejection swirl behind the dark irises that glared at her. The malevolence she had expected, but the hint of pain knocked her off balance. For Randall to be hurt by her words and her actions would mean that he actually cared about her on some level. The prospect staggered her mind.

"Tess, I don't want to punish you, but you don't seem to understand the gravity of what you've done. You've made a mockery of me and our marriage. You've wounded me with your disloyalty."

"I'm not your wife," she countered.

He captured her head at the base of her skull, and his fingers dug into her scalp.

Tess gasped in pain.

"You are in every way that counts! You leave me no choice but to put you back in your place. Perhaps you need a refresher course on how a woman serves her husband?"

The bite of his grip brought tears to her eyes. She shook her head. "No, Randall."

He released her so suddenly she fell back a step and bumped the edge of the bed. Randall unbuckled his belt, and her stomach tightened in fear. Again, Tess shook her head, panic building a dizzying maelstrom in her head.

Randall slapped her cheek, and her head snapped around from the force of the blow. The next lash came from his belt, landing across her arms and chest. Tess bit her lip to muffle her cries. Another lash followed, and another, as she balled herself up on the bed to protect her head and face.

Each stinging lick tore away another piece of the freedom and happiness she'd known far too briefly. The short period of joy and hope she'd shared with Justin had been a gift. Now it was over.

When Randall tossed the belt away, he pried her hands away from her body and ripped her clothes. Her eyes flew open, knowing he intended to have sex with her. She couldn't allow it. She wanted nothing to mar the memory of Justin's gentle hands, warm kiss, and whispered *You belong with me now.*

Clamping her knees together with every fiber of her strength, she raised tearful eyes to Randall's stern face. "No, Randall. I can't."

He grabbed her wrists and pinned them over her head, his lip curling in a snarl. "What do you mean, no? You're mine. I'll have you whenever and however I see fit. Open your legs, woman."

Choking on a sob, she shook her head. "Please, Randall. Please don't."

His face grew even darker, and he freed one hand to pry at her knees.

Kicking her feet and struggling against his grasp, she did the unthinkable. She fought him.

With a single-mindedness she'd have never believed she possessed, she battled. She struggled to save the body she'd given Justin, the body he'd cherished. She flailed and kicked. Her foot connected with Randall's hard body time and again. Finally, with a loud curse, he released her hands, and she glanced up to see him double over, clutching his groin.

His face contorted in pain, but he glared at her. "Stupid bitch! You'll pay for this!"

167

During his momentary incapacitation, she scrambled off the bed. Fleeing to the bathroom, she closed the door and sagged against it. Randall had designed the house so that interior doors could not be bolted from the inside, preventing her from locking him out of any room. She'd have a difficult time keeping him out if he came after her.

She listened to him grumble invectives. He finally left the room, shouting a harsh promise that he'd return and she'd suffer for her rebellion. Releasing the breath she held, she sank to the floor.

Her body ached, but her mind seemed numb. She refused to consider the implications of what she'd done. Drawing herself a cold bath, she hoped the cool water would ease the stings left by Randall's belt.

She stepped into the bathtub. For several long minutes, she merely stared at the ceiling. The water soaked the welts on her skin, while the will to live seeped from her like a slowly bleeding wound.

Drying off and dressing in a nightgown seemed too great a hassle, yet somehow Tess managed.

In front of her mirror, she dragged a brush through her damp hair, gazing bleakly at the hollow expression of the woman who stared back at her. She dreaded facing Randall again. How could she do it? What choice did she have?

But the choice was taken from her. The bathroom door had been locked from the outside. She was trapped, Randall's prisoner. A new sense of defeat left her muscles weak.

Tess slid limply to the cold tile floor.

Sleeping on the hard floor of her bathroom left Tess's muscles sore and tight. Added to the welts from Randall's belt, the bruises from his slaps, and the scars Justin left on her heart, Tess felt like hell.

But the worst part of the morning was the waiting. Randall would be back. Heaven only knew what other punishment he had in mind for her. The fact that he hadn't yet killed her didn't comfort her. She felt sure it only meant he hadn't yet decided how to dispose of her.

As the morning dragged out and passed into afternoon then evening, Randall still hadn't come. She began believing he meant to starve her to death. That would serve his purpose in a slow, agonizing fashion that he could blame on her refusal to eat.

At the end of her second day of imprisonment, with only water from the tap to sustain her, she grew more certain this was his intention.

Late on the morning of her third day, however, the doorknob rattled. She weakly lifted her head as Randall came into the tiny bathroom and leaned on the edge of the sink. In his hand, he held some type of book.

"Well, Tess. You surprise me. You're either an extremely good liar, or you've told the truth. We're about to see which is true." He grabbed her upper arm and yanked her to her feet. "Follow me."

Though her legs threatened to collapse, she trailed him down the stairs and through the living room, until he stopped to open the door of his private office. Her heart skipped a beat. Never before had she entered his office, by his decree. That he took her inside now terrified her.

Randall circled his large mahogany desk while her gaze swept a room filled with leather-bound books and antique vases, bought, she presumed, for their value, rather than an appreciation of art. On his desk, Randall's computer screen glowed with a blue screen and a blinking cursor.

Opening his desk drawer, Randall withdrew a handgun and set it in full view, a none-too-subtle threat. Her stomach rebelled, knotting in fear, though her mind said a bullet in the head would be a quick and painless way to end her suffering.

Next, Randall slapped the book he'd carried on the desk and extracted a stack of color photos. "I have here a yearbook for Wellerton High School. Rebecca Boyd did in fact live in Wellerton and attend the high school at a time that would make her your age."

He paused and arched an eyebrow in a manner that suggested his surprise that Tess had been correct. Then his gaze narrowed. "I'm going to show you the pictures of ten girls. If you can point out Rebecca to me, I'll believe your story. Although, I might remind you, believing doesn't mean forgiving."

Her chest tightened as Randall handed her blown-up images of ten girls of high school age. Apparently, he hadn't learned of Rebecca's death in his search. Or had he?

She glanced at the photos. All of the girls had black wavy hair and blue eyes. All were attractive. Tess concentrated. If she didn't recognize Rebecca immediately, Randall would never buy that they'd spent several days driving together.

She flipped one page then another and another. The fifth page stopped her.

Thank you, God.

Rebecca, for it could only be Rebecca, had the same devil-may-care grin as Justin. Her eyes, her nose, and the unruly waves of her raven hair were the spitting image of her brother. The face, so similar to Justin's, caused a flutter in her chest.

"This is Rebecca." Her voice remained calm and even held a haughty note of vindication.

Randall arched a dark eyebrow. "Bravo, darling."

Taking the pictures from her, he pushed away from the desk and rose from his chair. "You've earned your freedom from the bathroom. But I've had an upgrade to our security system installed that you may find interesting. No door or window in the house may be opened without instantly alerting me." He showed her a small device that resembled a pager on his belt. "And Henry."

"Henry?"

"Your new bodyguard. He'll be staying with you when I'm at the office."

Her body wilted as dejection settled in her bones. Randall crossed his arms over his chest while giving her a grin of satisfaction. "If you try to leave the house for any reason at all, a silent alarm will be triggered, and Henry and I will be alerted. You would be retrieved before you make it past the edge of the lawn."

In other words, he intended to hold her prisoner in her own house.

"What will you tell your friends and business associates?"

"They'll be none the wiser. You'll still perform all your duties as my wife, including entertaining, so no one has any reason to doubt that you're not still as faithful and loyal to me as ever. Only you and I will know what a deceitful bitch you really are."

Randall dragged a contemptuous gaze over her as if to punctuate the insult. Suddenly his face hardened, and his posture stiffened. "Where is your ring?"

She raised her naked hand to stare down at it, even though she knew it was bare. The ring, like everything else she'd had with her, had been in the Jimmy, in her suitcase, still in the pocket of her shorts from the day she'd stuck it there.

"It was in my suitcase when the car was stolen," she explained meekly.

Randall muttered a scorching curse. "If you don't have any more appreciation for the things I provide than that, perhaps you should do without."

Though too tired, hungry and numb to fully appreciate the subtle threat, when his gaze locked on her with a dark fury, fear raced through her.

He aimed a long aristocratic finger at her. "You've disappointed me for the last time, Tess. I won't tolerate any more of your treachery."

With that final warning, Randall returned the gun to the drawer of his desk and stormed out of the office, dragging her along by the arm. Once outside, he relocked the door and left her standing alone in the silent echoes of his wrath.

Her knees shook with fatigue, but she made her way to the kitchen. She fixed a sandwich and glass of fruit juice, which, despite her days without food, she still found difficult to choke down. Then, returning to her bedroom, she climbed onto the bed.

As they had so many times in the past three days, her thoughts turned to Justin. Where was he? Had he made it to Nashville yet? Was he really going to Nashville or was that part of his con? And why, after the way he'd betrayed her, couldn't she put him out of her heart and mind?

If she'd had the strength, if she'd had any tears left, she would have cried for the chance at love she'd lost. But she'd spent all her tears. She had nothing left inside but an emptiness so profound she doubted even time could heal her. She had nothing left. Not even hope.

In a Memphis hospital, the patient known as John Doe opened his eyes.

The nurse on duty leaned over him and smiled. "Well, hello, handsome. Welcome back. You gave us a real scare." She planted a hand on her plump hip and cocked her head. "Do you know your name?"

Chapter Fifteen

The blurry image of a middle-aged woman in pink surgical scrubs sharpened then dimmed again before coming into focus.

His head hurt. No, his head *throbbed*. But that was nothing compared to the pain in his side. Justin moved his hand to touch the painful place, an action that required most of his strength, and found a row of prickly stitches. He tried to clear his mind, tried to recall the events that had put him in the hospital.

He remembered a woman, a bearded man, a vise-like arm on his neck.

And he remembered Rebecca. He'd seen her. He was sure he had. But how?

"You lost a lot of blood, handsome, that's why you feel so weak. You've also been unconscious for a few days. In fact, you almost died. You're a real fighter, you know that?"

"Where am I?" His voice rasped from his dry throat.

The nurse in pink wrapped a blood pressure cuff around his upper arm and pumped the bulb in her hand as she answered. "Methodist Hospital. Do you know your name?"

"Justin Boyd."

"How old are you?"

"Twenty-eight."

"Who's the King of Rock and Roll?"

"Mick Jagger . . . and the Stones."

"Blasphemy! You're in Memphis, son."

He gave her a weak smile and closed his eyes in fatigue. "Ah, you're . . . looking for . . . ole Elvis."

"You're darn tootin', I am."

Justin tried to sit up, and the idea proved a bad one. Lightning bolts of pain shot from the stitched wound just under his ribs.

"Hold on, Justin. Where do you think you're going?" The nurse put a hand on his shoulder to ease him back.

He had the nagging feeling he had something urgent to do, something important he should tell the nurse. He furrowed his brow, trying to ignore the pain so he could concentrate.

"Well, Justin Boyd," the nurse continued, helping him adjust the bed to a better angle with a button on the railing. "Do you have any family we should contact about your condition? You had no identification on you when you arrived." The woman propped her hands on her hips. "And what exactly did happen to you, anyway? How'd you get that puncture wound in your belly? A knife? It cost you twenty-three stitches by the way. The gash wasn't as deep as you might have thought from the amount of bleeding. The blood came from an artery, a rather large, important artery, that got severed. That's been fixed up, too, but you won't be rock climbing anytime soon."

Squinting as he listened, he assimilated what the loquacious nurse told him while she was peeking under his covers to check his wound. When she paused and looked up at him, her expectant expression said she wanted a response. What had she asked him? About family?

"Uh, my parents are in Texas. So's my brother."

"No wife? Girlfriend?" the nurse prodded.

A woman's face flickered through his mind—a beautiful face that stirred an aching in his heart. Memories flooded back to him—memories of music and laughter and . . . car horns?

Icy fingers of fear clutched his heart. "Tess."

"Tess? She a wife or—"

"Oh, my God! Tess!" He bolted to a sitting position, unmindful of the searing pain in his gut. "I have to find Tess!"

"Whoa, mister!" Again the nurse caught his shoulder and pushed him back. "You're recovering from a nasty brush with death. Your body needs time to heal and strengthen and—"

"But she's out there alone! She has no money or car or—"

"Okay, calm down. We'll do something to look for her, but first you have to lie back and take a deep breath." The nurse, whom Justin estimated to be in her late forties, leveled an uncompromising stare on him. "Now, slow down and start at the beginning. Who is Tess, and why is she in trouble?"

Drawing a slow breath, he rubbed his face. His chin sported a short beard. "Tess is . . . my girlfriend. We were driving together and stopped for gas. Her car was stolen, a carjacking. I was held at knife point, and Tess was left stranded, without her purse or anywhere to go . . ."

He dragged a hand through his hair as more pieces of information flooded back to him. "She was on the run from her abusive husband. Except he wasn't . . . I mean, he wasn't her husband."

"The plot thickens." Cocking her head, the nurse widened her eyes.

"So, I was stabbed and left to die, and Tess is God knows where and in real danger of being found by the lunatic who already killed her sister."

When the woman's expression turned skeptical, Justin sighed.

"Are you sure you didn't hit your head?" she asked.

"I know how it sounds, but I swear it's true. Please, you've got to help me find Tess. She doesn't know where I am and what happened to me and . . . oh, hell."

Justin closed his eyes and groaned. He'd blown it again. He'd let his guard down, let those goons sneak up on him, and now Tess was alone or, even worse, with Randall Sinclair. He'd failed to keep her safe like he'd promised. She'd counted on him, and he'd let her down.

Just like he'd failed Rebecca.

Remorse and disgust wrenched inside him. If anything happened to Tess—

"Okay, handsome, let me get a pad of paper. I'll write down all the information and see what I can find out for you."

As the nurse headed out of his room, Justin called, "Wait a minute. What's your name?"

"Kathy. But you can call me anything you want." She gave him a flirtatious wink as she left.

Justin stared at the empty doorway, too concerned for Tess to see the humor in Kathy's outrageous flirting.

When she returned, she held her pen and pad poised, ready to write. "Okay. First, who in your family do you want me to call about your condition?"

Twisting his lips, he considered his options. When he thought of the less-than-harmonious state of his relationship with his parents, he hated the idea of calling them. But if he had Kathy call Brian, he knew his parents would know about his situation within the hour anyway.

"Do you have to call anyone?" he asked.

"You don't want to call your family?"

"I don't want them worrying. If you call, they'll fly up here to be with me. They can't afford the plane ticket or the stress. My mom's got a bad heart. Dad's got a business to run. And Brian, well, he could afford the ticket, but he's so busy with court, and—" Justin glanced up at Kathy as he realized he'd been thinking out loud. "I'm gonna live, right?"

"Better believe it. With a few days of rest and time for that gash to heal, you'll be good as new."

That settled it.

"Then don't call my family. When I'm better, I'll call them myself and tell them I'm okay. I want to concentrate on finding Tess, making sure she's all right." His head hurt worse, considering all that could have happened to Tess.

"When did you last see Tess? Where did you stop for gas?" Kathy sat down on the corner of the bed and balanced a clipboard on her lap.

"Just off the interstate outside of town. It was a small, independent kind of place. Not a national brand. Larry's Stop and Save, I think."

"And what does Tess look like? What was she wearing?"

"She's beautiful." His heart ached, seeing her face in his mind. He gave Tess's description, and Kathy wrote down everything he said.

"What's her last name?"

"Carpenter." Then, as Kathy started to write, he added, "Or Sinclair. Carpenter was her maiden name, and the one she's been using. Sinclair is her married name . . . sort of."

Although she wasn't legally married, Tess had used Randall's last name at least part of the time.

"Mm-hm." Kathy kept writing.

Dwelling on such small details, explaining the situation in all its sordid intricacies chafed Justin's raw nerves, wore on his short supply of patience. He needed to be *doing* something, looking for Tess, calling the police, going back to the gas station, talking to people . . . *something* besides lying on his ass in this hospital while Randall . . .

A sickening thought presented itself. Nausea gripped him

at the notion, but he had to cover every possibility. "She was from San Antonio. The man she lived with, the one who claimed to be her husband, is Randall Sinclair. Could you call information and get her home phone number? I've got to know if he found her, if she's back with him."

"Will do, sweet cakes. First, I've got to get some insurance information from you. Who's going to pay your bill, darlin'?"

Moaning, he sank back in his pillows. Things just got worse and worse.

Randall Sinclair's home phone number was unlisted, so Kathy called the number for Sinclair Industries that the phone company operator suggested she try. With an Oscar-worthy performance, Kathy managed to convince the switchboard operator that she was a relative of Randall's and there'd been a family emergency. A little more coaxing convinced the operator to give Kathy the Sinclairs' home number. Kathy dialed the residence, gloating over her success. On the third ring, a woman answered.

"Hello. May I speak to Tess Sinclair, please?"

"This is she." The voice was weak, hesitant, and sounded frightened.

The woman's soft gasp was followed by a loud, growling man's voice. "Who is this?"

"I'm calling to arrange a free makeover for Mrs. Sinclair, courtesy of the cosmetics counter at—"

"She's not interested," the man barked and hung up.

Kathy stared at the phone for a few seconds before she hung up. *Poor woman.* Pursing her lips, she headed for Justin's room to tell him the bad news.

Randall glared at Tess suspiciously. "Who was that?"

"I don't know. I didn't get a chance to ask."

"Stay off the phone," he growled. "Or better yet." He jerked hard on the phone cord and ripped it from the wall. "I want dinner ready no later than six."

He left Tess standing in the kitchen. She felt her world shrinking, her life collapsing. Moving like an automaton, she took a package of frozen steaks out of the freezer.

While she peeled potatoes, a thought jumped into her mind from nowhere. She and Justin hadn't used any form of protection during sex. Randall had had a vasectomy years ago, making birth control an unnecessary consideration. A dread so ominous it threatened to choke her clutched Tess.

The vegetable peeler in her hand clattered noisily into the sink, and her knees buckled. Mentally, she tried to calculate when she'd last had her period, and she prayed she hadn't been fertile during the four days she'd spent with Justin. She couldn't be pregnant. She'd never be able to explain it to Randall. For that matter, she'd never want to bring a child into the world to live the way she lived.

Please, God, she prayed. *Please, no!*

Justin's chest constricted in horror. "You're sure?"

"She answered the phone. At least, she said she was Tess Sinclair when I asked to speak to her. Then a man got on the phone, and I made up some cock-and-bull story about being from a cosmetics counter offering—"

"How did she sound?"

"Honestly? Kind of scared. She spoke real softly, and, well, I don't know what she sounds like most of the time, but—"

"Shit! I have to get out of here, Kathy. I don't care what the doctors say. Tess needs me." He threw back his covers and dragged his feet to the floor. The room spun, and he wobbled.

"Look, Sir Galahad, you're not going to do her any good if you leave here before your body is ready, and you drop from exhaustion a few miles from the hospital." Kathy blocked his path when he tried to climb out of the bed. "God didn't let you die last time. Maybe so you could go after Tess. But do both yourself and her a favor and give yourself a little time to heal, first."

Meeting Kathy's gaze, he crumpled his brow in worry. "Tess may not have time. Don't you get it? The guy's a real bastard!"

"I can appreciate that, hon. But you lost a lot of blood. You can't take off to San Antone to play hero until you can stand up by yourself." She arched one eyebrow. "Which reminds me, it's time for your shower."

Justin opened his mouth to protest, but something in her stance, her no-nonsense expression, told him it would be a waste of breath. He winced as he struggled to pull his body upright.

He knew it was silly to be embarrassed to have Kathy help him bathe. She was a nurse, after all. It was her job. But he'd bathed himself since he was five, and he shied from the idea of having a stranger helping him now.

Leaning on Kathy's arm, he hobbled into the adjoining bathroom. He tried to keep his mind off the awkward bath awaiting him by concentrating on the bigger problem facing him. He had no way to get to San Antonio and no money. "Kathy?"

"Do you think you can shave yourself, or do you want me to do it? I'm pretty good."

"I need money. How can I get some money?" He watched Kathy put a funny little plastic stool in the shower stall.

"Or did you plan to grow a beard?" She passed him the hand-held showerhead.

Justin scowled. "Did you hear me? I need money. Enough to buy a bus ticket to San Antonio."

She glanced over her shoulder and turned to take a towel from a shelf over the toilet. "I heard you. Will you answer my question?"

"I can shave myself."

"I'll wait out here. Call if you need help, and I'll think on the money problem."

Justin thought about the money problem, too, as he turned on a warm spray and doused his head. Brian would lend him some, but he hated to ask. He didn't even have his guitar to hock. In short, not a lot of options.

A pang of grief struck his heart. The guitar Becca had given him was gone, and though he'd have sold it to save Tess, losing it hurt. Another piece of Rebecca had slipped away. Another loss because of his incompetence. Why had he thought he could protect Tess? All his swaggering and big talk had been hot air.

The pain in his side paled in the shadow of the agony in his soul. A bitter taste rose in his throat, and he choked down the bile of regret and self-censure.

For Tess's sake, he would have to set his pride aside and borrow from his brother. He sighed then squirted a small amount of the generic-looking shampoo onto his hand. As he worked up a lather, grimacing at the pungent floral scent, he tried to refocus his thoughts. But the sweet smell made him think of Tess, and he gave up any hope of a distraction from his grief.

He missed her. God, he missed her. He tried not to think about what Randall could be doing to her.

His helplessness to do anything for her drove him nuts.

Think of something else.

A song came to mind, and he sang. Music had always been

a balm for him in the past, so he belted out the lyrics about a woman who walked out of his dreams and shined her light on his sleeping heart. While he rinsed soap out of his hair, he sang with a passion that was rooted in the ache of his own breaking heart.

"You finished yet, 'John Michael'?" Kathy called.

Justin grinned a little and finished the John Michael Montgomery song, singing louder.

From outside the shower curtain, he heard Kathy applaud. "I think I have an idea how you can get some money, Justin Boyd, if you're willing to take that act on the road."

"Ready, willing and able, ma'am."

"My heart is racing, and you're drivin' me wild. I should pull over, I can't handle the ride. I'm running on empty, but here you come again. Oh, baby, fill 'er up! With your sweet, sweet love. Fill my life, fill my heart, fill my soul. Fill 'er up!" Justin sang, a song he'd written. He added a special flourish for the smiling girl who was hooked to multiple tubes and wires. He pulled out all the stops to entertain the little girl whose dark eyes touched a soft spot inside him.

When he cut a glance to the doorway where Kathy stood, she grinned like a proud parent—or an agent who'd just discovered the next Garth Brooks. Having spread the word to the other nurses that a singer of considerable talent was in their midst, Kathy had helped set up private performances for patients whose families would pay a small fee.

Responses trickled in slowly at first, but after Justin sang a birthday concert for a woman whose husband wanted a special way to lift his hospitalized wife's spirits, business took off.

Word of the handsome, charismatic singer traveled like wildfire through the hospital, and Justin spent a large portion of his recovery time playing a borrowed guitar and singing from a wheelchair. His coffers grew along with his fame in the nurses' stations. He became especially popular in the pediatric ward, where parents were desperate for ways to entertain and comfort their sick children.

He even performed a complimentary concert for a little boy Kathy told him about, who'd lost both of his parents in the same boating accident that had landed the child in the hospital. The pediatric staff extolled his kindness, and he became nothing short of a hero to the moony-eyed nurses.

After a couple of days, his doctors reluctantly released him, ordering him to take it easy and drink lots of fluids. He'd earned enough cash to buy a bus ticket to San Antonio. Plus, a little extra for food.

Now at his last performance, another free concert for a little girl dying of leukemia, Kathy hovered nearby, waiting to tell Justin good-bye.

"Sing another one!" the girl begged, the excitement in her eyes making up for the weakness of her voice.

"Okay." He cast a look over his shoulder to the girl's parents who seemed tremendously relieved to see their daughter's response to the musician. "But only because I have a secret weakness for little girls with freckles." Justin reached out and tapped the girl on her nose. She beamed, and her smile filled his heart with a special warmth, like sunbeams streaming into a cold, dark room. He played again, another upbeat tune, while the girl watched him with stars in her eyes.

"All right, that's all. You need to rest now, sweetie." The girl's mother brushed past him and pulled a blanket up over the child's arms.

As he turned to set aside the borrowed guitar, the girl's father extended a hand to him. "Thank you, Mr. Boyd. I haven't seen my girl smile this much in weeks. I don't think you can ever appreciate how much this means to us."

Justin shook the man's hand. "I'm glad I could help."

"You're quite talented. Do you sing professionally?" the silver-haired man asked.

Justin shook his head. "Not yet."

The man nodded thoughtfully but said nothing more.

Facing the little girl again, Justin leaned close enough to kiss her cheek. "Hang in there, sweetheart. I'm pulling for you."

He gazed at the freckled face of the young girl, and his chest tightened with a bittersweet ache. She was too young to die. So young. A lump swelled in his throat as he headed out of the room, and he locked the memory of that little girl's smile in the dark recesses of his battered soul. Knowing his music had brought her just a few minutes of pleasure lightened the burden of guilt and despair he bore. By sharing his music with her, he'd eased her suffering a little bit. He'd finally done something right, something that helped, something that made a difference. He wouldn't soon forget the joy that seeped through the darkness inside him as he walked away from the girl's bedside. It was his first taste of real success.

"Thanks, Justin," Kathy said softly as they walked back out to the wide corridor.

"Thank you, lady." He startled her by giving her a hug. "I'll always appreciate what you've done for me."

"I'll keep one ear on the radio, waiting to hear you there."

"You've got front row seats at my first appearance at the Grand Ole Opry, pretty lady."

He handed Kathy the guitar that she had borrowed from a friend, and her face became serious.

"Be careful, Justin. Take care of yourself."

Backing away from her, he gave her a quick nod. Then

striding confidently toward the elevators, he left the hospital and headed out to the bus station to begin his trek back to south Texas.

To find Tess.

"I received an interesting phone call at work today, Tess." Randall stabbed a bite of chicken and turned his gaze toward her.

Over the past few days, she'd endured the pretense of a marriage that Randall insisted on. His manner remained cool and authoritative, but as long as she humbly submitted to his demands and played her part of the dutiful wife, he'd left her alone. After her refusal to have sex with him her first night back, he'd played the role of the wounded lover, too proud to try again until his hurt ego healed. Many nights he came home smelling of cigarettes and cheap perfume. His sideline trysts were a relief. As long as he found satisfaction else-where, he wouldn't bother her. But how long would it last?

Now, she raised her eyes to him, wary of what he had to tell her. Normally, they didn't speak at dinner, and she pre-ferred the silence to a tense guise of conversation.

"An Officer James Holton of the Memphis Police Depart-ment called. He asked for you. When I told him I was your husband, he informed me that your truck has been found. You'll never guess what was inside."

Chapter Sixteen

Tess's heartbeat stumbled, and her mouth became dry. "They found the Jimmy?"

"It had been stripped for parts and left abandoned on a road on the edge of town. Holton got your name and home number off paperwork in the glove compartment. Of course, when he called the home number, the call was forwarded to me."

Randall had set up a system that ensured that all calls to the home phone were routed to him. He stuck a bite of chicken in his mouth and chewed slowly, drawing out the suspense for Tess intentionally, she was sure.

"Holton said that the thief wasn't interested in your personal possessions," Randall continued, "and that they were left behind. I've sent a man to Tennessee to recover your things. It will be interesting to see what they found in your getaway vehicle. Don't you think?"

Her pulse pounded in her ears. Why had Justin abandoned the car after taking it? Had he been the one who sold the parts? Was he that desperate for cash? But why would he be, if he had the money from her purse? Her mind spun, trying to make sense of this turn of events.

Randall smiled smugly. "Oh, and he said they have a lead on who took the car. But then we already know, don't we?"

"What kind of lead?"

"Blood."

Her breath stilled.

"They can get a type on it and narrow the field of suspects, if we choose to pursue the investigation."

She barely heard Randall over the buzzing in her ears, and she fought the wave of dizziness that washed over her by gripping the edge of the table.

Blood.

Justin's blood? Was it possible that Justin wasn't the thief, but was as much a victim as she was? The possibility both delighted and horrified her. For Justin to be exonerated would mean that he could be hurt, even dead.

"I told him we would be pursuing the investigation," Randall said, and Tess gave him a curious look. "You seem surprised. You of all people should know that no one takes what is mine and gets away with it. Your friend Rebecca will pay for her misdeed. I've already sent my people after her."

Tess shuddered. Randall might discover that Rebecca was dead. Then what would happen? And what about Justin? Tess needed to know whether he was all right. The thought that he was injured or worse left a pit in her stomach.

"You're not eating," Randall said with a mocking edge in his voice. "What's wrong?"

She battled the tears that fought their way to her eyes, burning her throat and nose. She couldn't let Randall see her cry. Swallowing hard, she mumbled, "I'm not hungry, I guess."

Sliding his glass across the table, Randall sneered at her. "Then make yourself useful by fixing me another drink."

No matter what had happened to the car or to Justin, one unavoidable fact remained. She was trapped, stuck with Randall, imprisoned by the man she feared more than anyone on earth.

The next day, in Randall's absence, Henry answered the door when her possessions were delivered. Tess walked to the entry hall and stood back as a man she didn't recognize brought in her suitcase. Stooping, she ran her fingers over the small suitcase wistfully, and while she stared down at the piece of luggage, she heard Henry ask, "What's that?"

"They were in the car, too. Sinclair said get everything they recovered."

She looked up, and her breath caught. Justin's backpack and guitar. She clapped a hand over her mouth to suppress a gasp, but Henry eyed her suspiciously.

"That's it. No money. No purse," the delivery man said.

Henry produced an envelope full of money and paid the man for his services. "Want me to carry these things upstairs for you, Mrs. Sinclair?"

Her bodyguard—or rather, her babysitter—had proven to be polite, even respectful, but she didn't make the mistake of forgetting that Henry was on Randall's payroll and answered only to him. Henry had an intimidating physique with a barrel chest, thick neck and a bulldog-like face. He wore his blonde hair shaved close to his head, military-style, and despite his seemingly pleasant disposition, Tess knew he could be deadly. The bulge in his sport coat near his armpit was undoubtedly a gun.

"I can get them. Thank you anyway."

Henry turned and headed into the living room, where he resumed his guard duty. She watched him pull out a cell phone, presumably to report to Randall about the return of the items.

Lifting the suitcase and guitar, she took them up to her room first, before returning for the backpack. She would have precious little time to search the contents before Randall came home. Not that she could hide or dispose of anything incriminating. Henry had already seen the loaded backpack and guitar and would tell Randall about them.

Sinking down on her knees in front of the backpack, she slowly opened the first pocket with trembling fingers. She pulled out a small, framed picture of a woman Tess recognized immediately as Rebecca. Next she extracted the small notebook Justin had been scribbling in their last day together. Flipping through it, she studied the neat block-style handwriting that could only be Justin's. On the last page, she read the words he'd printed, and a knot swelled in her throat. It was the song he'd been writing for her.

You've been hurting far too long/ There's healing in the sky/ So spread your wings little bird/ It's time for you to fly. What would put the shine/ Back in your eyes of gold?/ You were meant to soar/ Despite what you've been told./ Love can be a balm/ That soothes a wounded soul/ No more need to run/ I want to make you whole.

Tears spilled down Tess's cheeks, and pain filled her heart. Justin hadn't abandoned her. He loved her too much to hurt her that way. She knew it now with certainty. The proof lay before her. He'd never have left his backpack behind. Or Rebecca's picture. Or his guitar.

Come sing, little bird/ There's music in my heart/ Let me show you love/ and make a brand new start/ Traveling together/ Our hearts will be our guide/ Don't be afraid now/ There's no more need to hide. Beautiful little bird, now that you're free/ Say that you will fly away with me. Tess finished reading, though her tears blurred her vision.

"Oh, Justin." She hugged herself as she cried. Moving to the bed, she opened his guitar case as if it was a treasure chest and lifted out his guitar. Stroking the instrument, she remembered how Justin's hands had caressed the wood and the strings as he sang to her.

She'd never told him how much she loved him. She'd been

afraid to, afraid of the feelings in her heart, knowing that one day Randall would find her. Justin was out there somewhere, and he didn't know she loved him. That knowledge clawed at her, left her bleeding inside.

She thought of the blood Randall said they'd found in the Jimmy, and her chest squeezed painfully. What if he was hurt? What if he was dead?

Clutching the guitar to her breast, she rocked slowly as she sobbed. "Oh, Justin, please be all right. Please, God."

"How touching."

Tess stiffened at the sound of Randall's sarcastic tone. She dashed away the tears from her cheeks as she whirled to face him.

Randall's menacing dark eyes traveled from Tess to the backpack propped against the wall near the head of the bed. "What have we here?"

Her palms sweated and nervous tension coiled inside her as he stepped over to the backpack and unzipped the main compartment. He pulled out a T-shirt, then a pair of jeans, eyeing them with suspicion. Then he dug out a stick of men's deodorant and a pair of Justin's briefs. His jaw tightened as he turned to Tess with the incriminating evidence. "This pack belonged to a man."

The simple statement and Randall's flat delivery of the words belied the rage Tess knew was building to lethal proportions. His face grew red. "You were traveling with a man. Weren't you?"

Tess hugged the guitar tighter as if it could protect her. When she made no response, Randall grabbed the neck of the guitar and yanked it from her arms. In one swift motion, he slammed the instrument against the wall, and it broke into several pieces.

Tess cried out in horror and grief. Randall aimed the piece

of the guitar neck still in his hand at Tess and screamed, "You lying whore! You ran off with a lover! Didn't you?"

When she shook her head, denying the accusation, Randall dropped the guitar piece in his hand and lunged for her with outstretched hands. Tess scrambled backward on the bed, but he caught her shoulder with one hand and back-handed her across the chin with the other. She bit her tongue and tasted blood. The chill of terror raced through her veins.

"You were humping him, weren't you? Weren't you? Answer me, whore!" Randall ranted with a rage unlike anything Tess had ever seen in him before. He was crazed, his eyes wild and deadly.

She trembled and stared at him in disbelief.

"Answer me!" Randall lunged again and wrapped his hands around her neck.

She would have gasped her shock if Randall's grip had allowed the flow of air. But his long, aristocratic fingers circled her throat and squeezed the breath from her. Tess clawed at his hands in a vain attempt to free herself.

"You bitch! I'll teach you not to screw around behind my back!"

His fingers dug painfully into her skin. Her lungs burned with the need for oxygen, and the room began to fade before her eyes.

"Don't do it, Mr. Sinclair! Not here. Not like this. There'd be too many questions," she heard, though she barely registered the fact that Henry had come to her defense.

"Stop it, Sinclair!"

Randall's chokehold broke abruptly, and Tess fell on the mattress weakly, sputtering and gasping for air. She peeked up in time to see Henry push a still-seething Randall out the bedroom door.

"Find out who that belongs to!" Randall pointed a finger

at the backpack. "Then hunt him down and kill the sonofabitch! Once he's dead, bring the body to me!"

"Yes, sir," Henry answered as he closed the door, leaving Tess alone in the room.

She had no doubt that Henry had just saved her life. But would he be around the next time?

And what would happen to Justin? Randall had just issued Justin's death warrant.

Chapter Seventeen

"Henry?"

The linebacker of a man looked up from the television screen and regarded Tess wordlessly.

"I just wanted to thank you for intervening on my behalf yesterday. You saved my life, and I—"

"I didn't stop the man out of charity for you. You may still die. That ain't my business. But I was hired to protect your husband's best interests, and it wouldn't have been in his best interests for him to kill you in his own house with his own hands."

Tess shivered. At least she now knew where Henry's loyalties were.

After Henry had stopped him from choking her, Randall had stormed around the house, ranting and breaking things. Then he'd left. He hadn't returned since last night, and Tess worried almost as much over his absence as his presence, especially in light of the contract he'd put out on Justin.

She prayed that Randall's men hadn't discovered Justin's identity from anything in the pack. Unfortunately, his name and Wellerton address were written boldly in the lid of his guitar case. Though she'd stashed the case under the bed, she held little hope that her hiding place would suffice for long.

Today, the pall of a funeral parlor hung over the house, and she jumped at every noise and shadow. She paced the living room, watching out the front window and waiting for

Randall's car, as if, with forewarning, she could combat any attack he launched upon his return.

She'd been back under Randall's guard for a little more than a week now. Though life still held little promise for her, learning that Justin had truly cared about her revived a part of her soul that gave her a spark of hope. In her mind, she replayed the hours of their time together, cherishing every memory, clinging to every word of encouragement he'd given her. Her memories of Justin were her lifeline.

Tess chafed her arms to ward off the chill that accompanied thoughts of her life with Randall, and she picked up her pace, wearing a path back and forth across the black, red and gold Oriental carpet.

"Do you have to do that?" Henry asked irritably, glancing up from the television. "You're driving me up the wall."

Tess stopped only for a moment to cast the man an apologetic look. With a grunt, he left the room. He disappeared upstairs, and she guessed he'd resumed watching the TV in the guest bedroom where he'd slept last night.

Sighing, she skimmed her gaze around the expensively furnished showroom that was Randall's den. He liked black, saying the color denoted power and control, and like Randall's fingerprints, the color stamped most everything in the room as his. Henry's large body had left a dent in the soft, black leather-covered cushions of the couch. Black lacquered lamp-stands dressed the glass-topped end tables, and on the matching coffee table, an onyx sculpture of a panther poised on the prowl held a prominent position. Without overwhelming the room, black featured prominently throughout the accent pieces, as well.

The primary relief from the oppressive color came from the cream and white brocade wing chairs and the white marble mantel above the fireplace. Tall windows allowed sunshine to flood the room on bright days. The walls, painted eggshell white, stretched to the cathedral ceiling and displayed modern paintings, comprised of bright splashes of paint with no particular form or purpose. She much preferred the impressionist works of Monet and Renoir, but Randall had given her little say in the decorating of his castle.

Fiddling with the diamond wedding band Randall had bought and demanded she wear to replace the one she'd lost, Tess bit her lip. The showy piece of jewelry perpetuated the lie, the farce of their marriage. She wondered at times like this why Randall didn't just marry her and make the union real. Why all the trappings of marriage without making it legal?

In his song, Justin had called her a little bird. A bird in a gilded cage, she thought morosely. All the opulence and finery surrounding her meant nothing.

Returning to her pacing, she worried about Justin's safety, fretted over her own fate, sweated over the mistakes she'd made, the lies that caught up with her, the—

She stopped short and spun toward the front window when a movement caught her attention. A white taxi stopped at the curb in front of the house, and the back door opened. Shadows inside the taxi hid the occupant, and she held her breath, waiting for the passenger to emerge. Had Randall sent one of his hit men to take her away? To kill her in her own house?

When the dark, lean form of a man stepped out of the taxi and into the sunlight, a tremor shook her to the core. Her hand flew to her throat, and she gasped. "Oh, my God!"

Running to the front door, she tore it open before the doorbell could alert Henry. She launched herself into the arms that opened at the sight of her, and she sobbed for joy.

"Tess! Oh, darlin', thank God you're all right!"

"Justin, oh, Justin." She buried her face in the crook of his neck. "How did you find me? How did you get here?"

"I was worried sick when I found out you were here. Has he hurt you? Oh, God, I've missed you!" Justin clutched her to his chest.

She stiffened and shoved away from him, her blood growing icy with fear. "You have to leave! He'll kill you!"

"Gladly, but I'm not leaving without you. I won't leave you with—" He stopped abruptly, his gaze narrowing on her neck.

Tess's pulse skittered, knowing he'd noticed the blue-black bruises Randall's chokehold had left on her throat.

Justin's eyes widened in horror before lifting to her face. "That sonofa— Randall did this to you?"

Flattening her hands on Justin's chest, she pushed him back toward the street. "You have to leave now! Henry will—"

"Henry? Who the hell's Henry?"

Instead of answering him, she spun to stare at the front door she'd opened without thinking. She realized Henry would be down any second to see about the breach of the security system.

Panic sluiced though her, and her heart thundered. She glanced around quickly, searching for someplace Justin could hide. "He can't find you. He has orders to kill you!" Her desperate tug on the front of Justin's T-shirt didn't give him the chance to ask the question on his lips. "In here."

Dragging him by the arm, she rushed him inside and shoved him into the front closet. He gave her a querying look but didn't put up a fight. She closed the louvered closet door then hurried to close the front door as thudding steps pounded on the stairwell.

"Mrs. Sinclair!" Henry shouted.

"Yes?" Pressing her back to the front door, she swallowed hard and tried to push down her rising fear.

"Did you open the front door?" An angry scowl puckered Henry's face. He'd already drawn his pistol, and she shivered as he waved the gun toward the door.

"Yes. I forgot about the alarm. There was a salesman . . . an encyclopedia salesman, and . . . I'm sorry. Please don't tell Randall."

"Your husband already knows. That's how the system's set up. He'll be here in less than thirty minutes, and he'll want a better explanation than an encyclopedia salesman." Henry glowered at her.

She wet her lips and struggled to steady her voice. "It's the truth. I got rid of him. He's—"

Henry's hand flew past her cheek, and she flinched. He punched a code in the panel of buttons by the front door and opened it to look outside for himself. "There ain't nobody in sight."

"He's probably already at the next house, or maybe he drove away."

The cold gray of Henry's eyes said he didn't buy her explanation as he punched a new set of numbers in the keypad. "Stay here. I'm going to have a look around the yard," he ordered and closed the front door behind him.

Justin stepped out of the closet a fraction of a second after Henry's exit. "Don't tell me. That gorilla is Henry, and he works for Randall."

She whirled around. "Justin, are you crazy?"

Shoving him back in the closet, she followed him inside. Huddled together in the dark, among the coats and umbrellas, she curled her fingers into his shirt. "Randall knows about you, Justin. He's already ordered a hit on you. If he found you here—"

"Then we'll leave now. Together. All we have to do is get by the goon with the gun and—"

"How did you know he had a gun?" she whispered.

"I watched him through the slats in the door. He's big and he's armed, but we've got to try to outrun him."

She shook her head. "Even if we could outrun him, we couldn't outrun a bullet."

"What about a car?" Justin smoothed her hair away from her face.

She trembled at his touch. Oh, God, how she'd missed his tender touch!

"Only Randall has a car now. He's not here . . . yet."

"Yeah, I heard. He's coming." Justin rested his forehead against hers. "Do you have any idea how much I missed you?"

Tess's heart swelled. "You're here. That says everything."

He captured her chin and angled her face to kiss her. She melted against him, putting her arms around his neck and holding fast to him as if her life depended on it. In a sense, it did, and that sobering thought forced her to lever away from him.

"Stay in here. No matter what happens to me." When Justin tensed, she soothed him with a gentle hand in his hair. "I'll be okay as long as you don't let anyone know you're here. We need time to plan our escape. We can't do something stupid that will get us both killed."

"Tess, I can't just sit in here while he—"

"You have to, Justin. It's too important. He. Will. Kill. You." She enunciated each word slowly and emphatically. "He'll kill us both if he knows you're here. Promise me you'll stay hidden, Justin. Promise me! No matter what happens!"

Silently, Justin stared into her eyes with a gaze that blazed with defiance, with affection, with frustration and anger. But he whispered, "All right, Tess. I promise. But only because I don't want to put you in any unnecessary danger."

Knowing Henry would be back soon, she gave Justin one more quick kiss. Then she hurried out of the closet to do battle for their lives.

"Like hell I'll stay here," Justin muttered under his breath as he peered out through the slats of the louvered door to watch Tess confront the big ape with the gun. He'd be prudent, sure. But there was no way in hell he'd sit back and allow Randall to hurt her without raising a finger to defend her.

That's what he'd done for Rebecca. Nothing. Well, never again. He'd made his sister a promise. He'd made God a promise, and the Lord in his infinite wisdom had seen fit to give him a second chance. He had no intention of letting another abusive husband take someone he cared about away from him. Sliding quietly to the floor, he watched the drama outside the closet unfold.

The armed henchman returned and punched the security code into the panel by the door.

"Did you see him?" Tess asked.

"No, not outside. But I haven't searched the house yet."

Justin's pulse quickened. He noticed the stiffening of Tess's posture, but had the goon?

"Go ahead." Her voice sounded strong and sure, and Justin admired her exterior calm, her bravery.

The man named Henry turned for the living room and scanned the area. Then, after checking behind the front window curtains, he began searching behind closed doors at the other end of the house. Tess stayed near the passage between the foyer and living room like a sentry guarding the closet. What would she do if Randall or his thug tried to look there?

A pang of regret for the jeopardy his presence put Tess in

plucked Justin's conscience, but he pushed it aside. She'd be in far more danger if he weren't there to protect her.

His thoughts flickered to the circle of bruises around her throat, and a fire blazed in his gut. Apparently Randall had already tried to kill her. Justin sent up a quick prayer of thanks that the man hadn't succeeded.

A door at the back of the house slammed, and a voice boomed from somewhere beyond the living room—a voice that brought Tess to rigid attention.

"Tess! Where are you?"

She cast a quick, panicked glance at the closet door then wiped her palms on the seat of her linen pants. "In the living room, Randall."

Justin's blood simmered with hatred for the man who came into view. Randall was tall and fit-looking, his brown hair graying at the temples. He had a chiseled, distinguished-looking face that was hard with anger and exuded arrogance. Justin's fist itched to smash the man's smug face then and there. But he waited. He bided his time. Timing could prove essential, especially since Randall and his armed sidekick had Justin out-manned and out-gunned.

"What's been going on here?" Randall asked as Henry walked into the living room, his gun still drawn. "Did she try to run?"

"She claims there was a salesman at the door. I checked outside and didn't see anyone. I'm searching the house now." Henry and Randall turned mutually distrustful glares on Tess.

Her knees trembled. "I forgot about the alarm. I'm sorry. Really, I am."

"Look upstairs," Randall ordered, and Henry strode past Tess and the front closet to search the bedrooms.

Randall's eyes narrowed to slits, and she took an instinctive step back, shrinking from the threat in his glare.

"Don't think I've forgotten your betrayal, Tess. You escaped with your skin yesterday, but any value you had to me as a wife vanished the minute I discovered you'd been giving it away to another man." He walked slowly toward her. "You're expendable now. Like Angela was."

She straightened her spine and lifted her chin, despite the quiver in her stomach. Justin was here. That knowledge gave her the strength, the courage to meet Randall's menacing eyes.

Don't let him win. Stand up to him.

His expression became a sickening leer. "However, when you breached the security system, you interrupted a meeting I was in with a representative from a promising jewel of a company I think I'll buy."

He stopped scant inches from Tess, but she stood her ground.

"This representative happened to be a woman with a magnificent body and a tendency to lean forward, giving me glimpses of her wares as we studied the paperwork. I'd have loved the opportunity to nail her. But since I'm here now, perhaps I should take advantage of my marital rights."

He gave her a suspicious glare before his hand snaked out and caught her by the arm. He hauled her forward and snarled in her face. "Unfaithful whores like you are only good for one thing, Tess."

With a yank, he dragged her toward the sofa while she wiggled to free herself from his grip.

"No!" she cried, frightened of what Randall planned to do and more terrified of what Justin might do, despite his promise to stay hidden.

"What?" Randall tipped his head in disbelief, his muscles taut. "What did you say?"

Tess mustered all her courage, all the hatred she felt for Randall, and leveled a challenging glare at him. "You heard me. I said no!"

An evil grin spread across Randall's face, and he delivered a slap across Tess's cheek that made her ears ring. "Now what do you have to say, slut?"

The closet door banged the wall as it flew open.

"I'd say someone needs to teach you respect for women, asshole," Justin growled.

Chapter Eighteen

"Justin, no!" Tess shrieked.

Randall released her and turned to face Justin with the misleading calm Tess knew so well.

"You must be the bastard who's been screwing my wife," Randall said, bracing his hands on his hips.

"And you're the prick who's been terrorizing her for years." Justin strode forward, his shoulders back. A fire blazed in his eyes that Tess had never before seen in their blue depths. "Didn't your mother teach you better than to hit a woman, Sinclair?"

"My mother was a bigger coward than Tess. All I learned from her was that I had to look out for myself. My father taught me how to keep a woman's respect." Randall's jaw tightened as he glared at Justin.

Tess shivered as the two men squared off.

"Intimidation is not the same as respect, you sonofabitch." Justin balled his hands into fists. "If you want to hit someone, hit me. But if you so much as lay a finger on Tess again, I'll tear you apart."

Tension coiled in Tess's chest, and her knees shook. She had to do something to stop the storm that brewed. But what?

Randall smirked. "How very noble of you, Mr. . . . ?" He paused in a manner that awaited a response.

"Boyd. Justin Boyd." Justin stepped forward, his posture as rigid and uncompromising as the tone of his voice.

Randall's face reflected a moment of surprise then understanding and recognition. "Ah, yes. Of course. I'm familiar with the Boyd family of Wellerton. Rebecca would be your . . . what? Sister?"

Justin's brow furrowed with suspicion. "What about Rebecca? How did you know about her?"

"Perhaps we could retire to my office to discuss this like gentlemen." Randall directed Justin toward the closed office door with a wave of his hand.

When he started in that direction, Justin followed.

Tess mentally assessed Randall's eerily polite manner. She knew things weren't what they seemed. Randall was plotting, or setting a trap, or waiting for Henry to return, or . . . what?

As she trailed behind the two men, she thought about the only time she'd darkened the door of Randall's hallowed office just a few days before. He'd tested her recognition of Rebecca's yearbook picture, blatantly intimidating her with—

The gun!

Already Randall was reaching for the top drawer of his desk. She threw herself on Justin and screamed, "No!"

A loud pop reverberated through the room. Pain seared her shoulder as she and Justin tumbled to the floor with a hard thud.

Justin scrambled to put himself in the line of fire, shielding Tess with his body.

Clamping a hand over the source of sharp pain in her shoulder, she found it damp. She drew back her hand and gaped at the blood darkening her fingers.

Randall rounded his desk, clearly enjoying the position of dominance his weapon gave him. His grin gloated his power with demonic glee. "Nice try, Tess. But I still have five bullets. I can put one in each of your heads and still have three left."

"You're sick." Justin breathed in quick, shallow pants, but his eyes blazed with defiance. "If you kill us in cold blood with your own gun, the cops will be all over you. You'll fry, Sinclair."

Her gentle cowboy's courage flooded her heart with love. If Justin was prepared to fight, then so was she. She had nothing left to lose and so much to fight for.

Knowing the gunshot would bring Henry downstairs, she thought fast. She had precious little time to plan.

"How sweet of you to be concerned," Randall said. "But I'm smarter than to let the pigs pin anything on me. You broke into my house and killed my wife. My killing you was a clear-cut case of self-defense."

While Tess listened to Randall's scheme, she scanned the area within her reach. She spied a decorative doorstop just past the reach of her fingers. But if she stretched . . .

She inched her hand across the Persian rug then hesitated. If she tossed the weighted sculpture at Randall and missed, he'd start shooting. They had to get the gun away from him. She could only pray Justin would follow the same line of reasoning.

And pray she did as she grabbed for the iron doorstop. The quick movement sent currents of pain shooting from her injured shoulder, and she bit back a moan. In a flash, she rolled on her back and lobbed the iron piece at a decorative mirror on the wall across the room from her. The mirror shattered with a loud crash, and Randall reflexively jerked his head toward the noise.

Justin seized the moment of distraction to kick a long leg up at the gun in Randall's hand. Randall spun back around as the gun flew from his hand and landed behind him. When

Randall turned to retrieve the pistol, Justin clambered up from the floor and tackled him from behind.

Tess searched the floor for the gun, but Randall managed to scoop it up before Justin grabbed him. The men battled for control of the weapon. Metal flashed. Hands grappled. Antiques shattered.

"Mr. Sinclair?" Henry shouted from the hall.

Tess gasped and scrambled for a plan. Quickly, she hid behind the office door. Snatching an Oriental vase from a bookshelf, she flattened herself against the wall, out of view. The minute Henry stepped into the room, she jumped from behind the door. Swinging with every ounce of her strength, she smashed the vase on Henry's head.

The burly man crumpled on the floor, and for a fraction of a second, Tess worried that she'd killed him.

The crack of Randall's gun grabbed her attention. In a flurry of fists and elbows, Justin still struggled to subdue Randall. Tess caught her breath and watched the deadly contest. Randall backed Justin against the desk and pinned him. Blood stained the front of Justin's shirt near his waist.

With a howl of pent-up rage and hatred, Tess charged Randall's back and jumped on him, clawing like a rabid wildcat.

"Get off me, bitch!" Randall grabbed at her scratching hands. Justin took advantage of the distraction to lift a well-placed knee to Randall's groin. Randall slumped, clutching his injured crotch. Justin wrested the gun from his opponent and aimed it at his head.

"Justin, no!"

"Why the hell not?" Justin's hands shook, and his eyes blazed with a wild fire.

"Because you're not a murderer. If you kill him, you're no better than he is," Tess squeaked, her throat tight with fear and tears.

She saw the turmoil swirling in his eyes. A muscle in his cheek twitched. "If I had killed Mac when I had the chance, Becca would be alive today." His voice sounded strangled. "But I didn't, and I've regretted it ever since. I won't make that mistake again."

Her heart beat double-time as the depth of his pain and conflict became clear. She reached for his hands and wrapped her fingers around his wrist. "Becca didn't want you to kill for her. And neither do I. I know you're hurting, but killing Randall won't bring Rebecca back."

Randall peered up, assessing the situation with dark eyes.

Justin cut a quick sideways glance at Tess. "But it would solve your problems."

"No. It would only make new ones. You'd be wanted for murder, and the gentle goodness I love about you would be destroyed."

The gun in Justin's hand drooped. The blaze in his eyes cooled. Behind her, Henry moaned and stirred. "Let's just get out of here," she said. "Please, Justin! We have to hurry!"

Justin aimed the gun and fired a bullet into Randall's foot. Randall screamed in agony, and Tess yelped, startled by the shot.

"At least I can slow him down," Justin said, backing toward the door.

When Justin grabbed her hand and tugged her toward the living room, Tess nearly tripped over Henry.

"Which way? Where's Randall's car?"

"Through the kitchen."

Stumbling, she headed for the garage with Justin on her heels. Flying down the flight of steps from the kitchen door to the ground level of the garage in one leap, Justin slid across the hood of Randall's Jaguar. Scurrying behind him, Tess plunged into the front passenger seat.

"Where's the key?" He groped the ignition and floor mat.

Tess groaned. "I don't know."

He flipped down the visor, and a key fell into his lap. He grinned smugly, but before he could crank the engine, a tall form darkened the kitchen door. Tess glanced up with a start. Henry plowed through the doorway and down the steps, while Justin coaxed the engine to start.

"Come on, baby, we've gotta roll!"

Tess locked the car doors with a flip of a lever as the engine roared to life. A rumble caught her attention. Henry had lowered the garage door and was punching in a code on a keypad. Tess mashed the button of the remote control in the car, but the door didn't budge. "Henry's locked us in!"

Henry moved to her car door and pounded her window with the butt of his gun. Holding her breath, she waited for the shattering of glass and the blast of Henry's gun.

"Hang on!" Justin shouted, gunning the engine. He popped the clutch, and the Jaguar rocketed toward the closed garage door.

Tess barely had time to shield her face before they crashed through the door. Splintering wood rained down, and metal crunched.

As the Jaguar flew down the driveway and bounced over the curb, Justin floored the accelerator. He gave a victorious whoop which was cut short as the back window shattered.

Swiveling in her seat, Tess watched Henry empty his pistol at the car. Bullets hit the car with ominous *thunks*.

"Get down!" Justin shoved her toward the floor.

When he took a corner too fast, the car nearly went up on two wheels. She whimpered and closed her eyes until she felt the wheels regain traction.

"We just got away from two guns. Try not to kill us now with your driving!" She glared at the sassy grin Justin flashed her. She clung to the edge of the seat and sucked in a deep breath, trying to restore her ragged heartbeat to a normal pace.

"You're bleeding. Are you hit?" Concern laced his tone, and he nodded toward her shoulder. Tess peeled back her shirt to examine her wound. "It's just a graze, a shallow cut. It's barely bleeding anymore. Keep driving!"

He frowned but didn't argue. The need to get some distance between them and Randall and company was an unspoken priority.

After a few minutes, Tess moved back up on the seat and looked out the window. "Any idea where we're going?"

"I'm working on it. I have a couple ideas."

"Such as."

"The police."

Tess shook her head adamantly. "I told you before, Randall has allies in the police department. He must. Too risky. We have to hide. Disappear."

"All right. Then plan B is we go to Austin."

"Austin?" She knitted her brow as she turned a stern gaze on him. "No, Justin. Don't get your brother involved. Don't put him at risk. It's bad enough I've endangered your life."

"Do you have a better idea? You've been shot, and I've ripped my stitches. If we go to the hospital, they'll have to file a report with the cops. We need money, food, rest, and time for a breather while we plan what to do next. I'm not suggesting we stay long, but we need to regroup."

Tess stared out the passenger-side window. She hated the thought of drawing anyone else into the horror show her life had become. Realizing how close she and Justin had come to losing their lives, she shivered. The notion of risking Brian's life, too, riddled her conscience.

But she trusted Justin and couldn't think of any other option. After a moment, she sighed and turned back to him. "All right. We'll go to your brother's. But just for one night."

Chapter Nineteen

"You've lost your wife again?" Tony Morelli worked hard to contain his amusement.

"Watch yourself," Sinclair warned. "Or I'll settle for your blood instead of Tess's."

Morelli drew a hand over his mouth to conceal a satisfied smirk. "Any idea where she might have taken off to this time?"

Who'd have thought that Sinclair's wife would have the nerve and the smarts to escape from her husband twice? Sinclair had had the fancy new security system installed, so Tess's escape surprised Morelli all the more.

Sinclair's wife had earned Morelli's respect. She had gumption and guts. The extent to which her defection riled Sinclair intrigued Morelli, as well. He'd known the businessman lorded his power with an iron fist and abhorred any defiance, but something about his wife's disappearance carried his vengeance to an extreme. Morelli had never seen Sinclair so obsessed with finding and controlling one certain person. Which meant either Sinclair thought he loved Tess, or Tess knew enough about Randall's operation to destroy him.

Morelli didn't waste time with the notion that Sinclair could love his wife. Not like Morelli loved his Maria. Cold and hardhearted, the bastard couldn't possibly appreciate what a good woman could mean to a man. So did Tess have

211

inside information about Sinclair that could help Morelli ruin the miserable bastard? Interesting . . .

Either way, Tess was a chink in Sinclair's armor, a weakness that Morelli could use to his advantage. Staying in Sinclair's circle of trusted employees remained essential until he knew he'd found Sinclair's Achilles heel. But now Tess had provided a promising possibility. How could he use the situation to bring Sinclair's empire down?

"She's got her lover with her." Sinclair slapped on his desk a grainy picture taken from the security camera at his house. The dark-haired man in the picture was young, tall, handsome.

Tess hadn't done bad for herself.

"His name is Justin Boyd, and I want both him and Tess brought back to me—dead or alive. Makes no difference to me." Sinclair's face seethed with rage. "But if I get my hands on them again, they'll wish they'd died when they had the chance to take a bullet in the head."

Morelli knew a moment of pity for Tess and the young man she'd escaped with. Randall Sinclair's legion of associates had any number of slow, agonizing ways to kill a person. He had witnessed, even caused, a number of those deaths himself. The sights and sounds of such torture were not for the squeamish.

Tess and her lover would be lucky if he found them before any of Sinclair's other men.

Although he had enough information about Sinclair's money laundering and drug smuggling operation to sink the powerful man, Morelli hadn't figured out how to expose Sinclair without bringing himself down in the process. Tess was the key, the avenue he'd searched for to exact his revenge against Sinclair, ever since the bastard had struck out at Maria.

"I'll find them." Morelli took the picture of the lover and

folded it before he stuck it in his breast pocket. Then with a smirk, he added, "Trust me."

Justin pulled the Jaguar to a stop in the driveway of an isolated house on the state road he'd been driving then killed the engine.

"Why'd we stop?" Tess asked, anxiety written in her wide, hazel eyes.

"Can you drive? I'm not feeling so good." Justin pressed his hand against his throbbing side. His stitches had ripped open during his struggle with Randall, and he'd grown progressively light-headed and weak as he drove, making it difficult to concentrate on the road.

Tess's eyes darkened with worry, and her gaze dropped to the drying bloodstain on his shirt. "Dear God, Justin, you were shot!"

"No, I busted open the knife wound I got from the two guys who stole the Jimmy."

Tess's mouth opened, and her eyes grew wider. "You were stabbed?"

"Yeah. But a guy found me at the side of the road and called for help. I've been stuck at a hospital in Memphis, or I'd have come for you sooner."

She covered her mouth with a trembling hand, and her eyes misted. "Oh, Justin, how could I have ever thought . . ." She brushed her fingers along his jawline. "I thought you had taken the car . . . because of the money." A tear spilled from her lashes as she leaned toward him. "I'm so sorry I doubted you. How could I have ever believed that you would do something like that?"

"I guess the circumstances were incriminating." Justin caught her fingers and kissed the palm of her hand. "How did Randall find you? What did you do?"

"I called Randall's secretary. She was my friend when I worked there, but she must have told him where I was, even though I begged her not to."

Justin dried the tears from her cheek with the pad of his thumb, his gaze thirstily drinking in the sight of her face. "I was so worried about you. One of the nurses called your house and found you there. I've never felt so helpless, so scared. As soon as I convinced the doctors to let me go, I caught the first bus to Texas."

He explained how he'd performed for patients for a fee and counted the days until his release. "I was so afraid I'd be too late."

"You almost were. Oh, Justin, how can I ever thank—"

He covered her mouth with his hand. "Don't thank me. All of this was my fault. I let those two jerks at the gas station snatch the Jimmy and your money right out from under my nose. I didn't even see them coming, because I had my mind on . . . I don't even remember what." He sighed and squeezed his eyes closed. "If I'd been paying attention, maybe those guys—"

"You said they had a knife! You were outnumbered and held at knifepoint. Justin, no car or money in the world is worth your life. I got you involved in this, and I'm sorry for—"

This time he muffled her apology with a kiss, hard and deep and full of gratitude that they were still alive. "Let's not debate faults, Tess. I'm just so glad to see you and know you're okay."

Pulling her closer, he took her lips in a gentle embrace, restlessly shifting, re-angling, relearning the soft curves and sweet taste of her mouth. Tess sank her fingers into his hair and held him near, deepening their kiss and responding to his lips with desperation and passion. Her mouth flowered under the light caress of his tongue, and she welcomed his tender invasion, sagging against him. She hugged his neck while his hand mussed her hair with loving strokes.

The sound of a passing car brought both their heads up and around in alarm. Justin recovered his composure, and he raked his hair out of his eyes, blowing a deep breath through pursed lips. "We should get moving again. Will you drive?"

Tess nodded.

He turned and opened the car door to get out, but Tess caught his arm. The wound in his side protested with a sharp ache as he twisted to face her again. Her eyes filled with tears, and his heart thudded anxiously.

Framing his face with her hands, she moved close enough for him to feel her breath as she whispered, "Thank you. You really came through for me when I needed you. You've risked so much for me, and I'll always be grateful."

Her words numbed him to any bodily pain, to their surroundings, to anything but the precious honesty in her eyes. She kissed him tenderly, sealing her declaration like a promise.

She still trusted and believed in him, despite his failure to keep her safe. He grappled with an awe that warmed him from the inside out. So much could happen to destroy that faith, and he knew losing her respect would be the most painful wound he could suffer. Yet, eventually, he was bound to disillusion her. A lucky escape from Randall was one thing. Providing lasting security and stability to a deserving woman was another. Much as he might want to consider a future with Tess, his conscience told him not to promise her anything he couldn't give. For now, she was stuck with him. She needed his protection until they could shake Randall's henchmen and find her a safe new home. That much he'd do for Tess, even if he died trying.

He heard his own heartbeat in his ears, heard his voice as he whispered his own promise. "You're going to survive this, Tess. Somehow. I swear."

The Boyd children had all been cut from the same cloth, Tess thought the minute the thirty-five-year-old version of Justin opened the front door of his suburban Austin home. Except for the conservative, short haircut and eyes better described as gray than blue, Brian resembled Justin and Rebecca in every way. His face registered surprise, then curiosity, then concern, and finally irritation in a matter of seconds as his silver eyes scanned his brother and the woman with him.

"Hey, Bri," Justin said softly.

Brian's gaze flickered out to the driveway where the Jaguar with the broken rear window and crumpled front fender sat, and his dark eyebrows snapped together.

"What the hell have you gotten yourself into now?" he said.

Wary of Brian's dark tone, Tess stayed behind Justin, scooting closer to him for reassurance.

"Whose Jag is that? Where have you been the past few weeks? And why haven't you checked in with anyone in the family?" He paused from firing questions long enough to give Justin a disgruntled look that morphed into a concerned frown. "Is that blood on your shirt? Dear God, are you hurt?"

Justin waved him off. "I'll be okay. Pulled some stitches, no biggie."

"Stitches. Why do you have stit—?"

Justin raised a hand to interrupt. "I can explain everything." He nodded toward the foyer. "Inside."

When Brian opened the door wider and stepped back, Justin waved a hand indicating Tess should go first. Hesi-

216

tantly, she stepped into the ranch-style home that smelled of cinnamon potpourri. The cozy, country decor immediately wrapped her with warmth and welcome, and she experienced a pang of regret that she'd never enjoyed the same sense of home and belonging in the house she'd shared with Randall for thirteen years.

She turned to Brian, who blinked at Tess as if noticing her for the first time.

"Oh. Hi. I'm—" He awkwardly stuck his hand out to shake Tess's then hesitated when his gaze landed on her shoulder. "You're bleeding too. What happened?"

"Tess, this is my brother, Brian. Brian, this is Tess." Ignoring his brother's question, Justin gestured with his hand as he made the introductions. An attractive blond-haired woman stepped out of the kitchen, and Justin added, "And this is Brian's wife, Hallie."

Brian, wearing neatly creased khakis and a yellow polo-style shirt, stared at his brother, clearly at a loss for words and waiting for Justin to start explaining himself. The smile Hallie had worn when she greeted her company was lost in a gasp when she dropped her gaze to Justin's bloody shirt. "Justin, what happened to you?"

If not for Justin's grip on her hand, Tess would have turned and left then and there. Her presence and the threat of violence that followed her violated the sanctity of Brian's home.

"Long story. Can we sit down?" Without waiting for an answer, Justin moved his hand to the small of Tess's back and guided her toward the front room. He showed Tess to the overstuffed sofa and dropped tiredly beside her.

"Why are you bleeding?" Hallie pressed. She hurried to Justin's side and tried to tug up his shirt. "Shouldn't you go to the hospital or something?"

Working his shirt back down, Justin shrugged away from his sister-in-law. "Soon. It's not as bad as it looks. I just . . ."

When Justin paused and sighed, Brian jumped in. "Justin, some roughnecks have been at Mama and Dad's earlier this week asking questions about Becca. Then yesterday, they were back asking where you were. Now you show up here in a trashed Jaguar, and the two of you are covered in blood and—"

"We've been worried sick about you!" Hallie added.

"I know. I'm sorry. I didn't want any of you involved in this, but I didn't know where else to go."

Brian sat on the edge of a chair across from them and dragged a hand down his face. "So start explaining."

"It's all my fault, I'm afraid," Tess said, casting an apologetic look at Brian.

Justin tensed and placed a hand on her knee. "No. None of this is your fault. You didn't ask for this, and you're not to blame. You did what you had to." Lifting his gaze to Brian's, Justin cut to the chase. "It's Tess's ex who's the problem."

Tess briefly met the eyes that turned to her in question before dropping her own gaze to the floor. Her stomach fluttered, and she sought the reassurance of Justin's presence by sliding her hand over his. He enveloped her fingers with a warm grip.

"What about her ex? Are you two involved?" Brian's tone sounded shocked, confused. "What about Amy?"

Justin sighed. "We broke up a few weeks ago. It's for the best. Neither of us was really happy."

"But I thought . . ." Hallie shook her head, clearly startled by the news of Justin's breakup.

Justin met his brother's dubious gaze without flinching. "Yes, I'm involved with Tess. We met on the road a couple weeks ago. Her ex is an abusive bastard who's tried to kill her more than once."

Hallie sucked in a sharp breath, and her gaze darted to Tess, taking in the bruises at Tess's neck and blood on the shoulder of her shirt.

Tess looked away. Telling Justin about her life with Randall had been hard enough. Hearing Justin spill her ugly secret to his family made a stinging shame heat her cheeks.

"He terrorized her," Justin continued, "until she had no choice but to run from him just to save herself."

"Thank God you got out," Brian said. "At least he can't hurt you now."

Tess didn't bother arguing about Randall's ability to still hurt her.

"When I found out about her situation, I couldn't turn away." Justin squeezed her hand. "I'd promised Becca I would never walk away again, and that's a promise I intend to keep. I let Becca down, but I can still change things for Tess."

Tess heard Brian expel a deep breath with a hiss. She wished she could crawl in a hole somewhere and hide.

"So this *is* about Becca. Justin, I feel as badly as you do that we didn't get Becca away from Mac before it was too late. But you can't change the past by taking on every abusive husband or boyfriend in a street brawl." Brian waved a hand toward Justin's bloody shirt.

Justin's grip on her hand became tighter, almost painful. "I know I can't change the past, but I can change Tess's future. And this—" he tugged at the edge of his shirt "—is the result of a lot more than a street fight."

Brian took a deep breath and softened his tone. "Look, I'm glad you could help Tess get away from her ex-husband, but—"

"They were never married."

"Okay, ex-boyfriend. Whatever. But now it's time to turn it over to the police. Let the court system handle it. Tess?"

219

She glanced up at Brian and met a gentle gaze much like Justin's.

"We can help put you in contact with counselors, professionals who can hide you in one of the safe houses—"

"No!" Justin shot to his feet, dropping her hand to clutch his side, which she was certain had suffered from his abrupt movement. He gritted his teeth but kept arguing with Brian. "It's not like that! This isn't like it was with Rebecca! Her husband is following us because he wants us dead. The lunatic has already tried to kill us! That blood on Tess's shirt is from where a bullet grazed her."

Brian tensed. "All the more reason to go to the police."

Justin shook his head at his brother. "It's not that simple."

"Damn it, Justin, grow up!" Brian shouted. "You have to think about what is best for Tess, not about assuaging your own guilty conscience over Becca!"

Tears welled in Tess's eyes, and she struggled weakly to push off the sofa. "Maybe we should just go, Justin. I don't want to cause more problems with your brother."

"I'm sorry you had to hear that, Tess. Why don't I, uh . . . get you something to eat? Are you hungry?" Hallie rose from the couch and put an arm around Tess. With a nudge toward the door of the kitchen, she escorted Tess out of the room. "There's a lot of history between those two that you may not understand. That's why Brian seems angry. But he's really not so much mad at Justin as he is worried about him. He's been worked up like this ever since his parents called and said that men were asking about Becca and Justin. He would have flown out to Wellerton last night if he wasn't in the middle of a huge case that he's spent literally years bringing to trial."

Hallie pulled out a chair from the kitchen table for Tess. "Would you like some coffee or a piece of lemon pound cake?"

Tess shook her head. "No, thank you."

Hallie's gaze dropped to Tess's shoulder. "Maybe I should take a look at that. I'm not a doctor, but I play doctor to a wide variety of injuries at school. I teach first grade. You'd be surprised at the inventive ways kids can get hurt." Hallie grinned, but her smile didn't cover the concern in her eyes.

Tess took a seat at the oak kitchen table. From the next room, she could hear Justin arguing with his brother, and compunction coiled tighter in her stomach. She'd caused so much grief and strife, and she hated it.

"Do you have any children, Tess?"

Tearing her attention away from the men's voices, she looked up at Hallie, who pushed Tess's shirt off her shoulder to examine her wound. "No, I don't."

Tess's thoughts jumped to the day she'd realized she could be carrying Justin's baby and the horror she'd known. Tess slid a hand to her lower abdomen and spread her fingers in a protective gesture. The possibility of a child, Justin's child, stirred a maternal longing in her heart. "I'd like to have children though . . . some day."

"Mmm. Me, too. We keep trying, but so far, no luck." Hallie smiled wistfully then dropped her gaze back to Tess's shoulder and winced. "Ouch."

"I think it's superficial. The bullet just nicked me."

Hallie's face blanched. "Your ex did this? He really shot at you?"

Tess wet her lips and nodded. "Except he was aiming at Justin. I knocked Justin out of the way before—" She stopped and met Hallie's eyes with a beseeching gaze. "Please, don't judge Justin harshly. I know it all sounds seamy and illicit, but it really never started out that way. Justin saved my life. Literally. He's the kindest, sweetest man I've ever met, and I never wanted him involved in the nightmare my life has become. But everything got out of hand so fast." She paused, and Hallie straightened from her examination of Tess's shoulder.

"I'm going to get some alcohol to clean this up before I bandage it."

Tess caught Hallie's arm. "Justin's not to blame. He's just trying to help me." She desperately wanted to repair the damage she'd done to Justin's relationship with his family, knowing how important they were to him.

Brian's wife sat back down in the chair across from Tess and covered Tess's hand with hers. "And we want to help you too. To help both of you. Our concern is just that Justin has always been a dreamer, an idealist, never quite in touch with the realities of life. Not that he's irresponsible, but he acts impulsively, based on his emotions, without thinking things through first. Just like when he took off hitchhiking to Nashville a few weeks ago. He's been especially unpredictable since Becca's death. Nothing he's done lately makes sense to us. Mac's trial ended and boom—Justin hit the highway. He broke up with his girlfriend of five years and was gone."

Tess raised her chin a notch. "I know about all of that. But Justin tells the story differently. Going to Nashville had been a dream of his for years. It wasn't a snap decision. I didn't intend to get him involved with my problems, but—" Tess bit her lip. "There's something special about Justin. He gave me something I needed. He filled a void in me. He was kind and understanding and fun to be with.

"I tried to leave him. I didn't want him in danger, but leaving got harder and harder the more I knew about him. Before I knew what was happening, I realized I was falling in love with him."

Hallie hesitated before answering, her expression dark

with worry. "We love him too, Tess. And we want him to be happy. If you make him happy, then I hope things will work out for you."

Tess felt a quick tug of regret in her chest. She debated whether to explain to Hallie that despite her fondness for Justin, planning a future with him was futile. She might never be truly free of Randall, and she couldn't stand in the way of Justin's dream of a music career by asking him to hide out with her. Nor could she ask Justin to saddle himself with a woman haunted by Randall's legacy.

"Justin has a lot to give," Hallie said, "but I have to warn you. There's a restlessness in him. He won't let himself be truly happy until he puts his demons to rest. How much has he told you about Rebecca?"

Tess narrowed her gaze. What else was there to the story about Rebecca?

"Justin took her death hard." Hallie turned her palm up as she explained. "Very hard. Much harder than the rest of us. We all loved Rebecca and were devastated by her death and how she died. But Justin was crazed with guilt and grief. He was especially close to his sister. They were kind of a team, and she spoiled him. He went to court every day of Mac's trial." Hallie's eyes had a faraway look as she remembered the days that had been so painful for the family, but especially for Justin. "Justin took so much blame on himself and has never forgiven himself for Becca's death. He can't let it go, just like he can't seem to let go of his notion that if he doesn't become a success in Nashville, he'll have let Becca down again."

"But he does have talent. Why shouldn't he try?" Tess argued defensively.

"Brian has talent too, but he also has the sense to know that if he wants to feed his family, he can't chase a dream that in all likelihood will never come true. Thousands of hopefuls go to Nashville and never make it. Justin has pinned all his hopes on a recording contract, setting himself up for heartbreak, and we don't want to see that happen to him. He sets such high goals for himself—"

"His optimism is one of the things I love most about him," Tess said.

"But optimism won't pay the bills. And when he doesn't reach the impossible standards he sets for himself, he believes he's a failure. If he were just more realistic about his goals, maybe he wouldn't see himself in such a dim light. We all see his potential."

"Meaning?"

"Well, before their falling out, his father offered him a share of the family's hardware business if he'd stay in Wellerton. Justin turned him down. Justin has talent in more than just music. He was working toward a degree in architecture when he quit college. And he's a gifted carpenter. He loves people, and he's as great with kids as he is with old folks. His personality draws people to him like a magnet. He has so many options open to him."

"But he loves his music. That's what he wants to do." Tess realized at that moment how much she wanted Justin to succeed too. She wanted him to have his dream, because she knew how important music was to him. His music came from his heart. "If his music makes him happy, why shouldn't he pursue it?"

Hallie leaned back in her chair, silenced by the subtle reproach in Tess's reply. The women exchanged glances that called a peaceable truce, an acceptance of their disagreement on the point. With a nod, Hallie stood. "I'll get the alcohol now."

"Thank you." Tess gave Hallie a smile she hoped mirrored her gratitude.

"Tess, I don't mean to sound so negative. I think the world of Justin. But Brian and I know Justin tends to act impulsively in some situations rather than responding rationally. Maybe that's not the case this time. Maybe his guilt over Rebecca's death didn't factor into his involvement with you. Maybe I've said too much." She frowned as she turned away. "I'm sorry. I have no right to pry in your business and Justin's."

Tess shook her head. "No, I appreciate your honesty. But maybe what Justin needs more than your worry is your faith. The idea that his family doesn't support him in his dreams, isn't proud of his willingness to try, can't believe in his judgment and trust him to do what he feels is right, hurts him more than you can imagine. It's in his eyes whenever he talks about his family or his music. He loves both and feels like he was forced to choose one over the other."

Hallie stared at Tess as if she couldn't believe what she heard. With a bewildered, deeply thoughtful look on her face, she turned her gaze toward the living room where Justin and Brian still argued, though in calmer voices now. "Is that how he feels? That we've forced him to choose? I never knew that. We never meant . . ." She tucked a short wisp of hair behind her ear as she snapped herself out of her daze and faced Tess. "I'll see to it he knows otherwise before he leaves here." She gave Tess a quick smile before disappearing down the hall.

Tess took advantage of Hallie's absence to look around the kitchen, sweeping her gaze from the refrigerator covered with family photographs to the white tile counter neatly arranged with baskets and appliances. The sunny yellow walls and floral wallpaper border lent the room an airy cheerfulness. The personal touches, like the cross-stitched picture of two white doves that declared Brian and Hallie's wedding date under the words "United in Love," gave the room warmth and spoke of the love Tess could feel within the walls of their home like a living presence.

Squinting, she examined the photos on the refrigerator more closely. She spotted a picture of Rebecca, mugging for the camera in her swimsuit with a sultry pose. Justin's sister had been a beautiful young woman.

Next she focused on a picture of Justin, wearing his black Stetson and grinning broadly while his arm curled around the shoulders of a dark-haired woman she assumed was Amy. Jealousy plucked at her before she thought of the affection she saw reflected in Justin's eyes whenever he looked her way.

Besides, she had no right to feel any possessiveness toward Justin. Not when she knew she had to let him go his way, eventually.

"What!" she heard Brian shout.

Turning from the photos, she focused on the conversation from the next room.

"Every officer of the law in Texas has heard of Randall Sinclair! He's dirtier than mud and twice as slick! The state attorney's office has been trying to find something they can make stick to him for years. Word is he's involved with organized crime. And you're sleeping with his wife? Have you lost your mind?"

"Would you keep your voice down?" Justin warned. "And she's *not* his wife!"

"Justin, do you have any idea what you've gotten yourself into? Do you realize Tess could have the information needed to put this man behind bars?" A thread of excitement tinged Brian's tone.

Icy dread trickled through Tess when she realized where their conversation was headed. Involving herself in criminal proceedings against Randall terrified her. Helping the authorities convict Randall would be suicide. All she wanted was a new life, her freedom, a chance to be happy again. But would she ever be happy without Justin in her life?

Somewhere in her mind, something clicked. All the seeds of hope Justin had planted twined their roots around her heart. Her need to escape Randall's injustice and malignancy had started her on this treacherous journey, and only faithfulness to her conscience could bring her the resolution she craved. The future she wanted included Justin. But before she could even think of spending her life with Justin, she had to do whatever it took to truly free herself of Randall. Not just the physical danger, but his emotional tyranny, as well. She would never have peace of mind if she didn't seek justice for Angela's death. She could never live with herself if she condoned Randall's evil with her silence.

Justin believed she had a core of goodness and strength within her. Somehow, she had to find that strength and courage to fight Randall. Could she find the woman inside her that Justin saw, a woman with merit, self-respect and dignity?

The promise of Justin's love and support gave her all the reason she needed to search her soul and choose her course of action.

The Tess whom Randall had demeaned and abused would give up. But the Tess whom Justin had nourished and cherished had to fight for her freedom and claim the right to hold her head high.

"If you could convince her to testify for the grand jury," Brian said in the next room.

"Haven't you been listening to me?" Justin's voice rose almost an octave, due to his frustration. "The man tried to kill us! Last time I checked that was reason enough to put him behind bars!"

"You have to call the police, Justin."

"Tess thinks Sinclair's got people on his payroll in the police department. She's scared stiff, and I don't blame her. The man's unstable, unreasonable. What we need first is a place for her to hide."

"So you came here? Justin, he's already sent men to Mama and Dad's! You think they won't be here next?"

Tess shivered at the possibility.

"Maybe so. I don't know." Justin spoke more quietly now, and Tess had to strain to hear. "If so, tell them you haven't seen us. We'll leave tonight if you want, but we need money. And wheels. Randall's crazy, and he's not going to give up looking for her. You saw the bruises on her neck, didn't you? He tried to choke her to death. Now tell me, how am I supposed to walk away from that? Even if I wasn't involved with her, how could I, in good conscience, turn my back, knowing she was in danger? I have to protect her, and not just because of Becca."

A long silence followed before Brian said, "All right, you've made your point. The first thing we should do is get rid of that Jag. It's a big red flag. I'll handle that. You're in no shape to run around scuttling cars. I can loan you some money, but you're going to have to figure out how to make ends meet when that money runs out. How are you going to survive? How long will it take to find her a safe cover?"

"I don't know."

"For God's sake, Justin. For once, you've got to think things through. How long are you going to hide out? What happens if Sinclair finds you?"

"I was hoping you could help us get a restraining order. It's not much, but it's a start."

"Here we are," Hallie said, returning with a bottle of alcohol and a few other first-aid items. "I'll have you fixed up in a jiffy."

She sat down and unscrewed the top from the rubbing alcohol. "Tess? What's wrong? You look ready to pass out."

"I can't believe the nightmare my life is. I hate myself for getting Justin involved. And now you." Tess put her head down on the table, burying her face in the crook of one arm while Hallie doctored the other.

"When I finish this, why don't you lie down in the guest room. You look like you could use a little rest."

"Thanks, I think I will." Tess sighed. She *was* tired. She was also scared and penniless and confused. But Justin had given her back the thread of hope she needed to fuel her will to fight. She wouldn't go quietly into obscurity and lose Justin. She would fight for the chance to stay with him.

Justin's music woke Tess from her nap in the guest bedroom. A check of the digital clock by the bed told her she'd slept for more than two hours. Her shoulder throbbed and felt stiff, and she decided to ask Hallie for some aspirin.

She found her hostess in the living room, where Justin and Brian were singing and playing guitars. Tess's heart sank, remembering the way Randall had smashed Justin's guitar in his fit of rage. She dreaded telling him what had happened to the gift Rebecca had given him.

For a moment she listened to Brian and Justin sing together about howling at the moon on a small town Saturday night. Hallie was right. Brian had talent too.

She smiled, watching the brothers who showed no sign of their earlier animosity. When Hallie noticed her standing in the doorway, she patted the sofa next to her. Tess moved to the couch and sat down.

Justin and Brian laughed when Brian missed a chord and mixed up the lyrics.

"So I haven't played in a while. So what? Let's see you get a continuance from Judge Matthews," Brian teased.

"Let's see you keep up on this one," Justin returned and began playing a song with an even faster rhythm. Hallie winked at her husband who tried to outdo his kid brother.

"Is the whole family musical?" Tess spoke loud enough to be heard over the dueling guitars.

"Even the dog." Hallie grinned when Tess wrinkled her brow in query. "She howls like a wolf when my father-in-law plays his harmonica. Funniest thing I ever saw. But there's no doubt Justin's the best, the one with the most promise."

"What about Rebecca?"

Hallie's smile turned sad. "Becca had an angel's voice and wanted to go to Nashville herself. Then she met Mac and put her plans on the shelf."

"She's the one who encouraged Justin to try his luck in Nashville, right?" Tess met Hallie's melancholy gaze when she turned back to face her, and Hallie nodded.

"Hey there, sleepyhead. How are you feeling?" Justin asked as he finished his song and spotted Tess on the sofa.

"All right, considering."

Justin raised the T-shirt he'd borrowed from his brother and showed Tess the fresh stitches on his midriff. "I've been to a weekend clinic while you slept. They said for me to take it easy so that I didn't bust this set of stitches. I told them I'd like nothing better than a calm couple of weeks to recover." He curved his lips in a half smile. "Wonder what our chances are for that kind of quiet."

"Probably not too good," Brian volunteered. "But your odds of staying lost go up the more you think things through, and don't let a careless error slip you up."

Justin cut an impatient glance to Brian before returning his sights to Tess. "It's time to make some plans."

As he stood, Justin held the guitar he'd been playing out to Brian.

"Keep it." His brother waved him off with a sweep of his hand. "You can't become a country legend without a guitar, now can you? It's just collecting dust around here." When Justin furrowed his brow with an incredulous look, Brian grinned. "Try not to lose this one."

Justin pulled the guitar back and looked down at it. "Thanks, Bri."

Brian chucked him on the shoulder lightly. "If a music career is what you want, what makes you tick, then go for it. Just remember all us little people who helped give you your start, okay?"

Without saying more, Brian took his own guitar toward a back room, leaving Justin staring after him with an expression that told Tess just how much his brother's gift and support meant to him. She glanced at Hallie, who smiled knowingly at Tess before rising from the sofa.

Hallie propped her hands on her hips. "What would y'all say to grilling burgers for dinner?"

"Sounds wonderful," Tess said. "Can I help?"

"I think they want you in on the big strategy powwow. I'll take care of dinner."

After Hallie left, Tess crossed the room to Justin and slid her arms around his waist, careful to avoid disturbing his stitches. Justin set the guitar aside so that he could pull Tess closer. He combed her hair behind her ears with his fingers then gave her a quick kiss. "Brian and I took the Jaguar to a junkyard on the way to the clinic."

Tess nodded.

"Brian's going to lend us some money, so we can rent a car or buy a plane ticket to Mexico or lay low on a cruise to Alaska or whatever you want. Whatever we think would be best. Brian will also talk to some of his lawyer buddies and get a restraining order in place for you."

When she bit her lip, he lay a finger across her mouth and rubbed the edge tenderly.

"And he'll go to the courts with what I've told him about Randall and his attempt on our lives. Brian will get an investigation started. With your testimony, Brian feels sure we can get Randall locked up. Then, when everything is safe, you'll come out of hiding and live happily ever after."

As Tess gazed into Justin's hopeful blue eyes, she tried to muster the same confidence in his plan. But she knew Randall's tenacity, the reach of his power, the infinite possibilities for something to go wrong. She knew the high probability that they would die before Randall finished with them. But for Justin's sake, because of all he and his brother were doing for her, she smiled at him and stood on her tiptoes to kiss him again. "Here's hoping."

Brian came back and rubbed his hands together. "Shall we get busy?"

Justin and Tess sat on the sofa. With Brian, they discussed all the options and stumbling blocks ahead of them. Over the next hour, the trio assembled a plan.

In the morning, they'd rent a car in Brian's name and drive north. Once well out of town, they'd switch cars and head to Dallas to catch a plane. From there, they'd fly to Maine, where Brian had a time-share cabin by a lake. Later, they'd move to more permanent lodging, using aliases. Once settled, they'd be in touch with Brian, and he'd let them know when it was safe to come out of hiding. When they needed more money, they'd drive to Connecticut or another location a few hours away from their new home, and Brian would wire the cash to them.

"All this is with the understanding that you name your

firstborn after me and I receive ten percent of all sales of your first record," Brian added as he folded up the map they'd been consulting.

"We'd better accept," Justin told Tess with a grin. "This is the same guy who used to extort my allowance from me in exchange for his silence about the trouble I got into as a kid. He charged me a dollar a day when I was kept for detention in seventh grade, and he came to pick me up after school because I missed the bus."

"He's lying, of course." Brian turned to Tess matter-of-factly. "I never took money from him."

Justin laughed. "Bull! You couldn't have taken Sandy Booth to your junior prom if you hadn't lined your pockets with all my money."

Brian's smug grin reminded Tess of the one that often graced Justin's lips. "Well then, maybe you should have stayed out of trouble."

"Why did you get detention?" she asked.

"I was caught cutting class."

"So that you could . . ." Brian prompted, and Justin scowled at him.

"Never mind why!"

"He was out behind the lunchroom with this girl—"

"Brian!" The tips of Justin's ears grew bright pink.

"—necking," Brian finished.

Tess raised an eyebrow as she regarded Justin with a teasing frown of jealousy.

"I'll see if I can help Hallie in the kitchen." Justin's face flushed fully as he stood and exited the living room.

"I have all kinds of stories about ole Justin, Tess." Brain sat back in his chair and laced his fingers behind his head with a cocky grin.

Tess smiled. "I'm all ears."

★ ★ ★ ★ ★

"So what kind of stories did my brother entertain you with?" Justin asked later that night as he eased gingerly into the double bed beside Tess.

"Sorry, but he paid me a dollar to keep my mouth shut. If you want to know, it'll cost you two dollars." Tess rolled to face him and grinned.

Justin patted his hips as if feeling for a wallet. "Damn. I left my money in my other pants." He tipped his head to peer at her. "What if I showed you some of the things I was showing Susie Smith behind the lunchroom?"

He wiggled his eyebrows, and she laughed. When he tried to sit up and turn toward Tess, the tug of his fresh stitches made him wince and fall back on the bed.

Tess scooted closer and hovered over him in concern. "Justin, are you all right?"

"Yeah, I'm fine. I just don't have the same freedom of movement until these stitches come out." He smiled up at her and drew a crooked finger along the line of her jaw. "How's your shoulder?"

"A little sore, a little stiff, but a small price to be alive and here with you."

She smoothed a warm hand over his chest, and Justin's whole body responded with a heightened awareness of every nerve ending.

He caught a lock of her hair and rubbed it between his fingers, kissed it, then moved his hand deeper into the thick tresses. Dipping her head, she pressed her lips to his in a tentative kiss that set a fire in Justin's belly. He slid his fingers around her nape and pulled her closer, opening his mouth against hers and drawing on her lips with a gentle suction.

Tess's soft, satisfied sigh sounded sweeter to him than any song he'd ever heard. When she pressed against him, he felt her nipples crest through the thin fabric of the nightgown Hallie had given her. His own body hardened in response, and he fought to keep the pace slow and easy.

Haste might frighten Tess. Haste might rip his stitches again. Haste would make it all over too soon. Being with Tess, holding her, making love to her was something Justin wanted to savor.

His limited movement proved less of an encumbrance than he would have expected, especially since Tess seemed eager to learn, to accommodate and to please him. She stroked and kissed him, hovered over him when he coaxed her into a position where he could suckle her breasts. When he rolled on his side and drew her to him, she cuddled close. He entered her from the back, cupping her breasts and nibbling her nape as he gently thrust and withdrew. Heat built in him, burning hotter and brighter until it exploded with a fiery force that shook him with its exquisite power. Tess moaned softly, and her body convulsed around him, prolonging his bliss.

When her body wilted in the aftermath, he held her nestled against him, their bodies still joined, his arms protectively around her. Holding her felt right. Making love to her was like a homecoming. How could he give her up and not go insane?

If he could know he'd made a difference, if he could feel certain he'd made up for his past mistakes, could he dare to believe in himself enough to promise Tess forever? More than anything he wanted to try his hand at a lifetime commitment. But she deserved more than an attempt. He had to have confidence in his staying power. He had to prove to himself he could take care of her before he would promise her the commitment she deserved. Until then, he'd give her all he had and savor the soft crush of her body next to his.

He slept in contentment until the early morning hours, when he received a rude awakening.

Two men flashing badges burst into the bedroom, past Brian who shouted about warrants and rules of conduct.

Tess screamed when the men hauled him from the bed and slammed him against the wall. Pain shot through his shoulder. Over Tess's cries and Brian's shouts, the man pinning him to the wall growled, "Justin Boyd, you're under arrest for kidnapping, car theft, assault with a deadly weapon, and breaking and entering. You have the right to remain silent . . ."

Chapter Twenty

Clutching the sheet over her bare breasts, Tess watched in horror as the policeman jerked Justin's hands behind his back and handcuffed him. When the other cop turned to her, she snatched her nightgown from the tangle of covers and tugged it over her head.

"Tess Sinclair?" the man said.

She stared mutely, too stunned and frightened to speak.

"You'll have to come with us too. You're wanted for questioning as a material witness."

Justin grumbled to the man holding his arm, "Can't I get some pants on?"

Brian picked up Justin's jeans and briefs from the floor and helped his handcuffed brother dress. "I'll be down to the station as soon as I can. Don't answer any questions until I get there." Brian raised a concerned but authoritative gaze to Justin then turned to Tess. "Same for you. Don't say a word until I get down there to straighten this mess out."

The man nearest the bed grabbed Tess's arm. He hauled her off the mattress, ordering gruffly, "Let's go, lady."

Justin studied the two men who'd burst into the room, and his jaw tightened. His eyes darkening, he turned a haunted expression to Brian. "I love you, Bri."

Brian was clearly as startled by Justin's words as he was touched. But before he could do more than give Justin a puzzled look, the men shoved Justin through the door. The men escorted them hurriedly out to a waiting car.

The dark sedan seemed vaguely familiar to Tess. She saw no emblem indicating the law enforcement division these men were from, and a niggling doubt and a tremor of worry formed in the back of her mind and tensed her gut. When the men pushed Justin into the backseat beside her, she met his gaze and read the same doubt in his eyes, and her pulse skittered.

Justin drew a deep breath and gave her a weak smile. "Brian will straighten everything out. We'll be fine."

Tess thought she heard doubt in his voice, as if he were trying as much to convince himself as her. For Justin's efforts to comfort her, she gave him the best smile she could and felt her cheek twitch nervously. As the car pulled away from the house, she inched closer to him, telling herself that as long as they were together, they would be fine.

An hour later, when they still had not reached the police station, Tess could no longer convince herself they'd be fine . . . together or not.

I love you, Bri.

Brian heard the words, the strange quality in Justin's voice, replaying in his head as he drove to the police station. "I love you" wasn't something men typically told their brothers out loud. It bothered Brian that Justin had felt the need to tell him now. He couldn't shake the idea the words held some other subtle message. But what?

As he climbed out of his Honda Accord and hurried inside the police station, Brian pushed aside that frustrating question and the image of Justin's haunted eyes. Clearly Justin was spooked, but why wouldn't he be? Having a man shoot at you, having two cops bust through your bedroom door while you slept, and being arrested were enough to spook anybody.

"I'm the attorney for Justin Boyd and Tess Sinclair, who were brought in just a little while ago," he told the officer at the front desk.

The man sat up and typed the names into his computer. "How do you spell that last name?"

"Boyd. B-O-Y-D." Brian shoved his hand in his pocket and jangled his keys. Ordinarily, he could be calm, assured, professional, even standing in front of Judge Matthews, whose reputation struck fear in lesser men. But tonight his heart beat erratically, and his hand fidgeted in his pocket. Tonight he was going to battle for Justin, and his brother's problems had him a little spooked too.

"No Boyd or Sinclair has been brought in here."

Brian cocked his head as if he hadn't heard right. "Pardon?"

"No Boyd or Sinclair has been brought in here." The officer glanced up at Brian blankly.

"Well, maybe they haven't made it down here yet. They just left my house a couple of minutes ago. Seems hard to believe I beat them here, but—"

"You can have a seat over there." The officer pointed to a short row of folding chairs. "I'll let you know when they get in."

Brian's gut twisted. *I love you, Bri.*

He took a seat on one of the cold aluminum chairs, and his mind replayed the whole incident from the moment he'd answered the door. The men had quickly flashed badges at him as they pushed inside. The brash entry of the cops into his house had clued him something was wrong. The police wouldn't have barged in unless they had reason to think their suspect or key evidence was about to disappear. Drugs flushed down the commode, convicts escaping through the back door, that kind of thing.

No such reason existed in this case.

And though he'd asked to see a warrant for Justin's arrest, one had never been produced. He'd been so distracted by the sight of his brother in handcuffs, the terror on Tess's face, and the disturbing way Justin said "I love you, Bri," he'd let the warrant issue drop.

Brian's heart thundered now, and he raked his fingers through his hair. After stewing for another minute, he stalked back to the front desk. "Are they here yet?"

The desk clerk shook his head.

"Damn," Brian muttered as a frightening reality dawned on him. Justin had known it. That's why he'd said he loved his brother. Justin didn't expect to see him again.

The men that took Justin and Tess away weren't policemen. They worked for Randall Sinclair.

The dark sedan pulled to a stop outside a warehouse in a downtown section of a city Tess didn't recognize. She didn't think they were still in Austin, considering the length of time they'd been driving.

The driver waited for a large sliding door to be opened then cruised slowly into a dim, cavernous warehouse. Apprehension rose like a fist from her stomach to her throat, strangling her.

Glancing at Justin, she met his eyes briefly, before he turned his head to survey the surroundings. She watched Justin's expression for some glimmer of hope, some indication that he had an escape plan in mind. Instead, his face reflected grave worry. His uneasiness unsettled her even more.

Suddenly, Justin's expression hardened. He straightened his back as his eyes narrowed on something outside the sedan. She turned her gaze in the same direction and met a dark, evil pair of eyes. She gasped involuntarily, her reaction rooted in the instinctive fear Randall always stirred in her.

The driver, his hand wrapped in a bandage, stepped out of the car and yanked open the back door. The second man who'd brought them like lambs to the slaughter leaned down and barked at Justin, "Out!"

When Justin ducked his head to climb out of the car, the driver sent the edge of his hand crashing down on the base of Justin's skull. Tess whimpered as he slumped forward and fell out of the car, barely conscious.

"That's for the whack you gave me at the fast food joint a couple weeks ago," the man grumbled, poking Justin with his foot.

Tess seethed at the unfair and brutal treatment but only had time to gape for a second in horror before the same man reached inside and seized her arm. She stumbled as she was dragged out of the car. Coming to her feet, she found herself staring into Randall's hard chest. Her gaze rose slowly to meet the unflinching, unforgiving eyes that glinted back at her.

"Tess, Tess, Tess," Randall clucked, as if speaking to an errant child. "What must I do to teach you once and for all that I won't tolerate your betrayal?"

She heard Justin groan in pain, and with a quick sidelong glance, she saw two men hoist him under the arms. They led him, stumbling, to one of two chairs set in front of the car, il-luminated by the headlights. The injustice of Justin's death at Randall's hands clawed at her conscience. That afternoon she'd sworn to fight Randall for Justin's sake, and the sight of her cowboy crumpled in agony fired that resolve. Tensing, she raised her eyes to Randall's.

"Go to hell!" she snarled.

Surprise, then rage, flashed in Randall's eyes, and he

raised his hand. Tess steeled herself for the stinging blow that was sure to come but swore to herself not to flinch. Leveling a hard gaze on Randall, she met his dark eyes head on, her chin high. Randall's hand stayed suspended in midair, poised, ready to strike. She didn't move.

Her passive submission to Randall's brutality and blind acceptance of his wrongdoing had fed his control over her and handed him power, carte blanche.

Don't let him win. Take back the control.

His gaze narrowed on her, shifting slightly as if seeing something intriguing for the first time. She stared back, her body stiff and unyielding, though her stomach swirled with trepidation. The certainty that she would die soon lodged a rock of terror in her chest. But she wouldn't go quietly.

Randall's mouth curled in a humorless smile. "I see you've finally acquired a little backbone. I'm impressed." He used the hand he'd raised to grab her chin, and his fingers dug into her skin. Putting his nose close to her face, he whispered, "Perhaps I will go to hell, but you'll get there before me."

Randall turned to Henry, who stood beside him. "Let's get on with this."

Henry wrapped beefy fingers around her upper arm and led her to the chair beside Justin, who blinked as he shook off the blow to his head. The short, stocky man who'd driven them to the warehouse pulled Tess's hands behind the chair and bound them with duct tape at her wrists.

The second man who'd taken them from Brian's house was taller and dark-haired. He walked behind Justin with another roll of tape. Tearing off a piece, he covered Justin's mouth and leaned into Justin's ear to growl, "Try anything stupid, and you're a dead man." He then tore off a second, longer strip of tape to wrap around Justin's wrists. Taping

Justin's hands seemed like overkill to Tess, considering he was still handcuffed. That oddity set off warning bells in her mind.

"Take care of them, and dispose of the bodies," Randall said. "I want nothing to connect me to their deaths."

She directed a defiant, hateful glare at Randall.

Randall barely glanced at her. "And, Morelli," he told the tall, dark man, "I want them to suffer."

Tess swallowed a whimper. Despite the bitter taste of panic and dread in her throat, she refused to let Randall see her fear. With a boldness that belied the chaos in her soul, she leveled a grim stare at Randall.

He met the challenge in her eyes with a sneer. Then, turning, Randall walked toward the car that had brought her to the warehouse. She noticed he limped and had extensive wrappings around the foot Justin had shot.

Randall opened the passenger-side door as Henry slid behind the steering wheel. Pausing, Randall touched his fingers to his brow in a mock salute. "Good-bye, darling."

Tess watched Randall climb into the car and close the door without so much as a flicker of remorse. The car backed out, and the man Randall called Morelli closed the large sliding door. The stockier henchman then turned to his prey and drew a revolver from under his jacket.

Chapter Twenty-One

Justin's mind raced. Why would Randall's henchman say something as absurd as "Try anything stupid, and you're a dead man" when it was clear he and Tess were going to end up dead regardless?

Why would that same man then unlock Justin's handcuffs while making a show of taping his wrists together? And why had the man wrapped the tape loose enough for Justin to wiggle his wrists free whenever he wanted? Although it would cost him some arm hair and a bit of pain, freeing his hands was definitely a possibility.

Caution kept Justin from taking advantage of the loose tape until he knew what they faced. He wanted to figure out what motivated the dark-haired henchman's peculiar actions.

The tall henchman, Morelli, turned to his cohort with the bandaged hand. "Dominic, go check outside. Make sure there's no unwanted witness who can hear anything and come snooping around."

With a quick nod, Dominic left to follow the order, leaving Tess and Justin alone with his accomplice.

Morelli turned to Tess. "We meet at last, Mrs. Sinclair. I'm honored to know someone with the grit and brains to have outwitted your husband . . . twice. If you cooperate and do exactly as I say, you may yet live to tell the tale to your grandchildren."

Justin fixed a hard, suspicious gaze on the man.

"What are you talking about?" Tess asked warily.

"I'm talking about the opportunity I'm giving you to get out of here tonight with your skin intact. You see, you're more valuable to my mission if you're alive. But the choice is yours." Morelli walked over to Justin and aimed a snub-nosed gun at his temple.

Tess gasped. "What do you want from me?"

"I want your help in destroying your husband."

"How?"

"Just make a simple promise. An oath that when the time is right, you will cooperate with me in bringing your husband down, however I see fit. That's it. But if you break that promise, I'll hunt you down and kill you myself. Of course, if you don't agree to my terms, you both meet your maker tonight." Morelli glanced toward the back door, where Dominic had disappeared, then continued. "Which will it be? We ain't got long."

"What are your terms?" Tess's voice trembled, and her eyes widened with hope.

Justin listened carefully, processing and analyzing the turn of events.

"After tonight, as far as the world outside these walls is concerned, you and lover boy here are dead. Your husband has to believe that I followed his instructions to the letter. No one except you, me, and your boyfriend will know our little secret. Ever. You are to disappear, never to be heard from again. At least, not until I'm ready to use you in my plan."

"I don't understand. Why would you do this?" Tess eyed the man cautiously.

"Let's just say I don't want to burn any bridges before I know if I may need them again. I think you have information that will prove valuable to me. This way, your husband thinks

I did what he asked, and I can keep his trust long enough to destroy him."

"Why do you want to destroy Randall?" Tess tipped her head, her expression bewildered.

"Because he hurt someone I care about. The bastard made an enemy when he touched my wife, and for that, he will pay. Now . . . do you want to live or do you want to talk about it until Dominic gets back and the choice is taken from you? Dom plans to turn you into fish food, so I'm your only hope. Do we have a deal?"

"Yes," Tess agreed quickly. She looked at Justin with wide, expectant eyes.

"That means you too, hotshot," Morelli said. "No one knows you're alive, ever. No one. Especially not family. That's the only way I'll agree to this." He pressed the gun harder against Justin's temple. "Hurry up, before my finger gets itchy."

Justin thought briefly of the pain his parents, Brian, and Hallie would be put through, believing he was dead. He thought of the music career he could never pursue. He thought about the dream he and Rebecca had shared, the dream that would die tonight in order to save his life and Tess's. Pain, like a million tiny shards of his breaking heart, filled his chest as he nodded his agreement.

What choice did he really have? Though he still saw himself as the wrong man for Tess, Randall's thug had forced his hand.

Morelli lowered the gun and stuffed it into the waistband of Justin's jeans. He ripped the tape from Tess's wrists, and she yelped in pain.

"Take this phone, and keep it on. When I'm ready to reach you, I'll call you and give you your orders." He handed Tess a small cell phone then braced his arms on the chair and leaned close. She shrank back with a gasp. "If I can't reach you, for whatever reason," he snarled, "I'll hunt you down and make you sorry you ever crossed me. I swear, Tess, if it is the last thing I do, I will find you. Got it?"

Her throat convulsed as she swallowed and nodded.

"You're on your own to take care of Dominic. As for my part, you're free to go. Now, Mrs. Sinclair, give me your wedding ring."

When Tess cast the man a questioning glance, he scowled impatiently. "Your husband wants proof that you're dead. Would you rather I send back your whole hand?"

Quickly, Tess fumbled to remove the diamond band on her finger then held it out to him.

"On the way to see your husband, I'll pay a visit to a friend of mine who works in the city morgue. I'll pick up a hand and your hubby's none the wiser. Unless there's no wedding ring on the hand. You follow?"

Tess gulped then nodded.

Morelli shoved the ring in his pocket. "Now remember, if I find out you've blown your cover or if I can't get you on that phone, I'll come after you. And Tony Morelli can find anyone."

He walked back to the sliding door and cracked it open. "So get outta here."

Justin needed no further invitation. He watched Morelli leave then wrenched his wrists free from the tape, gritting his teeth against the needles of pain. After ripping the tape off his mouth, he pulled Tess to her feet. "Let's go."

Retrieving the small gun from the waist of his jeans, he tugged Tess toward the back door of the warehouse. "Now I know Rebecca is with us," he murmured to Tess as they hurried to the door. "We just got handed a miracle."

No sooner had he said those words than the doorknob he

reached for rattled, and the door creaked as it opened. Yanking Tess behind the door with him, Justin pressed himself against the wall. Peering through the crack between the door and wall, he watched as the stocky man returned from his scouting expedition.

When the door swung shut, Justin cracked the butt of the gun on the back of the man's head and sent him down on the floor. "Sleep tight."

Without hesitating, he stepped over Dominic's sprawling form and pulled Tess out the door with him into the inky blackness of the late night.

"Now what do we do?" Tess asked, panting, after they'd run for several blocks. She cast an uneasy gaze around the dark alley where they'd stopped to catch their breath. The stench of garbage from a nearby Dumpster mingled with the smell of exhaust and the scent of her own fear. Her stomach pitched as she gulped the foul odors into her lungs along with oxygen.

"We need more clothes for starters." Justin rubbed his hand over his bare chest as if to prove his point.

Tess wrapped her arms around her middle, trying to calm the tremors that shook her body. She had only the thin nightgown Hallie had loaned her, and Justin had only his jeans. Shoes were a priority, as well.

"How do we get more clothes? We have no money. We have nothing, Justin." She sighed miserably at the thought. Shaking her head, she gave him a short, humorless laugh. "How ironic would it be if, after all this, we died of starvation or exposure or—"

"Hey!" Justin said with an edge in his voice. He aimed a finger at Tess, and his expression bore his trademark determination. "We've come this far and survived. I, for one, have no intention of dying on the streets from starvation. We'll survive. Trust me to take care of you, okay?"

A chill slithered down her back. She realized what he'd lost in their bargain with the devil, and she forgave his chastising tone. Because she had no one but Justin, she'd had nothing to lose by playing dead. Justin, on the other hand, had sacrificed everything, everyone he loved. Because of her. Because he'd had no choice. Because of the mess she'd made of his life.

Remorse clutched her chest, squeezing painfully. She didn't want to cry, knowing it would solve nothing. But her emotions had been on such a roller coaster for days, and knowing the pain Justin had to be suffering from his losses made holding her tears at bay impossible. "I'm sorry. I trust you. I'm just so scared."

Justin pulled her into his arms. The warmth of his skin and the security of his arms made a haven where Tess gladly would have spent the rest of her days.

He pressed a kiss to her head. "We can either steal the clothes, or we can try to find some kind of Goodwill place and hope we can get something there."

"I'm not a thief, and don't intend to become one if I can help it." Tipping her head back, she peered up at Justin.

A gentle smile found his lips, and he rewarded her with a soft kiss. "Then let's start looking for a charity where we can score some clothes and maybe a little traveling food. If anyone asks, we were burned out of our house last night and got away with only these clothes. Agreed?"

She nodded. When he started to back away, she tightened her hold on him. "I know how much you gave up for me, and that means everything to me."

Justin's eyes grew sad. "Forget it."

Clutching at the hard muscles of his back, she shook her

head. "I can't forget it, Justin. I know what your family and your music mean to you. I've robbed you of them."

He grasped her chin, and his blue gaze penetrated hers. "This is not your fault. That guy gave me no real choice, now did he?"

Swallowing past the lump in her throat, she formed the question that sliced at her heart. "But if he had given you a choice . . . if he'd given you the option of giving me up while I played dead . . . if you'd had to choose between going into hiding with me and the chance to go to Nashville, to keep your family . . ." Her throat closed, and she couldn't finish the question.

Justin's eyes grew dark with emotion, and he sighed. "Life is funny, huh? Three weeks ago, I'd have sworn nothing could keep me from Nashville and that I'd never do anything that would hurt my family. Suddenly I'm scraping in the streets to survive with a beautiful woman who means more to me than my next heartbeat." He slid a crooked finger along the bridge of her nose. "I could never give you up, Tess. You're far more important to me than Nashville."

She caught her breath, and her heart twisted with a bittersweet tenderness. "I don't deserve you."

He closed his eyes and rested his head against her forehead. "You deserve better than me, but for now it looks like you're stuck with this poor cowboy."

"What about your family?"

Pain crumpled his face, and she bled inside for him, her empathy a gaping wound that filled her with a searing sorrow.

"You're my family now," he said.

When he kissed her, Tess's tears came faster, wetting his cheeks and hers. She returned his kiss, praying that he felt the depth of her love. He'd given her life hope, joy and meaning.

He'd renewed her spirit, giving her the fullness inside her that made it necessary for her to share her soul with him.

Now it was her turn to give something back to him. Her liberation from Randall had cost Justin his dream. Compensating him with her heart, her soul, and her devotion was the sweetest debt she'd ever had to pay.

Justin held Tess's hand as they walked the streets until sunrise. As dawn broke, turning the sky a misty gray and pink, they found an old, regal church where they camped on the front steps, waiting for someone to come and open the doors for the morning service. Waiting gave Justin time to think, to remember.

"I saw Rebecca," he said without preamble as they huddled in silence on the concrete steps.

"What?"

Tess's voice sounded drowsy, confused, and he realized his comment had roused her from a light sleep. She raised her head from his shoulder and blinked groggily at him.

"Last week, after I was stabbed, I saw Rebecca. I almost died. Maybe I did die, and she sent me back. Maybe to help you. Maybe for some other reason. I don't know. But I saw her. I'm sure of that much." Even to his own ears, he sounded tired and rambling. He stared at the cracks in the sidewalk, while the changes in his life tumbled in his mind like clothes in a dryer.

"I believe you."

He turned his face toward Tess, letting her see the dampness that crept to his eyes. "I miss her so much sometimes."

Tess caressed his cheek gently. "I know you do." Her lips curved into a weak semblance of a smile. "And I miss Angie, but I know she's in a better place. Knowing that helps me. She's not hurting or afraid now."

Justin closed his eyes with a sigh. "If only I'd insisted that she—"

"Stop it, Justin." Tess touched his lips with her fingertips. "Enough is enough. Hindsight is always clearer, but there's nothing you can do to change the past. And you can't keep punishing yourself for what happened to her."

He tried to turn away, but she caught his chin and held his face toward hers, not letting him avoid her gaze. "Mac killed Becca. Not you. You did your best to make her leave him, but the decision to stay was hers. It's not your fault she died."

Her admonition made sense, logically, but he'd heard and rejected the same sentiments before. From counselors, from his family, from his own mouth when he tried to justify his lack of action. Logic didn't heal his broken heart or ease the burden of his guilt.

But Tess's eyes shimmered with tears, affection, and pleading that echoed in the black vortex that had swirled inside him since Becca's death.

And he listened. He let the wisdom of the words seep in for the first time.

She wet her lips before she continued. "I know that when you met me, you saw a chance to make amends for what happened to your sister."

He started to deny her claim, but her hazel eyes stripped away his pretenses, leaving his soul naked and exposed. Her fingers traced the lines of his face as she spoke, hypnotizing him with her caress, her soothing voice. "But I can't absolve you of your guilt, Justin. Only you can do that. You have to forgive yourself. No one blames you but you. Don't let your guilt mar your memories of her anymore. It's not what she would have wanted. I know it's not."

His throat ached as he struggled to suppress the grief that wanted to swallow him. He mourned not just for Becca but for a lost dream that had started when she placed a guitar in his hands and told him to go the distance. In his quest to right the wrong he'd done her, he'd dropped the baton and lost the race. "I wanted to succeed with my music for her. I wanted to make her proud. But I failed again."

"Oh, Justin," Tess whispered, capturing his face between her palms. "How could she not be proud of who you are? You have a beautiful, loving spirit, a rare compassion and humanity. You're not a failure. You're a treasure, Justin, and even if Nashville never knows it, Rebecca did. And I do."

"Then why do I keep letting people down? I try to help, try to make a difference, but it seems like I always come up short."

"You haven't let me down. And I don't think Rebecca would feel you let her down, either. You kept your promise to her, even though it was the wrong choice. You both made mistakes. But mistakes don't make you a failure. They make you human."

Tess's reassurances tangled around his heart, weaving through the fabric of his memories, his hopes and his guilt, unraveling the threads that had bound him. Yet some fiber of misgiving held fast.

Covering her hand with his own, he pressed her soft palm to his cheek. "I hear what you're saying. I appreciate what you're trying to do, but writing off my mistakes as being human isn't enough for me. There's still a void inside me. I have this restless yearning in me that—"

"I know. You absolutely hum with restless energy." She smiled, and her eyes glowed as she gazed back at him. "You're like a hot air balloon with a fire inside that makes you strain against the ropes, waiting to break free and soar into the blue."

"Are you saying I'm full of hot air?" He managed a half smile.

"Well—"

"Don't answer that."

The humor left her expression. "But your guilt is a sandbag, Justin. It's holding you back. You're clinging to a weight that limits your freedom to fly. You've spent enough time and energy punishing yourself. It's time to let go, to rechannel that wonderful fire inside toward something more positive, more productive."

He lifted his chin and narrowed his gaze on her. A strange tingling prickled the back of his neck. "Like what?"

"Like . . . I don't know. Only you can decide that. Whatever it is, I bet it's the thing that will fill that void for you. When all is said and done, when people look at your life, what do you want them to see? What do you want them to say?"

She'd given him a lot to think about, and he knew he would spend hours mulling over what she'd said. But as the sun rose higher and spread its golden fingers over her face, he focused on only one thing. Tess.

He flashed her a lazy smile. "I know one thing they'll say about me when I'm gone."

"Oh?" She hesitated, eyeing his grin curiously. "What's that?"

"That I was the luckiest damn man in the world to find you."

She ducked her head to stare at her toes. "I don't know about that. I've been nothing but a burden so far."

"Tess," he said sternly, and she looked up. "I'll make a deal with you."

She groaned. "What?"

"I'll *rechannel that wonderful fire toward something more positive*—" he wiggled two fingers of each hand as if drawing quotation marks, and she gave him a lopsided grin "—if you'll promise to work on rebuilding your self-esteem."

Her expression shifted abruptly to one of incredulity and incomprehension, but he didn't have a chance to pursue his meaning.

An elderly man arrived at the foot of the steps to the church. "Can I help you folks?"

Tess turned her attention to the gray-haired man. "We . . . we were burned out of our house last night." The lie bothered her, but wasn't a lie better than stealing? "We need clothes and something to eat. Is there an emergency shelter around here or some kind of Goodwill center?"

"Well, let's see." The man rubbed his chin. "Yes and no. There's a place a couple blocks from here, but they're closed on Sunday. I think we might have something to tide you over until Monday. The youth group has been collecting things for a rummage sale, and there's always coffee, juice and doughnuts for the Sunday school classes. You can help yourself to whatever you can use."

Justin took a deep breath. "Thank you, sir. You're a godsend."

An hour later, after they'd scrounged clothes and a backpack full of other items from the rummage sale collection, Justin and Tess flagged down an eighteen-wheeler along the interstate, hitching a ride out of town. Justin grabbed Tess's arm as she started to climb into the cab.

"You sit by the door," he murmured in her ear.

"Why?"

Justin shifted his gaze to the man behind the steering wheel. "I'm sure he'd love to have you squished up against him, but I'd prefer you weren't."

A tiny grin tugged the corner of her mouth as Justin

climbed into the truck and shook the trucker's hand. She struggled up to the ripped seat and closed the door. The stale odor of cigarettes filled the truck, and country music twanged over the radio.

"Where ya goin'?" the trucker asked.

Justin gazed out the windshield at the highway. "Anywhere."

Randall sat behind his antique desk and stared at the human body parts that Morelli had brought him in plastic bags. He would have been convinced that Morelli had finished off Tess and her lover if Dominic La Bosa hadn't reported back that morning that he'd been ambushed and knocked out. Dominic recounted that when he woke up, Tess, Boyd, and Morelli were all gone.

Randall played it close to the chest, revealing nothing in his expression or his tone. He gauged Morelli's behavior, his responses.

And decided the man was a traitor.

Gritting his teeth, he hid his anger. "Well done."

Morelli grinned. "The little woman put up a fight, but she won't be giving you no more trouble."

Randall scoffed. "That's all. You can go."

The hit man frowned. "What about my payment?"

"You'll get what's coming to you. Don't worry."

Morelli scowled as he backed away from the desk then turned on his heel and marched out of the office.

Randall weighed his options before dialing his phone. "Henry, I think we need to pay Maria Morelli a visit. Get the car. And bring your gun."

Chapter Twenty-Two

Brian lowered the evening newspaper, a tidal wave of nausea washing over him.

"Honey, what is it?" Hallie asked, glancing up from the needlepoint in her lap.

"They're dead." He stared in stunned silence at his wife, who gazed back at him with wide eyes.

"Who's dead?"

Her expression said she knew perfectly well whom he meant. He'd told her about the police station.

He handed her the paper, folded to display the small article that included a head shot of Tess. According to the newspaper, Tess had been found dead in her bedroom, the victim of an apparent suicide following a long bout with depression. A memorial service had been scheduled for the wife of businessman and millionaire Randall Sinclair that afternoon in San Antonio.

"There's nothing about Justin here, Brian. Maybe he's—"

"They were together. You know as well as I do that Tess didn't kill herself. Sinclair or his men killed her. And Justin." Brian dropped his gaze to the floor. "If Justin were alive, he'd have called by now or contacted me somehow." Sighing to suppress the knots of grief choking him, he covered his face with his hands. "Justin knew those men were Sinclair's. He didn't put up a fight when they came for him, because he didn't want anything to happen to us."

"But maybe—"

"I know my brother, Hallie. I know, because I'd have done the same thing. I know because of the way he looked at me, the way his voice sounded when he told me he loved me." Brian's voice cracked, and Hallie rushed over to him and put her arms around his neck.

His gut twisted, and his chest felt as if his heart had been ripped out. He'd lost another sibling to a vicious crime. Even though he'd dedicated his life to putting criminals behind bars, Justin and Becca had both been stolen from him by the savagery of criminals. That irony added sting to the wound in his heart.

After indulging himself in a few minutes of grief, Brian focused his despair on the man responsible for his loss. Randall Sinclair.

Calling the state attorney general, one of his golfing buddies, at his home, Brian told him everything Tess and Justin had confided about Randall Sinclair. Brian laid out his suspicions about Tess and Justin's disappearance, and his friend promised that a full investigation would be launched first thing in the morning. The attorney general said he was as eager to put Sinclair away as Brian was.

But Brian knew better. Randall Sinclair had murdered his baby brother. For Brian, it was personal.

After several hours on the highway, the driver of the eighteen-wheeler finally made a pit stop at a truck stop. Tess climbed out of the truck and headed straight for the women's restroom. The relief of emptying her aching bladder blinded her to the blood at first. When she did see the crimson spotting her panties, her heart lurched. Blood served as a vivid reminder of her bullet wound and Justin's stab wound. She stared, trembling for just a moment, before understanding crept in. Her period. She'd simply gotten her period.

Two days earlier she would have greeted her period with relish. Now, however, the knowledge that she wasn't carrying Justin's child brought a momentary pang of sadness. She sobered quickly, though, admitting that the timing was wrong for a pregnancy. Not while they were on the run.

Still, she had a new problem. She had no tampons. And no money to buy any. She grunted in disgust at the inconvenience. Sighing, she headed out to find Justin. She hated the idea of stealing the tampons from the convenience store and weighed the embarrassment of explaining the situation to the teenage boy behind the counter.

She spotted Justin, pumping gas for a white-haired woman and smiling at her with a disarming charm. When he replaced the gas nozzle, he washed the lady's windshield, and the woman virtually swooned. Tess watched curiously, wondering what he was up to, until he opened the car door for the woman, and she handed him a tip. He flashed her another charming smile and waved good-bye.

Tess crossed the pavement to him and grinned. "So, Casanova, how much did you get?"

"Three whole dollars."

His cocky smile made her laugh.

"I'll take that." She plucked the money from his hand and turned toward the convenience store.

"Get me something to eat," he called to her as she walked away. "I'm starving. I'll go hustle a few more dollars before we have to leave."

She didn't answer him. Her stomach begged for food, too, but tampons were her priority. First things first.

After buying the smallest pack of tampons she could find, she only had enough money left for a pack of cheese crackers. She took her purchases and met Justin by the gas pump.

"What did you get?" He held out his hand for his dinner, and she plopped the crackers in his palm. His eyebrow arched in question. "That's it? I gave you three bucks."

"I bought something else with the rest." She rolled down the top of the small paper bag and started across the parking lot for the ladies' restroom again. She felt his incredulous stare following her.

"What about food?" he called after her.

"Sorry," she tossed over her shoulder without stopping.

The heels of his newly acquired boots thudded on the pavement behind her, and he grabbed her shoulder, halting her escape to the restroom. "Tess, I'm starving. I told you to get us some food!"

Crediting fatigue, hunger and frustration for the sharpness of his tone, she drew a slow breath and lifted her chin. "I said I'm sorry. This was more important than food."

"What did you buy?" His eyes shots sparks, and the volume of his voice drew looks from other customers. A twinge of familiar ill-ease started deep inside her.

"Never mind," she mumbled through clenched teeth.

He pressed his lips tighter. "Tell me what you did with my money, Tess!"

His tone, his phrasing, the angry glint in his eyes were all too familiar. A frisson of panic spiraled through her gut. Then something inside her snapped like a rubber band stretched beyond its limits. She'd risked her life to free herself from the cruelty and control Randall wielded over her, and she'd be damned if she would give up that freedom from male dominance now.

Squaring her shoulders, she met his penetrating gaze with a determined one of her own. "Back off!"

Justin's temper rose along with hers. "What did you buy, Tess?"

She balled her fists and glared at him. "Tampons, you big jerk! I got my period! All right? Satisfied?"

Knowing that with Justin she was safe to express her anger, safe from retribution, she stomped her foot and jabbed his chest with a finger. Yelling at him felt good. So good. Like a cork popped on years of bottled emotions, she savored the release. "Would you like for me to go without tampons?"

Red stained his ears as his pique drained from his expression, replaced with almost comical discomfort. "All right. Easy. I didn't know. Keep your voice down."

Shifting his weight from one foot to another, he glanced nervously at the people who had stopped to stare.

Drilling her finger into his hard pectorals, she furrowed her brow. "I'm as hungry as you are. I know we need food, but how am I supposed—"

He grabbed the finger she poked at him and pulled her up against his body with a firm tug, silencing her argument with a kiss. Stunned by his tactic, she gave him no resistance. When he broke the kiss, she blinked at him, uncertain what to say.

A lopsided grin blossomed on his face. "That's the spirit. Good girl."

"Huh?"

"I acted like an ass, and you let me know it. I'm proud of you." Amusement sparkled in his eyes.

She opened her mouth, but no sound came out.

Smiling broader, he tweaked her nose. "I consider it an honor to keep you in tampons." He paused, and his brow wrinkled with wry humor. "Although I can't believe we're having this discussion in the middle of a parking lot."

Twisting her lips in a droll grin, she curled her hand around the back of his neck. Her fingers wound through the thick waves of his hair. "Frankly, neither can I."

Her heart swelled as she gazed up at the blush of embarrassment staining his cheeks. She wasn't sure she could admire anyone more than she admired Justin at that moment. True chivalry, true heroism, she decided, was when a man scraped up the money to buy a lady in distress a box of tampons.

Kissing her soundly, he sent her off to the restroom with a wink. "Don't be too long, or our trucker friend might leave without us. I'll see about earning us some dinner."

When she returned from the bathroom a second time, she met Justin at the store's front door, and he handed her a sandwich wrapped in cellophane. "Ham and cheese."

Tess rose on her tiptoes and rewarded him with a peck on the lips. "Thank you."

He grinned. "Anytime, gorgeous."

Tony Morelli opened the door to his apartment and strolled inside, carrying a small bunch of daisies he'd bought for Maria. A lingering guilt lived inside him for what she'd suffered through no fault of her own, and he looked for little ways to try to make it up to her. Not that any amount of flowers and promises could make up for the brutality Sinclair's men had inflicted on her. But he did what he could, just the same.

He lived for the day that he could bring Randall Sinclair's empire crashing down around his ears.

"Maria, *caro*," he called, using the Italian endearment she loved. "Where are you?"

Only silence answered his call, and an uneasiness inched up his spine. She made a point of being home to welcome him, and when she greeted him, she did so with volume and verve.

"Maria?" Morelli poked his head into the kitchen and

found a pot of what had probably been spaghetti sauce, charred and smoking on the stove. Snapping off the burner, he turned to head down the hallway toward the bedroom, his apprehension growing.

Had she left him? Had she finally had enough of his erratic hours and secretiveness? Had she connected her kidnapping and mistreatment to his work and blamed him?

"*Caro?* I'm home." As he put distance between himself and the burned pot, he smelled the metallic scent he'd learned through his own grisly profession. Blood. A lot of it. A chill arced through him.

Gasping for a breath, for his lungs were suddenly leaden, he lumbered to the door of the bedroom. "Maria!"

He found her on the bed with her throat slit and a note on her bloodstained stomach. Shock rendered him still for a moment, then grief tore an animalistic cry of despair and rage from his throat. Cradling her limp body in his arms, he wept like a baby for his wife, the only woman he'd ever loved.

Sometime later, he took the note from her stomach and opened it with shaky hands.

"YOU ARE NEXT TRAITOR" was scrawled in red ink.

A hatred so strong he shook from it filled his veins and blazed with a white-hot fury. He no longer wished to bring Sinclair's empire down. Destroying his business was not enough.

He would kill him. A life for a life.

With a contract now on his own head, he had to lay low. He knew Randall Sinclair was too well-protected for Morelli to off him and escape with his own life. First he would hunt down Tess Sinclair and her lover for breaking their bargain, for that was the only way Sinclair could have found out. Their treachery had cost Maria her life. Tess and lover boy were the bait he'd use to trap Sinclair. He'd bring them back, offer them as evidence of his continued allegiance, and worm his way close enough to Sinclair to exact his revenge. Then once Sinclair was dead, he could finish off Tess and her boyfriend. Once and for all.

As Justin watched the scenery flying by the window, he ran his and Tess's future through his mind. The muffled trill from the small backpack puzzled him until he remembered the cell phone from Morelli.

Could Morelli be calling in his favor already? *Hell.*

Tess leaned against him, asleep, and he tried not to wake her as he dug in the pack and pulled out the phone.

"Hello?" he answered hesitantly as the trucker cast him a sidelong glance.

"You stupid sonofabitch! I told you to kill Dominic! Now my Maria is dead, and Sinclair is on to me." Hearing the venomous voice, Justin stiffened.

"So help me, I will find you and—"

Justin jabbed the disconnect button and stared at the phone with his heart thumping.

Damn it! He should have known their luck wouldn't hold. He gritted his teeth. Time to make his own brand of luck. Glancing sideways at the driver, whose attention was fixed on the road, Justin reached behind the seat and stuck the phone under the trucker's bags. Maybe, just maybe, Morelli would chase the eighteen-wheeler *and the phone* across the country, buying him and Tess time to hide.

Justin cleared his throat and enacted the next part of his plan to throw Sinclair's thug off their trail. "I don't suppose you're headed toward Nashville, are you?" he asked the trucker. "I've got a friend there I think we'll stay with for a while."

"Sorry. Minneapolis."

Justin grunted acknowledgment, satisfied he'd planted a feasible, though false, destination for them in the driver's memory should Morelli track down the phone. "Thanks anyway."

Tess slept on, and with a weary sigh, Justin put a hand on her knee. The next stop the trucker made would be where he and Tess got out.

Chapter Twenty-Three

Later that night, the trucker pulled off the interstate at a sparsely populated exit near the Missouri-Arkansas state line. He parked his rig behind a tiny motel that reminded Justin of the Catch-a-Wink motel, where he and Tess had spent a memorable night several days before.

After thanking the driver for his help, Justin and Tess climbed down from the cab and headed toward a small diner across the street. When they slid into a booth, a waitress handed them menus.

Justin gave the woman his most disarming smile. "Mind if we just sit here for a minute and talk? We don't have any money, and we're trying to figure out what to do next."

She nodded. "Go ahead. It's not like there's anybody else gonna need the table at this hour."

As she walked away, Justin rubbed his eyes tiredly. "Okay, here's the deal. The way I see it, the sooner we stop and find work of some kind, the sooner we can afford a place to stay and something to eat." He raised a weary gaze to Tess. "So how does Samson, Arkansas, strike you as a new home?"

She reached for his hand and laced her fingers with his. "My home is wherever you are."

He quirked a small smile. "Then Samson it is. Now, how about we get some rest?"

"Where?"

"When you were a little girl, were you ever a Girl Scout?"

Tess frowned and shook her head. "We didn't have a lot of money, and the Girl Scouts weren't a priority."

"Well, then, I guess tonight will be your first experience camping under the stars." Smiling, he opened the backpack to show her the quilt he'd brought from the church rummage sale items. "We can throw this down on the ground in the woods behind the motel. It's a pretty night. Perfect for camping."

Meeting his eyes, she stroked his cheek. "Ah, Justin, who else would take a situation as bleak as being homeless and call it camping under the stars? You make hunger and poverty sound like a romantic vacation."

"Attitude is everything." He tweaked her nose and slid out of the booth. "Let's go. I'm bushed."

On the way out, she spied the restroom and grabbed his arm. "Hang on. Nature calls."

"Again?" Justin shook his head. "Women."

While Tess availed herself of the facilities, Justin browsed through the postcards in a tiny stand by the checkout counter. He found one that had a picture of a National Historic Monument in Samson. He wanted so much to send Brian a card, to let him know he was all right.

He'd sworn to Morelli not to let anyone know he was alive. But that was before the phone call.

I told you to kill Dominic!

Morelli was probably already looking for them. He rubbed the back of his neck and tried to stay calm. He wouldn't let Tess know. Yet. She deserved some peace of mind.

He glanced at the cards again, and an idea formed in his mind. Digging in his pocket, he found the change left over from the sandwiches he'd bought at the truck stop. He had enough for the postcard but not quite enough for a stamp, too. He looked up to find the waitress watching him with something akin to pity in her eyes.

"Not enough for the stamp." He shrugged and put the card back. "So what's the point?"

"I've got a stamp, if that's all you need." She reached under the front counter and pulled out a large purse. After fishing around for a moment, she pulled out a tiny change purse and, finally, a dirty but functional stamp.

Justin gave her a bright smile of thanks. Slapping the change for the postcard on the counter, he reclaimed the card from the rack.

After sticking the stamp on the blank postcard, he addressed it to Brian in block letters and handed it to the waitress. "Would you mind dropping that in the mail for me?"

"Aren't you going to write anything on it?" she asked, giving Justin a quizzical glance.

"Nope. He'll get the message."

When Tess came back from the bathroom, they crossed the road, hand in hand, and hiked into the woods until they couldn't see the lights of the motel anymore. He took the quilt from the backpack, and they spread it out over a pine needle carpet.

She settled on the makeshift bed. "So I take it you were a Boy Scout?"

He carefully stretched out on his back, favoring the side where his stitches were. "Naw, not me."

"But you've been camping, right?" She rolled on her side and peered through the inky darkness.

Justin stacked his hands under his head. "Brian and I used to camp out plenty when I was a kid. He's nine years older, so by the time I was old enough to camp with him, he was already in high school. He always acted more like a second father than an older brother. He was real serious, all business most of the time. But when we'd camp, he'd act more like my brother, a friend, a kid. I loved it."

"Did Rebecca ever go with you?"

"Are you kidding? She was a girl!"

Tess grunted. "So?"

He laughed. "Eight-year-old boys don't want their sister camping with them. Besides, that was my special time with Bri."

"So when did you and Rebecca get close?"

Justin took a deep breath. "After Brian went off to A&M, and Rebecca started thinking she was going to be the next Loretta Lynn. She gave me my guitar for Christmas the year I was ten, and she began training me to be in her backup band." He chuckled. "We practiced and practiced until Dad got worried that I'd be a wimp, because I didn't play as much baseball as the other kids on the block."

"What are your parents like?" A note of wonder colored her voice, and he remembered that she had lost her parents at a comparatively young age.

"Dad is like Brian. All business, very serious. I think I told you he owns a hardware store?" He tipped his head toward her, and she nodded. "Mom is the buffer in the family, always trying to bridge differences and keep the peace. We didn't fight any more than I'd imagine any family does, but it was always about the same things. Dad wanted me to buckle down and get serious about schoolwork and 'real life.' He thought I had my head in the clouds when I talked about Nashville. By the time Rebecca was sixteen, she was constantly battling Dad over curfews and dating. Typical stuff."

"Mmm." Tess rolled on her back and stared up at the sky through the branches of the trees. "Did you ever work for your dad?"

"Summers in high school and college. Then I worked construction jobs up until the day I headed out for Nashville. That was right after Mac's trial ended. I had nothing left to keep me in town. Except Amy. But she didn't support my ideas about Nashville, and we finally broke up."

The stillness beside him gave away the track of Tess's thoughts. He found her hand and brought her fingers to his lips. "She's history, babe. You are my future." He glanced at her sideways. "You want kids, don't you? I've always seen myself having a large family."

Her breath caught. "Children? Oh, yes. I want your children."

He heard the tears in her voice. "You okay? Did I say something wrong?"

"I've ruined your life, taken away your dreams, and you're talking about having children." She sucked in a deep breath. "You don't have to stay with me if you'd rather not. I'll be okay. I don't want you to feel like you have to—"

"I love you, Tess."

He heard her fight for a breath. "What?"

"You heard me. I love you." He rolled to face her and dragged a finger along her jaw. "I'm not going anywhere. You haven't ruined my life. You gave it meaning. I may have forced my way into your life because of Rebecca, because I thought I had to make amends to her, but I stayed because I fell in love with you. It's senseless to deny it."

"Oh, Justin—"

He put a finger over her lips. "I can't promise I won't ever disappoint you, and God knows you deserve better than I can afford to give you right now. I don't know if I have what it takes to build a life with you. But I have to try. I can't walk away. You mean too much to me not to try."

In the moonlight, he saw tears shimmer in her eyes. "You've already given me more than I dreamed possible. All I need is your love, Justin. Just your love."

Leaning down, he pressed a kiss to her cheek. "Done."

He wiped away a tear that trickled down her cheek. "You okay?"

"I'm fine. I was just thinking how strange it was that I had to die, so to speak, to have the life I've always wanted."

Drawing her into his arms, he cradled her head against his chest. "Funny how facing death makes you take stock of your life, when in reality, we face death every day."

Winding his fingers through her hair, he closed his eyes. In his mind's eye, he saw the face of the last little girl he'd played for at the hospital and the smile she'd worn. His heart hammered at the memory. He remembered what Tess had said to him earlier that morning about refocusing his energy, and the feeling he'd known when he played for the freckle-faced girl at the hospital stirred to life again.

Cheering up the little girl had made him feel good, had given him a sense of purpose and direction. Giving her something of himself had ministered to his own dying spirit.

At the beginning, helping Tess had been a means to assuage his guilt over Becca. The feelings that had blossomed between them had changed his motivation for helping her but hadn't been the most significant change he'd experienced.

Seeing Tess struggle with the emotional scars of her marriage took his involvement to a deeper level. Watching her overcome the inner battles she faced, one step at a time, gave him a gratification and pride that rivaled anything in his past. She'd done the hard work, of course, peeling away the layers of garbage that Randall had imposed on her and uncovering the gem inside. But he didn't discount his contribution to her growth. He knew he'd given her the tools to find herself.

Although she still had discoveries to make, the "tampon incident," as he liked to think of it, proved she'd come a long way. She'd finally begun to discover her self-confidence and shed the cloak of intimidation and doubt. Breaking her emotional chains took more courage than walking out the door on Randall.

The surprise he'd received in witnessing her progress was the satisfaction that now filled his heart. Before, only his music had filled the void left by Becca's death.

Lying there under the stars, he considered for the first time that his healing would come not from living to make amends for the past, but from building a brighter future. He couldn't change things for Rebecca, but he could make a difference for women like Tess. He could use his music to bring joy to people who needed hope in their dark lives, like the dying girl at the hospital.

He tensed, clutching Tess tighter as something inside him shifted, pointing his life in a new direction, showing him his world in a new light.

His music wasn't the goal. It was the means.

His talent was more than a gift to exploit. It was a responsibility and a tool. Reaching people, touching lives, sharing hope was what his soul cried for. His dream hadn't died when they'd gone underground. It had transformed.

"Justin? What is it?"

"That's what I want to be remembered for," he murmured.

"What? Justin, what are you talking about?"

"Rebecca didn't die in vain, Tess. Not if I can tell other women about her and wake them up to the reality of domestic abuse."

She angled her head to peer up at him, and her soft breath caressed his face. "How?"

"However I can. I'm taking your advice, honey. I'm refocusing my energy on what matters. People matter. Hope matters." He ducked his head and brushed her lips. "You matter."

"You know what I think?" She nestled closer, and his body answered with an acute awareness of every inch of contact between them.

"What?" he asked, his voice a little husky.

"I think your decision would have made Rebecca very proud."

Justin and Tess spent the first day of their new life in Arkansas walking from business to business, asking for work and filling out applications. Because they had no references, no Social Security cards, and no address to list, the hope of finding work began to look dim. Justin even knocked on several doors in a small neighborhood near the interstate and offered to mow lawns. He had one taker, a kid who saw Justin's offer as the golden opportunity to get out of the job he hated. The kid paid Justin twenty of the twenty-five dollars he said his parents would pay him. The twenty dollars bought their dinner and another box of tampons for Tess.

After their second night of camping, they wandered out of the woods and into the bright morning sunlight, blinking and stretching the kinks from their backs and legs.

Justin plucked a leaf from Tess's hair and speculated aloud on their best options for follow-up visits on their applications. A man's shouts drew her attention to the sidewalk behind the run-down motel where the truck driver had slept. The thin, balding man yelled at a woman dressed in a housekeeping uniform. From the snippets Tess caught, he'd worked himself into a tizzy about the woman's tardiness and her general lack of responsibility.

At first, Tess watched with almost a morbid fascination, because she empathized with the woman, because the shouts held her nearly paralyzed in remembrance.

"Tess? What's wrong?" When Justin spotted the man and

woman, his body tensed. He started forward, but Tess put a hand on his arm.

"Wait," she whispered, noting the negligent way the woman leaned against the side of the motel and ignored the man's ranting.

"This is the third time this week you've been late." The man's face grew redder as he shouted. "If I wasn't desperate for help, what with the regional manager coming later, I'd fire you on the spot!"

The woman gave her boss a bored look.

"Not only that, three customers complained last night that their rooms were dirty. One even said the sink was full of someone else's hair. You have to be more thorough!"

"You want it done better, then do it yourself!" she snapped then stalked off.

"Crista, come back here! You can't just leave like that! Crista! I won't give you a good reference!"

Justin started toward the road again, but Tess grabbed the back of his shirt. "Justin, wait! This is just what we've been looking for. The man said he was desperate for help. I can clean a motel room, and maybe we could get a room where we can stay thrown in as part of my salary."

Smiling her excitement, she saw Justin raise his gaze to the balding man. His eyes brightened. "Why not?"

She hustled across the parking lot with Justin at her heels. "Excuse me, sir," she called, "but I couldn't help overhearing your discussion with that woman about your need for help."

"I'm sorry. Did we wake you?" He smoothed a hand over his bald spot.

"No, nothing like that. I was hoping you'd consider hiring me to clean for you. I need the work badly, and I'll be thorough and quick and—"

"You're hired." An expression of immense relief crossed

the man's face. He turned to Justin. "How about you? Are you willing to change sheets and vacuum? I'll pay you each two hundred dollars a week."

Justin's eyes widened in surprise at the suggestion that he clean motel rooms, too.

Tess grinned. "How about it, cowboy? A little domestic work never killed a man."

Grimacing, he arched an eyebrow. At the same time, his mind raced. Two hundred a week was slave wages, but if they were paid under the table, so to speak, there'd be no paper trail. "Pay us in cash and throw in a free motel room, and you've got a deal."

The motel manager's eyes widened, then he nodded. "Follow me. You can start right now. My regional manager is coming later today, and I need the place to be in top form. Oh yeah, my name's Jim Beam, and no, I'm not kidding. My mother didn't drink, so she didn't know what she'd done to me until it was too late."

The man expelled a frazzled sigh, and Tess glanced at Justin, who was working to hide an amused grin. "And you two are?"

"Jus—"

"David," Tess interrupted, before Justin could finish. Both Justin and Jim Beam looked at her with curious expressions. She cleared her throat and squared her shoulders. "David and Mary . . . Camper." She held out a hand to Jim, and he shook it.

Justin muffled a chuckle, and she elbowed him. Fortunately, she poked him in his good side, since she realized her mistake too late to recover the jab.

Jim shook Justin's hand, too, then turned to lead them to the office.

"Camper?" Justin asked under his breath.

"It was the first thing I thought of, okay?"

"Okay, *Mary.*" He grinned and followed their new employer inside.

"I have a healthy new respect for housewives who do this every day." Justin dropped onto the bed in their motel room and heaved a tired sigh. They'd cleaned several rooms, dividing the chores and conquering the work in an organized and efficient manner.

Justin made the beds, vacuumed the floors, and emptied the trash, while Tess, who drew the short straw, cleaned the bathrooms.

"Housewives only have one house to clean. We cleaned the equivalent of three or four whole houses today." Tess propped herself up on the bed next to Justin, who flipped on the TV and clicked through the channels. He stopped briefly on a music video channel and watched a man in a black cowboy hat sing about watching the taillights of his woman's car fade in the night.

Justin sighed again and changed the channel.

Though he said nothing, she could see the pain in his eyes, and she shared a longing ache for what he'd given up. He stopped on a cartoon and watched absently for a minute.

"I just don't get it," he said suddenly. "Coyote keeps on buying stuff from Acme, even though every single device he's ever ordered from them has backfired or not worked in some way. If he's stupid enough to keep buying things from a sorry company like that, he doesn't deserve to catch the Roadrunner."

Tess furrowed her brow. "Pardon me?"

"Coyote and Roadrunner. Don't tell me you've never heard of them?"

"Yeah, I guess I remember them from when I was a kid. I

just never analyzed them to such an extent." She grinned up at Justin, and he smiled back. As always, Justin's attitude was good, his teasing in place.

"Well, think about it. Has anything Coyote ever bought worked like it was supposed to?"

Tess rolled on her side and swung one leg over his. "I'd rather think about you." She kissed him on the chest and trailed roaming lips down the plane of his stomach. Justin sucked in a sharp breath and turned off the TV.

"Mercy," he mumbled as she worked her way back toward his lips and settled more fully on top of him. The Coyote's buying habits were quickly forgotten.

"Hmm. That's weird."

"What is?" Brian looked up from the evening newspaper at Hallie, who browsed through the day's mail.

"You got a postcard from Samson, Arkansas, but there's nothing written on it."

He arched an eyebrow. "I don't know anybody in Arkansas. Let me see it." She handed him the card, and he turned it over to study the postmark. When he saw the handwriting, his pulse screeched to a stop. "Oh, my God! It's from Justin."

"What? But I thought—"

"This is his handwriting. I'm sure of it." Stunned, Brian stared at the card another moment, examining every detail. "The postmark is only two days old. He's alive! That's what the card is for. To tell us he's okay and where he is." Relief as pure and sweet as anything he'd ever felt rushed over him. "I knew he'd contact me somehow, but . . ."

"But?"

"He doesn't want anyone else to know where he is. Otherwise, why use such strange and vague means to contact us?"

"Do you think that means Tess is all right, too?" Hallie's tone sounded as hopeful as the light in her eyes.

"I don't know." Tapping the card against his palm, Brian narrowed his eyes. "But I intend to find out." He shoved out of his chair and stalked toward the back of the house with Hallie trailing after him.

"What are you going to do? Brian, if Justin's being this secretive, doesn't it stand to reason he might not want you to blow his cover? I doubt he sent you the card to have you come after him."

He threw his suitcase on the bed while Hallie fussed.

"He's my brother. I just have to make sure he's okay. I'll be careful, I promise."

"I don't like it. It could be dangerous for you."

Turning, Brian pulled Hallie into his arms. "If it's dangerous for me, then it's dangerous for Justin. And that's all the more reason for me to try to help him."

"Oh God, Brian. I couldn't stand it if anything happened to you." Hallie hugged his waist and turned worried eyes to his.

"And I couldn't stand it if anything happened to Justin, and I hadn't tried to help him."

She sighed sadly. "I understand, but I don't like it. Not one bit."

Squeezing her tighter, he kissed the crown of her head. "I love you," he murmured into her hair then turned to finish his packing. "I'll leave first thing in the morning."

Hallie's scream jolted Brian from his sleep.

"Don't give me a reason to kill her." The gruff male voice sent panic sluicing through him as he spotted the dark figure holding Hallie from behind.

Shadows shrouded the man's face, but the gleam of the gun aimed at Hallie's head was unmistakable.

Brian's heart leaped to his throat. Raising his palms slowly, he said, "Okay, easy. Don't hurt her. What do you want?"

"I want your little brother and Tess Sinclair. Where are they?"

"I don't know." Brian prayed his courtroom training would help him out-bluff the man holding his wife at gunpoint.

The click of the gun cocking reverberated in the dark room. Hallie whimpered.

"Come on, guy," Brian begged. "Let her go. We don't know anything about where Tess is." That was almost true.

"Why don't I believe you?"

Brian pulled in a slow breath. *Don't panic.*

"Look, I read about Tess's death in the paper. We assumed that meant Justin was dead, too. Some men dragged them out of here the other night and—"

"I know all that, asshole. I was one of those men. But I made the mistake of trusting your punk brother and the Sinclair woman when they couldn't be trusted. Now Randall Sinclair's after my neck and theirs. I don't plan on dying. I plan to find Tess and your brother first. And you're gonna help me."

Listening carefully to the man's explanation, Brian gauged his motives and calculated the risks. "What if you do find them first?"

"I'll ask the questions, pal. Tell me where they are, or I'll blow blondie's head off." The thug nudged Hallie with the gun again, and Brian's gut clenched.

"I don't know where—"

"Don't lie to me!" The man jerked his arm tighter around Hallie, and she gasped.

The sudden volume and desperation in the man's voice

alarmed Brian. He played a dangerous game for his brother's life, but Hallie's danger was immediate.

"I'll kill her! I saw the suitcase. Where are you headed?"

"A business trip."

"Bullshit!"

Brian heard Hallie sniffling. He fumbled quickly for a plausible story. "Nashville."

The man didn't answer. Brian held his breath.

"I don't believe you."

"I swear to God. Justin always wanted to go to Nashville. If he's anywhere, he's there."

"What if I said I was going to take blondie here along for the ride? If I don't find little brother in Nashville, blondie dies."

Brian's palms were sweating. "Take me instead."

"Not a chance. Your brother and Tess betrayed me and cost my wife her life. If I don't have my wife, why should you have yours? Last chance, brother. Where are they?"

Knowing he only had one chance to save Justin and Hallie both, Brian sent up a prayer for assistance and courage. He had to tell the man what he wanted to know then hope he could find Justin before this maniac.

"I got a blank postcard from Samson, Arkansas, today. I think he's there."

The thug remained silent as if considering the information. When he finally released Hallie, she slumped to the bed, sobbing. Brian rushed to her.

"You've been most helpful," the intruder said as he backed toward the door with the gun still aimed at them. "Do yourselves a favor. Don't say anything to the cops about this, or I'll be back. Blondie won't be so lucky next time. Got it?"

He disappeared into the hallway, and Brian wrapped his arms around Hallie. She trembled violently in his embrace. Or was that him shaking so hard?

"I want you to go to your parents' house. Wait there for me. I'll check in with you tonight. If you haven't heard from me in twenty-four hours, it means something's gone wrong. In that case, call the police and tell them what you know . . . everything that's happened."

Levering himself higher, he peeked out the bedroom window to watch the light-colored sedan pull away from the front of the house. He dressed in a hurry while Hallie gaped at him in horror.

"You're not still going after Justin, are you? Brian, you can't!" Her voice was high-pitched and hysterical.

"I have to get to him before that creep does! Get dressed and get out of here! Go to your parents, and don't talk to anyone unless you don't hear from me." He snatched up his suitcase.

"Brian!" Hallie screamed in panic.

He stopped long enough to blow her a kiss. "I love you, babe."

Chapter Twenty-Four

"Morelli just left the brother's house. You want me to rough up the brother and find out what he told him?" Dominic asked his boss via cellular phone.

"No. Follow him." Randall fumed at Morelli's betrayal. "Once you have an idea of where he's headed, call me back. We'll meet you. I think Mr. Morelli will lead us straight to Tess and her boyfriend. Then we can pop all three at once."

"Yes, boss."

Randall disconnected the call then leaned back in his desk chair to wait for further news. Ten minutes later, Dominic called back.

"Morelli seems to be headed out of town. Going north. You think he's going to that little podunk town Boyd's from?"

"That's what you're to find out. Don't lose him! We'll be right behind you."

Night encroached on the horizon by the time Brian passed the sign that welcomed him to Samson, Arkansas. His eyes scanned the town with a heightened sense of awareness, and apprehension wound inside him. What if Justin had merely been passing through town on the way to Nashville or Canada or . . . ?

Stopping at a red light, he dragged a hand over his face and sighed. He was bushed. He'd driven nonstop after being awakened early that morning by the thug with the gun. Lord, his life had been turned upside down. When he found Justin, he'd kill his little brother himself!

Spying a small motel, Brian pulled in to get a room. He couldn't do much to find Justin until tomorrow, so his first order of business was sleep.

Tess walked up behind Justin, who hunched over a notepad at the tiny table in their motel room, and she rubbed the muscles in his shoulders. She glanced at the paper he worked on while so deeply in thought. "What are you doing?"

"Hmm, that feels good." Justin rolled his shoulders as she massaged them. He tossed his pen down and handed her the pad of paper. "I'm trying to reconstruct a few songs I'd written. I thought maybe I could use a different name and try to get them recorded, even if I can't be the one to sing them."

Tess moved around to the edge of the bed and sat down with the pad, meeting Justin's bright blue eyes with a smile of admiration. "Never say die."

"Huh?" Justin wrinkled his nose as he absently scratched his stubble-darkened chin.

"You. Your never-going-to-quit attitude. Your faith and doggedness."

"Are you calling me stubborn?" Justin tipped a wry grin at her.

"Yes. Charmingly stubborn. Don't ever change, Justin. It's one of the reasons I fell in love with you."

The grin on his lips slipped, and his eyes flashed with emotion. "Say that again."

"Which part?"

"You used the 'L' word."

She glanced down at her hands and furrowed her brow. "I did, didn't I?"

"Yeah."

She did love him. So why was it so hard to say the words? He'd pledged his love to her, sworn to stand by her, proven his trustworthiness. What was wrong with her?

"Justin, I—"

"It's all right. I understand."

But the pain in his eyes and the disappointment in his voice said he didn't understand. And she'd hurt him. Regret sliced through her. Dropping her gaze to the notebook, she read what Justin had scribbled on the page.

I tried and tried to play the chords she taught me/ I was just a kid learning the hard way/ More than anything, I wanted to make her happy/ For my sister, I'd practice night and day

Sayin'— Next time I'll do better/ Experience is a teacher/ A second chance is all I need/ If you'll believe in me/ I won't let you down/ Oh, I promise I'll do better/ Next time.

A dull ache lodged in her heart. "You wrote this about Rebecca."

He angled his head and released a slow, deep breath. "Yeah. Right after she died."

Tess read aloud. " 'Well, we grew up, and big sister got married. She was just a wife learning the hard way. More than anything, she wanted him to be happy. For her husband, she'd give both night and day. Saying, "Next time I'll do better. Experience is a teacher. A second chance is all I need" . . .' "

She stopped when her voice broke, then with a deep breath, she went on to the third verse. " 'The first time he got angry, she forgave him. But in the end she learned the hard way. How I wish I'd done more to convince her. Not to give the man who'd hurt her one more day. But she believed him when he'd say, "Next time I'll do better. Experience is a teacher. A second chance is all that I need. If you'll believe in me, I won't let you down. Oh, I promise I'll do better. Next time." Now when the cold night wind blows. I only hope Rebecca knows. What I'd give if she could have had a next time.' "

Tess sat silently, absorbing the love and grief that had prompted Justin to write the song. Finally she whispered, "You know, you gave me a next time. You gave me a reason to want a second chance. You've given me what Rebecca was denied. In a way, I feel like Rebecca gave it to me too."

Justin turned his gaze up to find hers. His expression reflected a degree of surprise, a touch of sadness. "That's what I prayed for the night she died. A second chance to do better. The opportunity to make up to Rebecca for not being there for her. God sent you to me. I know he did. You've helped heal me." His gaze bore into her. "Do you know why I fell in love with you?"

Her heartbeat tripped. "Why?"

"Besides the fact that you're the best-looking woman I ever met, and you have a smile that could stop traffic . . ." He paused, and the smile he sent her felt like a soft caress. "I loved your heart."

His voice and gentle expression held her mesmerized.

"Despite all the reasons you had to not trust the world, despite all the pain you'd suffered, despite the right you had to harden your heart and be bitter, you didn't. The woman who offered me a ride that rainy day was trusting and kind and generous and sweet and witty and—"

She held up a hand to stop him. "I think I was naive and foolish and sympathetic and frightened, and you just saw all my flaws in a positive light, being the optimist that you are. I had selfish motives for picking you up." She ducked her head and bit her lip.

"And you don't give yourself enough credit." Justin pushed himself out of the armchair and knelt in front of her.

"Don't underestimate yourself, Tess. Randall has dimmed your vision of your worth, but I can see all you have to give, all the virtue in you. You're a warm, intelligent, wonderful woman, and don't you forget that." He pressed his hands to her cheeks and lifted her face.

She couldn't hide from the intensity in his eyes, and her heart turned over. Her troubled conscience split wide and poured at his feet. "For so long, I turned my back on what I knew was wrong. I gave up my self-respect. I sold what was good about me to survive. How do I ever forgive myself for that?"

"One day at a time, baby. You did what you had to, what you felt was best at the time. But you didn't lose everything good to him, or you wouldn't be here now. You have courage and strength and a sense of justice that led you to act when the time was right." He stroked her cheek. "Remind yourself of that when you want to doubt what you have inside."

She gave him a weak smile, and his mouth descended to hers. His kiss filled her with warmth and hope and promise. When the tip of his tongue traced her lips, the warmth heated, and the most basic of longings burgeoned from inside.

Easing back onto the bed, she took Justin with her, and his body blanketed hers while their hunger for each other grew. As always, Justin's patience and attention to her fulfillment awed her and touched her heart. His hands stroked gently, slowly, and his kiss explored intimately, thoroughly, until Tess quivered with desire to be one with him.

And as before, when Justin joined their bodies, she experienced the union to her core, in her spirit. Each time Justin made love to her, she lost a little more of her heart and soul to him, just as he gave his own heart and soul to her.

He became an extension of her, an amazing phenomenon Tess wanted to spend the rest of her life exploring. He stirred to life the hope that she could find all the good in her once more and cling to those qualities when doubt reared its head.

In Justin she'd found her safe harbor, her home. But more importantly, he'd helped her find herself.

She realized then the reason she withheld the words of love he needed to hear. The gift of love he gave her was whole, unblemished, complete. She wanted to offer the same to him. But Randall still haunted her. Before she could offer her love to Justin, she had to truly free herself from Randall and his hold on her soul.

Brian waited patiently while the man at the five-and-dime studied the picture of Tess.

"Pretty woman," the man said. "Why is it you're looking for her?"

"Long story," Brian replied with a sigh. "Have you seen her or the other guy around here in the past couple of days?"

The store clerk handed the pictures back to Brian. "Afraid not. I'd remember a woman who looked like that."

Brian huffed in frustration. If he'd shown the picture to one person, he'd shown it to 500, and he sensed that his time was running out. "Okay, thanks anyway."

When he climbed back into his car, he crossed the address off the list of stores and restaurants that sold the postcard of the National Monument.

The secretary at the small printing company that distributed the postcards had helped Brian construct the list he worked from, but after a full day of showing Justin's and Tess's pictures around town, Brian's patience had worn thin.

The last three names on his list included a diner near the interstate, and since he'd skipped lunch, he decided he'd visit the diner next.

Once there, he noticed the rack of postcards at the cash register before he slid into one of the booths.

A waitress with her hair pulled back in a ponytail handed him a menu.

"Hey, I like the haircut," she said and smiled. "But it does sort of make you look older. Don't you think?"

Brain looked at the waitress. "How old do I look?"

"About thirty-five, maybe thirty-six. I like it better long, but then that's not for me to decide, huh? What does your girlfriend think? She *is* your girlfriend, right?"

"Who?"

The waitress tapped her pencil against her order pad. "Who do you think?"

"I really don't know." He watched her face as she narrowed her gaze and wrinkled her nose.

"Hey, whatever. Forget I asked. You want the regular? Chocolate chip pancakes with extra syrup?"

"God, no! Why would you say that?" His stomach turned over at the thought of so much sugar. He only knew one person who liked sweets enough to eat a meal like that.

His breath stilled in his lungs.

"Aren't you—Oh, I'm sorry." She blushed and waved her hand in dismissal. "I thought you were someone else. God, you look just like him. It's spooky."

Brian's pulse quickened, and he fished out the picture of Justin. "You thought I was him, didn't you?"

Chapter Twenty-Five

The waitress set down her order pad and took the picture. "Yeah. That's the guy. He's been in here a couple times over the last few days. Him and his girlfriend."

Brian pulled out the picture of Tess. "Is this her?"

"Yeah, that's the one. Real pretty hair. You know them?"

"I'm his brother."

The waitress laughed. "I should have guessed. You could be twins. Except that you look older and stuffier."

"Do you know where I can find them?"

"I think they're staying at that motel." She aimed her pen across the two-lane road.

Snatching the pictures back, energized by his good fortune, Brian rushed toward the door.

"Aren't you gonna eat?" the waitress called after him.

"Not right now." Brian moved his car across the street and hurried into the front office of the motel. He waved the pictures at the man behind the desk. "I'm looking for these two people. Are they staying here? What room are they in?"

The desk clerk put on a pair of reading glasses and took a look at the pictures. "That's Mary and David Camper. They're staying here, but I can't tell you which room. That'd be an invasion of their privacy."

"This is an emergency, damn it!" Brian slammed his hand down on the front desk. "Either you tell me where they are, or

I'll disturb every one of your customers by knocking on all the doors until I find them!"

"Try it, and I'll call the police." The man took off his glasses and matched Brian's impatient glare with one of his own.

Brian sucked in a breath to steady his rising temper. "I'm his brother, and it's imperative that I talk to him right away!"

The man behind the desk twisted his mouth and crossed his arms over his chest.

"In ten seconds I'm going to start knocking on doors, and then none of your guests will have any privacy." Brian leveled a no-nonsense stare at the clerk.

The clerk scowled. "Room twenty-one."

"Thank you." As Brian jogged out to the sidewalk, he spotted a familiar-looking sedan, an old green Thunderbird. The car stopped in front of the motel, and he watched the thug who'd terrorized Hallie emerge from the vehicle.

Ducking behind a tall bush, Brian waited until the thug disappeared inside the motel office. Then he ran down the sidewalk, searching for room twenty-one.

Let them be there. Please, God, let them be there, he prayed.

"Hello, can I help you?"

The brusque manner of the man behind the motel desk irked Morelli. He set his jaw but let the rudeness slide . . . this time.

He took out the pictures of Tess Sinclair and the Boyd man and slapped them on the counter. "Have you seen these two hanging around here?"

His lack of success frustrated him. He'd had no luck all day, not so much as a nibble.

The balding man behind the desk frowned. "Are these two

in some kind of trouble? You're the second person in five minutes to ask for them."

"So you know where they are?"

"Are you a cop? You know, I could get in real trouble for giving out this kind of information."

"You could say it was official business, yeah. Where are they?"

"Come on. I'll show you." The clerk stepped out from behind the desk, but as he did, the telephone rang. "Just a minute."

Morelli gritted his teeth and suppressed the urge to choke the life out of the clerk.

"Okay, this way." The clerk hung up the phone and started for the door. "What'd they do? Why are the authorities looking for them?"

Morelli curled his lip in a snarl. "They got a woman killed. And now they have to pay."

"Brian?" Justin's jaw dropped open in shock. "What the hell are you—"

Brian put a hand on his brother's chest, pushed him backward into the room, then slammed the door closed. Tess gasped and scrambled off the bed.

"You two have to get out of here now." In a flurry of motion, Brian gathered things into a backpack. "One of Sinclair's hit men is in the motel office as we speak. He broke in our house the other night and held a gun on Hallie."

Justin's gut twisted.

"I had to tell him about the postcard you sent, or he'd have killed Hallie. But I beat him up here, and now we have to get out of here before he finds you."

"Postcard?" Tess cast Justin an accusing look.

"Move!" Brian roared. "You don't have any time to waste!"

Tess flew to the bathroom sink, raked a few possessions into a paper bag, then shoved it into the backpack Brian held. He passed the pack to Justin.

"I'll get the car," Brian said, running to the door. "Be ready when I pull around."

Justin poked a small stack of cash into his jeans pocket. "We're right behind you, Bri."

As Tess climbed into the backseat of Brian's Accord, Justin spotted Morelli coming out of the motel office with the clerk. Morelli's gaze found his, and Justin's stomach pitched. "He saw us! Burn rubber, Bri!" Justin jumped into the backseat with Tess. Brian tore out of the parking space before Justin could even close the car door.

As Brian raced from the motel parking lot, he nearly flattened Morelli, who ran in front of the car, trying to stop them.

"Well, that'd be one way to get rid of him," Justin muttered. He clung to the seat as Brian sped out onto the two-lane road.

Morelli made a break for his own car.

The Accord's tires squealed as Brian turned on the entry ramp to the freeway. Justin turned to watch through the back window as Morelli's green Thunderbird screeched from the motel driveway in hot pursuit.

"Here he comes, Brian. He's right behind us."

"Hang on!" Brian gunned the engine, and they sped toward the interstate. He pulled in front of a Mack truck, and the truck driver blasted his horn.

Tess clapped a hand over her heart. "I see your brother shares your driving skills."

Justin reached into the backpack and pulled out the snub-nosed gun that he'd been given a few days before by the same man now chasing them.

"Where did you get that!" Brian's eyes widened in disbelief as he used the rearview mirror to stare at the gun. He swiveled his head to look again, as if he doubted the image in the mirror was right. "You can't shoot him! That's called murder, Justin! I'm not saving your butt so that you can spend the next fifty years in prison for murder!"

"I'm gonna shoot at his tires."

Brian shook his head. "Don't try it. There are too many other cars on the road. I'd rather try to outrun him. Save the bullets, in case you have to defend yourself or Tess."

Justin lowered the gun but didn't put it away. Anything could happen. He wanted to be ready.

"Bingo!" Dominic said with a satisfied laugh. He watched Tess and Boyd get in the brother's car then Morelli jumped into his wreck and sped after them. Cranking the engine of his Camaro, Dominic pulled out of the motel lot and gave chase. He dialed Sinclair and told him that his wife and Morelli were both within his sights. He reported their location and direction.

"Good work," Sinclair said. "Now it's time to bring them in. We've got our end covered. You know what to do."

Dominic hung up and gave the Camaro more gas. Within seconds, the Thunderbird and Accord were within two car lengths. How simple it would be to shoot and have this over with. Dominic cut his gaze to the .38 on the seat beside him. He had his orders. He knew what to do.

Brian watched in his side mirror as the Thunderbird changed lanes and made up some of the distance that had separated the cars.

The Mack truck he'd angered when he pulled on the road now drove in the passing lane beside him. The truck trapped his Accord behind the Sunday driver in front of him. He gritted his teeth and flashed his lights to tell the car in front that he wanted to pass. Still they poked along. Finally, as the Thunderbird drew nearer, Brian used his last available option.

"Hang on! I've got to get pass this jerk, and it may get bumpy." Brian cut the wheel hard to the right and floored the accelerator as he passed the poky driver on the shoulder. The Accord's right tires bumped over the uneven ground at the edge of the road, and Justin muttered a curse.

Jerking the steering wheel back to the left, Brian cut between two cars with mere inches to spare. His heart pumped wildly, and his body shook with adrenaline, but the maneuver seemed to work.

For about one minute.

In his rearview mirror, Brian watched the hit man use the shoulder to pass the same driver and pull alongside Brian's car. "Damn!"

"Get on the floor, Tess!" Justin yelled as he climbed from the backseat to the front and opened the glove box.

"What are you doing?" Brian fought to keep his distance from the bumper in front of him, waiting for an opportunity to pull into the passing lane. The Mack truck sped up and blocked him again. On purpose, no doubt. *Damn him!*

Justin grabbed Brian's tire gauge, his windshield scraper and a bottle of aspirin from the glove compartment and rolled down his window. The Thunderbird chose that moment to swerve into Brian's car, bumping them halfway into the next lane. The Accord scraped the side of the Mack truck.

Finally the truck driver backed off, which gave Brian the opportunity he needed. Pulling into the passing lane, he shot past two more cars. The Thunderbird continued down the shoulder then cut in front of a Jeep to pull alongside Brian again.

"Damn it!" Brian shouted.

The Thunderbird side-swiped him again, trying to force him off the road. His hand grew sweaty and slipped on the steering wheel as he struggled to stay on the road.

"Steady." Justin turned toward the window and lobbed the bottle of aspirin first. It struck the windshield of the Thunderbird but didn't slow it down. Next, Justin launched the ice scraper and the tire gauge at the Thunderbird's front window. The green sedan swerved back into the right lane and lost some momentum.

"Good shot, little brother." Brian seized the chance to speed up. He put some distance between his car and the Thunderbird, but not much.

Justin twisted in his seat to look out the back. "You okay, honey?"

"Define 'okay,' " Tess answered.

With another check of the green sedan's progress, the brothers let out a mutual curse. The persistent henchman had regained most of the space they'd earned and rammed the Accord from behind.

Brian cut the wheel to the left and changed lanes with the Thunderbird on his tail. "Damn, he's still with us. I'll get off the highway. Maybe we can shake him better in town."

Justin grunted. "It's worth a shot."

Switching back to the right lane, Brain watched the road for an exit while the Thunderbird rear-ended him again and again.

"He's not going to give up, Justin." Tess's fear resounded in her voice.

"Neither are we. Understand? I'm not giving up, and I won't let you either. We'll be okay."

Despite the confidence of his brother's words, Brian heard an equal amount of anxiety in Justin's tone. He knew his brother was trying to buoy Tess's spirits and maybe his own, but the situation looked grim. His gut clenched.

Sinclair's thug must have seen the exit ramp when Brian did, because he swerved into the left lane, forcing another car off the road. Then, passing the Accord, he cut in front of Brian as Brian eased off the main road. On the sharp rise of the exit ramp, the driver of the Thunderbird slammed on his brakes and spun sideways.

Brian stood on his brakes. He cut the wheel hard to avoid a collision and missed the Thunderbird by inches.

Seconds later the thug plowed his car straight into Brian's door. The impact pushed the Accord off the embankment on the far side of the exit ramp.

Tess's scream filled Brian's ears as the two cars rolled down the short hill. The Accord rested upright when it stopped. The Thunderbird lay on its side.

A sharp pain shot up Brian's leg. He tried to move, but the crush of metal pinned him. He looked down and found blood pouring from his thigh where the driver's door had been shoved in.

"Justin, you're bleeding!" Tess reached across the seat for Justin's forehead.

"I'm okay. It's just a nick from the broken window. Brian, are you okay?"

Brian shook his head. "My leg's trapped. I can't move it, and it hurts like hell."

"Justin, look!" Tess pointed to the Thunderbird where the relentless henchman struggled out his side window.

Justin groaned. "That guy is like the Terminator. He just keeps coming."

"Get out of here!" Brian shouted. "Run!"

Bending, Justin fumbled on the floor of the car for the gun.

Tess scrambled from the backseat, but Justin turned toward Brian with defiance in his eyes.

"Go!" Brian said before Justin could voice his objection.

A dark concern clouded Justin's eyes, but he opened his door. Turning back, he grabbed Brian's hand and slapped the gun in his palm. "To defend yourself. I won't leave you here like a sitting duck."

Justin climbed out of the car and raced away.

Brian watched helplessly as his brother and Tess clambered up the hill toward the road at the top of the exit ramp.

Sinclair's thug watched, too, and renewed his struggle to get free from his car.

Flexing his fingers around the small gun in his hand, Brian knew that Justin would need the weapon more than he did. His brother's valiant gesture may have cost Justin and Tess their lives.

Chapter Twenty-Six

Tess's lungs ached. She'd climbed the steep hill of the ramp embankment at a breakneck speed. Fear sucked her breath from her. Justin tugged on her arm, urging her to hurry as they crested the hill and scrambled to their feet.

Justin took off across the pavement at a clip. She stumbled as he pulled her along behind him. He led her toward the overpass, where the road at the end of the exit ramp crossed the interstate. Her feet pounded the hard pavement as she tried to keep up. Speed was their only defense now.

She hazarded a glance over the waist-high concrete wall that buffered the drop to the highway below. Their height above the interstate increased her sense of vulnerability, and she edged closer to the middle of the overpass.

A black Camaro wheeled past her. Screeching its tires, the Camaro spun to a stop at an angle, blocking their path.

She and Justin staggered to an abrupt stop. Justin squeezed her hand as the Camaro's driver emerged and started toward them.

A cry ripped from her throat when she recognized the man as Dominic, one of Randall's lackeys. He'd been at the warehouse.

As Dominic came toward them, Justin stepped between her and the new threat.

"Back this way!" Justin shouted, spinning on his heel. He

started back in the direction they'd come, but a dark blue sedan squealed to a stop in front of them, halting their progress.

The man behind the wheel of the sedan removed his sunglasses, and Tess shivered. "It's Henry!"

"And Randall," Justin added.

She shifted her gaze to the menacing man in the backseat. "We're trapped!"

Justin's expression reflected the same fatalistic conclusion.

And a stark, cold terror flooded her veins.

Henry shifted the car into park and cut the engine. Reaching into the holster at his chest, he drew his gun.

"You idiot, you can't flash that thing around here! There are too many witnesses!" Randall barked, pointing at the interstate. "And we sure as hell can't kill them here! Get them in the car, and we'll finish them later. Can you handle that much?"

Henry sheathed his weapon. "Your call, boss."

He stepped from the car, slammed the driver's door and stalked toward Justin and Tess.

Randall's men outnumbered them. Even if he thought he had a chance of beating them in a hand-to-hand brawl, Justin knew better than to think he could take them both at the same time.

Play it as it comes.

With a cold and merciless gleam in his eyes, Dominic squared off. Justin planted his feet and balled his fists. Keeping his gaze pinned on Dominic, Justin pushed Tess out of the way. Her whimper of fear twisted inside him.

Tess was what mattered. He'd put his body and soul in

harm's way to save her. He loved her more than any other reason to live. Failing her now was not an option. No test of his ability to protect and defend her, to come through in the crunch, had ever mattered more. A primal, protective instinct surged through him as he stepped toward Randall's ape.

He deflected Dominic's first punch then stepped back to regain his footing. Lowering his head, Justin charged Dominic, shoulder first. He sent the other man back a few steps. But when his opponent recovered his balance, he attacked Justin with a brutal force. Dominic's meaty fist caught Justin in the jaw. Another blow found his gut. Shaking off the pain, Justin landed a punch in Dominic's ribs. Stunned by the returned hit, the henchman staggered back.

Seizing the moment, Justin lunged, tackling Dominic around the waist and working to bring him down.

Tess's scream jerked his attention from his fight. Henry hauled Tess backward, his arm around her waist and his hand on her throat. Prickling horror raced through his blood. "Tess!"

The momentary distraction allowed Dominic to land a solid blow to Justin's cheek. His ears buzzed from the force of the hit. He staggered backward toward the concrete wall at the edge of the overpass. Dominic blurred before his eyes. Without moving his sights off his opponent, Justin braced for the next round. He planted his feet and swung at the approaching man, throwing all his weight behind the punch.

Pain streaked through his hand with the impact. He quickly regained his bearings and readied himself for the next attack.

When his vision cleared, he found Dominic stretched face down on the pavement. *One down.*

Tess kicked and struggled as Henry pushed her head down and forced her into the backseat of the blue sedan. Henry closed the car door, and she whirled to face Randall with her heart in her throat.

His dark eyes held the same condescending glare they had for years, and something inside Tess snapped. Justin had shown her respect, and she knew she didn't have to take Randall's demeaning treatment anymore. In the light of Justin's love, she knew all Randall had shown her was selfishness and disrespect.

"Trust yourself," Justin had told her more than once. "Don't let him win. There's a spark in you. Draw on it."

Randall lifted one eyebrow and shook his head. "You surprise me, Tess."

She raised her chin and met his evil glare without blinking. "No, Randall. You underestimate me. The sad thing is, you even made me underestimate myself." She swallowed hard, focused on the happiness and support she'd found with Justin, and felt a wave of new energy spiral through her blood. "Well, no more."

Randall lifted a corner of his mouth in droll amusement. "Well, if it isn't the mouse who roared."

Tess shook her head. "You're the mouse, Randall. The one hiding behind intimidation, terrified of losing power, and using other people's fear to boost your inflated sense of self-importance. But you miscalculated two things, and now you're scrambling to regain your false sense of control."

"Miscalculated? I wouldn't be so sure. I seem to have the upper hand here."

Randall's smug assurance should have infuriated her. Instead, she knew a moment of pity for him. He was a brilliant man, an influential force in the business world. If only he could have used his strengths and influence to build rather than destroy, to love rather than hate.

"Oh, yes, Randall. You miscalculated me." Her voice resounded, deep and strong, in the confines of the car. "And you miscalculated the power of love to break the chains of intimidation and dominance you used against me for so long. Justin has shown me the strength of love, and I will fight you to the bitter end to defend what I have with him and win my freedom from you."

Randall scoffed. "You think he loves you? That punk just wants the free sex you're giving him. I'm the one who laid the world at your feet." He poked a finger at her, and his face grew florid. "I gave you everything money could buy, invested thirteen years of my life, and asked only for your loyalty."

"But did you even once love me?"

As if she'd pulled a plug on him, Randall appeared deflated. "I tried, but you were so weak. Like my mother."

"Weak? Randall, you tortured me! You hit me and demeaned me and stole my self-respect! That's not love!"

He snatched her upper arm and drew her closer. "None of that matters now, does it? You betrayed me, and for that, you're going to die."

His dark eyes glittered with evil intent. Self-preservation erupted inside her. Tess launched herself at him, clawing his face like a cornered alley cat. Her arms flailed, her body thrashed, and her legs kicked as he tried to subdue her. A sound she barely recognized as her own voice growled and screamed like an injured animal. She raked Randall's face and arms with her fingernails.

"Stop it, bitch!" he yelled, when she jabbed at his eye. "Henry, tie her hands! Henry!"

Randall seized one of her hands and twisted it behind her until she cried out in pain.

"Stop fighting me, or I'll break your arm!"

302

Gasping for breath as lightning-like pain shot up her arm, she met his glare. "I won't let you win. You may kill me, but I won't just roll over and die." With a yank that cost her another sharp bolt of pain, she wrenched her arm from Randall and twisted away from him.

"Henry!"

While Randall yelled for his hit man, she scrambled for the door. He sank his fingers into her shoulder and hauled her back. Spinning to free herself from his grip, she met his hard eyes.

He tore his gaze from her, presumably to look outside the car for Henry. When an evil grin curled his lip and he leaned forward to peer out the front window, she followed the direction of his gaze.

Henry and Justin, locked in a struggle, inched dangerously near the edge of the overpass. They lurched and pitched as they fought each other's wrestler-like stranglehold. A chilling dread arced through her, paralyzing her briefly.

Randall's satisfied chuckle goaded her into action. Grappling for the door handle, she rocked backward into Randall's chest with a force that knocked him off balance. Throwing open the door, she scurried from the car. "Justin!"

Randall caught her shirt before she made it two steps. He jerked her back against his chest and wrapped his arm around her waist. A hard lump poked her back with a menacing jab. Randall had a gun hidden under his suit coat, she realized, and trembled.

"Stand back, people," Randall said, and only then did she notice the small crowd of curious onlookers. "These fugitives are dangerous. Let us handle it." The cool authority in Randall's voice, his businesslike attire would have fooled her, too, if she hadn't known better.

She swung a desperate look to the crowd. "No! He's not the police. Please, someone help!"

No one moved. Not that she blamed them. What they witnessed had to be terrifying.

Justin's grunt drew her attention. As she watched, Henry shoved Justin up against the short wall, pinning him. Justin's knees buckled tiredly.

Her breath caught in her throat. *No!*

Grabbing a leg out from under Justin, Henry hoisted his opponent over the side of the short wall. Justin clutched the top edge of the wall, while Henry pounded him in the back with his elbow.

"No! Stop!" Tess struggled against Randall's grip as foreboding settled on her chest. She wrenched her body desperately, trying to free herself. She had to help Justin, had to help him before he fell. *Please, God!*

Even as she thought it, she heard a gunshot. Then a second. And a third. She stiffened with alarm.

Henry's body jerked and slumped forward until the weight of his massive body pulled him over the concrete wall. As he slipped over the edge, he grabbed for Justin. Henry dragged Justin's legs with him as he fell, and Justin slid farther over the wall.

Tess screamed in terror.

Randall released her and ran to look over the wall. On rubbery legs, she rushed toward the spot where Justin clung precariously to the edge of the overpass.

She grabbed for his wrists. "Justin, hold on! Don't let go! Please!"

His arms trembled with the effort of supporting his weight as he dangled. He kicked his legs up at the wall as he tried, unsuccessfully, to gain a foothold.

Randall appeared at her side and smirked as she tried to

save Justin. Snaking his arm around her again, Randall hauled her back toward the car, and her hands slipped from Justin's wrists.

"Justin, hold on!" she wailed, kicking and scratching Randall's arm.

"Sinclair!" The male voice distracted Randall long enough for Tess to bite the arm that hooked across her chest. With a vicious curse, he dropped her. She fell with a jolting thud to the pavement. She cringed as Randall reached for the pistol tucked in his waistband and swung his arm up to fire.

Rapid gunfire rang in her ears. Something warm and wet sprayed her clothes and hair. A large red stain spread on Randall's chest, and his eyes became fixed and glazed. A small dark circle marred his forehead, and he crumpled on the pavement beside her. Shock rendered her mute and numb. On some level she knew he was dead, knew his blood and tissue dripped on her, but she couldn't move. Horror welled inside her and choked her breath.

When a dark shadow spread over her, she looked up with a start, jolted from her daze by a new terror.

"That's for Maria," Morelli said calmly.

Tess gaped at the new threat anxiously. Her heartbeat pounded in her ears. She blinked at Morelli in confusion. "You killed him."

"He killed my wife. I returned the favor."

Morelli's flat, unrepentant tone sent a shiver down her spine. Then his gaze shifted to her. For a moment, hope flickered inside her. This was the man who'd freed them from the warehouse, after all. Maybe—

"You're next, Mrs. Sinclair. You broke your word. You didn't stay dead, and now because of you, my Maria is dead. "

"No," Tess argued. "I didn't tell anyone. I swear! I don't know how Randall found out."

"He found out from Dominic. I gave lover-boy a gun so he could eliminate Dominic, but he didn't finish the job. And the phone I gave you, the one you haven't been answering. Where is it? And your smartass boyfriend sent his brother a postcard. Bingo! Brother knows where he is and that he's alive." Morelli crouched down and stuck his nose in her face. "You tell me. Does that sound like you kept your end of the bargain?"

"I didn't know about the postcard. I swear I didn't." Tears burned her throat. She glanced to the concrete wall where she could still see Justin's fingers as he clung to the edge for dear life.

"Whether you knew or not, I told you what would happen if I had to come after you. Remember?"

She whimpered and squeezed her eyes shut as he raised the gun to her temple. "How sweet," he mocked. "You and Randall get to die together."

She heard the cold steel click as he cocked the gun, and she held her breath. Her body convulsed with tremors of fear. Did it hurt to die? She prayed it would be quick.

"Ciao, Tess."

She winced, waiting for the pain, the darkness.

"Police! Drop the weapon and put your hands where we can see them!"

Tess's heart lurched.

Morelli swung the gun away from her, toward the source of the new voice, and fired his weapon. Answering gunfire rent the air. Tess opened her eyes to find Morelli sprawled on the ground, a pool of blood spreading from under his back. Two uniformed policemen rushed forward, their guns aimed at Morelli.

One policeman checked him then Randall. "They're dead."

The second policeman rolled Dominic over and felt for a pulse. "This one's alive. Cuff him until we find out what's going on."

Tess sucked in a deep breath of relief.

"Are you all right, ma'am?" the officer hovering over Morelli asked.

She nodded, hugging her trembling body. "Justin." His name rasped from her throat. She turned her gaze toward the overpass wall and pointed a shaky finger. "Help . . . Justin."

The police officer pivoted to look where she pointed.

But as she watched, Justin's fingers slipped from the wall.

"Justin!" Tess screamed in anguish.

The nightmare she'd fled had claimed an innocent man—the man she loved.

Justin's blood was on her hands.

A black veil shrouded her eyes.

Chapter Twenty-Seven

Tess stood alone beside the casket draped in flowers. The tears streaming down her cheeks cleansed her heart. She grieved for more than the man in the casket. She grieved for his wasted life, the unrealized potential. She mourned also for all the loved ones who hadn't escaped his brutality and for the naive and desperate young woman she'd been when her nightmare with him began.

Today she buried that former self, as well. Justin had helped her rediscover her strength and her joy for life. With her tears, she released all that was past, forgave herself for the sacrifices she'd made to survive, expunged the bitterness and resentment that no longer had a place in her life. From now on she would look forward.

For all the tragedy and trauma, the past weeks had taught her the value of hope and love. She'd discovered love with a man who'd risked everything to give her back her life. But most importantly, she'd learned to love herself.

By choice, there would be no official funeral. Tess wasn't prepared to answer the inevitable questions, questions she still asked herself, questions for which she had no answers. The only thing she knew with certainty was how much she longed for Justin's arms to comfort her now. The violent resolution to her days of living in fear weighed heavily on her heart. Though free of Randall and his menace, she would always live with a graphic memory of what her liberation had cost her and others she loved.

Still, she felt Justin's presence. He was a part of her new self. His love had changed her, transformed her, helped her find an inner peace.

She stared through her tears, watching as men in dark suits loaded the casket in the back of the hearse, ready to make its journey back to Texas. Stepping nearer to the casket, she dropped a white rose on the lid. A lonesome chill washed over her, and she tried to feel something other than the emptiness in her heart as she bade her last good-bye, but she could find no emotion for the deceased. Not even hatred.

Somehow, such bitterness toward the man who no longer posed a threat seemed a waste of energy, a pettiness to which she refused to stoop. She'd given too much of herself away because of him. Now, she reserved her energy for healing, for rebuilding, for new beginnings.

With a final deep breath to cleanse her mind and spirit, Tess turned away and headed back to the cab that waited for her. She needed to hurry to the hospital to meet Hallie, who would arrive from Texas any minute to join her injured husband.

Tess waved when she spotted the blond woman stepping off the elevator. She made her way over to Hallie, whose face reflected the worry she'd suffered since Brian left on his mission to save his brother.

"Tess!" Relief melted the harsh lines in Hallie's expression.

To Tess's surprise, Hallie hugged her with a firm grip. "Oh, thank God you're all right! Where's Brian? Do you know which room he's in?"

Smiling, Tess nodded. "Of course. This way. I know you're eager to see him."

Hallie clutched Tess's hand, and they hurried down the hall. With a sideways glance, Hallie asked softly, "How are you holding up? I know this has been a terrible ordeal for you."

"I'm surviving. I know better days lie ahead, and that's what pulls me through. That and Justin's love."

As she and Hallie entered Brian's room, Tess sought a familiar pair of blue eyes. When she found them, her heart gave a giddy leap.

"Did I hear my name? My ears are burning."

"What are you doing out of bed?" she chided, though a grin split her face.

Despite the purple and blue bruises that distorted his face, the repairs needed to his stitches, and the fresh cast on his leg, she thought Justin had never looked better.

"We're comparing casts," Brian volunteered.

"Yeah, he's all cocky 'cause his cast is bigger. But I keep telling him that size doesn't matter." Justin flashed his brother a devilish grin.

Hallie flew to her husband and wrapped him in an embrace.

"Oh, Brian, I was so scared. When you said you were in the hospital . . ." She pressed her hand to her mouth and shuddered.

"As you can see, I'm alive and well except for a shattered femur. I'm going to need surgery later, but, for now, the doctor said just rest my leg and let it heal."

Hallie turned to her brother-in-law, sitting in a wheelchair beside Brian's bed. "And what about you? You look like heck warmed over."

Justin lifted an eyebrow. "Gee, thanks."

"I didn't mean . . ." She huffed impatiently and propped a hand on her hip. "What did your doctor say?"

"He said I broke my fibula." Justin propped his forearms

on the armrests of the wheelchair. "He said most of my stitches needed redoing, hopefully for the last time. All these bruises are nasty-looking but superficial. Nothing broken up here." Justin aimed a finger at his face. "I can get out of here tomorrow, if I promise the doctor to get a good night's sleep tonight."

Heaving a heavy sigh, Hallie settled on the edge of the bed next to her husband. "Tell me the whole story. Leave nothing out. What exactly happened to all of you?"

Brian explained to her how he'd been pinned in the car and watched Justin and Tess's ordeal on the overpass, unable to do anything for them. When Henry had tried to push Justin over the side of the overpass, Brian had used the gun Justin left with him to shoot Henry.

"And he called the police from his cell phone," Tess added, when Brian omitted that detail. "If the police hadn't arrived when they did, I'd be dead today."

Tess explained how Morelli had shot Randall and how the police had arrived before Morelli could kill her.

"What about Dominic?" Justin asked. "The police come up with anything on him yet?"

"A rap sheet as long as my arm and outstanding warrants on numerous other charges. He won't be a free man anytime soon," Tess told the group.

Brian whistled. "Little brother, when you get in over your head, you really do it up right."

"That reminds me. Have I thanked you yet for coming after us and saving our asses when the heat was on?" Justin cuffed his brother on the shoulder.

"All in a day's work." Brian smiled glibly and stretched his arms over his head.

"Yeah, right!" Hallie chortled. "Your *Lethal Weapon* days are over, buster."

Tess heard Brian mumble something to Hallie about showing her his lethal weapon when they got home, and she blushed as she swatted him. He pulled her down, and they locked in a deep kiss that made Tess want to blush. Moving her gaze to Justin, she found him watching her.

"What did your lawyers say when you talked to them?" he asked.

She sighed, remembering the meeting she'd had earlier that morning. "They said that according to Texas law, I was Randall's common-law wife and am entitled to his estate, even though everything except our small joint account was in Randall's name. The authorities have frozen his assets until they can figure out how much of it was illegally gotten or used in the commission of a crime. Which could take years to sort out. In the meantime, I get the money I can prove I earned and deposited in our joint account. In other words, not much." She scoffed and shook her head. "Not that I care. I don't want any of Randall's money. I don't want anything from my old life. I told the lawyers, when they release Randall's assets, to give everything to a shelter for abused women. I asked them to set up special funds in Rebecca and Angela's names."

The last revelation clearly touched Justin. He took a deep breath before smiling at her warmly. "Becca would have appreciated the gesture. And so do I."

"Ditto," Brian said softly.

Hallie cast Justin a curious glance. "I still don't understand how you broke your leg. Did that happen in your brawl with this Dominic person?"

"Naw. I broke it when I dropped from the side of the overpass."

Hallie's eyes grew round. "Excuse me?"

Tess shivered at the memory of watching Justin's hands disappear as he fell.

"I got pushed off the overpass. I held on for a while, but—"

"The driver of an eighteen-wheeler saw Justin's predicament," Brian explained when Hallie furrowed her brow. "The trucker stopped his truck under the overpass, significantly cutting the distance Justin fell when his hands slipped."

"It was still a rough landing. That's how I broke my leg." Justin's face hardened, and he met Tess's gaze. "What really hurt was knowing that I'd let you down . . . again. I promised to take care of you, and I dropped the ball. My failure almost cost you your life."

Tess crossed the room and knelt in front of him. "That's where you're wrong. You were with me. During our time together, you helped me find that part of myself that I thought had died. You've done more than save my life. You've given me the courage and strength to fight for myself." She stroked his cheek and saw the impact of her words written in the moisture in his eyes. "You've made a difference, Justin. You've succeeded in changing my life and winning my heart."

Justin was silent for a moment, absorbing what she'd said. Then he narrowed his eyes with a mischievous grin. "She don't need no stinkin' bodyguard. My lady can take care of herself."

"Darn right, she can," Brian said.

"But I still need you," Tess continued. "You're very much a part of the woman I've become. I love you, Justin."

He sobered quickly and met her gaze with a blue fire in his eyes.

She squeezed his hand. "I couldn't say the words before, even though I felt them deeply. When I gave my love to you, I wanted it to be a gift free of encumbrances and not tarnished by the past. I can do that now. I can give you my whole heart and a perfect love."

With a hungry groan, he tugged her close and captured her lips with his. "I love you, Tess," he murmured between kisses.

"You hurry up and get out of this hospital, Justin Boyd," she whispered back. "Nights are awfully lonely without you. Besides, you have some unfinished business to attend to." At his quizzical look, Tess grinned. "Nashville is waiting for you."

Justin's features softened, and he ducked his head. "I don't know if Nashville is where I belong. I've realized I can reach people and make a difference with my music anywhere. I think Becca just wanted me to use my gift in a way that made me happy. Helping people makes me happy. My music is just a tool I use."

"Nothing says you have to give up Nashville in order to help people." Brian cleared his throat. "Think of the platform you'd have as a musical celebrity, the number of people you could reach with your message if your name is on the Billboard hit list."

"He's right, you know," Hallie said. "The two goals are not mutually exclusive. The one could serve the other. And think of the good work you could do with all the money you'll make."

Justin frowned. "Money was never what it was about for me. You know that."

Brian shrugged. "But there will be money, and you can use it to help people, if you hit the big time."

"When he hits the big time, you mean," Tess corrected and smiled at Justin. "He'll take Nashville by storm. I'm sure of it."

A slow, lazy grin split Justin's face, reminding Tess of the blue-jean-clad cowboy she'd met on a rainy Texas highway only a few weeks before. "Fine. I'll go to Nashville, but only if you go with me."

Tess kissed him softly. "I wouldn't miss it for the world."

Epilogue

Justin picked up his guitar and headed toward the waiting area in the lobby of the record producer's office. He'd bought a new guitar but still preferred the one Brian had given him for sentimental reasons. Over the months they'd been in Nashville, Brian's old guitar had gone with Justin to every audition.

"Well?" Tess asked, peering up from the magazine in her lap.

He frowned and shook his head.

Tess sighed. "Don't get discouraged. There are other producers in this town."

He gave her a wry smile. "I'm not discouraged. I'm hungry. How about lunch?"

"Yum." Sliding her arm around his waist, she walked with him toward the elevator.

"Mr. Boyd? Wait!"

With a glance over his shoulder, Justin saw the producer's secretary wave and motion him back to her desk.

"Mr. Turner wants to speak to you. He's on his way out. Can you wait?"

Justin exchanged inquisitive looks with Tess and shrugged. "Yeah, I guess."

When the door behind the secretary's desk opened, a tall, silver-haired man strode out. "Justin Boyd?"

The man looked vaguely familiar, and anticipation mingled with curiosity inside Justin, starting a flutter in his gut. "Yes, sir. That's me."

He stepped forward and offered the man his hand to shake.

The man continued eyeing him, then, as if satisfied by what he saw, he motioned for Justin and Tess to follow him into the office.

Once they'd sat on a long leather couch, Mr. Turner took a picture down from his bookshelf and passed it to Justin. "I don't know if you remember my daughter, but you made quite an impression on her."

Justin looked at the picture. Turner's daughter couldn't have been more than ten or eleven years old. Red hair, freckles, and a bright grin.

"You made an impression on both of us really," Turner said. "I'm glad I caught you before you left. If I'd realized sooner who you were, I'd have had my secretary send you right in."

Justin handed Turner the photograph. "I'm sorry, but I don't recall meeting your daughter. When would that have happened?"

"Several months ago in a hospital in Memphis. You played and sang for her. She didn't look the same then, though. She was in the final stages of leukemia at the time." Turner's face grew sad.

Recognition dawned on Justin. "I remember her now. She has such a pretty smile. I admired her ability to smile in the face of her illness." Justin hesitated. "How . . . is she?"

Turner drew a slow breath. "She died about a month ago."

Justin exchanged a quick glance with Tess. "I'm sorry."

"But she never forgot what you did out of the goodness of your heart to brighten her last days. Most people fear dying patients and avoid them like the plague."

"I'm glad I could help."

"I want to repay your kindness. Not only did you do something kind for my little girl, but I think you've got real talent, and I like your enthusiasm. If you want to give it a shot, what do you say we reserve some studio time and see what develops?"

Gratitude, shock and excitement rendered Justin mute. Tess beamed at him like the lights of the Opry stage.

"He says yes!" Tess answered for him.

"Then you have a deal, son." Mr. Turner stuck out his hand and pumped Justin's in a hearty shake. "Welcome to the Sunshine label!"

Two Years Later

Tess sat in an audience full of country music stars and fans, watching with a heart full of pride as her husband performed "Little Bird" for the crowd. A few weeks before, the song he'd written for her had made it to number one on the country charts. They'd celebrated, first with the record company executives and honored guests then later, privately, with his family.

One person had been conspicuously missing from the celebration. Tess had seen the regret of Rebecca's absence in Justin's eyes. That night he'd decided to donate a large percentage of his profits from his debut CD to the battered women's shelter fund set up in Rebecca's name. It was Justin's way of sharing his success with his sister.

Now, dressed in his black Nero-style tuxedo and black cowboy hat, he held the audience enthralled as he sang. "Beautiful little bird, now that you're free. Say that you will fly away with me."

His eyes met Tess's as the last chorus faded and the crowd cheered and applauded. She blew him a kiss, and he headed offstage as Andy Griggs and Jo Dee Messina came to the microphone with an envelope to announce the next award category at the annual Country Music Association awards.

Andy and Jo Dee read the list of names for Best New Male Artist. The list included Justin Boyd.

Tess's heart pounded. As she waited nervously for Jo Dee to rip open the envelope and announce the winner, she slipped a hand over her lower abdomen. Even if Justin didn't win, he'd have another surprise when they got home. She would tell him tonight what her doctor confirmed earlier that morning. Justin was a daddy.

Her grin grew broader, thinking of the other new father in the family. Hallie and Brian had adopted a three-month-old girl the month before, and baby Kate had turned her attorney father into mush. Hallie called every day, giggling over the newest way Kate had wrapped Brian around her chubby finger.

Finally, Jo Dee finished fumbling with the envelope, glanced at Andy Griggs with a grin and read, "The winner is Justin Boyd!"

The music from the speakers and the roar of the crowd blurred as Tess shot to her feet along with the record company people around her. She clamped a hand over her mouth in joyful surprise.

Justin strutted back out onstage, obviously overwhelmed himself, and took the small gold statue Andy Griggs handed him. The audience sat back down as Justin stepped up to the microphone to make his acceptance speech.

"Holy cow!" he said breathlessly as he stared at the award in shock. "This is really the icing on the cake for me. It's been such an incredible year. I have to thank Bud Turner for giving me my big break, my band for all their hard work, and the fans who supported me and have been so great."

A cheer rang from the balcony as the fans whooped their support.

Justin took a deep breath and shook his head in disbelief. Tess knew her husband well enough to detect the subtle change in his demeanor, even if no one else in the audience did.

"I want to dedicate this award to someone who couldn't be here tonight," Justin continued. "She taught me to play the guitar when I was ten. She inspired me and encouraged me . . ."

Tess's eyes filled with tears when she heard the emotion in Justin's voice. He tipped his head back and looked toward the lights above him.

"This one's for you, Becca." His voice cracked as he held up the award. "I did it."

Swiping at his cheek, he dropped his gaze to the audience again. The crowd had grown reverently quiet. His blue eyes connected with Tess's, and she held her breath.

"Last, but far from least, I want to thank my beautiful wife for all her love and support. There's not a day that goes by that I don't thank God for bringing you into my life. Despite all that we went through together, I'd do it all again for the chance to be with you."

Tess knew the television camera had swung to focus on her, but her gaze stayed on Justin. Tears rolled down her cheeks, unchecked. Let America see her cry. They were tears of joy, tears of affection for the raven-haired cowboy who'd stolen her heart and showed her the real meaning of love and happiness.

"Tess," Justin said from the stage, "all of this would mean nothing without you. You are my dream come true."

Author's Note

This novel is fiction. Unfortunately, the problem of domestic violence is all too real. For more information or help with an abusive relationship, call the National Domestic Violence Hotline at 1-800-799-SAFE. A portion of the sales of this book are being donated to help battered women make a new start.

About the Author

Award-winning author Beth Cornelison worked in public relations until she moved with her husband to Louisiana, where she decided to pursue her love of writing fiction. Since that time, she has published two romantic suspense books and has won numerous honors for her work, including the coveted Golden Heart, awarded by the Romance Writers of America. She lives in Louisiana with her husband, one son, and two cats who think they are people. She invites readers to visit her Web site at www.bethcornelison.com.